"In her book, AN IRISHMAN'S SON, author Kathy Aspden shows us the ripple effects of one decision and its lasting impact on many lives. Her prose is crisp, her characters speak to you, and the journey she takes you on will stay with you long after you've finished reading.

AN IRISHMAN'S SON is a penetrating and well-crafted tale."

~ Casey Sherman, New York Times Best-selling author of "The Finest Hours"

"Can even the most devoted love withstand the trauma of a devastating betrayal? This question is at the heart of AN IRISHMAN'S SON. In Kathy Aspden's moving novel of a marriage under siege, Daniel and Teressa Muldaur must not only confront the truth about the child Teressa is carrying, but also the truths about themselves, and the many contradictions and complications of the human heart."

~ Anne D. LeClaire, Best-selling author of "The Halo Effect" and "The Orchid Sister"

"An exceptionally insightful story of a husband trying to save his marriage after his wife's infidelity. Set in a multicultural community and spanning events in Greece and Italy, Teressa and Danny hope to survive while they wait for the birth of their son. A good read, and a model for the power of love."

~ Madeline Miele Holt, Producer, *Books and the World* – A Cape Cod Writers Center Television Broadcast, enjoying more than 40 years of literary programming.

Enjoy the journey
Kathy Aspden

AN IRISHMAN'S SON

the love story behind the lie

Kathy Aspden

Katharine
Celli
Books

Katharine Celli Books

50 River Road
Marstons Mills, Massachusetts 02648
www.kathyaspden.com

ISBN: 978-1-7350592-3-5

This book is dedicated, with love and admiration, to my husband, Bill Aspden - a man who knows the value of patience, kindness, and quiet strength. Thank you for being the cornerstone of my world.

"Giving in is not the same as giving up.

Bending is not the same as breaking."

Kathy Aspden

CONTENTS

PART I

1992

SCITUATE, MASSACHUSETTS

February 8, 1992

DANIEL MULDAUR SLAMMED on the brakes, swerving to a halt just inches behind his wife's Lincoln Continental. The force of his stop caused the Honda Civic he was driving to rebound backward a couple feet before he could yank up the emergency brake. Miraculously, both he and his wife had managed to stop before hitting their friend's car, which lay freshly mangled under the bluish tint of the street light. Danny jumped out of the Honda and ran toward the accident, the inadequate soles of his dress shoes causing him to fall in the snow as he slid toward the wreckage.

Dr. Gregory Costa was hanging out the smashed window of his rolled sports car, the driver's side door facing the dark sky. His scalp was pulled away from his skull, blood flowing onto the snow in a steaming hot puddle.

"Teressa, don't come any closer!" Danny yelled when he saw his wife approaching the bloody scene. "Get back in your car and drive to the police station!" He felt Gregory's neck for a pulse. It was thready. *Stop the bleeding* Danny's mind commanded. He put his hand under the doctor's head and gently lifted the scalp back into place, trying to apply pressure without moving Gregory's neck, which looked to be broken. He saw a shadow in the headlights. It was Teressa.

"What are you doing?" he shouted. "You need to go now!"

She stood there, her eyes frozen on Gregory's face.

"Teres, don't look at him. Look at me. It doesn't matter why you're here. Whatever you came for can wait. We've got to get Gregory to the hospital. And be careful! The roads are getting worse." Danny spoke calmly, as though she were a child and not his thirty-nine-year-old wife of nearly twenty years. It worked. She ran to her car and took off toward the Scituate Police Department, a half-mile away.

Gregory made a gurgling sound. His eyes fluttered open.

"I've got you, Doc. Don't try to move. Help is coming."

"Danny," Gregory struggled to speak.

"Shh. It's okay, it's gonna be fine," Danny reassured.

"Danny," Gregory repeated, his eyes focused despite the bright red hemorrhage cascading over them. "Promise me you'll take care of them … the baby is … yours." Then he was gone.

A siren sounded in the distance. Danny tried to assess whether there was anything he could do. Attempting CPR meant dragging Gregory through the broken window to get him onto the ground, impossible without help. He scanned through the falling snow for something he could use as an airway. There was nothing.

2

"Jesus, Doc!" Danny cried in anguish. He was sobbing, shaking, and still cradling the deceased man's head when the ambulance arrived a few minutes later. Gregory Costa was pronounced dead at the scene. Daniel Muldaur was taken to the hospital in a severe state of shock.

February 9, 1992

Teressa Giannopoulos Muldaur stood in the doorway of her husband's hospital room. Danny laid motionless in the type of slumber only medication could provide. *So handsome* was her thought. The blue of the hospital gown accentuated his slightly silver hair. Had his eyes been open, the color would have made them appear deeper in tone than their water-like azure. Teres had loved his eyes from the first time she gazed into them, all those years ago at the edge of a worn mountainside road in Nea Makri, Greece. *Don't think about that now.*

"Mrs. Muldaur," the nurse said softly from behind her. "I know it's been a long night. I can have a cot wheeled in for you."

The nurse's expression changed from sympathy to annoyance when Teres reached for the clipboard in its slot by the door. Teres ignored the look and pushed her blurry eyes to focus on the words and numbers. Upon arrival, Danny had been in tachycardia and his temperature was dangerously low. She looked at the monitor above his bed. Everything looked normal: O2 sats, heart rate, blood pressure. "You are aware that my husband underwent open heart surgery only seven months ago, yes?" Teres' slide back to a thicker Greek accent was the only indication of the terror she felt. "Have you performed another EKG?" she asked the nurse.

"The nurse responded, an edge to her voice. "We're waiting for a consult from the cardiologist before we order another."

Cardiologist. The word knocked the air out of Teres. She leaned forward to stop herself from passing out. Danny's heart problems had pervaded the full duration of their marriage, beginning with a heart attack just months after they wed, and culminating in quadruple bypass surgery – performed last summer by Dr. Gregory Costa. *Gregorio.*

Teres lowered herself into the bedside chair. Her head began to spin, and a suffocating heat flooded her body, the telltale signs of an impending anxiety attack. She sensed the nurse's stare as she flung her arms out of the fur coat she had been wearing for hours. Her sleeveless silk dress, perfect for Danny's birthday party the night before, was now ridiculously inadequate and soaked with perspiration; the matching silver heels had become a vice. She began to shiver uncontrollably and put her head to her knees. It was eight hours since she had eaten anything, a few passed hors d'oeuvres. Teres looked up. The nurse was still there.

"Can you get me a cracker and ginger ale. I am pregnant." *There. I have said it out loud.* The nurse nodded and left. Teres shakily stood and went to the bedside. Unable to stop herself from touching him, she brushed the hair from his forehead, let her hand glide down his face to his jawline. A wave of nausea swept over her. Like an outsider in someone else's slow motion dream, she watched her hand go from her husband's face to the baby in her stomach. She backed away from the bed, horrified at where she was, *who she had become.*

Teres Muldaur took one more look at her sweet Danny, the love of her life, the gentlest man she had ever known, and ran from the room, taking all her secrets and lies with her.

*

Danny had been awake for some time, but didn't have the courage to open his eyes. Even with them closed it hadn't taken a minute to grasp he was in the hospital. After eighteen years as a respiratory therapist, a previous twenty as a Navy medic, and countless days as a patient, he recognized the hospital sounds around him better than most people recognize the sound of their own name. It was the consistent beep of the heart monitor that penetrated his consciousness first, soon followed by *last night wasn't a dream.* Keeping his eyes shut was his way of dealing. It would become real in the daylight, and night becomes day when you open your eyes. In the safe darkness of his mind, Danny let himself remember the birthday party Teres had given him the previous night.

*

His wife had insisted they celebrate his renewed health with friends, food, and music, which seemed crazy to Danny if his suspicions turned out to be true. And the evidence was mounting: the hidden pregnancy test, a mailbox full of coupons directed at new mothers, no wine at dinner. Teres was pregnant. He was hanging onto the fact she had not already run off with someone as a sign she planned to stay with him. None of it made sense, but he knew she still loved him. Her birthday toast was more proof of that love. Nothing was as true or as touching as her speech had been …

"Thank you, everyone, for coming to celebrate Danny's sixtieth birthday. My husband is a special person to many people. He is a man who spent two decades serving his country as a medic in the Navy. Just when he thought he would be retiring to a carefree life, he met me. And I have run over that calm life he had planned for himself, much like a Sherman tank. But to be fair, he ran over me first." There was a flurry of laughter about her reference to the car accident that brought them together. *"He has put up with my bullish behavior with grace and patience. I have dragged him into adventures, made plans he hated, and then stomped around like*

General MacArthur when he didn't see things my way. My husband, as you all know, is a true gentleman. He is quick with a smile, a joke or a shoulder, a man with modest wants and needs. Danny is happy if the people he cares about are happy. He is the same man I married all those years ago. Please raise your glasses in a toast to my husband, Daniel Muldaur. This day is for you, Danny! Happy Birthday, my sweet man. I love you!"

*

It was a perfect night – until he saw her speed out of the restaurant parking lot without telling him she was leaving. He had no choice but to grab his friend Ron's car and follow her.

The images in Danny's mind were vivid: Gregory's bloody scalp, the look on Teres' face, the intimate spark of awareness that passed between the two men with Gregory's revelation. *"Promise me you'll take care of them ... the baby Is ... yours."* For the briefest of moments, Danny thought by some miracle the baby *was* his. But no. A sperm abnormality and a vasectomy said otherwise. The baby was Gregory's. *But she loves me.*

Danny had enough rehashing. He was ready to force his eyes open, knowing Teres would be sleeping in the chair next to his bed. He wasn't afraid to face her. He had known about the pregnancy for nearly a week. His worst fears were already behind him. *She loves me.*

He opened his eyes. The chair beside the bed was empty. Danny began to cry.

*

Ron Watters was used to seeing dead people. As an emergency room physician, he had seen all types of accidents and tragedies, along with the inherent sadness that accompanies each one. None of that prepared him for the sight of his friend and colleague, Dr. Gregory Costa.

6

Gregory was bigger than life in every way: looks, arrogance, determination, and charm. Ron couldn't think of any situation in which Costa had not managed to propel himself to the top - and he had the credentials to prove it. He had seen Gregory's ascension first-hand when they were med students at Tufts. The guy was an effortless learner who quickly grasped the correlation between medical specialty and financial reward. Costa had chosen cardiothoracic surgery despite a major league pitch from plastics. For a guy like Gregory, cardiac surgery was the best of both worlds: the intricate, precision-based mechanics of plastic surgery, along with the extreme life-and-death control of cardiology. Gregory Costa was a power-hungry perfectionist.

It was for all those reasons Ron fell apart when he saw Gregory in the morgue. His beautiful face was a mass of bruises. The detachment of his scalp began slightly above his right eyebrow and followed a jagged path into the left side of his hairline, a hairline notorious for its thick, dark curls. At some point after being pronounced dead, his scalp was reattached with what Ron could only think of as Frankenstein-like sutures. Had he not already been dead, Ron was sure Gregory would have killed the person responsible for those stitches.

After a few brief words with the pathologist, Ron excused himself and hurried into the hallway to cry. It was a reaction he hadn't expected. Yes, he had known Gregory for years. And yes, they had seen more of each other in the months since Gregory operated on Ron's best friend, Daniel Muldaur. But they weren't close. Nobody got close to Gregory. He wouldn't allow it.

Ron headed to the elevator. He assumed Danny would be in coronary care. Teres would have insisted. She was a guard dog about her husband's health. When it came to the people she loved, Teres didn't respond well to the word *no*. Ron was grateful for his place in her tightly protected circle. Not only were Teres and Danny his closest friends, they were also his business partners in a private ambulance company.

When Danny had bolted out the door in search of Teres, Ron did what any best friend would have done – he stayed and enjoyed the party. Not only was the band great, but the group had dwindled down to all the right players. Most of their Accelerated Ambulance employees were still there, partying strong. A few ER nurses were doing shots at the bar with the EMTs. What started out as a very high-class, sophisticated sixtieth birthday party had become your quintessential hospital bash. Stepping in as host was a sacrifice Ron was glad to make. *What are friends for?*

Then suddenly it was a nightmare. Ron got the emergency page from Doug, the paramedic on call for Accelerated Ambulance, telling him about the accident and that Danny had been taken to South Shore Hospital. Even if Ron had his car, he wouldn't have risked driving. Scituate was a coastal town, the roads ice up quickly. He'd seen too many versions of what they referred to in the ER as *The Winter Olympics of Intoxication*. Ron waited for the storm to pass, then had Doug pick him up in the ambulance. The delay hadn't changed anything. Gregory was dead, and Danny was admitted. *But, where was Teres?*

*

The elevator door opened into the reception area of coronary care. Ron could hear the commotion before he stepped off the elevator.

"Mr. Muldaur-"

"I said, I'm fine! I just need you to find my wallet, so I can get outta here."

Danny was standing at the nurse's station. He was re-dressed in the blood-soaked white shirt and black dress pants he had arrived in the night before. His arm was bleeding from the self-removal of his IV. Ron rushed over.

"Hello, eh," he looked at her tag. "Tammy. I'm Dr. Ron Watters from Quincy City Hospital. Could you do me a favor and have someone grab a set of clean scrubs for Mr. Muldaur? We'll wait for you in his room." Ron turned to his friend. "Come on, Danny, let's get you out of those clothes and then I'll drive you home."

They walked back to the room in silence. Danny sat down on the bed.

"Tough night. I just saw Gregory … downstairs. None of that could have been anything but horrible. You okay?"

Danny didn't answer. His head was down, shoulders slumped.

"Danny, you're going to have to talk to me or I'm gonna think they're right to keep you. Shock can be a dangerous condition for a guy with a cardiac history."

Danny continued to look down. Ron couldn't decide if he was watching the blood drip from his IV site or completely unaware of its presence. He stepped out of the room in search of gauze, tape and alcohol preps. When he came back in, Danny finally spoke. There was nothing frantic or illogical in his voice.

"I need to get home, Ron. I have to find Teres. She was there last night. It was … traumatic for us both."

Relieved by the sound of normal, Ron pulled a chair in front of Danny, sat down, and began cleaning his arm. Danny's nurse walked in with the scrubs. Ron spoke before she could express her displeasure at the scene in front of her.

"I'm Dr. Ron Watters, Quincy City Emergency Room Director. If you'll wait a minute, I'd be happy to show you my ID." He continued to apply a pressure bandage on the arm and directed his next words to Danny, "It's the blood thinners you're on. Don't go ripping this off in a big hurry. It should be fine by the time you get home."

"Mr. Muldaur has not been discharged."

"I know," said Ron. "But it appears he's leaving AMA, so let's get him ready to go, shall we?" Ron stood and took the scrubs from her. She hesitated a few seconds, then turned on her heel and left, presumably to alert someone of the situation.

*

Danny was ready to lose his mind. He and Ron had been standing at the nurses' station signing paperwork for fifteen minutes. Releasing him against medical advice required a complete documentation of his current vital signs, all normal except his blood pressure, which was rising a few points with every minute of delay. Somewhere near the last signature it occurred to Danny he had no idea where Ron's car was, having been carted away from the accident scene in an ambulance. *Jesus! Could getting out of here be any more complicated?*

The nurse handed him a packet. Inside were the keys to Teressa's car.

"Your wife left this for you earlier."

Why did she leave her car? Where is she? A pit formed in his stomach. He wondered how it had taken so long to form. He palmed the keys, and took off at a run, Ron on his heels.

"Danny, give me the keys. We'll stop at the impound and pick up my car. It's on the way."

*

The Lincoln was parked in a handicapped space near the emergency room entrance. Danny looked without comment at the parking ticket attached to the windshield. He waited for Ron to unlock the passenger door. As he got inside, he noticed an unopened white envelope on the floor of his wife's unfailingly

10

clean car. He picked it up and read the one word written in Teres' perfect handwriting: *Gregorio.* His stomach pit deepened. He folded the letter in half and stuffed it into the back pocket of his newly acquired scrubs. Ron got in, parking ticket in hand. They drove to the impound lot in silence.

*

Gregory's 1990 arrest-me-red Ferrari was the first thing Danny saw when they pulled into the lot. It was sitting on the back of a flatbed tow truck, no longer on its side. Upright, it looked hardly able to inflict the damage it had. *Blood doesn't show on red paint.* Danny looked away. Ron pulled up to the tow company office and left the car running while he went inside. After a minute, Danny got out and went over to Gregory's car.

Other than the damage, Gregory's car, like Teres', was impeccable. "Another thing they have in common," Danny muttered to himself, *aside from their child.* The sports car was low. Even on a flatbed Danny could see everything inside: the blood, Gregory's hospital badge miraculously still hanging over the rear-view mirror, and the doctor's ever-present, black leather backpack. Without thinking, Danny reached through the shattered window and grabbed the backpack. He walked back to Teres' car and threw it into the passenger seat. He looked toward the office and saw Ron still engaged in retrieving his car. Danny got behind the wheel of the Lincoln and drove away.

*

It was clear the house was empty, but he yelled her name anyway as he came through the mud room, into the kitchen. His yell wasn't mad, or desperate, or sad. It was the way he yelled for her anytime she was in the house before him. "Teres! I'm home."

Danny wasn't a guy with a lot of tricks. He had a way or two of doing things, but not an entire arsenal in his bag. It was part of

11

his charm. He was steady, the kind of man you could count on when things were good, and when things were bad. That didn't mean he was a rescuer. Other than his shifts on the ambulance or in the ER, he didn't come swooping in to save the day. But he was there in all the ways that mattered. He had let Teres run the show, encouraged it really, when it became obvious shortly into their marriage that she had the drive and desire to make their life into something more. *As if I could stop her.* Sometimes, that 'something more' was a circus. But part of Danny's steady persona was his ability to zig and zag through commotion. Teres was a force of nature. He had spent much of their marriage worrying if he were enough for her: young enough, rich enough, athletic enough, handsome enough. His answer to all those questions was no. Hers was to assure him that she didn't love him because he was perfect, she loved him because she loved him. *She loves me.*

Danny walked through the house. The sun streamed in through every window, no need to turn on a light. It was ten o'clock in the morning and he was exhausted. He headed for the sunroom and fell into his favorite chair, only then realizing Gregory's backpack was still clutched in his hands. *It would be so easy to close my eyes and forget about all this* he thought despondently. He tried it. Images of Gregory's bloody face came immediately. Danny got up and went to the kitchen to make a cup of coffee.

"I'm going to set up the coffee maker for tomorrow. If you wake up before me, just push the button," Teres had said, probably knowing they would both be tired after Danny's big party. Or knowing what? That she would be gone? Her last good deed to him, a decent cup of coffee? He pressed the button and then opened the cabinet that contained his morning pills. Teres had set them up in two locations – the kitchen for the morning, the master bath for his evening pills. *She loves me.*

12

He sucked the pills down in one handful with a quarter-glass of water, something his wife hated. He could hear her lecture in his mind. "You need to drink a full glass of water with those pills! And wait thirty minutes before drinking your coffee!" Yeah. That wasn't happening this morning. He was ready to slide into a coma again. Actually, a coma was the one thing he had never been in. He'd been in traction, cardiac arrest, a seizure, but not a coma. Unconscious for a bit, yes, but not in a coma. Danny put the backpack on the breakfast bar, opened it up and unceremoniously dumped out its contents. He went through the shaving kit first: deodorant, razor, toothpaste, hair gel, aftershave. No surprises there. He stopped and poured himself a cup of coffee, adding an extra sugar, and half and half instead of skimmed milk. *Take that, Teres.* His thought was hollow. He knew his health was the one thing that tortured his wife because she couldn't control or predict it. He thought about the anguish he had put her through, but she'd gotten him to the other side of every health scare. Teres was the food Nazi, the exercise Nazi, the take-your-medication Nazi. Always for his own good. Danny felt immediate guilt. *Seriously? My wife is pregnant with another man's baby and I feel guilty about using cream in my coffee? How the hell does she do that*, he wondered?

He abandoned the backpack and brought his coffee into the bathroom. Normally his morning routine consisted of reading the newspaper on the toilet, a shave, and a leisurely shower. Today he stripped off the hospital blues, jumped into full-force hot water, and tried to scrub his body from head to toe without closing his eyes and inviting unwanted images. No luck. He saw her shadow in the headlights, her face, staring with unblinking eyes as the snow fell onto her dark halo of hair.

Danny shut off the water. The bloody bandage had fallen from his arm onto the floor of the shower and was causing the water to pool. He stepped over it. While toweling dry, he saw Teres' letter, still in the scrubs' pocket. He plucked it out and put it on the bathroom windowsill. The word *Gregorio* stared back at him. He ignored it and went to the bedroom to get dressed.

*

Lacing his hiking boots was an effort. He felt beat up. With a deep breath and loud exhale, Danny knew it was time to plan his next move. Was he going to go find his wife or curl up in a ball? The choice was easy. He couldn't live without her.

He grabbed his heavy, wool, Navy-issue pea coat, along with the scarf his mother-in-law, Katharine, had knit for his birthday, and prepared to leave. At the last minute, he went back to his room and threw together a bag with a change of clothes, his medication, and his passport - just in case there was no coming home from whatever happened next. It wasn't until he was leaving the bedroom that he thought to look and see if anything of Teressa's was missing. Everything she would have taken was there: her suitcase, favorite boots, and her passport, which he shoved into the overnight bag next to his. Without it, she wouldn't be able to run back to Greece.

Then, out of habit, he removed his coffee cup from the bathroom and threw the clothes in the hamper. He left Teres' letter to Gregory on the sill, unable to touch it again. But he had no problem throwing everything else into the dead man's backpack and slinging it over his shoulder on the way out the door. Danny felt oddly invigorated. For the past week, since discovering his wife's pregnancy, he'd been in a mental and physical purgatory, bordering on hell. He had conjured up so many scenarios about how and why she was pregnant, yet somehow avoided putting a

14

face on who she was pregnant by. Now that the face was Gregory Costa's, a man Danny respected, admired – perhaps even loved – the path to the truth was in sight. Not that Danny was always a fan of the truth; he was a fan of status quo, the path of least resistance. Teressa Muldaur never took the easy road. And now she was dragging him down that hard road with her.

*

His wife referred to Saint Mary's of the Nativity as "relaxed Greek Orthodox." It wasn't. It was Irish Catholic at its finest. On the short drive to their little church, Danny envisioned Teres kneeling alone in a pew, head down, praying for forgiveness. She was religious. It was not the kind where she preached the gospel or felt terrible if she missed a Sunday. It was the type that drove her to bow her head in times of adversity and times of joy. Danny knew his wife had logged plenty of hours making deals with the Lord while waiting for him to wake up, recover, or heal. Her love for God was like her love for him, devotional. *Just keep telling yourself that, idiot.*

He forgot it was Sunday; the parking lot was full. She wasn't going to be in there with all those people, but just in case he parked his Jeep Cherokee where he could watch the parishioners leave the church. While he waited for Mass to end, Danny went through the rest of Gregory's backpack. His wallet was in there, Gregory's driver's license tucked into the appropriate clear-view slot. Danny pulled it out and put it in his glove compartment. Everything else was what you'd expect a doctor to carry: stethoscope, ID badges for three different hospitals, rubber gloves, some mail. Danny looked through the mail. There was a letter from Joseph Costa, return address Sorrento, Italy. Brother? Father? Someone would have to notify him of Gregory's death. He'd give the mail to Ron later. The last item, which Danny had been deliberately pushing aside, was Gregory's calendar.

It was a small brown leather datebook with gold embossing. The words *Gregory A. Costa, M.D., F.A.C.A. 1992* were centered on the front. Danny had one, too. All Gregory's patients got them last year for Christmas. Before looking into the monthly activity, Danny flipped to the back pocket where a black and white photo was tucked.

It was an ultrasound, the embryo in it hardly a baby. The scan was dated February 4, 1992, five days ago. The name at the top: Teressa Giannopoulos. Estimated gestational age: 11 weeks, 2 days.

Danny stared at the image, frantically trying to decide how to feel. Devastated? Pissed? Betrayed? Scared? It was all there. But along with those emotions was a sense of wonder. This little being was growing inside his wife. It was the miracle that had been snatched from them nineteen years ago by fate and an old case of the mumps. His heart sank. This wasn't their miracle, it was hers – hers and the man she had slept with. Danny wanted to tear up the picture, but he carefully put it back in the datebook.

The windshield was fogged. Between that and his tears he couldn't see the people coming out of Saint Mary's. It didn't matter. She wasn't there. He knew where she was. Danny retrieved the license from the glove box and read the address: *24 Oyster Bay Road, Apt 607 Boston.* He took off his new scarf – *blue to match the color of your eyes* Katharine's birthday card had said – and wiped down the windshield, threw the jeep into drive, and took off.

*

The guy behind the desk was young and stupid.

"I need to grab some keys off the key chain of that red Ferrari," Danny said upon entering the impound lot office. Without asking

16

one question, the kid turned around and unlocked the metal panel that housed all the keys. After watching him stare at them for a minute, Danny reached over the counter and grabbed the only set of keys with Ferrari's famous prancing horse logo on its key chain. *Bingo.* He slipped off the car key and flipped it to the boy, keeping the key chain and the rest of the keys.

"Thanks," he said and walked out.

*

Danny knew where he was going. Twenty-Four Oyster Bay Road was the address of Harbor Bay Point on the Bay, a complex of luxury apartments.

When Harbor Bay Point was still under construction, one of its first tenants was Sylvia Pierce. At fifty-two and in total renal failure, she was a three-times-a-week regular at Beth Israel's hemodialysis clinic. Sylvia didn't like cabs, or cab drivers. One day, when her ride to the clinic cancelled at the last minute, she called for an ambulance rather than miss her three-hour dialysis session. At that point, the building she lived in wasn't half-finished, most of the units empty or being worked on. The elevator was sometimes filled with stacks of tile or a couple of kitchen cabinets, as was the case when Danny came to pick up Sylvia that first time. He walked the two flights up to her apartment. She opened the door before he could knock. He assisted her down the stairs, buckled her into the jump seat in the back of the ambulance and then he and Tony drove the five miles to Beth Israel Hospital. Sylvia didn't utter a word. Four hours later, they returned to the clinic and brought her home, still without a word. She must not have hated them, because soon they were doing the job every Friday. For two years – until Sylvia Pierce died of an electrolyte imbalance while on dialysis – Danny was privy to a weekly, first-hand construction update. The complex had four top-of-the-line models. Their price differences were generated mostly by the view. He once told Teres if he ever had to live in an apartment again, he wanted it to be Harbor Bay Point on the Bay. *How ironic* Danny thought as he rounded the corner on the sixth floor and saw that number 607, Gregory's apartment, was the one he had secretly picked out for himself. It had the best view of the Boston Harbor skyline.

*

The place was dark and empty. Disappointed, Danny decided to look around a bit. He didn't know what he was searching for, maybe a note or an airline ticket – or a journal entry that read *this is what I plan to do about getting my patient's wife pregnant* ...

The kitchen was so clean it looked unused. There was a glass jar filled with protein bars on the counter. Danny took one out and put it in his pocket. Then he walked through the sterile living room and into the bedroom. Gregory's bedroom. *Their bedroom.* He was done. He sat on the bed, lowered his head to his hands, and prepared to cry himself into unconsciousness.

She was right in front of him. At first, he thought his eyes were playing tricks. The louvered blinds were positioned at an angle creating slats of light throughout the room. Danny closed his eyes and reopened them. It was Teres.

She was sitting on the creamy, plush carpet, leaned into a corner created by the wall and Gregory's bureau. Her knees were pulled up to her chin with her arms curled around them, her head resting on her forearms. She was barefoot, but still wearing the dress from Danny's party. She looked frail for such a powerhouse of a woman. Danny mistakenly thought she was asleep. He stared at her, waiting for his blood to start boiling. It didn't. He was frozen, on the brink of a moment to which he couldn't imagine the ending. Neither of them moved.

"You know everything." Her words were a statement, not a question. She didn't raise her head.

"No, Teressa. I don't know everything, just enough to get me to this apartment."

She looked up at him, her beautiful face distorted by pain and tears. "It would have been easier if you had not found me – if I just disappeared from your life."

Danny's anger found him.

"That's your fucking plan? Disappear on me forever? Let me worry about you for the rest of my life? Wonder if you're alive? Search for you?" His body had risen from the bed in a towering gesture of fury. "You owe me a hell of a lot more than that!"

Teres remained silent.

"Answer me!" he shouted in a voice he had never used before. "That's your fucking plan?"

"I have no plan," Teres said, her tone empty. "I have slept with another man. I am carrying his baby. It is over for us."

A switch flipped in Danny's brain. Every moment became this one. Every decision they had ever made, inside and outside their marriage for the past twenty years, became this decision. He couldn't stop the sudden rerouting of his mind, the explosion of change that happened like a biblical awakening – a lightning bolt of clarity. *No. You don't get the last word on this one, Teressa Giannopoulos Muldaur.*

"Have you eaten anything?"

Teres looked confused by his question. "What are you talking about? You need to go! This is not a good place for you … to be here … in this room." He ignored her, reached into his pocket, and pulled out the protein bar.

"It's not all about you, Teres. Not anymore." Danny opened the package and half-knelt in front of her, not an easy task with the stiff left leg he acquired years ago in a car accident. He lifted her chin so her confused eyes could meet his controlled stare. He was momentarily ashamed by how good it felt to touch her, expecting revulsion. "Eat this. I'm going to the kitchen to get you something to drink." He dropped the bar into her hand, got up and left.

*

What just happened? Horrifying images of this confessional moment had been projecting through her head for six weeks. She had come up with hundreds of scenarios, all ending in disaster; her most terrifying version culminating in Danny's death of a heart attack from the shock of finding out she had betrayed him. Teres had imagined every possible reaction – except the one she had just witnessed. She was confused and too drained to make sense of it.

*

Danny walked into the room with a glass of orange juice. Teres was still clutching Gregory's protein bar. It was difficult for him to look at her. She looked scared, wild-like, with her wrinkled dress and tangled mass of hair. He had never seen her like this, with eyes so empty he couldn't find a connection to them. It scared him. *I should call Ron. Maybe she needs to go to the hospital.*

"Danny, go. We cannot fix it. I have no explanation … for this."

He set the juice on the nightstand and sat down on the bed. "Teres, whatever you have to say is too much for me to handle right now. We'll talk about it when we get home."

She looked up at him like he was insane. "There is no *home* for us! Please! Just leave me here!"

He had enough. He bent down to pick her up from the floor. "Come on. Where's your coat and shoes? Let's go." She went crazy.

"Do not touch me!" She began kicking and scratching at him. Danny tried to grab her arms but lost his balance and fell on her.

20

By the time he righted himself she was in full hyperventilation. She flipped herself onto her hands and knees and began gasping for breath through croup-like sobs. The old Danny of a week ago would have wrapped his arms around her and comforted her while she calmed down. This Danny backed away, scared but amazed at her strength and violence.

"Okay, okay! I won't touch you." He pulled the expensive down-filled quilt off Gregory's bed and put it over her. She leaned back onto her folded shins and began coughing. Danny retrieved Kleenex from the bathroom and, keeping his distance, handed her the box.

"I cannot … I cannot …"

He thought she was going to say breathe.

"… have you look at me," she gasped.

Danny stood over her in silence.

"Please, Danny. Go!" she choked out.

His mind raced through options: *call Ron, call 911, sneak off to the living room and wait it out, slap her, do nothing.* He surprised himself with his next words.

"No. I'm the one you fucked around on. If you think you're gonna decide how this plays out, you're wrong, Teres. I'm not going anywhere."

His words snapped her out of something, and into something else. Teres collapsed into a fetal position, no longer panting and crying. Her eyes closed, and her face became expressionless, almost peaceful. Danny knelt beside her and checked her pulse. It was rapid, but steady – normal under the circumstances. *Now what?*

He decided to call Ron. There was a phone on Gregory's nightstand, Danny picked it up and began dialing Accelerated Ambulance. He put the phone down. He couldn't handle even the friendliest of interrogations from his staff about last night. He would call Quincy City. Ron wouldn't be working, but they'd get a page to him.

"Hello. This is Danny Muldaur. I'd like to page Dr. Ron Watters in emergency." He could hear the operator announcing the overhead page in the background. An ER nurse picked up.

"This is the emergency room. Dr. Watters is not in today. Can someone else help you?"

"Tina, it's Danny Muldaur. Can you leave a message for Ron to call me at this number?

"Danny! Oh my God! Are you okay? We heard about last night!"

"I'm fine," he lied, looking on the phone base for Gregory's telephone number. "I know Ron's not in, but can you send him a page to call me at six-one-seven, two-six-five, oh-eight-nine-two?"

"Will do."

"Thanks, Tina." He hung up. Teres hadn't moved. Danny looked around the room. He was bone tired but sure as hell not going to sleep in Gregory's bed. He headed to the kitchen in search of something to eat.

*

The expiration date on the package of English muffins was February fifteenth, a week away. Gregory must have bought them yesterday. It was impossible to believe that yesterday had been his birthday – a lifetime ago. Danny remembered how good it felt to wake up next to Teres. They had made love the night before, their first time in ages.

*

After Danny's bypass surgery, there had been one complication after another. His recovery wasn't easy. Sex had flown out the window. He wanted Teres, but his body wasn't a cooperative player. All that changed the night before his birthday.

They had gone to bed early, both exhausted. He suspected she was tired from the effects of being pregnant. He knew his exhaustion was from the stress of anticipating a confession that would ruin his life. They fell asleep immediately with Danny conformed behind Teres, his arm thrown over her waist. Uncharacteristically, he dreamt:

The scene was real. He and Teres were in the field beside her parent's villa in Nea Makri. They were sitting in the grass, her head on his shoulder, Danny's arm wrapped around her. He could hear the noise from her grandfather's funeral feast going on in the background. It was joyous, lilting laughter and conversation. Danny was surprised to find he understood the conversations even though they were being spoken in Greek, a language he could never master. The sun was shining, the air clear and crisp, he could smell the Mediterranean Sea. His overwhelming sense of peace was both physical and ethereal. He turned to his wife and lifted her chin. She was so beautiful. Their eyes met, held, and exchanged a secret. Her hand was resting protectively over her stomach. Danny covered her hand with his. She put her head back on his shoulder.

He half-awoke with a lingering sense of contentment and expectation. The woman from his dream was right in front of him, already in his arms. Danny felt his body respond to her closeness. He reached under her t-shirt and cupped her breast, feeling its additional fullness. His urgency increased when her nipple responded to his touch. Danny felt his wife press her body against his, the beginning of a familiar dance. They rocked like that, on the brink of their dance, for an achingly long time. When she turned to face him, her eyes were still closed, but wet with tears. He watched her face as he ran his hands over her skin. Then he lowered his head

23

to her breast, gently sucking and teasing, while she arched toward him. When he knew she was ready, he entered her. And like a carpenter working on a house he called home, his urgency was replaced with patience and skill. When Teres climaxed, she called out to him. Danny felt his heart expand and heal at the sound of his name on her lips. He held her tightly and shuttered his orgasm.

That was the moment Danny realized he could love another man's child. It wouldn't matter to him who the father was, as long as the mother was Teressa.

He continued to cradle Teres while she fell back to sleep. "I know, sweet girl," he whispered in the darkness. "It's been a long time and I'm sorry for that. I'll make it up to you."

*

The telephone rang in stereo. Thankful he wouldn't have to talk to Ron in front of Teres, Danny scrambled toward the muffled ringtone in the living room. By the time he located the feminine, aqua-colored, princess-style telephone – on the floor, tucked partially underneath the couch – it had stopped ringing. *Damn!* Danny picked it up and slammed it down on the side table. It looked out of place. *It was probably purchased by one of his women*, Danny thought, trying to decide if it were his wife's taste. Everything else in the room was expensive and masculine. The dining room set, end tables and matching bookcases were all Scandinavian teak; the couch, a dark, overstuffed tweed with pillows to match. Danny looked at Gregory's recliner with a touch of envy. It was a chair purchased with comfort as its only criteria. The phone rang, again.

"Thank God you called back," Danny said, expecting Ron's voice.

"Gregorio? Questo non suona come te? Ho ricevuto una chiamata da un avvocato."

24

Danny panicked and almost hung up the phone, but he couldn't do that to whoever was on the other end.

"Hello. No. I'm sorry this isn't Gregory. This is ... I am a friend of his." Danny was surprised to hear the man reply in perfect English.

"Ah! Well, hello! This is Joseph Costa, Gregory's father. It's nice to hear that my son has friends. He is such a serious man. He works too hard, I tell him, always."

Danny responded with a voice that should not have been audible to someone so far away.

"I'm sorry, Mr. Costa. Gregory died last night in a car accident." There was silence on the other end. "Mr. Costa? Are you there?" Danny heard something that sounded like throat clearing. He worried the man on the other end of the phone might collapse. "Mr. Costa, is there anyone you need me to call for you?"

"There is no one. I will return the call to Gregory's attorney. Thank you ... Gregory's friend." The phone went dead.

Danny stood, still holding the receiver in his hand. *Oh, God.* Another layer of misery descended upon him. *I can't do this.* This misery had a familiar feel. Despite years in the medical field, Danny had only given 'the worst news ever' one other time. As a respiratory therapist, it wasn't his job. There were times he was present at the telling, but never the actual bearer of bad news – except for *Tommy Wilkinson.*

April 1971
SERE *Survival, Evasion, Resistance and Escape*
New Brunswick, Maine

Danny had been best friends with Tommy's oldest brother, Teddy, since first grade at Squantum Elementary School in Quincy. The Wilkinsons were Danny's true family, providing him with after school daycare and the siblings his parents never gave him. That included Tommy, Mrs. Wilkinson's happy accident, who was just a baby when Danny joined the Navy. Eighteen years later, Tommy's draft number was picked. By sheer coincidence they ended up in the same construction battalion – Danny as a medic, Tommy as a heavy equipment mechanic. Their Seabees team was scheduled to leave for Vietnam immediately after SERE training. The thirteen-man unit had been assigned to work with the South Vietnamese to build an access road up Takou Mountain in Mui Ne. Although SERE had been brutal, Danny would have stayed there forever rather than go to Vietnam. He was apprehensive, Tommy was terrified.

*

"Di chuyển xe tải"

"Doc, I think it's Bạn phải di chuyển xe tải," Tommy said to Danny.

"What's the difference?" asked Danny.

"One is 'move the truck.' The other is 'you must move the truck," Tommy explained patiently.

"This is bullshit! I don't care where they put the goddamn truck!"

Their unit had been in foreign language training at Port Hueneme for four weeks. They had two weeks left and Danny was no closer to being able to speak Vietnamese than the first day he walked into class. *How the hell am I gonna be in charge of anything if I can't even speak the language?*

"I speak Vietnamese." Tommy quizzed the next sentence.

"I wish," said Danny.

"Doc, you gotta try."

"Okay. Tôi nói tiếng Việt," Danny replied.

"You got it!" Tommy hollered.

Danny grinned at the kid's enthusiasm. He had to admit; he wouldn't know a thing if Tommy hadn't offered to tutor him. Studying together also seemed to have pulled the kid out of whatever abyss he had been in since getting the orders to go to Nam. Tommy had been a mess: crying on the phone to his wife, not eating, drinking too much. *He looks alright, now*, thought Danny.

"Doc, you okay if we call it quits? I wanna call Sheila before it gets too late."

"Good luck with the line at the payphone. You got enough change?"

"I just reverse the charges." Tommy saluted. Danny grinned.

"Sounds good. Thanks for the help." Danny watched him walk away. *He seems fine*, Danny decided, unconvinced it was true. *Nobody wants to go to God-forsaken Vietnam.*

*

For the fourth night that week, Sheila didn't take Tommy's call.

His bunkmates found him the next morning, smelling like Jack Daniels and hanging, dead, from the high threshold of the latrine utility closet. It turned out his wife wanted to surprise him by paying off their bills with the second job she had taken, working nights at Stop and Shop. She was going to tell him right before he left for Vietnam, so he'd have one less thing to worry about while he was away.

Everyone knew the drill. Uniformed officers would present themselves at the front door. The minute Mr. and Mrs. Wilkinson saw the dress blues, they would know their son was dead. It had already happened twice; three years ago with Teddy, and the second time when the state police came to tell them their son, Jerry, had been killed in a car accident on his way back from a hockey game. The Wilkinsons surely knew the drill.

There is an unwritten rule in the Military about notification of next of kin. Danny broke it. It was the hardest call he had ever made, but he couldn't bear the thought of another uniformed ambush at his best friend's parents' door. He owed them more than that. He should have kept their baby boy safe. He was a medic for chrissake - part of his training was to recognize the signs of suicidal depression. Danny's guilt was narrowly outweighed by his sorrow.

February 9, 1992

I'm trained to see the signs of suicidal depression ...

Teres was scaring him. She had taken a few sips of water at his insistence. Actually, it was a little more than insistence.

"That's it. I'm calling an ambulance and taking you to the hospital."

"I am fine. You need to go." Like a broken record, every sentence ended with a plea for Danny to leave. She was still on the floor in the corner. He wasn't budging.

"This is ridiculous, Teres. You have to let me help you. I'm not leaving."

"Please, Danny." And the crying began again; this time not a wail, more like whimpering, quiet and heartbreaking. It was too much. He picked up the phone and began to call for an ambulance.

"What do you want me to do?" she cried, pathetically. "Just tell me and I will do it. I do not want to go to the hospital!"

Danny stopped dialing. "Let me take you home."

"No!" she sobbed.

He turned his back to her and resumed his call for help.

"Do you not see, Danny? I cannot go back to the house we made. I have ruined it for us." Danny put the receiver down and turned around.

"Okay. We'll stay here for now. But Teres, you need to do what I say or I'll call someone to bring you in – by force if they have to." She didn't argue. "I'm gonna help you into bed." He waited for a sign of compliance. He wasn't up for another hysterical wrestling match. "Do you have to go to the bathroom, first?" he asked, as he pulled her to her feet. She shook her head no.

"That's because you're dehydrated. It's not good for your baby. *There, I've said it – your baby.* Danny shifted Teres toward Gregory's bed, while at the same time pulling the covers back. He sat her down gently. "I'm gonna find you something to wear. Do you need help taking off your dress?" She, again, shook her head no. But then she did need help. His wife, like all wives, needed help with her zipper.

The simple act of unzipping her dress was Danny's unraveling. He had zipped up this very dress twenty-four hours ago. Zipping and unzipping were actions filled with promise: the promise of a wonderful evening, followed by the promise of an intimate night. Danny couldn't remember zipping up his wife's dress the previous night. He knew he had done it, but he couldn't remember the details. Was it in their bathroom? Did it happen in the kitchen? Had Teres walked out to the sunroom, found him in his chair, and presented her back to him. Danny couldn't remember. In fact, the entire week leading up to his sixtieth birthday had gone missing. There were two things he remembered clearly: finding the pregnancy test hidden in the bathroom and watching Gregory die. Everything in between those two moments was a blur of anxiety and questions. Danny unzipped the dress. The two sides sprang apart, exposing a glimpse of her matching bra and panties. He walked to the bureau and opened the drawer in which every man keeps his t-shirts and boxers. Gregory was no exception, although his underwear was rolled, not folded. Danny grabbed a white V-neck and a pair of Calvin Klein boxers, and walked back to the bed. He pulled the dress over Teres' head. Other than lifting her arms, she didn't help. He unhooked her bra and tried not to think about what he was doing. *I'm putting my wife in her lover's underwear.*

Teres immediately curled onto her side as Danny pulled up the covers.

"No, you don't. Sit up, I'm gonna make you an English muffin. You have to eat something." She dutifully sat back up against the pillows.

*

The tea kettle whistled as the English muffin popped up from the toaster. Gregory didn't have butter, just peanut butter. Danny ignored the kettle and slathered the muffin while it was still hot. It felt strange cooking in another man's kitchen. Admittedly, it felt strange cooking in his own kitchen – Teres' kitchen. He hardly ever did. Sometimes, when he sat at the counter with their evening wine, she would ask him to do something, maybe rinse the lettuce or grab olive oil out of the cabinet if her hands were messy. He cooked meat on the grill because, by some unwritten couples-law, he was supposed to. Teres didn't need him in the kitchen – or the yard, or the office. She was good at things. Danny couldn't say he had been outsourced, because he had never actually been insourced. Their first house was the first time Danny lived in a dwelling he owned. Up until then, he had never painted a room or done a day of yard work. Teres' enthusiasm for hard labor and home improvements outmatched his by a mile. She was a one-man show. Sure, they did random projects together, but in truth, the only room she needed him in was the bedroom. *And now I've been outsourced from that.*

He added honey to her tea and carried the plate and mug back to Gregory's bedroom, miserably wondering if she had eaten in this bed before today.

*

The ringing phone startled him into spilling the tea while setting it on the nightstand. With Teres watching, Danny didn't dare rush to the living room to answer the call. On the third ring he picked it up and waited for whoever was on the other end to speak.

"Hello?" Thankfully, it was Ron.

"I'm here with Teres." Danny said, wondering if Ron knew *here* meant Gregory's apartment. "She's not good. I think you might need to come over, or maybe I should bring her to you."

Danny stared at Teres while he spoke. Her look of panic was immediate. He put his hand over the receiver and mouthed, "Let Ron help you. He's your best friend."

"No! Please, Danny. I am begging you! I need time ... to figure out where this is going, before we say to people ..."

"Hold on, Ron." Danny palmed the phone's mouthpiece and sat on the bed next to Teres.

"Teres, he can give you something to help, something that won't hurt the baby. Ron knows what he's doing. Yesterday was ... a trauma."

"Please, Danny! Just if you stay here – I can be okay."

She's asking me to stay. Danny felt strangely hopeful. He didn't care if it was a trick to make Ron stay away.

"Teres doesn't want you to come, you know how stubborn she is – yup, I'm okay. How are you doing with all this?" Danny waited for Ron's answer. "Yeah, a nightmare. I spoke to Gregory's father. I guess he got a call from Gregory's attorney." Danny watched his wife's eyes widen. Neither of them had said Gregory's name since the accident. "Can you ask Martha to cover for Teres at work? We're gonna need some time – yup, I will. Thanks." Danny hung up the phone. Teres was crying again. He pretended not to notice.

"Eat your English muffin and drink your tea before it gets cold." Then he escaped the room, unable to witness her grief for another minute.

*

Teres choked down bites between bouts of sobbing and sips of tea. Eating felt like a betrayal of something unidentifiable. To be taken care of by Danny compounded the betrayal. Her anguish wasn't wholly centered around Gregory. *He's dead. I saw him die on the road, running from my decision.* Another wave of nausea and heartache ripped through her as the guilt and confusion deepened. *Why does Danny know Gregory's father?* She shut her eyes and slept. Her peanut butter English muffin slid to the floor, staining Gregory's perfect, cream-colored carpet.

*

Pacing didn't help. Danny could feel his hypertension escalating. He eyed the recliner and began to bargain with himself. *If we're staying here for a while, I'm gonna have to sit somewhere.* Sitting in another man's chair was always tricky. Sitting in the chair of a man who's slept with your wife bordered on treason. Danny sat down. The chair was wonderful. He reached to the side to hit the recline lever and saw there was none. He gripped the arms and attempted to push the seat back. When it didn't budge, he foolishly realized it was electric and found the remote in the drawer of the end table. It was a small mistake, but it made him feel like Dr. Gregory Costa was continuing to get the better of him. *My enemy is dead but his chair fits like a glove.* The massage feature lulled Danny into a dreamless sleep.

*

He awoke five hours later, disoriented and confused. The apartment was pitch black and soundless. His heart began to race but was soon slowed by the beta blockers his doctor prescribed.

While his eyes adjusted to the darkness, Danny's mind reluctantly brought him up to speed. *Teres.*

He carefully made his way to the kitchen and turned on a light – easier than stumbling around looking for a lamp in the living room. Danny was not a guy to go recklessly off without a plan. He didn't stumble around looking for things. His wife's frantic energy made him appear overly cautious, but he had learned early on that a big guy doesn't want to trip and fall; it's a long way down.

The clock on the stove read 9:45. *No wonder I'm hungry.* He decided he would check on Teres and then, since there was little else in the refrigerator, he would make fried egg sandwiches. But first he needed to pee.

*

The bathroom was upscale marble and stone tile. The large, glass enclosed, walk-in shower was to the right of the toilet. Danny looked at it as he urinated. His wife's brand of shampoo rested on the built-in ledge next to a bottle of Head and Shoulders. He felt nauseous. *What are you doing here? Go home, dummy.* He washed his hands and opened Gregory's medicine cabinet in search of an antacid. There was a half-empty bottle of Pepto Bismol. Danny gave the bottle a shake, opened it, and took a long swig, visualizing Gregory doing the same thing. What difference did it make? His wife's lips had already connected them. Unlike their bathroom at home, this cabinet was sparse: razor, shaving cream, deodorant, *his and hers toothbrushes.* He took another swig. He was momentarily lifted by the thought of Gregory having indigestion.

There were two doors in the bathroom: the one he had entered through from the hallway, and the other leading to the master bedroom. Danny opened the second one a crack and peered inside. The bathroom light fell across the bed revealing Teres curled on her side and sleeping soundly. Danny was torn between checking

33

to see if she was breathing and knowing if she wasn't there was nothing he could do about it. *She's fine* he assured himself, people don't easily die of misery. Either way she looked peaceful. As he quietly closed the door, he sensed a slight resistance from the doorknob. He reached his hand around to the other side and felt Teres' pocketbook hanging over the knob. He pulled it into the bathroom and sat on the toilet seat, preparing to rifle through it for answers he didn't want to questions he would never ask.

Teres' pocketbook was big. Danny always gave her shit about it. He used to tell everyone to look in his wife's purse if they needed anything from a corkscrew to a paper cutter. Teres always came prepared. The guys at work were still kidding her about the time she pulled a piece of blueberry pie out of her pocketbook at a staff meeting.

Teres had tucked her small evening purse into the large, leather hobo bag. The little purse was old and probably worth a fortune. Made of red silk tapestry, it depicted intricately stitched blue peacocks with bezel-set garnets adorning their fanning tail feathers. It had been a present from her grandmother, Yaya, after Teres' grandfather, Papus, died. Yaya insisted her own days of dressing up for joyous events had come to an end with the death of her husband. She made Teres promise never to take for granted any day that required a special purse. Danny opened the silver clasp to reveal Kleenex, lipstick, and her small, newly-necessary reading glasses. Seeing the glasses would have made Danny chuckle a week ago, remembering how mad she was about having to get them. Not today. Today he wanted to smash them under his heel and kill himself with the shards of broken glass. He tossed the purse aside and went on to the larger bag.

Danny saw nothing to indicate an attempt to run away after his birthday party. The silk shawl she had worn over her dress, a pair of flat shoes in case her feet got tired, he had watched her pack both. Yes, she had the checkbook which was normally stored in the desk drawer in the kitchen. After years of not recording – and occasionally bouncing – checks, the Muldaurs used a duplicate check system. There was a carbon copy for every check written. The latest check hadn't been torn out. It was made out to the Mill Wharf Tavern to pay for his birthday party, with no dollar amount filled in. Danny went through the other carbons one-by-one: utility company, credit cards, grocery store, deposit to Mill Wharf Tavern; all explainable. Then he found a co-pay written out to Brookline Bay Obstetrics. It was dated February 4, 1992 – the same day as the ultrasound. He wondered vaguely if her OB was any good – he hated her current gynecologist, Dr. Ruff, who spent the first year of their marriage giving out bad news in his dispassionate, monotone voice. Knowing Gregory, this new guy was top in his field. Dr. Costa was used to nothing but the best, *and now that includes my wife.*

There was a business card tucked between the checks, *Marion Lamoreaux-Aarons, Ph.D. Specializing in family therapy and women at risk.* Danny slipped the card in his pocket. Teres' calendar, which she carried everywhere, wasn't in her purse. He quickly went through her wallet where he found an appointment card for her next OB visit, along with a business card of Gregory's. He took them both. After reassembling her leather bag, Danny opened the door and slipped it back over the doorknob. She was still asleep. He walked to the bed and put his hand on her jaw and neck, feeling her pulse, *feeling her soft skin.* He would have checked the pulse on her wrist, but she had both her hands curled under her cheek. *She sleeps like a child.* Danny suddenly saw how small she was. Perhaps she had always been this small, but her powerful personality made her seem bigger. He refused to consider that he might look smaller than his six-foot-two-inch, two-hundred-fifteen-pounds as a result of his own laid-back personality. Danny liked being tall. His height and weight carried the illusion of force and power, while letting him stay true to his passive nature. He knew quiet guys were seen as strong and silent, *even if they let their wives run over them like wildfire in a national park*. Teres murmured in her sleep. Danny fought the urge to crawl into bed behind her. He was mad at himself for wanting to. It wasn't about sex; it was comfort he sought. Outside Gregory's bedroom window, the moonlight reflected off Boston Harbor and bathed his wife's face in an otherworldly glow. Danny experienced a moment of pure terror when he realized Teres was the only person he had ever let comfort him – and now the reason he needed comfort. *I can't live without her*. He left to make egg sandwiches.

February 12, 1992

They were out of food. The eggs, tuna, frozen Lean Cuisine, and English muffins were gone, along with the orange juice and the two beers in the back of the fridge. All that was left was half a can of Maxwell House, but no coffee filters, and a couple of Earl Gray tea bags. Gregory's pantry was bare, and Danny was no closer to getting Teres to leave the apartment. But at least she was out of bed.

After two days of watching her lie there, reluctantly lifting herself to a seated position for the food he brought in, Danny suggested she get up and shower. She stared back at him with blank eyes, threw the covers away from her body, and swung her legs out of the bed. Then she sat there, slumped and silent, looking unable to create the next move.

From anyone else, this would have appeared to be a case of attention-seeking drama. But Danny knew better. Teres was dramatic in all the ways a passionate European woman can be. She loved something with the same fury with which she hated the next thing. Everything was black or white, right or wrong, but not both. She possessed a convicted opinion on most topics and wasn't shy about letting those around her know how she felt. No matter what crisis they had been through as a couple, Teres was the one to take the bull by the horns, and wrestle it to the ground if need be. Unless she had become an entirely different person overnight, Danny knew her affair fell into the black and white category for her. Her lethargy wasn't a trick to gain sympathy. She was devastated by her own deception. Why else would she be this non-functional? *Because her lover is dead,* his mind yelled back.

Danny helped her out of bed and walked her to the bathroom. She pulled down Gregory's boxers and sat on the toilet to pee while he adjusted the water temperature in the shower. She got up, kicked the boxers away, pulled off the t-shirt, and walked into the water without so much as placing her hand under the stream to check the temperature. As she stood there, motionless, Danny wasn't sure what to do. Should he get in the shower with her and help her wash up? He sat on the toilet seat and began taking off his hiking boots. When he looked up from the task, she had lifted her face to the water and begun washing her hair.

*

For as far back as Teres could remember, taking a shower was her do-over. It was her Mikvah, her sacred bath. The shower was where she sorted it out, both the ideas and conclusions of her life. In the steamy cocoon, she had washed away sorrows and anger, along with the frustration at simply being an imperfect human. The flowing water was restorative. Once she began her affair with Gregory, the healing effects of the shower stopped working. It became her crying place. No amount of water could wash away her guilt, especially in *this* shower. Standing for a thousand years under the large rainwater-showerhead wouldn't change what she had done. But hair washing was reflexive. With her eyes closed, Teres reached to the shelf she knew would be there, for the shampoo her lover had bought her.

November 19, 1991

"I cannot use your man shampoo. My hair will be a nest of frizz," Teres stated, as Gregory began to pour the thick blue shampoo into his palm to wash her hair.

"It won't kill you this one time." Gregory replied with his usual dose of know-it-all arrogance.

"And now you are an expert on my hair?" Teres shot back, not kidding.

It was like this every time. They made love, her body frantic for his, and as soon as it was over she hated him. She knew she was turning the disgust she felt for herself onto Gregory, but he gave her so many reasons for wanting to choke him. The notion that he knew her better than she knew herself, *better than Danny knew her*
...

"I am done." Teres shut off the shower and stepped around Gregory toward the door, leaving him holding the shampoo and covered with soap.

*

"Teressa, don't be ridiculous! Where are you going?" Gregory turned the water back on and quickly rinsed himself. By the time he got out of the shower, she had left the bathroom. He was ready to kill her but at the same time her fury excited him. He glanced at his erection in the mirror as he toweled off.

Gregory had had a lot of women in his life. Most had been easy to get and quick to go. He knew his appeal: handsome, rich cardiothoracic surgeon with a mysterious background. Little did people guess his mysterious background was a triple decker in the poor section of Dorchester, along with a father in an Italian prison. Teressa had been a hard win – *a very hard win.* As the wife of his patient, she was strictly off limits according to the list of rules he had adhered to in the past, a list designed to keep his life as hassle free as possible. Their relationship broke two rules: Don't get involved with patients, and don't date married women. Now here he was, standing in his bathroom with an erection for a married woman who drove him crazy. And he had become friends with her very likable husband, whose heart he repaired three months ago. *This is stupid,* he berated himself. *Just end it!* But he knew he wouldn't. For the first time in his life, Gregory Aldo Costa was in love – and it was killing him.

*

She was dressed and swinging her hair into a knot as Gregory entered his bedroom.

"I am done."

"You said that already," Gregory replied as if it didn't matter to him. He flicked off his towel and casually walked past her to get a pair of boxers from his bureau. Even with his back to her, he felt her staring at him. His stomach flipped, and his erection twitched. Gregory couldn't control either bodily function. Being out of control was like a return to his childhood. There had been many things he couldn't control back then, *like having a father who was a criminal, or a mother who was mentally ill, or sisters ...* Using well-practiced compartmentalization, Gregory pushed the dangerous stream of thought from his mind and concentrated on her.

"I have no say over the circumstances of our relationship, Teressa." *No control.* "Only you do." For a man to whom integrity with women was of no consequence, Gregory was alarmed by his involuntary honesty when it came to this woman. It pissed him off. He could sense she was gaining the upper hand. Gregory's dominant personality had made him familiar with the swap of power from lower to upper hand, but never the reverse. And to make it worse, she was holding all the cards in a game she was ready to fold. It took everything in him to stay calm, look placid. He knew from past experience she would run if he baited her with his anger. Their trysts had become a one-man contest to see how long he could keep her from leaving after they made love. Typically, she fled within thirty minutes. Gregory looked at the clock on the nightstand – twenty-eight minutes and counting.

*

Teres searched the bedroom for her shoe. *He probably kicked it under the bed*, she decided angrily, ashamed by her memory of how quickly they had undressed. Gregory was still standing at the chest of drawers with his back to her and his underwear in his hand. She stopped looking for her shoe and stared intently at his back. It was beautiful. There was no denying Gregory was handsome in a Greek God kind of way, thick dark hair, slim hips, strong upper body – kept that way by daily trips to the gym. He once told her that surgeons fall apart at the end of their careers because of an inability to stand for hours and operate. "All it takes is strength," he had said cavalierly. Teres knew Gregory was the king of self-discipline. Which was why it suddenly struck her as comical that he was standing there naked, with his back to her, trying to control the anger she knew he was feeling. She began to laugh.

"What's so funny?" He turned to face her.

"You are. You would do anything to not join me in this fight I want to have with you." She sat on the bed, a smirk on her face.

"What fight? The one about your shampoo?"

"Yes," she said, a lie and he knew it.

Gregory walked to the bed and stood in front of her, his naked body inches from her. He reached down and pulled her hair out of the knot, letting it fall across her shoulders. He picked up a damp curl and put it to his face, breathing in the scent. "What shampoo do you use?"

"Mane and Tail." Her voice was breathy, a traitor to her own ears.

"Head and Shoulders, Mane and Tail. I think our shampoos have a lot of body parts covered." Gregory pushed her back onto the bed, her wrists clasped above her head in his one-handed grip. "But not all of them." He lowered himself onto her, began kissing her neck and working his body against hers. She knew she was losing to him again, but just then she didn't care.

February 12, 1992

The funeral. Danny hadn't even thought about Gregory's funeral.

Whenever someone as young as Gregory died, people came out of the woodwork to attend the services. His wake was going to be a stampede: colleagues, alumni, and anyone whose heart Gregory had ever tinkered with – *did that include my wife's?* – would be in attendance, along with random people whose vague connections allowed them to mourn the tragic loss of someone so young and talented. Ron had called a half-dozen times before mentioning the arrangements. The concern in his voice was obvious. But to his credit, Ron didn't bombard him with questions beyond asking if there was anything he could do, to which Danny replied, "No," but thought, *Yes. Help me drag my wife home.*

Danny hadn't turned on the TV or picked up a newspaper since Gregory's death. He had barely gone out to the Jeep to grab his clothing; that accomplished in the middle of the night when he was certain Teres was asleep. But now they needed food, and Danny wasn't convinced she wouldn't take off the minute he went out the door. "Well, this is stupid," he mumbled to himself. "If she takes off, she takes off," as if he could let that happen.

Danny quietly opened the bedroom door. It was noontime and she was asleep, again. His mind went to blood clots. He needed to get her up walking, but for now this worked for him. He crept around the room and gathered her shoes, coat, and purse. He knew not having her wallet wouldn't stop her from leaving, but having no shoes might make it tougher. Teres had graduated to Gregory's workout sweats and thick white socks. When he saw she hadn't even rolled up the sleeves to effectively use her hands let alone adjusted the pants, Danny had twisted each pant leg up tight and stuffed it into the sock, so she wouldn't trip. She was lying there, all curled up with the covers thrown off, and didn't move a muscle when Danny pulled the blanket over her.

Before he left the room, he took one more look around – the way you would if your patient were in the psych ward – and concluded his wife was the only dangerous thing in the room. He tiptoed out in search of a good hiding place for her things. After a few minutes of entertaining ideas like the kitchen cabinet and under the couch, Danny emptied his duffel bag of everything but his medication and put Teres' purse and clothing inside. He would just take it all with him. *Now to find a grocery store.*

*

It was good to be outside. Danny took a few deep breaths of the cold air. There were remnants, now gray and dirty, of the snow that had fallen just four nights ago, *the beginning of my new reality.* He pried open the frozen Jeep door, threw the duffel bag inside and started the engine, giving it a few minutes to heat up while he chipped away at the windshield with the scraper. This warming of the engine was a concept he could never explain to his wife. She insisted if she was fine with riding in a cold car, what difference did it make to the car? Every movement or thought led to Teres. It had been that way since the moment he laid eyes on her. She permeated his existence, both undermining and defining him, as his life before her never had. For thirty-nine years, he was Danny Muldaur, the big, easy-going guy with no worries. His world had been small and controllable, the way he liked it. Then Teressa Giannopoulos came along and changed everything.

1972
US Naval Communication Station
Nea Makri, Greece

The Karmann Ghia didn't sound like it would make it up the hill, but always did. With over 200,000 miles on the odometer and on its eighth owner, the little car owed nothing to anyone. It had been passed down from one Navy sailor to another for most of its life. Danny had a list of men willing to buy the car off him when he was ready to pack it in. He was going to miss this car. The Karmann Ghia was a treasure. Its simple engine design made it the kind of car an idiot could fix, and Danny was no idiot. Within two weeks of buying it from the last guy, for the bargain price of three hundred dollars, he had the car running like a charm. This was why when his prized possession coughed and sputtered a bit, he took his eyes off the road and looked down at the tachometer, worried about the transmission. A moment later Danny looked up, just in time to hit her.

The girl was unconscious. He hadn't hit her hard. The steel bumper of the Karmann Ghia had barely grazed the bicycle, making her foot slip off the pedal and wedge itself between the spokes of the bike's front tire. Then the momentum of her trapped foot caused her body to catapult over the handlebars and slap viciously to the ground. The event took a matter of seconds. In just a few seconds more, Danny had vaulted from the offending car and was assessing the young woman's injuries. Her forehead was split open, deep into the hairline of her raven black hair. She probably had a concussion. Her foot was bloodied and most likely fractured. *Think! Think, stupid! What do you do next?* For reasons he couldn't fathom, Danny was paralyzed. It wasn't the slow-motion version of a disastrous dream, but something close. He was floating through it, not in a detached way, more of an intensely-attached way. He was part of the blood coming from her head. He was thrown from the bike with her. Danny was confused. Was it possible he, too, had hit his head when he swerved the car? The young woman moaned. "Damn. Damn. Damn." With her thick accent, Danny thought she was saying his name. *How does she know my name?* Later, when it was too late for him to not be in love with her, he would realize "damn" was her favorite curse word. Then the girl opened her eyes and brought her hand up to touch her bloodied scalp. She looked right into Danny's eyes and said, "I was blinded by my tears." It was like that. It was that rapid, that breathtaking, that devastating. And it was too late. His soul had recognized hers and there was no turning back.

February 12, 1992

The distance from Dr. Costa's apartment to Beth Israel Hospital was five miles and a boatload of traffic. Danny couldn't imagine how Gregory handled emergencies given the logistics of his commute. *Knowing Gregory, he had the helicopter pick him up*, Danny brooded, fighting his way through Morrissey Boulevard. He decided to turn toward Dorchester where he knew there was a Stop & Shop – and hopefully, an ATM.

Danny rarely went to the store without a list from Teres. Her lists were a riddle most of the time, written with little lessons and commentaries:

"Tomatoes – do not get the kind you like because they are the one with lots of acid," or *"One pound of beef – except if it is on sale – then get 1 pound and 2 pounds."* Danny would try to guess the meaning of her cryptic note and inevitably fail, bringing home a two-pound package of ground beef only to find she meant what she had written: a one-pound package for today and a two-pound package for the freezer, which she would then divide into two separate containers. And it was peppers that gave him indigestion, not tomatoes.

Finding the ATM was easy, located inside the doorway of the bank next to Stop & Shop. Danny took out the same conservative one-hundred dollars he would have grabbed if his wife had sent him on this shopping trip. *How much can you take out of an ATM at one time* he wondered; but more importantly, *how much food do I buy when I don't know how long we'll be holed up in Gregory's apartment?* Which brought him to the one-million-dollar question: How much longer would he put up with this situation before he called in reinforcements to drag Teres home or to a hospital? Danny didn't know. He felt like his head was going to explode. The sudden blinding headache reminded him how badly he needed a cup of coffee. He looked through the glass doors of the bank and saw they had a complementary coffee station in their lobby. Danny went inside, downed two tiny paper cups of black coffee, then made a third the way he liked it, plenty of cream and sugar. He was ready to face the grocery store.

*

Grocery shopping had gone unexpectedly well in his opinion. He had purchased the basics, including donuts – one of which he was now eating in the car. On his trip through the medicine isle for ibuprofen, he had noticed a section with prenatal vitamins. Danny knew folic acid was important for fetal development, but he couldn't remember why, or which foods contained it, so he picked out the brand highest in folic acid – a one-month supply.

The ride back to the apartment was quick, one-thirty in the afternoon and no traffic. His stomach churned with two kinds of urgency: Teres was probably awake by now, and he needed to use the bathroom. He was happy to see a parking spot close to the apartment building. Danny had bought three filled-to-the-brim bags of groceries. He took Teres' pocketbook, dress and heels out of the duffel bag and stuffed it with two of the grocery bags, then threw the duffel bag and her purse over his shoulder and grabbed the last grocery bag. He was loaded up like a mule, but at least it would only be one trip. He carefully walked across the parking area. It was cold out, with patches of ice still on the blacktop and walkways despite the midday sun. At the main door of the building, Danny realized he had left Gregory's keys on the hook in the kitchen. *Jesus Christ! Now what?* In that moment, the hopelessness of his current situation descended upon him, not just the locked door – all of it. He envisioned dumping everything on the ground at his feet, walking back to his car, and driving home to Scituate.

"Can I give you a hand? Looks like yours are full."

Danny hadn't heard the man come up behind him. He was wearing a gray suit and carrying a black leather briefcase. Danny responded with a lie. "Only if you've got a key. I think mine's at the bottom of this duffel bag." The man produced a key and opened the door. They made small talk as they waited for the elevator.

"This is a great apartment complex. Have you lived here long?" the man asked.

"No. Not very long," Danny replied, trying to stick to some semblance of the truth. They were both headed to the sixth floor. The man offered to carry one of Danny's grocery bags. Danny let him and then shifted his wife's purse to the other shoulder without making any excuse for having a woman's purse. Once on the sixth floor, they continued around the corner together, Danny assuming the man was following, not leading. At apartment 607, he stood awkwardly in front of the door. *What if Teres doesn't open it?* thought Danny, hesitant to knock in front of the man.

"Thanks for the help. You can just leave the bag on the floor. My wife ran up ahead of me … to use the bathroom. I don't know how long she'll be in there, but you don't have to wait. You know how women are."

"Mr. Muldaur. Allow me." Danny's jaw dropped as the man produced a key, unlocked Gregory's door, and pushed it open in a gesture that said, "After you."

February 10, 1992

Ron's money would have been on Cathedral of the Holy Cross as venue for Gregory's funeral service. It was the mother church of the metropolitan see of Boston and considered a more important church than Saint Leonard's on Hanover Street in the North End. But what did Ron know? As a lapsed Presbyterian with a lifestyle deplored by most religions, the Unitarian Universalist Church was the only house of God he had entered since trading seminary college for medical school. Saint Leonard's Church proved to be an unexpected surprise.

When Father Giovanni Ambrosoli called Ron at the hospital on Monday to ask if he would do Gregory's eulogy, his Italian accent was so thick Ron was tempted to page the emergency room interpreter. Eventually, they agreed to meet at Saint Leonard's after Ron's shift, which ended at seven a.m. the next morning.

*

"It is my pleasure to meet you, Doctor Ron Watters," the priest said, rushing toward him with arms outstretched for an embrace. Father Ambrosoli was a little man, not nearly as robust as his booming voice would imply. Ron raised his left arm to match the handshake he had extended with the right and went in for the hug.

"Thank you, Father Ambrosoli. Your call was an unexpected surprise."

The little priest frowned. "How so, Dr. Ron? It is an honor, as an oldest and dearest, ah, *amico*, that Dr. Costa chose you to speak at his funeral."

What is this guy talking about? Dearest friends? We were colleagues who didn't even work in the same hospital. Danny's surgery was the first time Ron had laid eyes on Gregory since graduating med school. By that point he knew Costa only by his reputation as an excellent cardiac surgeon. Questions shot through Ron's mind, not the least of which was how did this priest get his name? "Father, how did you get my name?"

"When Philip made the arrangements."

"Who is Philip?" Ron asked, further confused by this conversation.

"Philip Dixon, of course. Gregorio's attorney. *Evidentemente* Gregory provided *istruzioni* ...direction to him in the event of this sad moment. Mr. Dixon handled also the paperwork for Gregorio's donation of the *bellissimo* statue in our Peace Garden in... ah... *onore* of his madre, Louise. Dr. Costa has provided much for our Parish, as well as *sostanziale* support to one of our *preferito* charities, Italian Home for Children."

48

Jesus, I knew nothing about the guy. Ron considered telling Father Ambrosoli he couldn't do the eulogy, but there had to be a reason Gregory chose him. He wasn't flattered, he was mystified. And Ron loved a mystery. It was fortunate he had the next two days off. It appeared he was going to need every minute of that time to research a guy who thought of him as an *amico.* "Father, do you have Philip Dixon's telephone number?"

"Please, follow me to the parish office and I will have Kelly Jo provide it for you, then we will visit the Peace Garden."

Ron followed Father Giovanni Ambrosoli through the beautiful church, genuflecting like a devout Catholic as he passed the alter. *When in Rome ...*

February 12, 1992

Ron looked into the sea of faces in front of him, searching for, but not finding, Danny and Teres. The church was filled to capacity. *Maybe they're out there somewhere.* He took a deep breath and began:

"Gregory Aldo Costa was a man of many faces. As a world-renowned cardiothoracic surgeon, he was the face of success, innovation, and hope. Two years ago, Dr. Costa accepted an appointment as head of cardiac surgery at Beth Israel Hospital, only after the administration assured him it would not interfere with his commitment to patient care. Caring for the heart was his number one priority. I'm certain there are many people in this church today whose hearts Dr. Costa touched – and I mean that literally." Ron paused to accommodate the low rumble of laughter.

"As an Italian immigrant, Gregory arrived in Boston at the age of fourteen. At just sixteen years old, his father, Joseph Costa, was deported back to Italy and Gregory became the sole support of his mother and twin sisters. From those meager beginnings, Gregory

Aldo Costa crafted himself into the epitome of the American dream, going to college on a merit scholarship and then paying his way through medical school by working as a mason and cement contractor, trades he had learned from his father."

"It was a tough start with endings that weren't all happy. His mother, Louise, died shortly after Gregory graduated high school, from complications of a ruptured appendix. His sisters, Maura and Maria, were sent back to Italy to live with an aunt. Gregory was left behind in Dorchester to sink or swim. Anyone who's met Dr. Gregory Costa knows he was not one to sink. He flourished, creating a life any man would be proud of.

I wish I could say these were things I knew about Gregory before his death. I can't. The person I met during our first semester at Tufts School of Medicine was the same person we honor here today: tough, smart, confident with colleagues, charming with women – the type of man you want in your corner during a crisis. But there was another side to Gregory, a side he hid from others. This other side included his philanthropic nature, giving generously to charities that spoke to his heart and were a nod to his history. One of those charities is this church, Saint Leonard of Port Maurice Parish, a church built in 1899 for, and by, the Italian immigrants of Boston. Another was The Italian Home for Children, whose original purpose was to care for the many Italian children orphaned during the 1918 influenza epidemic, but now serves the special needs of all children in the Greater Boston area. His loss leaves a hole in our hospitals, our communities, and our hearts. There will be no replacing Dr. Gregory Aldo Costa.

As I look around this room, I wonder about the people we think we know – people with hardships, burdens, and traumatic stories, hidden under perfected exteriors. Perhaps the silver lining in the dark cloud of Gregory's death is that I truly got to know my friend.

Perhaps his journey on this earth wasn't only about fixing the physical heart but getting to know and accept the spiritual heart. What if the lesson Gregory leaves us with today is to let people see us for who we really are, and not the polished masks we wear every day? Wouldn't that be amazing?"

Ron made his way off the alter and back to his pew knowing exactly what he had just done. *Looks like I'm finished hiding my homosexuality behind my Mardi Gras mask. Thanks a lot Gregory – and to think, you were my first serious crush.*

February 12, 1992

"Who are you and what are you doing here?" Danny was rattled, and it showed.

"I'm sorry Mr. Muldaur. I didn't mean to startle you," said the man, entering the apartment with Danny. "I wasn't certain, at first, it was you. Where is Teressa?"

"Where is Teressa? None of your god damn business! That's where my wife is!" Danny threw the groceries and his wife's purse on the couch and came at the man with a menacing stance.

"Danny – may I call you Danny – I'm Philip Dixon, Gregory Costa's attorney."

Danny immediately backed away, knowing he was the one with some explaining to do.

"Just give me an hour and I can have us packed up and outta here," Danny countered, already stuffing the last grocery bag into the duffel bag.

"That's really not necessary," Dixon said. "I'd like to speak to your wife. Is she still pregnant?"

Danny's face went from red to purple as rage flooded his body. "That's none of your business, you fucking little shyster!" He went at the man just as the door to the bedroom opened.

"Danny? Is everything alright? Who is this man?" Danny froze and took in the sight of his wife: wild hair, wearing oversized sweats that hung on her yet still showed the tiny bulge of her stomach. She looked emaciated, but in control. He let go of Philip Dixon.

"Gregory's attorney," Danny replied in an emotionless voice. "He wants to talk to you."

Philip came forward and extended his hand, "Philip Dixon, Teressa – Mrs. Muldaur." She ignored his hand and gestured to the couch for him to sit, then shrugged her shoulders when she saw it was covered with upturned grocery bags. "I'd like to speak with you privately about the estate and last requests of Gregory Costa."

Teres swayed like she was going to fall, then pulled her posture into a defiant rod. "Anything you have to say to me, Mr. Dixon, can be said in front of my husband."

"I can leave," said Danny, pissed that his wife was suddenly all about honesty and full disclosure. Her look was pleading. Danny hesitated, then caved, pulling the groceries off the couch so she could sit before she fell down. Philip Dixon sat in Gregory's chair and opened his briefcase onto the coffee table. He placed a pile of paperwork in front of Teres and began speaking in an official capacity.

"First, Mrs. Muldaur, I need to see a copy of your license to verify your identity." Teres looked at him as if he were crazy. Danny pulled Teres' wallet from the purse at his feet, opened it to reveal her license and slapped it on the table in front of the attorney. Teres shifted her look of disbelief to her husband.

"Have you been going through my purse?"

"Yup. And I cashed a check at the grocery store," he said defiantly, even though it wasn't true. Danny stared her down for a second, then they both turned their attention to Dixon.

"This is a copy of the Last Will and Testament of Gregory Aldo Costa, dated January 23rd, 1992, two weeks prior to his death." Danny stopped himself from glancing at Teres' face to gage her grief. "You, Mrs. Muldaur have been named as a beneficiary of his estate, along with his father and two sisters. Gregory has bequeathed this apartment and a bank account with five-hundred-thousand-dollars in your name to be used at your discretion. The unborn child you carry is further named as a beneficiary. Gregory established a sizable trust fund which will be released ..."

"I've heard just about enough of this bullshit. Thank you, but no thank you, Mr. Dixon. I can take care of my own damn family! We don't need any money from Gregory Costa!"

"I'm sorry, Mr. Muldaur, but this really isn't up to you. You are not mentioned in any capacity, other than as part of my initial briefing when the will was redrawn in January. You have no rights to this child, and should Mrs. Muldaur be unable, or unwilling to care for the baby ..."

Danny stood. In a low voice with an explosive undercurrent he said, "Gregory gave me this baby as his dying wish."

"Mr. Muldaur!"

"Daniello?" Teres' voice was a whisper. Danny sat down on the couch. He took his wife's hands in his. He spoke softly, as if they were alone in the room.

"Teres, it's true. Right before Gregory died, he made me promise to take care of you and the baby. He said the baby was mine."

"Mr. Muldaur, you have no legal standing when it comes to this child. I'll admit, this is an unusual situation, but you have no proof of that conversation ever taking place."

Teressa stood. "We are finished here. Thank you, Mr. Dixon. Please leave your card and our attorney will contact you about the transfer of this apartment and the funds." Her words were final and inarguable. Both Danny and Philip Dixon watched her walk back to the bedroom, shutting the door behind her.

"I really do need a signature," Dixon said.

"I'm sure you'll live," Danny replied, getting up to usher the man to the door.

The attorney organized his paperwork, leaving a stack on the table and efficiently loading the rest into his briefcase, which he closed with a resounding clap. He put the key to the apartment on top of the papers and walked briskly to the door.

"You can take that with you. We're not keeping this apartment."

"Again, Mr. Muldaur, that's not up to you." Danny held the door for Philip Dixon and locked it behind him. Then he strode past the rubble of the living room, barely making it to the bathroom in time. He could hear Teres' wracking sobs through the bedroom door. Seated with his pants around his ankles and his face resting in his palms, Danny could no longer hold in his own pain, so he joined his wife in a symphony of tears with Gregory's last words its lyrical refrain: *The baby is yours.*

*

Pull it together! Teres was out of control and unable to reign it in. The crying increased her nausea and made her scared for the baby. She was headed for the bathroom when she heard the exhaust fan go on and the door slam shut. *Danny.* Teres swung the wastepaper basket under her face as her sobbing transitioned to gagging. Knowing he was on the other side of the door escalated her hysterics. This would be so much easier with Danny's arms wrapped around her. It was a foolish thought, but part of the pattern they had created together; Teres was the instigator, Danny was the smoother. She thought about last year when she had insisted, over

54

Danny's objections, they needed a swimming pool. She did all the leg work, hired the contractors, and made the decisions. Halfway through the project, her frustrations with its progress turned her into a ranting lunatic. Danny had held her in his big embrace and assured her it was going to be fine. Then he said a few simple things to the owner of the pool company and the problems disappeared. She needed Danny to get her through the pain of Gregory's death.

Some primitive survival mechanism wouldn't allow Teres to dwell on Gregory. Whenever the bloody vision of him entered her mind, she'd feel a chest-crushing pain and the image would vanish. She would have let go, let the pain take her down the dark abyss of insanity, if not for the life she was carrying. She had made a vow to Gregory, and to herself, to keep this baby safe; a vow more important now that he was dead.

December 24, 1991

It was on Christmas Eve morning Teres found out she was pregnant. She had purchased the pregnancy test the day before, certain by the ache in her uterus she wouldn't have to use it. She was wrong. The ache was not the result of an impending menstrual period. It was the ache of a uterus expanding ever-so-slightly to accommodate and protect the embryo which had recently attached itself to the uterine wall. A miracle had happened. She was having a baby. She had wanted to rush into the other room and tell Danny. That was when the full force of her guilt hit her. *I want to tell my husband I am pregnant because he is the only one who will truly know what this means to me.* She couldn't make herself leave the bathroom.

When Danny came to check on her an hour later, she told him she was sick but feeling a little better. The truth was she was sick and feeling worse, almost to the point of ending her life. There were enough medications in the Muldaur medicine cabinet to kill a small army. Teres had taken them down, one by one, analyzing each one's effectiveness as a life-ender. But to kill herself would be to kill the life that was growing inside her. An abortion and ending her affair would also resolve her problem. Neither Gregory nor Danny would ever have to know. *But I will know, and my life will be over.* Teres put the medications back onto their shelves. She knew she could never harm this baby, no matter what cost to herself.

So she did the only thing she could do, take a shower and finish the preparations for Christmas dinner. It was the best she had in the way of a plan. There would be plenty of time to reflect upon this miracle her deceit had created, starting with midnight Mass at Saint Mary's, where she and Danny went every year to celebrate the birth of Christ.

February 12, 1992

Danny realized he needed a better plan than feeding Teres and listening to her cry, especially with Gregory still fucking with him from the grave by bestowing a gift that made it easy for Teres to stay in this apartment forever. He remembered a time, just days ago, when he thought of Gregory as a savior: *The Great Gregory Costa – Cardiothoracic Superhero.* He had saved Danny's life twice, once with the bypass surgery, and the second time when Danny went into cardiac arrest two days after the operation. Gregory had stuck with him, trying medication after medication in an attempt to control the post-surgical arrhythmia his heart had developed. *A lot of TLC to get my wife into bed.*

But Danny had to admit he felt great. Sure, he was on a lot of meds. His strength and energy levels were still building, but the endurance-limiting exhaustion he felt before the surgery was gone.

Climbing stairs wasn't embarrassing. He could picture a day that included twenty-seven holes of golf once the weather broke in the spring. He and Ron had talked to Gregory about making it a threesome on the course; Gregory had a membership to The Country Club of Brookline, Ron and Danny were members of Scituate Country Club. *Another disappointment* thought Danny, ironically. *Looks like I'll never play the nation's first country club.* Danny wanted to hate Gregory, but somehow, he couldn't. He was appalled to realize he felt more hatred for Attorney Philip Dixon than he did for the man with whom his wife had cheated. It didn't make sense. None of this made sense. Teres wasn't a cheater. She was a big pain in the ass at times, but not a cheater. Lying made her crazy. Danny thought about the lie they had told her parents in order to get permission to marry: Teres was pregnant. The guilt had almost killed her, especially when it turned out they couldn't have children.

This walk down memory lane wasn't getting Danny anywhere. He needed help. He shoved his hands in his pockets and jingled his change, a gesture he made unconsciously when he was nervous or upset. Right now, he was both. Along with his coins was the business card he had taken from Teres' wallet. He pulled it out. *Marion Lamoreaux-Aarons, Ph.D. Specializing in family therapy and women at risk*. Teressa was at risk. Danny dialed the number on the card and left a message with the answering service, then went to check on his wife. She was sitting up in bed, asleep again, clutching a small trash bucket to her chest. He went back to the living room, pulled the ugly phone closer to Gregory's chair and fell asleep, hoping to be woken by a phone call.

*

Marion Lamoreaux-Aarons didn't fool around.

"Yes, Mr. Muldaur, I know who you are. Is your wife alright?"

57

Danny hesitated. He had been prepared with a speech to explain everything, now it didn't look to be necessary. "No, Doctor. I don't think she is. She hasn't left her bed – that is to say the bed in this apartment – in four days." *Why am I making a thing about this not being her bed? The lady doesn't care whose bed my wife won't get out of – only I do.*

"Has she taken anything? Pills? Tranquilizers?"

"No," Danny answered, "I can barely get her to eat."

"Give me the address and I'll be there as quickly as I can."

"Twenty-four Oyster Bay Road, apartment six-oh-seven in Boston. Do you mean you're coming now, or quickly tomorrow morning?" It was eleven-thirty at night.

"Now. I'll see you in thirty minutes." Dr. Lamoreaux-Aarons hung up the phone. Danny got up from the chair to make himself a cup of coffee. *It looks like it's gonna be a long night.*

*

Marion Lamoreaux-Aarons knew better than to begin her patient intake by gathering information from family. It wasted valuable time, and past experience had taught her the only perspective that mattered was that of the woman in crisis. When Daniel Muldaur opened the door, she was prepared to brush by him, and whatever he had to say, with a simple, "I'm Dr. Lamoreaux-Aarons. Where is Mrs. Muldaur?"

To her surprise, she was greeted with, "Thank you for coming. My wife is right this way." He ushered her to the bedroom door and before he opened it asked, "Is it better for Teres if I introduce you or is that something that works better if you do it?"

His question told her three things: His wife was his primary concern, he had nothing to hide, and he was scared enough to put his faith in a stranger's ability to help. Her gut instinct, a trusted tool but not the last word, told her this was a good guy. Marion

58

touched his arm reassuringly. "I've got it from here, Mr. Muldaur. But stay close in case I have questions or need you to come in the room."

"Danny. Just call me Danny."

"Lamoreaux-Aarons is a mouthful. Call me Marion."

*

They were making progress. Mrs. Muldaur was awake, her affect a bit guarded but not paranoid. She was answering questions.

"Mrs. Muldaur, do you know where you are?" The question brought immediate change to her features. *Defensive? Stoic?*

"Yes. I am in Dr. Gregory Costa's apartment."

"And who is staying here with you?"

"My husband," The woman answered.

"Do you feel safe?" It was sometimes the first question she asked if the patient was agitated or showed obvious signs of fear. Mrs. Muldaur did not appear scared. She was disconnected and lethargic, although it was difficult to determine lethargy with a new patient having just woken up.

"Yes. Doctor, what do you already know about me?"

Direct. Good. "Nothing. Just that your husband is worried about you and he found my card among your things, so he called me."

"I'm pregnant."

"Congratulations, Mrs. Muldaur," Marion responded cautiously, unable to read this as good news or bad.

"Your husband is my doctor. He gave me your card," She said without looking at Marion. "There are things about my pregnancy … have you seen my records?"

"Until you give me permission, or I determine you're a danger to yourself or others, your records are private," Marion responded. "Is there something in particular you would like me to know?"

59

Mrs. Muldaur hesitated, one hand pulling at the other as if she were wrestling with a stubborn doorknob. *Pull it open and let me in,* the doctor pleaded telepathically. But Marion kept silent, knowing one false word could take the current question off the table. She had seen admissions swallowed back down from the tip of a patient's tongue because the wrong question had followed too closely to the right one. *Is there something in particular you would like me to know?*

*

Four days ago, Teres was prepared to tell the world this baby was Gregory's. The deception was killing her. She had planned to confess everything after Danny's party, beg his forgiveness, and take whatever fate was due her. But that was four days ago, when she knew Gregory would never give up having a life with his child. Four days ago, when he threatened to fight her for custody. Four days ago, when he was alive. Now she was on the verge of telling this woman about the baby's real father and she couldn't do it. *Does that make me a coward on top of being an adulteress?* She wanted desperately to lie back down, curl herself into a ball, and go to sleep. A part of her brain was functioning in command mode, looking for a plan, a way out of this moment. If she wasn't careful, she would end up in a psych unit. Why was it so difficult to tell this doctor the truth about her pregnancy? Anything had to be easier than the day she told Gregory…

January 7, 1992

No one at Accelerated Ambulance expected Teres to be in the office on Tuesdays. It was sales and service day, her time to scout new accounts and check up on those the ambulance company already had. Teressa loved Tuesdays. It gave her a chance to meet new people, roam around unfamiliar hospitals and clinics, and eat lunch by herself. "This is my most productive day," she would declare to Danny and the staff. For a woman driven to succeed, turning Tuesdays into 'Gregory days' was a professional failure second only to her personal failure of infidelity.

*

"I do not want to go back to your apartment." Teres watched Gregory's hands tighten on the steering wheel, his look became sullen. *He's such a baby.* "Why can't we have a day that is not about having sex?"

His face brightened with a superior grin. "This is progress. Looks like you want a relationship with me, not just an affair."

She hated him. Whatever she said he twisted to his advantage. He knew she loved her husband. He knew she spent every moment they were together trying to end this affair. And yet he arrogantly acted as if their Tuesdays could result in a lifetime. The news she had for him would push him further toward that delusion. *What am I going to do?* Running away had become a viable option, but how could she run from Danny? She couldn't.

"Please can we go somewhere for lunch and have a normal moment?" she asked, as if that could happen. The conversation she had planned was anything but normal.

Teres' stomach lurched as Gregory down shifted his ridiculous red Ferrari and swerved off the exit toward his apartment. It reminded her of the nausea she experienced each morning; nausea which didn't allow her to put the pregnancy out of her mind, and eventually cemented her decision to tell him about the baby. *Apparently, it wasn't quick-set cement* she thought to herself, mentally listing the reasons not to tell him today. Teres hated how indecisive she had become. After a lifetime of knowing exactly what she wanted and being somewhat scornful of people who weren't able to nail down their choices, it was humbling to be powerless and vacillating. She hated herself for her weakness. And she hated him.

"Where are you going? I said I do not want to go back to your place."

"Relax, Teressa," he replied in his controlled voice. "You've made that abundantly clear."

Teres reclined the seat and closed her eyes, hoping to stem both her anxiety and her queasiness. An involuntary smile crossed her face when she imagined how Gregory would react if she were to vomit all over the beautiful leather upholstery of his prized possession.

*

The Union Oyster House had a history that dated back to 1826, the décor being a blend of early Americana and old-world Europe. Composed of brick, beams, wainscoting, and dark wood, and located between the Boston Seaport and Government Center, it had been Gregory's go-to place for years. He first discovered it as a student at Tufts. The bar was both anonymous and inviting. No one there cared or kept track of the women he was with, but they knew his favorite drink and enough about him to refer to him as "Doctor Costa." Going to lunch with a new woman would raise no red flags. The weather on that day was good for January, temperature above freezing, but windy. He and Teressa blew into the doorway to the familiar greeting of Jerry, behind the bar. It made him smile, but caused Teressa to hiss, "Why did you bring me here to where everyone knows you?"

"Nobody cares who I have lunch with but you, Teressa."

"And I do not care either," she spat at him, as if he were trying to make her jealous. He wasn't, but it was gratifying to hear the thicker European accent brought on by her obvious jealousy. *She never makes it easy*. Maybe that was the attraction. After years of having women fall at his feet, this woman was more likely to take him out at the knees. They fought about everything. Gregory had never been one to back down from a verbal sparring match, until now. His fight strategy had become retreat rather than advance. After wooing her for nearly three months, Mrs. Muldaur wasn't a disappointment, she was a challenge.

"We're heading upstairs," Gregory said to Jerry, grabbing a couple menus from the hostess stand.

"Great. I'll send Sharon up to grab your drink order," he responded. Gregory appreciated Jerry not making him look like the frequent flyer he was by offering to open a bottle of the wine The Oyster House stocked especially for him.

At the top of the stairs, he maneuvered Teressa toward his favorite booth, number eighteen, which bore the inscription: *This was the favorite booth of John F. Kennedy when he dined at the Union Oyster House.*

"You should have the oyster stew. It's delicious."

*

Teres couldn't imagine gagging down oyster stew right now, no matter how good it was. "Gregory, I have an idea. Perhaps you can worry about your order and I will worry about mine," she replied gently, trying unsuccessfully to make a snotty comment sound less biting. Gregory had already ordered them a bottle of red wine without asking her if it was what she wanted. Granted, two weeks ago it would have been. *I hope he has fun drinking the whole bottle himself* she thought, as Sharon, the waitress, poured a tasting into his glass. Gregory nodded his approval and Sharon reached over to fill Teres' glass. "No thank you," Teres said with her hand covering the rim. The waitress gave Gregory a full pour and left them to look at their menus.

63

"Teressa, if you're mad at me, I'm mystified. You don't normally hate me until after I've satisfied you beyond your wildest dreams." Gregory's tone was light, but his eyes were dark. "Are you okay?"

Am I okay? Of course, I am not okay! I am a married woman having an affair! What could be okay about that? "I am just tired," she lied, and felt her face redden under his intense stare.

"Are you pregnant?"

Teres was stunned. Every instinct told her to laugh it off, lie to him. Once Gregory knew, he would insist on control of the situation, perhaps even push for an abortion; something she would not do.

"Yes."

She couldn't read his face.

"Don't lie to me."

"I am not," she said without breaking eye contact.

"So, you're pregnant?"

"Yes," she said, again.

"With my baby?"

"Yes."

"You're sure?"

"Yes."

"You've had a pregnancy test?"

Teres was finished with this game. She swung her coat over her shoulders and stood up to leave. Gregory grabbed her hand to stop her. His face broke into a radiant smile.

"This is wonderful news! Teressa, do you know how happy this makes me?" She burst into tears and ran past him in search of a bathroom. She was going to throw up.

February 12, 1992

"The baby is not my husband's." Teres waited for the doctor's face to change. It didn't. She continued. "The father died Saturday in a car accident." Still no change on the woman's face. "My husband ... knows ... he is ..." Teres faltered. *What is Danny?*

"Worried about you," Dr. Lamoreaux-Aarons filled in as though she were giving a gift.

"Yes. I am unable to function through this." *Go ahead. Put me in a straitjacket.*

"Describe to me what 'unable to function' means," the doctor requested.

"I am ... there is a fog in my head. I want to sleep and not ... think about what will happen next."

"Do you care what happens next?"

"I think so. But I need a plan. I am someone who needs a plan." Her words sounded and felt pathetic to say. "I am ... normally the one who decides ... things, for Danny and myself. I cannot think straight."

"What if you didn't have a plan? What if you just let things be for a bit? Does anything need to be decided today?"

Teres couldn't answer her. It was unfamiliar territory, letting life happen without a plan. She didn't know what that meant.

"What does your husband want you to do?" the doctor asked.

"He wants me to come home," Teres answered without hesitation. She was surprised by how simple it sounded. That was all Danny wanted. He had not asked her for one other thing, not an explanation or an apology. He certainly had not wanted details. *Just come home.*

"And?"

"And I can't. Our home is for us – me and Danny. I have ruined it for that."

"What happens if you stay here?"

Teres was confused by the question, so she didn't respond.

"Mrs. Muldaur, are you a danger to yourself? Do you have feelings of wanting to end your life?"

"Yes. But I would never hurt this baby … so I guess … no. I am not a danger to myself."

*

There it is. The piece I can use as a bargaining chip. She won't hurt the baby. Marion didn't need to figure out everything on the first visit, but she did need a negotiating tool, an attachment to a person or idea more important than the patient's own wellbeing. It was difficult to leave a patient to their own devices if she hadn't uncovered a reason to live.

"Mrs. Muldaur, you know this baby needs attention, even now. He needs you to nurture and sustain him through exercise, nutritious food, and fresh air. Lying in bed could cause complications. There is more to the health of an unborn child than not harming it. He needs you to be mentally healthy."

"Yes. I know this." Her response sounded like she was throwing in the towel. But which towel? *Have I made it sound like more than she can handle right now, or was her resigned tone a sign of compliance?* Marion took it back a notch.

"How about if you take a break from planning and we go with my plan. It's simple, with just a minimum of effort on your part. Want to try it?" Mrs. Muldaur nodded her head. Marion pulled two pieces of paper out of her bag and handed one to her patient. "This is an agreement we will make to assure both of us that you and your baby are getting what you need. It's a step-by-step guide on how we will accomplish that goal." Marion read aloud.

"I will get up in the morning before 9:00 a.m.

I will eat three healthy meals a day and drink at least four 8-ounce glasses of water.

I will go outside for fresh air and a walk every day, weather permitting.

I will take my medication – in your case pre-natal vitamins.

I will communicate with my caregivers.

When feeling anxious I will try not to sleep, instead I will use four-square breathing –
which I will teach you if you don't know.

I will not watch or read anything that makes me anxious.

I will not leave by myself without clearing it with my caregiver – Mrs. Muldaur, this is not jail. It's just a way to make certain you're safe until you feel stronger.

I will visit my obstetrician regularly and follow his or her recommendations.

If at any time I feel unsafe, I will call 911 and then my therapist at 555-3047."

The last rule she said with purposeful eye contact. "Does this sound like something you could agree to, Mrs. Muldaur?"

"Yes."

"Is there any part of this you don't understand?"

"I understand all of it."

Marion took a pen from her purse and handed it to her. "Let's both sign this and then I'm going to go out and talk to your husband. Is that okay?"

"Yes."

"You should go back to sleep. It's two o'clock in the morning. Do you need a glass of water or to use the bathroom first?"

"Were you going to teach me the breathing method?"

Fabulous. It looks like she wants to cope and not sink. "Yes, absolutely. This is something you can do anytime, anywhere. Lay down and place your hands over your abdomen. Take a deep breath in to the count of four, letting your stomach expand instead of your chest. Good. Now hold it in to the count of four. Okay, now breathe out slowly, again to the count of four. And then count to four without any air in your lungs before you start all over again. Think of it as a box." They did the breathing exercise together two more times. "I have a card with the four-square breathing directions in my bag." Marion fished around her purse and produced the card. As she reached over to place it on the nightstand, the woman grabbed ahold of her hand.

"Thank you."

"Teressa, it was nice to meet you. I'll be back to see you in a few days. You can call me if you need anything before that."

Now, let's see if I can help Mr. Muldaur.

*

"When is her next appointment with my husband?"

"Who's your husband?" Danny asked, confused.

"I thought you knew. My husband, Dr. Abel Aarons, is your wife's OB-GYN. That's how she got my card. He must have sensed she was going to need it."

"I know she has an appointment," Danny responded. "I don't remember when, but I'll make sure she gets there."

Danny felt Marion's stare. She was sizing him up. He started to ask her a random question to fill the space when she interrupted him with a question of her own.

"Danny is there anyone else who can help you with this?"

"No. Teres is very private," he hesitated. "So am I." *Just say it.* "The baby isn't mine."

"She told me."

"Until we figure out which way this is going, I think the less people who know, the better."

Danny watched the doctor think for a minute. She pulled a pen and paper out of her bag.

"This is the agreement your wife signed. It's pretty self-explanatory, but you're gonna need help – someone to be here when you can't, or to go grocery shopping for you. I'm writing down the name of a woman who works for Abel and me. She does errands and transcription, she's smart and kind. Perhaps she can spell you when you need it. I'll let her know you're calling. Do you work?"

"I … we own an ambulance company. It can run without me when it has to," Danny replied misleadingly. *But can it run without Teres is the real question.* He made a mental note to call the office tomorrow and set up some long-term coverage; it didn't look like either of them would be back any time soon.

"And what about this apartment? Can you stay longer?" Dr. Lamoreaux-Aarons asked.

Danny kept it simple. "Yes."

"Good. She's not ready to face going home. Today's Wednesday – Thursday really – I'll plan on coming back Monday. Call me if you think I need to be here sooner." She extended her hand. He took it. "Danny, I know it seems like a lot, but my instincts tell me this is going to be okay."

Danny felt better, more in control. Dr. Marion Lamoreaux-Aarons had given him the resources he needed to take care of his wife.

*

Note to self - call Lori Stanley first thing in the morning to let her know Mr. Muldaur might be calling.

The pieces were fitting together: *Gregory Costa's apartment, baby's father died Saturday.* Costa was Abel's golfing buddy. Marion only knew him as the guy Abel said had the world by the balls, or at least thought he did. *Well you don't anymore, Dr. Gregory Costa. But what kind of hell have you left in your wake?* Marion was leaving Gregory Costa's apartment with more questions than answers. For now she would shut this story off and get some sleep. Nine a.m. was coming up fast.

February 14, 1992

Lori Stanley had never thought of herself as a victim, even when her husband was using her as a punching bag. Somehow, she had rearranged the culpability to excuse him and implicate herself. Evidently, that psychological mechanism made her the very definition of a victim. She was still in denial when she met Dr. Lamoreaux-Aarons. By then she was pregnant with a baby her husband didn't want. He was already supporting two children from a previous marriage to a woman who had ended up in the hospital when she tried to warn Lori. Looking back, it was all so classic. Through counseling and commitment, Lori managed to stop looking back and had begun looking forward. Occasionally she had relapses of fear, like when she thought about her ex-husband being released from prison.

Whenever the paralyzing anxiety overtook her, she would call Dr. Marion, or sometimes her lawyer, Jesse Rand. Each time they would talk her off the ledge, re-explaining the court's decision to consider the assault and battering death of an eight-month-fetus to be a capitol murder crime. The verdict was still out as to whether Ed, her ex, would receive the death penalty. Lori didn't necessarily want to see him dead; she just didn't want to see him ever.

A few months after Lori got out of Spaulding Rehab in Quincy, Dr. Lamoreaux-Aarons offered her a job. She had an associate degree from Quincy Junior College and no real skill set. Before she knew it, Lori was trained as a medical transcriptionist. She passed the CORI background check, memorized Dr. Marion's privacy oath, and began transcribing recordings of patient visits into documents. At first it was hard. Not the typing, the stories. By then, she had begun to see a new therapist who was devoted to her whole life and not just her crisis. Her therapist told her she could look at things one of two ways: she could be traumatized by every woman's trauma, or she could see it as a way of recognizing she wasn't alone – violence happens to a lot of women. Lori continued to transcribe the women's painful histories, until her tale began to take a backseat to theirs.

Now, Marion was offering her a front-row seat to one of those stories. Lori wasn't sure she had what it took to look directly at a life that might be a mirror to her own.

*

"How sure are you that the husband isn't a monster?" Lori liked to get right to the point these days.

"Very sure. He's just a nice guy caught up in a crazy situation, with a wife who's not doing well. Although I'm not at liberty to say much, abuse has never been their problem. If you take this job, I'll have someone in Abel's office handle the transcription of her file. And Lori, she's pregnant. If that's a problem I completely understand."

Yeah, that's a problem. Lori had a good friend, due in a few months, who she was already avoiding. *Here we go again, baptism by fire.* "Did you tell them how much I make an hour? And I don't do windows," she added for the comic relief.

*

Today was day two. So far nothing was happening. Mr. Muldaur had run out to do errands and Mrs. Muldaur was taking a nap. Lori had already checked on her three times. She didn't dare turn on the television for fear she wouldn't hear her, so she cleaned

71

the kitchen and then took her cleaning products to the bathroom, tiptoeing through the job so as not to wake the woman. After their initial meet-and-greet, Lori wasn't convinced they'd be bonding any time soon.

*

She had accompanied Marion on Monday and was sitting on the couch, a safe distance from the husband, while the doctor was in the bedroom with the wife.

"So how long have you known Dr. Lamoreaux-Aarons?" the man had asked.

"A couple of years. You?"

"A couple days – one time really. She seems … smart," he said, waiting for confirmation.

"Yup. She's smart." The ensuing silence was awkward. Lori didn't try to fill it; another tangible sign she was done making life easier for a man.

"Is there anything you want to know about us?" Mr. Muldaur asked, adding a self-depreciating half-grin. It made her smile. *This guy's gonna be okay.* Lori let her guard down a bit.

"Yeah. How'd you get an apartment as cool as this?" She watched a controlled sadness flash across his face. *Ugh. Why did I ask? It's probably from his dead sister or something.* Then the guy flashed a smile.

"Lori, it's one of those stories you wouldn't believe if I told you." They both left it at that.

*

Meeting Mrs. Muldaur was more difficult. It wasn't the tear streaked face that let Lori know she was in pain; it was her eyes. They were vacant, yet filled to the brim with emotion. *Familiar.*

"Hello, so happy to meet you." *Clearly, she wasn't.*

72

"Thank you, Mrs. Muldaur. I'm happy to meet you, too." *Clearly, I'm not.* "Dr. Lamoreaux-Aarons said you could use a little help." No answer. "So, I hope I can be of help." Still no answer. *Been there. Done that.* She owed Marion, but it was one thing to read a report about someone's private hell. It was another thing to look it in the eye. "Okay. Well. I'll be back on Wednesday," Lori said, preparing to run from the room.

"Wednesday? Why Wednesday?" the woman asked.

Lori hesitated. *Does she even know why I'm here?* "I don't know. It's the day your husband said he needs … help … it's …" Lori let her words dwindle down to nothing.

"Yes. I will see you Wednesday," the woman said firmly, as though it were her idea. Lori bolted from the room.

February 19, 1992

Danny had managed to avoid all but one call from Ron, which he picked up by mistake, thinking it was Marion. He kept the conversation short, "Teres has made herself sick since witnessing Gregory's death, I'm waiting for her doctor to call back." *All true.* Ron had insisted on coming over. Danny still wasn't certain if Ron knew where *over* was. "Ron, really, we're good. *Don't come here to my wife's love nest.* I'll call you after I hear back from her doctor," which he didn't do. Keeping the truth from Ron was hard, but it was something Danny might have done even without Teres asking him to.

They had been friends for more than ten years. Like a lot of men, their relationship appeared to be superficially based on their shared love of golf. Their weekly conversations didn't cover deep topics, but their sidebar comments contained nuggets of gold. In a sentence, Ron could sum up an entire week at the hospital. "This week was a shit-show." *Did it really require more than that?*

Danny doubted it did. That's not to say his friend wasn't one of the best trash-talkers he had ever known. Ron could ride Danny's ass for eighteen straight holes of tormenting, especially if Ron was winning. But most of their important conversations could be summed up in a line or two: Teres is pregnant. Gregory is the father. *How the hell am I going to say that?*

*

Danny was on his last errand. He had been gone from the apartment for two hours. Lori could stay till three o'clock. It was two, now. "Maybe I don't have time to see Ron," he mumbled to himself as he pulled into the parking lot of Quincy City Hospital. Ron was expecting him. Danny hurried in through the lobby doors.

The ER looked bright and loud, a shock after being out of it for a while. It was the middle of February, flu season. Danny hated flu season for all the reasons every respiratory therapist hates flu season. It was nasty business; the frustration of watching old people and kids take a turn for the worse, running out of vents and croup tents, doing breathing treatments. Just thinking about it made him wonder why he picked respiratory for a career. As a medic in the Navy, he had loved the variety of his responsibilities. He could diagnose, suture a wound, give shots, prescribe medicine – all tasks restricted to physicians, once back in civilian life. He surely didn't choose respiratory for his love of mucus. On the wrong day, a bad gob of noxious phlegm still had him fighting the urge to gag. But the technical piece, like assisting in bronchoscopies or putting in a Swan-Ganz catheter, was what he really loved – not thumping some poor kid with Cystic Fibrosis for forty minutes until he hacked up what was left of his very diseased lungs. Danny's stoicism made people think he was immune to suffering, but watching the same kids come in month after month was heartbreaking. By the time he stopped working at Quincy City he had had enough.

Danny thought about how mad he had been when Teres tried to convince him to leave his respiratory job and work full-time for their ambulance company. It was an epic battle ending with her screaming, "Why do you always fight me on the things I know you will love?" She was right. Every run was something new, leaving little time to dwell on a patient's outcome before he was called out to the next accident, heart attack, or transport. It had been exactly the change he needed. *She always knows what I need - right up until she doesn't.*

*

Ron Watters spotted Danny the minute he walked into the emergency room. He didn't rush over to him. Instead, he took a long, appraising look. It was a technique he used with his patients: observe them when their guard was down. It amazed him how quickly a patient could change their affect in one direction or another. Sometimes a person looked wracked with pain but would immediately put on their game face when Ron rounded the corner and introduced himself. Drug seekers were the opposite. Danny looked good. Ron had expected to see him aged and worn from the events of the last ten days. Strangely, he looked the best Ron had seen him look since his heart surgery – stronger, less frail, taller. *Could it be he looked younger?* Maybe it was the clothes. Danny was wearing hiking boots and a dark wool Peacoat, two items Ron had never seen him wear before.

Heads were beginning to turn. Ron decided to nab his friend before the ER employees began anointing him with their goodwill questions and condolences.

"Hey. Perfect timing. I was worried you were gonna bail on me," Ron said, with just a note of humor. They embraced, Danny letting go last. Ron ushered him into a cubicle and got straight to the point. "How's Teres?"

"She's a mess," Danny replied, instant anguish in his voice. "She blames herself for Gregory's death."

Ron couldn't hide his look of surprise. "I don't get it? Why?" He watched Danny take a deep breath, saw indecision flicker across his face. It was an easily readable emotion for any good ER doc – *Am I going to tell this doctor the whole truth or just what he needs to know?* Ron waited for Danny to decide.

"It's complicated, but I think Teres and Gregory had a fight at my party and he left in a rage."

"You think? She didn't tell you?"

"No," Danny replied. "She's barely talking, barely anything really."

This sounded serious, intervention kind of serious. Ron knew better than to appear riled. When situations looked dire his modus operandi was to lower his voice and make an impact statement. "Danny, I think you need to bring her in. Teres could be having some kind of breakdown."

"No."

Ron was taken back by the force of the reply. This wasn't like Danny at all. Although the last time Ron saw him was when he left the tow yard without a word – and he didn't come to Gregory's funeral. Maybe *he* was having the breakdown.

"Ron, I know you're concerned. I am too. But Teres is seeing a doctor, a psychiatrist, who is helping her through it. You'll have to trust me. I'm keeping her safe and if that changes, you'll be the first person I call."

I can live with that, Ron decided, saying simply, "Tell me what you need." He watched Danny release a deep breath, clearly relieved about not being further pressed.

"I need help running the company. Teres won't be back for a while, and we both know I'm useless with the day-to-day crap. It doesn't make sense for me to step in when Teres needs me with her."

"Right. You are useless." Ron's half-hearted attempt at a joke didn't make either of them smile. "I'll get Martha to nail down how much time she can put in and fill the rest with staff from the hospital. Don't worry about a thing. And you tell Teres I have this covered; I know how she worries about the company running like a finely tuned-"

"Ron," Danny interrupted, "she hasn't mentioned the business at all."

That was the sidebar comment, the one that made Ron realize the gravity of the situation. His friend didn't have to say another word. "Don't worry, Danny. I've got this. Just take care of Teres and check in with me from time to time." A handshake, a pat on the back, then Danny left. Ron remained in the cubicle for a couple minutes, his mind racing, his anger rising.

Seriously Gregory? You had to put the moves on my best friend's wife? You fucking misogynistic asshole. Ron wasn't one to think ill of the dead, but it was the only explanation: Gregory made a pass at Teres, she turned him down, and he left in a rage. It would be just like her to feel guilty – as though there's a nice way to shut down some guy who hits on you at your husband's birthday party. *What the fuck were you thinking, Costa?* Ron shook his head, miserable about the whole situation. He left the cubicle and headed back to the emergency triage area, anxious to deal with other people's problems.

*

Mr. Muldaur didn't say anything about going for a walk.

Lori had been organizing the pantry closet, lost in her own head, when she realized Mrs. Muldaur was standing behind her. It startled her enough to knock a can of baked beans from the shelf.

"I'm supposed to take a walk every day," Mrs. Muldaur said in an expectant monotone.

Lori retrieved the can and turned around. Mrs. Muldaur was dressed in layers and wearing brown Frye boots, too nice for the snow. She looked like a bag lady without the bags, overly long sweatpants, sleeves of the sweatshirt hanging past the arms of her fancy fur coat. *Well, at least she won't need gloves* Lori thought to herself, trying to decide if taking Mrs. Muldaur out of the apartment was wise. The walking thing made sense to her. She had been given Marion's live-to-fight-another-day list. But it was a risk. *What if she bolts?*

"Why don't we wait until your husband comes home?" There was no response. *What the hell.* "You know what? I think a walk will do us both good."

*

The sidewalk was clear, and Mrs. Muldaur was a surprisingly fast walker. In fact, the minute they got outside, she seemed to perk up. Lori was hoping it wasn't an act to put her off-guard. They walked in silence for five minutes. Finally, Mrs. Muldaur spoke.

"Do you have children?"

The question Lori dreaded; it was the first thing people asked. She wanted to reply, *it's none of your fucking business*, but said, "No. I can't have children."

"We can't either," the woman replied, staring straight ahead.

Lori was shocked, then pissed. *Why do all the lunatics get to have babies?* She was so sick of hearing about pregnant women who had no business bringing a child into the world. And this crazy woman was no spring chicken – with an even older husband. The desperate unfairness of it began to take over. Lori wanted to push Mrs. Muldaur off the curbing and into oncoming traffic. She took a few controlled breaths, utilizing the technique her doctor had taught her.

"My husband and I tried for years. We couldn't adopt. He had … health issues."

Lori waited for her to continue; admit she was pregnant. She didn't. They walked in silence. Lori wanted to ask questions but couldn't, knowing her questions wouldn't make sense if the woman hadn't admitted to being pregnant. *Maybe she doesn't know.* It was a thought that opened a list of possible scenarios, keeping Lori's mind occupied for the rest of the walk.

Eventually, they made their way back to the apartment complex and into the elevator. Mrs. Muldaur turned to Lori and said, "That was a lovely walk. Thank you."

*

Lori had left a playing card between the latch and the doorway to stop the apartment door from locking. It was gone. Mr. Muldaur must be home. She knocked, and he whipped open the door.

"Where have you been? I was just getting ready to call the police!"

"Mr. Muldaur …"

"You should've left me a note!"

"I did," explained Lori. "I left it where you would see it the minute you got home – the bathroom." Danny looked at her like she'd lost her mind.

"The bathroom?" He looked confused.

"Yeah, it's the first place every guy goes the minute they get home. I didn't feel like I could write a note right in front of your wife …"

Their argument was stopped dead in its tracks with the sound of Teres' snorting laughter.

"Oh, Danny! That is the funniest thing I have ever heard! She is right. A note for a man should be left by the toilet!" She walked past Danny's open mouth and into the bedroom. Danny looked at Lori, who was smiling broadly.

"Thank you, Lori. Looks like the walk did her good. Can you come back on Friday?"

"Yes. Mr. Muldaur."

"Call me Danny."

March 1, 1992

A new routine had emerged: breakfast, showers, daily walks – four days a week with Danny, three with Lori. Teres could feel herself getting stronger. She used her breathing at night when her mind filled with fear. She sat by the window and read Gregory's medical journals during the day. Since she couldn't talk about the important things, she said nothing. For the first time in her life, she was letting everyone else do the talking. In spite of the blank look her face carried, her mind whirled with images and thoughts, projections and unresolved outcomes. One morning, she realized she didn't know the date. She knew the day because Lori came on Monday, Wednesday, and Friday. Since this was the second day she had not come, it must be Sunday. She and Danny were taking a walk. Danny was, as a dictate of the new usual, doing all the talking.

"After I dropped off the car for the oil change, I remembered that we hate that guy. Remember Teres? The guy that overcharged me for the timing belt? I know I should just get a new car, but it drives me crazy to get used to something new when I'm not unhappy with the Jeep-"

"What day is it?"

"It's Sunday."

Teres watched the way his face changed when she spoke. He looked hopeful. She hated what she was doing to him. "What is the date?"

"March first," he answered. They had stopped walking. She felt him reading her face, anticipating and guessing if there would be next words. *March first.* Is something happening on that day? She forced her brain to operate through the fog. *March second.*

"I have a doctor's appointment tomorrow."

"Yes. At three o'clock," he answered, still searching her face. "I'll bring you."

"When were you going to tell me?"

"Tomorrow. I didn't want to give you too much time to worry about it."

Teres let her protective veil slip away. She looked into her husband's eyes with an instinctual connection, the kind that says *you get me, and I know it.* It was done by accident, before she could take it away. His recognition of their shared moment was instantaneous. His face lit up. Teres looked away, ashamed she had led him to think the old Teressa was still in there. She wouldn't let it happen again.

"Okay." She turned away from Danny and resumed walking.

March 2, 1992

"Ms. Teressa Giannopoulos?" the nurse called into the waiting room. Teres and Danny stood as she motioned them to follow her.

"It's Muldaur," Danny corrected while they walked. "My wife's name is Muldaur."

"Oh, congratulations! You got married!" the nurse responded without turning around to look at them. Danny didn't reply. They were led to an examining room where the nurse took Teres' blood pressure and got her weight. "One-twenty-four. You've lost seven pounds. You're going in the wrong direction," she said brightly, as though this were no problem at all. "It will turn around soon enough. First three months is nauseating." Teres didn't reply. Danny didn't know if it was helpful to tell the nurse his wife was no longer vomiting. She didn't seem to care, either way.

"There's no need to change out of your clothes, today's just a chat!" The nurse left, closing the door behind her.

Danny was a wreck. Uncomfortable social situations put him on edge, and this was the epitome of uncomfortable. He had given Marion permission to talk to her husband about him, but neither of them had broached Teres on the subject of shared information. Perhaps she assumed they all communicated. Perhaps she had told Dr. Aarons about him at her first OB visit. *Perhaps she doesn't care.* He would just have to wait and see how Teres handles it. For all he knows, she'll ask him to leave when the doctor comes into the office. At this point Danny would welcome a little good-old-days assertion from his wife, even if it meant her kicking him out.

*

One month ago, Teres had a meltdown in this very room – a full blown anxiety attack, brought on by her deceit, but triggered by the suffocating way in which Gregory was handling her pregnancy. He had shown up at her appointment when she had told him not to, sat right there in the chair Danny was now sitting in. She had been furious, but then softened in spite of herself when she saw his reaction to hearing the baby's heartbeat. Everything with Gregory was like that. Right when she was ready to kill him, literally put her hands around his throat, he would do something genuine and uncalculated, showing her a side she couldn't resist. Even when his goal was to manipulate her to get his way, Teres was able to see right through him. For the entire appointment, she had wished it was Danny by her side instead of Gregory. *Be careful what you wish for.*

*

"Teressa. It's good to see you," Abel Aarons liked to enter the room on an up note. It was going to be especially important today. He extended his hand to Danny. "You must be Danny. Marion told me to expect you." The two men shook hands. Abel noted the grateful look in Mr. Muldaur's eyes, relief at an easy introduction, he assumed. "How's the weather out there? I wouldn't know. I opened these office doors before sun-up today. Looks like we're in for a lot of spring babies this year." Neither of the Muldaurs responded. Abel picked up Teressa's chart, quickly catching himself up. "But yours will be late summer, early fall," he said directly to his patient, hoping it didn't sound too obvious they all knew the baby wasn't Danny's. He pressed a button on his countertop. The nurse appeared.

"Heidi will you show Mr. Muldaur to my office while I chat with his wife?" He addressed Teres. "Good? And we'll catch up with your husband in a couple minutes?" Teres nodded. Danny left. *Let's see what we can find out* thought Abel, sitting in the chair Danny had just vacated.

*

Well that went well. Fifteen minutes later Dr. Aarons was ushering the Muldaurs toward the reception desk to set up their next appointment and some additional bloodwork. He and Teressa had covered her weight loss, nausea, and general well-being. She had signed a form giving him permission to exchange information with his wife, along with an emergency contact form listing Danny as next-of-kin. Neither one had mentioned Gregory's death. Teres was almost sixteen weeks along. She had agreed to have her alpha-fetoprotein screening next week to rule out spina bifida and potential for Down's syndrome, despite insisting she would not terminate the pregnancy regardless of the results. Just as he was putting the final farewell on the appointment, Mrs. Muldaur began to speak candidly.

"Aside from Danny, you and your wife are the only people who know this baby is Gregory's." Abel nodded, waiting for more. "It would have been conscionable to tell the world and let people judge us – if Gregory were still alive. Now it seems pointless, almost cruel, to ruin his reputation. But to keep a secret like this forever is a pain I cannot endure." Abel waited for her to continue. She didn't.

"Teressa, are you religious?"

"Greek Orthodox. But I go to Catholic Church."

"I'm Jewish," Abel said to her, as if she might not know. "In Hebrew there are two words that are like your word, confession. *Yādâh* means to confess sins and give thanks. It's used in a general way for all sinners, as well as expressing all thanks to God for his grace and mercy. *Teshuva* is repentance. It's more than "I'm sorry." It's the act of a true repentance by making something whole again, restoring it to its original form. Think of it as, *I've broken the vase. I'm sorry* – there's your confession. But then you painstakingly glue the vase together to make it whole. This is the importance of *teshuva*, making it right.

Teressa, you have one God to confess to, and one person you've wrong. What difference does it make whether the rest of the world knows, or doesn't?"

*

This cannot be fixed! I can't undo my affair or this pregnancy. Her mind tried to make sense of what Abel was proposing: making amends to the one person she had wronged, Danny, thereby fixing the thing she had broken, her marriage. Somewhere in that equation was the unmentionable paradox of her pregnancy. Could she take back the affair, and still keep the pregnancy? No matter how much she chastised herself for the sin of the affair, she was grateful for this baby. Is this pregnancy worth her marriage? Her lover's life? Every thought brought her to the event she couldn't change. Sleeping with Gregory had ruined three lives. No, it could not be fixed, but she appreciated Dr. Aarons for trying.

"Thank you, Dr. Aarons," Teres said. *And thank you, Gregory, for your arrogant insistence on choosing my doctor.*

*

The ride home was quiet. *Home.* Danny realized he was beginning to refer to Gregory's apartment as home. "I'll be home in two hours," he'd say to Lori. Or, "Tell Teres we can go for a walk when I get home." Danny knew how quickly a person could make a bad place into home. He had done it over and over again in the Navy. The difference between now and then was in how easy it had been to do before Teres. Up until then, Danny didn't have a place he called home. The middle floor of the triple decker apartment he grew up in always felt shared. The whole building was loaded with relatives. Both his parents were working poor. There hadn't been money or time to feather the nest, a saying his wife was fond of using every time she bought something new and unnecessary for their home. Teres had loved taking care of their house. *Now it's me and Lori doing the cleaning.* Well, Lori, if he had to be brutally honest.

Gregory's apartment was simple, easier than living at home. Maybe Teres was right. They were in such a mess that *home* had been ruined for them. Scituate wouldn't feel the same, even if he dragged her back with him. But how ridiculous was it that the very place where she had ruined their lives had now become the only place he could stand to be. He had gone back to their house a couple times, to grab clothes and more pills, and found himself anxious to leave. It was just a building if Teres wasn't there.

*

"Oh shit. I forgot to put out the laundry," Danny said as he and Teres rounded the hall toward the apartment. There was a sorry-we-missed-you-slip stuck to the door.

On week one of the Muldaur's new life, Danny had answered the two-rap knock of a kid holding a duffel bag of clean laundry along with a half-dozen white shirts in dry cleaning bags.

"Great. You're here," the kid had said to Danny. "You owe for last week, too." He handed over a slip and waited for Danny to lug Gregory's laundry into the apartment and grab money.

"Do I usually tip?" Danny asked the kid, in disbelief he was now paying for his wife's lover's laundry.

"You're not that great a tipper," the kid replied, giving Danny a weird second look.

"Well I am now," said Danny, trying to one-up Gregory on something. "What day is pickup?"

"Mondays. Drop off is Wednesday." The kid looked at the five-dollar bill. He didn't look impressed, but Danny was. The problem of how to do their laundry had been solved.

*

Teres was still in survival mode. Although she had moved past having to read Marion's list, her goal was the same: stay alive and give birth to a healthy baby. The night of her appointment, her sleepless thoughts turned to what Dr. Aarons had said about *teshuva*. Teres' mind, normally an equal mix of analytical and emotional, rejected the possibility of doing a penance that would free her of guilt. There wasn't one. She would hate herself for the rest of her life for what she had done to Danny, what she was still doing to him. If only he would give up on her and make her self-loathing complete.

As a little girl, Teres remembered locking herself in her room after her brother was mean to her. She sat pouting while her father sang to her through the door.

"Who are you punishing, little Teressa? Whoever it is, they're off playing in the fields. Looks like you're doing half their mean work for them." Whose mean work was she doing now?

She had closed her world down to this apartment and a walking route – no work, no ambulance company, no friends, *no Gregory* – just her and Danny. Every day she punished herself by shutting him out. What this was doing to him was easy to see and added to her guilt. It was the opposite of making whole, putting back together. Maybe her penance, her *teshuva*, wasn't something she could orchestrate like the conductor of a symphony. Maybe the debt she owed her husband needed to be repaid in whatever way *he* chose. Maybe none of this was up to her.

She got out of bed and knelt on the floor in an act of formal confession. The first part of her prayer was a painful recognition of what her refusal to leave this apartment, *his bed*, must be doing to her husband. Teres recited the Prayer of Repentance in her native tongue.

"Κύριε Θεέ μου, ομολογώ ότι αμάρτησα ενάντια σε Σένα στη σκέψη, στη λέξη και στην πράξη.

Παράλειψα επίσης να κάνω αυτό που απαιτεί ο ιερός νόμος σας από μένα.

Αλλά τώρα με τη μετάνοια και τη λύπη γυρίζω πάλι στην αγάπη και το έλεός Σου.

Σας παρακαλώ να μου συγχωρέσετε όλη την παράβασή μου και να με καθαρίσετε από όλες τις αμαρτίες μου.

Κύριε, γεμίστε την καρδιά μου με το φως της αλήθειας
Σου. Ενδυναμώστε τη θέλησή μου με τη χάρη σας.
Με διδάξτε τόσο να επιθυμούν και να κάνουν μόνο ό,
τι σας ευχαριστεί. Αμήν."
*O Lord my God, I confess that I have sinned against
You in thought, word and deed.*
*I have also omitted to do what Your holy law requires
of me.*
*But now with repentance and contrition I turn again to
Your love and mercy.*
*I entreat You to forgive me all my transgression and to
cleanse me from all my sins.*
*Lord, fill my heart with the light of Your truth.
Strengthen my will by Your grace.*
*Teach me both to desire and to do only what pleases
You. Amen.*

Teres knew this was just the beginning of the confessional
process in the Greek Orthodox church. The sinner must then,
without justification or self-pity and using the ten commandments
as his guideline, examine his life and recount his sins, using pen
and paper if necessary. *There isn't enough paper in this apartment.*

The last time she had been to confession was as a young
married woman. She had become consumed by the guilt she felt
about lying to her parents. An out-of-wedlock pregnancy had been
the one thing Teres knew would force her father to agree to a
marriage between his only daughter and a foreign stranger. She
had assumed her fake pregnancy would turn into a real one in no
time. When Danny's sperm abnormality was diagnosed, Teres
became obsessed with the idea it was divine retribution for the lie
told to her parents, a lie further cemented in a ceremony before God
and his church. No matter how many times Danny urged her to

forget about it, reminding her the damage to his sperm happened before she was born, Teres couldn't shake it off. She was certain God was punishing her.

Her confession to Father Mistakidis was a disaster. Teres had poured her heart out and was ready to receive her absolution, when the old priest told her it would only be a true confession if she were to confess to those she had wronged – her parents. That ended that. Her mother had already mourned the loss of her grandchild, Teres couldn't put her through the loss of her daughter's integrity as well. At least this time the person she had wronged already knew he was wronged.

Teres began mentally compiling her list, beginning with every time she had manipulated her husband into seeing things her way. Because she had been good at making him think certain decisions were his idea, there were too many offenses to count. But she had to begin somewhere.

*

The Bruin's game ended just before the eleven o'clock news began. Danny wasn't certain he was up for tonight's gloom and doom report. Between Mike Tyson's rape conviction and this whole Jeffrey Dahmer thing, the news was a little tough to stomach lately. Sitting alone in the living room would have been a treat a month ago, hockey with no interruptions. Now all he felt was lonely. At least they were eating their meals together again. He had tried to convince Teres to watch the game with him after dinner. It was a long shot since she wasn't a fan of hockey – *a stupid game where you were called off-sides even though no one went out-of-bounds* was her assessment of the sport. She loved baseball. She'd watch any game, anywhere. It didn't matter who was playing. They had become big supporters of the Scituate Sailors over the years. If he had to guess, he'd say Teres liked high school sports better than pro, although she'd never pass up a chance to see the Red Sox play. His heart surgery had been in August last year. The Sox lost the American League Division in October. Teres joked about their loss being the toughest thing she'd been through all year. She was funny like that; she'd cry about things that weren't important and somehow hold it together for the real problems.

Danny could write a book, entitled: *What I Know About My Wife ~ but never told her I knew.* He had been quietly observing her for twenty years. She'd take issue with that concept, insisting he didn't pay any attention. *Well, you've got my attention now, don't you Teres?*

It was time to go check on her, another part of his new routine. He'd take his pills, put his water glass in the dishwasher with the dinner dishes, and then go in the bathroom and get ready for bed. The last thing he did every night was tiptoe into the bedroom and check on Teres, listen to her breathe for a minute or two, then slip out to his bed on the couch. Why he didn't just get in the king-sized bed beside her was beyond him; it was big enough for them both to feel alone.

*

The bed was empty. Danny rushed into the room, his immediate thought that she had jumped from the window. She was on the other side of the bed, on her knees with her hands folded in front of her on the floor, forehead resting on them like a yoga pose.

"Jesus Teres! What are you doing?" he asked, making his way to her.

*

Teres raised her head in time to see Danny snag the corner of the quilt with his slipper and go flying head-long into the dresser landing unconscious at her feet, blood pouring from the laceration on his head.

"Danny!" Teres screamed. She ran to the bathroom and grabbed a towel. She turned the cold water on, soaking the towel along with her pajama's and the floor, then raced back to the bedroom. He came around as soon as she applied the towel to his head. "Oh my god, Danny! Are you okay? Can you hear me? Is your neck broken?"

*

"No. I mean, yes, I'm okay. I think my neck is fine." He tried to sit up.

"Just lay there until I know you are alright!" Teres reached up to the nightstand and turned on the lamp. Danny winced at the light in his eyes. "Look at me!" she commanded. "I need to check your pupils." She waved her index finger side-to-side, then up and down. "Follow my finger." He almost laughed at how serious she looked. "You are going to the hospital," she declared.

"Teres, I'm fine."

"No, you are not! Your pupils look even, but that was so I could know if I need to have an ambulance come or is it me to drive you! You need sutures!"

Danny knew there was no arguing with her, not when she was at this level of Greek-speak. Once Teres' accent showed up, the determined girl he met all those years ago was close behind. His head hurt, his ear was ringing, and he didn't know the size of the cut. *She's right. I need to go to the hospital.*

*

In ten minutes, they were dressed and in the car. Teres' hair was clipped into a French twist; she was wearing her fur coat. Danny had pulled his jeans and a wool sweater over his flannel pajamas and was sporting his Navy pea coat. They looked like an attractive couple out for the night, except they had left behind a blood-spattered bedroom resembling a crime scene. Teres was driving, Danny holding a clean wad of paper towels to his head. Within one minute of leaving the apartment, they were flagged by a police officer for failure to come to a complete stop at the stop sign; *or maybe it was a red light*, Danny wasn't paying attention. Either way, it was like the good old days watching Teres kick into defense mode.

"Here is my license and the registration to my husband's car. If you are going to give me a ticket, you should give it to me in a quick manner. My husband has had an accident and I would like to get him to the hospital before he has a brain bleed."

The officer peered in at Danny, who grinned back like a man with no control over the situation.

"He looks fine to me," the officer said. Danny pulled the clean paper towel away to show off the gash on his head. The bleeding had stopped, revealing its depth, down to his skull. The cop handed back Teres' credentials. "Be careful. The roads are icy. Do you need an escort?"

"No thank you," Teres replied. "I own an ambulance company and I am able to drive in any type of weather."

What a load of bullshit, Danny thought, happy to see the return of Teressa's spitfire persona. True, she had gotten her paramedic's license. True, every once in a while she took an ambulance for a spin. But no, she could not drive in any type of weather. Sometimes she couldn't back her own car out of their garage at home, let alone back the ambulance into a bay. His wife wasn't a good driver, so she had determined that she *hated* driving, rather than admit to the fact she *can't* drive. Teres hated anything she wasn't good at. Danny knew the list of those things was small, which was why he rubbed it in when he could. *I have to. I'm the husband, it's my job* he thought, trying to decide if it were too early in her mental health recovery to give her shit. It wasn't.

"You're able to drive in any kind of weather?" he wisecracked, the minute she pulled the car back onto the road.

"No. We both know I am a terrible driver." She said, quietly. "I am done lying to you about things. Even if they are small."

Danny wasn't expecting that. *Wait? What else does she lie about? I mean other than the affair?* He was afraid to ask her. He didn't have to.

"There have been many times I have misrepresented the truth. I have told you things that were in the family of true, but not true. Most of the time I did it to get my way," she stared straight ahead as she spoke.

"Teres, this is silly. I know you're not perfect. None of us are." *Jesus. Why am I defending her?* "We don't have to do this right now. Maybe we should just concentrate on getting me to the hospital in one piece."

"No, Danny. I have to say this." She turned to look at him. He wanted to hear her out, but not at the expense of his life.

"I'll listen if you keep your eyes on the road."

"Okay," she responded, facing straight ahead. "When I told you that our attorney, Seamus, thought opening an ambulance company was a no-brainer, he did not say that. He said just that he would help us with the permits."

Danny was confused. Why was she bringing this up now? "That was ten years ago. What difference does it make? The ambulance company was a great idea, and you think I didn't know you were making up shit to convince me? I know I'm not easy to convince."

She pulled into the hospital parking lot, shut off the car and turned to him. "Please, Danny. Stop making it hard for me to confess who I have been. I am not a saint." She was starting to cry.

Danny would have said anything to stop her from dissolving into a fresh batch of tears.

"Teressa, I know you're not perfect. But you were a good wife before you cheated on me. I had no complaints. I don't know what this affair thing was – but don't make our whole marriage about it. We had a good marriage. And don't act like I was some stupid guy who was blinded by you. I wasn't. I know what a mess you can be, I just never said anything – cause – I love you, and I'm not a mean guy."

His speech, long for him and designed to make her stop crying, had the opposite effect. She was bawling. He opened the passenger door, saying, "You should stay here and try to pull it together."

Teres caught up to him before he reached the main entrance to Quincy City. Her red eyes were the only sign of her tears. He opened the door and let her enter first. The place looked quiet. *Good.* He didn't recognize the triage nurse; she must be new. *Good.* Teres was subdued enough to let him speak for himself. *Unusual and good.*

"Hi. I think I need stitches. I fell and hit my head." The nurse motioned him around the corner to a chair. Teres stayed on the other side of the glass. Within minutes, Danny was logged in and on his way to the back. Teres followed behind. In the cubicle, Danny sat on the gurney, Teres took the chair, still quiet. The doctor walked in. This was where her silence ended.

"My husband is going to need a CT scan. He lost consciousness when he fell."

*

Pete Eldredge was not so new to Quincy City Hospital that he didn't know who Danny Muldaur was. He had begun working the nightshift a week before Christmas. The paramedics from Accelerated Ambulance were well known. Their medical director,

Ron Watters, was the ER doc who had shown Pete around during his first couple shifts. Six or seven weeks later, the hospital was abuzz about the accident that killed a cardiologist who was at a party for Danny Muldaur. So although Pete had never met either of the Muldaurs, he recognized Danny's name the minute he saw it on the chart. To confirm his suspicion, he looked to see if there was a reference to Accelerated Ambulance. There was. Pete extended his hand to Mrs. Muldaur, since she spoke to him first.

"I'm Dr. Eldredge. You must be Mrs. Muldaur?"

"Yes." Her grip was firm, somewhat masculine for such a small woman. Pete didn't shake Danny's hand because he was using it to secure a paper towel over his wound. He looked at the paperwork on the clipboard.

"Looks like we have a head laceration as a result of a fall."

"Yes. My husband tripped on the edge of a quilt and hit the bureau. He was knocked-"

"Thank you, Mrs. Muldaur. I'm going to need to hear the details from your husband. I'm sure your version is the same as his, but part of the exam for a head injury is cognitive. I get a better feel for things if the patient speaks."

"Of course."

Pete noted the wife didn't appear offended. She turned her attention to look at her husband as though she, too, wanted to hear his side of the story.

"Like my wife said, I tripped on the part of the comforter that was dragging on the floor. I'm a big guy, when I go down, I go down hard. If she said I passed out, I must have. I woke up to a cold towel on my head."

Danny pulled the paper towel away from the cut. Pete took a gauze square and touched the wound, checking to see if he could detect any damage to the skull beneath it. It looked good. He pulled the penlight from his pocket and checked Danny's pupils: equal and responsive.

"Dizziness?"

"No."

"Headache?"

"Just some ringing in my right ear."

"Neck pain?"

"No." Mr. Muldaur smiled. "But you know how this is, I'll wake up in the morning and feel like I've been hit by a truck. Ha, maybe you don't know how this is. At your age, nothing bothered me – now I trip over a blanket and end up in the ER."

"Since the injury is right along the mastoid process, and you're already having a little ringing – which is not abnormal for the fall you took – I am going to order a CT scan. We'll get that first, and then I'll suture you up. For now, let's get a bandage on that cut so it doesn't reopen during the scan."

"Thank you," the married team said in unison. Pete opened a two-by-two, taped it on, then left to alert Radiology they had a customer. He had been about to suggest to Mrs. Muldaur that she wait in the exam room, possibly get a little sleep. She looked exhausted and he couldn't shake the feeling she was pregnant. At the last minute, he took his mother's advice and kept his mouth shut.

"Never ask a woman if she's pregnant," Beverly Eldredge would say. "I don't care if she's standing in a puddle of amniotic fluid, gripping her husband's hand, and timing contractions – wait until she tells you." It was advice that had kept him from more than a few embarrassing moments. Maybe Mrs. Muldaur just had a pot belly, he decided. A lot of women her age do.

*

They drove home from the hospital with very few words, not alarming considering how tired they both were. A 'Danny calamity' – a term Ron had coined in reference to his endless health emergencies – had put Teres in action mode and opened a window between them. Danny wasn't going to let her close it back down.

"Well that's good. No fractured skull," he said to her.

"A concussion is serious enough," she answered, not taking her eyes off the road. It was two-thirty in the morning, no cars in sight. They were home in no time. The bloody mess they had left greeted them at the door. *Gregory would be pissed,* Danny thought, but didn't say.

"Look at this place. Gregory would be pissed," Teres said for him, as though speaking of Gregory was now commonplace between them. She went directly to the kitchen in search of a cleaning product that would remove blood from white carpet. Danny peeled off his outer layers, getting back down to pajamas.

"There isn't a drop of blood on me. Go figure. What can I do to help?"

"Sit there and do not get into trouble," she replied.

There's my girl, thought Danny, heading straight for the recliner. Teres came out of the kitchen with white vinegar and the box of baking soda that Gregory, or whoever cleans, had put in the fridge to keep it smelling fresh. *Where has the cleaning woman been?* There wasn't a chance in hell Dr. Costa cleaned his own toilet. A person or company should have shown up by now. Another mystery. He watched Teres go into the bedroom, ready to remove his DNA from the carpet. He wanted to fall asleep but began to feel the throbbing he knew would greet him as soon as the Novocain wore off. He thought about concussion protocol and got up from the chair.

*

97

"Why are you taking the alarm clock?" Teres didn't look up from her scrubbing. She knew Danny had come into the room, she felt him staring at her. When he walked in, she experienced a precognitive moment. It had happened many times in their marriage, always when Danny was on the verge of doing something she would consider ridiculous or dangerous. He hadn't touched the alarm clock, yet somehow she knew he was planning to unplug it and take it. He had accused her in the past of being a witch. She knew it unnerved him and she took advantage of that fact. Once, when they lost their electricity after a big snowstorm, Danny got up from his chair and walked toward the kitchen. In a flash she could see him going to the mud room, pulling on his boots, and heading to the garage to start the car.

"You know you cannot run the car for heat, right? We will both be asphyxiated."

"I know that," he had answered, his irritation showing. But her suspicion was confirmed by him retreating back to his chair. Later, he told her what his plan had been, to open the garage window and fire up the car. He asked her how she knew. Teres had just smiled, as if she had a secret talent. But the truth was, she had no idea. When it came to Danny, she just knew. This return of the knowing both calmed and jolted her. She had to decide soon which way this relationship was going.

*

"I need to wake up every couple of hours to make sure I'm okay," Danny said, realizing the flaw in his plan as he said it.

"Danny, that is crazy. A person with a head injury does not wake themselves up to see if they can. What if you cannot? What if the alarm goes off and you are busy having a brain bleed, so you are not interested in answering the alarm and checking your vital signs? Is this the advice you would give your patients?"

98

"I wouldn't give advice for concussions. I'm a respiratory therapist, not an ER doc." Danny's voice was rising. He hated being called out on his less-than-logical plans. Teres' changed her tone.

"Danny, just sleep in here with me. That way I can check on you. I am too tired to go to the living room a bunch of times. We can set the alarm for two hours, good?"

This was what he wanted, to climb in bed with his wife. She was offering it, not pushing him away. He couldn't remember what he was supposed to do. *Do I resist and make her force me into it, then we'll both know it's her idea? Do I take the alarm clock like I don't care what she thinks of my plan? Do I get into bed before she changes her mind?* He used to have a handle on this kind of situation. She would say *this*, and he would do *that*. They had a pattern of responses that kept their marriage going in a steady direction. Danny looked down at Teres. The patch she was scrubbing had become a reddish-brown puddle of vinegar and baking soda. He hated the smell of vinegar. He couldn't decide what to do. Suddenly it wasn't up to him. Without warning, he vomited down the side of the bed and onto the floor, barely missing Teres. The vomit nailed down two decisions: he was sleeping in bed with his wife, and they needed to hire a cleaning company.

March 8, 1992

Teres woke with the instant heaviness of knowing it had been a month. It felt like a lifetime. One month ago, she came to this apartment. One month ago, her life had been different. One month ago, her husband trusted her. Now she couldn't go outside without supervision. She liked Lori. She liked their walks along the harbor. Sometimes they chatted, but most of the time Lori let her stay lost in her own thoughts. It was no substitute for running, which was quick, effective and solitary. In the past, Teres would have run in weather like this: cold, windy, still patches of icy snow. Even if she were allowed – *and who says I'm not* – to run by herself she wouldn't have because of the baby. Everything was about the baby. Danny had begun saying "the baby" frequently and easily after her appointment with Dr. Aarons.

*

"Teres, I'm heading to Stop & Shop. I'm gonna grab some salmon. I know you like it, and it's good for the baby. Are you up to cooking? I'll end up butchering it. Or maybe Lori can..."

"I will cook it. Can you get sweet potatoes and spinach?" It was the first time she'd asked him for anything, but she was getting tired of sandwiches and eggs. He looked happy.

"Why don't you throw on your coat and come with me? We can grab a salad at Lambert's."

"No."

The look on Danny's face was crushing. She wanted to say more, but couldn't. She wanted to tell him how panicky she felt at the prospect of leaving the apartment. What if they ran into someone they knew? She wanted to say that going somewhere normal, like Lambert's, was too normal for their situation. It would feel like the old days, and there were no more old days. She wanted to say, "If I do this you will want more from me, and I already feel bad about the hope I give you."

Her *teshuva* plan to let Danny be the one to decide how she would make amends had dissolved. Their relationship had taken a step forward, or *backward*, with his concussion. Neither of them suggested he move to the couch once he was feeling better. Danny came to bed every night after she was asleep. They weren't touching, but things had changed. Because he was a constant snorer, quiet meant he was awake. He was awake a lot. Teres felt

100

him watching her in the dark. She measured the energy between them, could judge the distance. She wanted to touch him, be held. Her husband was now the forbidden fruit in her life. The nights became as difficult as the days. It took everything to keep him emotionally at bay. Somehow the baby had become the safe topic between them, although their conversations didn't follow the pattern of a typical couple. Neither was asking for predictions. "Do you think it's a boy or a girl? I hope the baby has your eyes." They spoke of her health, and the health of the baby. He brought her to the lab for her bloodwork, was with her when the nurse called to say her tests were normal other than borderline anemia, requiring she take additional iron. He ran right out to get the supplements. Every nice gesture layered more guilt upon her soul. The iron made her constipated, such a tiny punishment. It was something she would have complained about endlessly in the past. Now it was barely nothing.

*

The minute Danny left for the store, Teres picked up the phone to call Martha.

Martha Bertakis was Teressa's oldest friend. They had met at Saint Catherine's Greek Orthodox Church in Quincy shortly after Teres moved to America. Martha and her husband, Bemus, were the Muldaurs go-to couple. The foursome had spent two idyllic weeks traveling the Greek Islands in the spring of 1987 and they'd had numerous adventures since then. Teres had not spoken to any of their friends and had no idea what Danny had been telling Ron. The outside world was an off-limits topic for them. But Martha had been good to her, good to them both. She had taken Teres, a young foreign bride with barely a grasp of the English language, under her wing. The Bertakis had helped launch Accelerated Ambulance and still jumped in when needed. Teres owed her some kind of explanation for dropping out of sight. This would be a good time to call. It was Sunday, Martha would be at church. Leaving a message on her answering machine was all Teres could manage.

"Martha. It is Teressa. I want to let you know that I am okay. *We* are okay. We are just… we are just… beat up about what happened on Danny's birthday. I will get in touch with you when I can." As an afterthought she added, "We might go to Greece." Teres hung up. An idea had taken root: *I will go home to Greece.*

March 12, 1992

"Will you bring me to my attorney?"

Danny was startled by the request. *Why is she saying 'my' attorney and not 'our' attorney?*

"Do you have your own attorney?" he asked before he could stop himself. He had checked himself at every sentence for almost five weeks. It was exhausting. Danny wasn't accustomed to weighing his words. Most of the time he didn't say enough words worth putting on a scale, and when he did say something stupid, Teres had long-since stopped losing the show over it. He waited for her to reply. It came slowly.

"Do I need my own attorney?" She looked hurt. It wasn't the defiant comeback Danny expected, although his expectations of her responses had been altered to an unrecognizable state. For a man not known for amazing communication skills, he thought he had been doing a pretty good job holding his own through all this.

"No, Teres. You don't need your own attorney. It's just not the way you usually refer to Seamus – 'my attorney.'"

"Yes I do."

"Yes I do what?" Danny was losing track of where this was going. "Yes, you need your own attorney?" His confusion made her look at him like he was the crazy one.

"Yes. It is how I say things. *My* attorney. *My* business. *My* house. *My* friends. *My* garage. You give me a hard time for being possessive with our things and our people. Please tell me you have not forgotten this is how I talk."

Danny let a grin cross his face. Maybe things hadn't changed as much as he thought. Conversations with Teressa were always a challenge. There were battles fought in the early days where an hour (or a day, or a week) into it he would realize they were on the same side of the argument. Most times it had little to do with English being his wife's second language. It was more about an inability to continue listening once either of them heard something they didn't like; a bad trait to have in common.

"I need to see our attorney, Seamus, about this apartment," she said, deliberately.

The legal packet was sitting on the coffee table where Philip Dixon had left it. Overcoming his fear enough to read it had taken Danny weeks. It contained no real surprises, just gut-wrenching references to "the child," making him hate Philip Dixon even more. The money part didn't interest Danny at all. Ownership of this apartment was so far down the list of their problems it didn't have a number. They hadn't even discussed it. Who was he kidding? They hadn't had discussions of any kind, just a necessary word here and there. Maybe Teres was ready to talk? Maybe-

"I will have Lori bring me." Teres stated then vanished to the bedroom, leaving Danny choking back his hope and his anger. *Fuck it!* He was done swallowing his words. In one motion, Danny grabbed the paperwork from the table and burst into the bedroom behind her.

"Is this what you want to discuss with *our* attorney!" He flung the papers on the bed. "Staying in this apartment and divorcing me? Is it? Answer me for Chrissake!"

"Yes!" she screamed back at him. "We cannot just sit here and do nothing – waiting for a baby that is not yours to be born!"

If she had used a machete it wouldn't have hurt as much. He sat down on the bed and wondered if his lung was collapsing. He knew it was irrational, but air had gone out of his chest and would not fill back in. It was like watching a patient take their last breath, which in his experience was never in, only out. He felt lightheaded and in pain.

*

Teres knew she had gone too far. Of course she had thought about divorce, but only as a theoretical idea meant to save Danny, not herself. It wasn't her reason to see an attorney. She just wanted to find out if transferring her share of the business to Danny could be done without his knowledge or consent. The inheritance from Gregory seemed a good excuse to see Seamus. Teres watched Danny lay himself back onto the bed, his feet planted on the floor, one hand on his forehead, the other on his solar plexus. *I have already killed Gregory. Now I am killing the man I love.* She tried to visualize the kindest thing she could do, the thing with Danny's best interest as the heart of her intention. She envisioned herself sitting next to him on the bed, lying down and wrapping her arms around him, soothing him with reassurances, repairing the broken vase of their love. Her feet wouldn't move. Without permission, her lips settled on the most compassionate choice:

"Yes. I am going to take ownership of this apartment and I think we should get a divorce."

March 19, 1992

Danny had been home for a week, another routine quickly settled into: make a sandwich, throw out the rest of the pot of coffee, watch the news, go to bed alone.

World News Tonight was currently the backdrop for Danny's misery. The television spewed from morning till night, mostly on the same station. It helped him feel less alone. Danny thought back to the glee he used to feel when Teres headed off to work in the morning, leaving him behind to sit around and watch whatever he wanted, for as long as he wanted. *What an idiot.*

Did he feel guilty – like he should have been better at being a husband? Maybe a little. But Danny still couldn't shake the feeling the affair had nothing to do with him. It wasn't an inability to accept responsibility that made him feel that way. His gut told him nothing he might have changed would have stopped this affair from happening. Danny shut his eyes, normally the first step of his nighttime ritual: falling asleep in the chair. With the news humming in the background, he let his mind wander and found himself thinking about Gregory. His thoughts didn't hurt. Instead they traveled the path of reminiscing the start of their friendship.

July 13, 1991

Danny thought it odd that Gregory had known him for eight days before they officially met. By then Gregory had opened his chest, fixed his heart, and won over his wife.

*

"Danny, I want you to meet your doctor," Teres said, holding the arm of a handsome, dark-haired man in a suit and tie. His hospital badge and stethoscope were the only indication of his profession. "This is Gregory Costa, the brilliant surgeon who saved your life and to whom I am forever grateful." Teres' introduction was formal enough to require Danny to stand had he been able. Instead he grasped the right hand of Dr. Costa with both of his. He would have pulled the hand to his lips and kissed his ring except the doctor wasn't wearing a ring, and Danny wasn't convinced saving his life had been wise, given the amount of pain he was in.

"Thank you. I don't know how you did it, I thought I was a goner when I went down."

Dr. Costa removed his hand. "You have your friend, Ron, to thank for keeping you alive until I could operate. I can fix anything, but I do need my patients to start out alive."

"Gregory is Ron's friend, too, Daniello! Isn't that wonderful? We are so lucky!" Teres' gratitude appeared uncontainable. Danny wished he could amp up some enthusiasm for this great man, but he felt awful. Every part of him was in pain: his chest, his leg where they took the donor graft, his arm with the blown IV site – and his stomach! He felt so nauseous that it was an effort to hold back his gagging. He hoped the doctor's visit would be brief. But no, his heart began racing out of control and the monitors tattled the news to his doctor, who pulled the stethoscope from around his neck and began to bark orders.

"Teressa, get the nurse in here!" Dr. Costa commanded as Danny watched in astonishment. His wife was not a woman people ordered around. The nurse, alerted by the same alarms, entered before Teres had a chance to move.

"I'm going to need a stat EKG and ECHO. Get me four milligrams ISDN and a crash cart!"

Crash cart? Danny had a good beat on what medical overreacting looked like, and this situation was heading there fast.

"No need for a crash cart, Doc. I'll take the nitro, get the EKG and ECHO, but I'm not gonna have you jumping on my chest with paddles." Danny kept his voice calm and reasonable. Dr. Costa ignored him. The crash cart came screeching into the room. Danny raised his voice.

"We both know it's just a little AFib. You can stop scaring my wife."

"Mr. Muldaur, if you think I'm going to let you die after all my hard work, you're mistaken. It's probably AFib. But since you've already had one post-surgical heart attack, I'm not taking any chances."

Holy shit. No one had told Danny his heart had given out again after surgery. *I'm a mess! They should have let me die on the putting green.* "Well, okay, Doc. But let's give this a little time to settle down before you go cardioverting me. I really think it will pass."

"Do you, now? Is that what you think with all your cardiac expertise?" The doctor was still listening to the damaged heart, his face inches from Danny's, his look furious, determined – and kind of ridiculous. Danny couldn't control himself. He burst out laughing, which caused his heart to self-cardiovert into a normal sinus rhythm, much like bearing down to mimic a bowel movement might do.

There was a moment of frozen silence as they realized what had happened. Danny watched Costa's face go from furious to disbelief, then back to an overall aggravated look. *At what?* Danny thought. *That I was right? That he didn't have to pull out the big guns?* They stared each other down for ten seconds as the sounds of the heart monitor simmered back to normal. Then something crossed between them, an imperceptible nod. Danny might have taken it for medical comradery, or the begrudging admiration bestowed when a lesser opponent wins the match. Either way, Gregory Costa's look changed, and he started to laugh. Soon they were both acting like this had all been an exercise in male bonding – two men jumping off a high bridge into the river. Teres did not see the humor. Danny realized late that she was shaken to the core.

"You think this is funny? Almost dying, again? Laughing like idiots? Like a couple of … stupid assholes!" She ran from the room. Danny was again deflated by how much pain his health had caused his wife. Costa looked more contrite than aggravated, as well.

"I'm sure she didn't mean it." *She meant every word.* "I've put her through hell over the years with this heart of mine," Danny said by way of apology.

"Don't be too sorry. I think your outburst pushed you out of AFib. Want me to go check on her?" his doctor asked.

"She's probably fine, but if you can I'd appreciate it."

"No problem," Dr. Gregory Costa replied, then hurried away, leaving Danny to conclude his health emergency was over.

March 19, 1992

"No Problem," Danny muttered, slipping out of his non-judgmental dream state and into his judgmental reality. *That was my first mistake, asking a heart surgeon to console my wife.* Every hospital cliché proved real. Cardiologists are considered cocky bastards, and surgeons, self-centered assholes. *Apparently, Gregory Costa, you were both.*

"The former Yugoslav Republic of Macedonia came under scrutiny from Greece again today in its bid to become a member of the United Nation…" the newscaster's droning voice continued. Danny's ears perked up. Teres had spent considerable time trying to explain to Danny why the Greeks didn't want a Yugoslavian defector country using its ties to Macedonia as its new republic's name. The conversations had been lost on him, primarily because the argument begins in ancient Greece and has nothing to do with territory, but everything to do with culture. He listened to the rest of the news story, not learning any more than he already knew, with

the exception of one internal revelation: *Teres is going home to Greece.* The thought felt closer to a premonition than a guess. Danny jumped from his chair and headed to the mud room where he had dumped his duffel bag a week ago. His passport was still there. Hers wasn't.

*

Forty-five minutes later, Danny had booked a flight to Athens and a rental car for the hour's drive to Nea Makri. If he had taken the time to think it through, sleep on it until morning, he knew he would talk himself out of chasing her. The red-eye flight from Logan Airport was Friday at eight p.m., less than twenty-four hours from now. It didn't give him much time to dwell on his plan, but it would be enough time to present himself at Seamus' law office and see what he knew, maybe take a trip to Accelerated Ambulance. It had been six weeks since either of them had stepped foot in their business. Money was being deposited in their account, payroll and expenses coming out, presumably by Martha. He'd go in, listen to a few condolences, and tell whoever was in the office that he and Teres were going to Greece. He would call Ron later, maybe a lot later – like from Greece. Danny went back to the mudroom, dumped the contents of his duffel bag on the floor and repacked for his journey. He could feel himself becoming energized and optimistic. For a man to whom action was the avoidable choice, moving forward had become the lesser of two evils. The probability of another rejection was better than the bottomless depression of a life without Teres.

As if to cement his decision, the television had switched to a late-night talk show with Michael Bolton singing his remake of Percy Sledge's *When a Man Loves a Woman*, Teres' favorite song. Danny, never one to listen to lyrics, stood mesmerized. The song was about loving a woman so much you'd turn a blind eye to her affair. He should have been depressed by it. Instead it gave him hope that what he was feeling was somehow universal, he was not alone in the world. Danny Muldaur didn't always understand the mechanics of relationships and marriage, but he knew about love – and he was in it. He went to bed electrified and eager to begin his mission, a state reminiscent of his days in the military. The funny thing was most of those missions didn't scare him as much as this one did. A wife and a baby were a lot to lose.

*

Dr. Marion Lamoreaux-Aarons wasn't buying it. Teres' plan locked her into decisions she wasn't in any shape to make.

"Teressa, Greece will still be there in a month. What's your rush?"

"If I'm going to leave this country, have my baby in Greece - perhaps live there the rest of my life - I should get settled in before this child arrives." Her answer sounded reasonable, but Marion knew better. Mrs. Muldaur was running from her life and making irrevocable choices on her way out the door. Marion had seen this happen many times. Those first decisions after a trauma were like rebound boyfriends: regrettable Band-Aids, taped over unresolved situations.

"Why can't you leave your business as it is? It seems to be running fine and no one has asked you for anything since the accident. Have you been there at all?"

"These weeks… have given me some distance," Teres replied. I cannot get involved with everything again or I won't be able to leave."

"Do you realize what you're saying? Your business is your baby. You love it so much that seeing it again will make you unable to abandon it. What about Danny? Could you leave if you saw him again?"

*

Teres wanted this session over. Her mind was made up. Today she felt strong enough to leave. And yes, seeing Danny would derail her plans. She wasn't sure seeing Ron wouldn't do the same. Or Martha. But they were part of her old life, a life she lived unashamed of her actions – a life she could never have back. She would walk away from all of it, concentrate on the health of her baby. If she needed to be back in the States for anything, there would be Gregory's apartment and the money he had left her. Handing over the business and the Scituate house was the only way to make a clean break. Logistically, it wasn't going to be as easy a transaction as she thought. Seamus said he would process the inheritance but wouldn't transfer the business and residence without a much better explanation than, "I need you to not ask questions." Seamus, like everyone else, loved Danny. Teres had deliberately left her coat on and kept the visit brief. She knew the documents she was leaving behind would reveal everything with its reference to her pregnancy and the trust fund allocated for her child. Perhaps after he read them, Attorney James Flannigan, Seamus to his friends, would be calling Teres to say he'd be glad to help her hand over her assets, then recommend a good divorce attorney – for her husband.

"I have had nothing but time to think, Marion. It is decided. I am leaving tomorrow night.

March 29, 1992

In January, Trans World Airline filed chapter eleven to financially reorganize and save the company. Danny had followed the news story with interest. The airline had made a monumentally bad decision when it concluded there was no money in freight service or transatlantic flights. But Danny's guess was the airline

111

had never recovered from the terrorist hijacking of its Boeing 727 out of Athens, in 1987. He knew his wife hadn't. They had returned from Greece on Trans World just eleven days before the hijacking. Teres stayed glued to the television for most of the seventy-five-hour hostage ordeal and had not flown since. Danny didn't love flying, but the hijacking hadn't added to his dislike since it was based more on annoyance than fear. His flight this evening was booked on TWA. They had the lowest fare for his last-minute booking. Danny was frugal. No matter how much money he and Teres made, he couldn't override his financially insecure upbringing. There were two other elements factoring into his decision to fly a struggling airline: Based on the law of averages they wouldn't get hijacked again any time soon, and the chances of Teres using TWA were slim. Danny was playing the odds.

*

Normally Danny loved popping into Accelerated Ambulance and was always greeted with hearty hellos. He was 'good cop' to his wife's tight-ship management style. Danny never understood how Teres could be so tough, yet so loved by the staff. They bent over backwards for her, and she got away with saying things that would have made him hated had they come from his mouth. He planned to slip in early, before the night shift left, reducing the need for chitchat and explanations. He had prepared a hand-written note for Martha, thanking her for pitching in and relaying their plan – or maybe just his – to go to Greece. Then he would scoot out before anyone noticed.

He parked in the back lot and headed for the employee door. For a brief second, just before he turned the key, Danny pictured some new guy mistaking him for a burglar and bashing him over the head with a fire extinguisher. He dismissed his ever-cautious, slightly paranoid thoughts and unlocked the door. The motion-sensor light came on just as he was tripping over the first of many items that didn't belong in the hallway. Teres would have lost her mind over the mess. There were rolling oxygen tank carts, boxes of supplies, and a milk crate stuffed with odds and ends that obviously came out of somebody's car. The wall-peg coat rack was filled with more jackets than the staff owned, along with items clearly meant for the laundry bin. None of this made Danny mad. The grin across his face was unstoppable as he imagined his wife's fury. Her outburst would have produced one of two responses: employees running to fix it, or employees running for cover; those pitching in garnering a gold star from Teres, with Danny admiring anyone with enough smarts to run.

"Hello! I hear you back there!" *Shit. What's Martha doing here this early?* This was not part of Danny's plan. He poked his head into the office. She jumped up from behind the desk.

"Danny!" Martha hugged him thoroughly. Danny didn't realize how badly he needed such a hug. She was a friend he complained about, a woman even pushier than his wife. Teres threw Martha's opinion into every argument like she was the tie-breaking vote, never seeing how it only made him dig his heels in deeper. Although Danny hated having a not-so-silent partner in their marriage, he did love Martha. She was a pain in the ass and their dearest friend. And she came with the greatest husband, Bemus Bertakis, a man of high intellect and humor.

"Hey! You're in early. Teres and I appreciate what you've done for us." He almost kept going. *This pregnancy hasn't been easy ... with Gregory's death ...* It suddenly occurred to him Martha might know about the baby. His instinct said no. If she knew she would have insisted on being at Teressa's side through this hell. Danny broke from the embrace.

"What's going on?" Martha demanded, hitting Danny with her *don't lie to me* look. He haltingly began his lying reply.

"This accident took a lot out of her, triggered something… like an exhaustion breakdown. She's getting help, but she's depressed. Doesn't want to leave the house." He should have stopped one sentence earlier.

"She's not at the house. I went there many times," Martha's look said she knew he was lying. Danny felt like a husband trying to explain his wife's dead body.

Jesus fucking Martha. "Yeah, that's what I mean. She's been in her room, lights off, lying in bed or sitting at her desk. I would've answered the door, but maybe you came by while we were at the doctors. She sees a therapist twice a week. I go to the grocery store …" *One more question and I'll tell you everything. We both know I'm no match for you.*

"What can I do?"

"You're doing it," Danny replied, trying not to let his relief show. "This is what she really needs – to not worry about the business – and you're the only one she can count on to keep things going around here." Danny knew it was a lot to ask. His gratitude overshadowed any irritation he felt toward Martha. "It's not good for her to stay home much longer, but she's not ready to come back here. I'm taking her to Greece to visit her parents."

"Yes, Danny. Teressa left me a message saying that," Martha responded, smug to be in the loop.

Danny tried to keep his face even. His hunch had been right; his wife was leaving him without a word. But she had told her best friend. *I do hate you sometimes, Martha.* He had to stop himself from fishing for details. He gave Martha another hug to signal he was done.

"Could you get Ron up to speed for me? He was with a patient when I stopped by." *Another lie.* "I'll call you from Greece." Danny said, then rushed away from Martha's prying presence.

*

"What a load of bullshit," Martha said out loud to her empty office. She rarely swore, even in private. She had a certain image to uphold as the secretary of Saint Catherine's Greek Orthodox Church. Plus, she didn't like swearing. It sounded ugly. But this was bullshit, plain and simple. Martha had been to their house a half dozen times before she finally heard from Teres. She and Ron speculated constantly about what was happening with the Muldaurs. In fact, the last time they spoke, she couldn't shake the feeling Ron was keeping something from her, too. "What the hell is going on?" *Swear number two.* Martha made the sign of the cross while determining to push Dr. Ron Watters into telling her everything he knows. *There's more to this story.*

*

Danny's visit to Accelerated Ambulance was a bit of a bust, but nothing compared to his stop at their attorney's office.

*

Attorney James "Seamus" Flannigan had known Danny and Teres Muldaur since the fall of 1982, when he represented Danny in a personal injury case after he was half-crushed by a city garbage truck while running one summer's day. Against his client's better judgement, Seamus had gone after the city of Quincy with a case so filled with negligence it was settled in a matter of weeks. The check was written before Danny could rid himself of his cane. The Muldaurs felt indebted to Seamus and, as such, embraced him into their fold. He was guest to every event and party, both professional and personal. He and Colleen invited them to their wedding, and later, the baptisms of their three daughters. Both Colleen and

Seamus had left large families behind in Ireland and were happy to be part of *The Band Muldaur,* as Seamus jokingly referred to Danny and Teres' entourage. He knew they had a good life, a solid marriage, which was why reading the brief prepared by Attorney Philip Dixon shook him to the core.

Seamus skimmed the paperwork three times, each time hoping for a different story to become apparent. *Teressa is pregnant. Dr. Gregory Costa is the father. Gregory Costa is dead and had a boatload of advance directives in the event of his death.* It was a lot to wrap his head around. Seamus wasn't naive. He knew people had affairs. More's the case they were people he would have pegged for divorce anyway. Teres and Danny were his aspiration couple. They had weathered storms and come out on top. Seamus had wondered why they were childless, but it was never mentioned or explained. They were godparents to baby number three, Teresa Rose, and doted on all the Flannigan children. The Muldaurs were the perfect blend of open and private, fun without drama. If Seamus had to choose a side, he couldn't. He was in the middle of drafting a letter to Teressa recommending another attorney when the phone on his desk buzzed. He pressed the button.

"Yes."

"Mr. Flannigan, Daniel Muldaur is here to see you," his secretary, Deidre, said, with more recent Irish lilt than Seamus carried.

"Cac!" Seamus blurted, realizing too late he was on speakerphone.

"Mr. Flannigan?"

Seamus picked up the receiver and buzzed Deidre's phone on line one, forcing her to abandon the intercom and pick up the receiver.

"Deidre, tell Mr. Muldaur I am sorry, but I've gotten me-self an emergency call from home and I have had to leave. Please tell him I'll ring him tomorrow first thing." Seamus hung up before she could reply, feeling every bit the chicken *cac* he was.

*

Danny stood there in disbelief as Deidre worked at her answer.

"I'm sorry, Mr. Muldaur. It slipped me mind that just moments before ye entered, Mrs. Flannigan called … in quite a state, she was … something was amiss with one of the *leanbh,* I gathered." Deidre's face was bright red. Danny felt bad she was stuck in such a lie. He should have just left politely, but he couldn't rise above it.

"Deidre, hand me the phone. I'll have an ambulance sent to their house in case the child has to go to the hospital." And then he stared her down, as if any of this were her fault, as if his wife wasn't responsible for the entire mess.

"Mr. Muldaur …" she stammered. Silence hung. The door behind her opened and Seamus rushed through.

"Daniel, my friend. I'm sorry about this, and the way in which I put you to thinking I was leaving. Come in and set. Let's *ceap* through this a bit." Danny didn't move.

"Just tell me, Seamus. I know she was here. Do you know everything?"

Danny watched Seamus hesitate. It pissed him off, but he held it. Deidre and her desk were between the two men, but their locked eyes barred her from the room. Seamus responded quietly.

"I know some. I've read the paperwork she left off. It isn't good, but it's not unfixable."

"Did she ask about a divorce?" Danny broke to the heart of it.

"No, Daniel. It was a property transfer. I was just setting to write a letter suggesting a different lawyer."

Danny's heart rate slowed a bit. "Sorry you're in this, Seamus. She trusts you. Don't get a different lawyer. Just do me a favor – process the paperwork slowly. Give me time to change her mind."

"I will, Daniel. There's nothing slower than a good probate case. You have my word."

*

Ever cautious, Danny had time to spare after he got through airport security and customs. He pulled his carry-on to a quiet seat a slight distance from his gate. It felt good to relax after all the disappointing running around he had done that day. His calm lasted approximately sixty seconds when he realized it wasn't totally out of the question Teres could be on his flight, or any flight out of this terminal, since most of the international flights originated from terminal E. Panic set in. If she spotted him now, before he got to Greece, she would blow up and abandon her plan, surely ruining his only chance to win her back. Danny got up, scanned the room like a criminal casing the joint, and walked to the gate for his flight. *Time for more lying.*

*

"Hi Samuel, I have a little dilemma that I'm hoping you can help me with," Danny said to the gate attendant, whose name tag read *Shmuel*. "My wife is headed to Greece on business and since it's our twentieth anniversary I've decided to surprise her by meeting her in Athens." Shmuel didn't seem impressed or responsive, clearly waiting for the part where the need for his help becomes apparent. Danny continued.

"I want to make certain her company didn't book her on the same flight as mine – it would ruin the surprise. *To say the least.* Is it possible for you to look on your list and make sure she's not on this flight?"

"No. We're not allowed to give out passengers' names," Shmuel said with zero affect.

"You don't have to give me any names," Danny countered. "It's a yes or no question. Yes, you'll be seeing your wife on this flight, or no, she's not listed." Danny pulled out his boarding pass and his passport. "Am I the only Muldaur on this flight?" Shmuel looked at the boarding pass, ignoring the passport. He ran through the manifest on his screen.

"No."

Danny's panic rose. "No, I'm not the only Muldaur on the plane?"

"No. You will not be seeing your wife on this plane." Shmuel looked aggravated, as though he could not have made his answer any plainer. "Is there anything else I can do for you?"

"No. Thank you. I appreciate it." Shmuel ignored his thank you, as if bored. Danny stood there, trying to decide if he should check out other airlines, or hide in the men's room until they called his flight.

"You could check United." The blank face of Shmuel said.

"Huh?" Danny replied.

"United is part of Star Alliance. They fly with Lufthansa to Greece. Your wife might be booked on a connecting flight to New York. There's one going out later tonight at gate E11."

Christ. This was E4. It was a country mile between the two gates. Danny hesitated, thinking about the cranky wheel of his carry-on bag.

"You've got time," Shmuel said, suddenly invested in Danny's faux romantic plan. "If there's nothing you need from it, I'll gate-check your bag and you can pick it up in Athens."

Danny thought about his meds and the mess he'd be in if they lost the bag. Then he thought about how much better it would be to know Teres wasn't going to be standing at the same baggage carousel as him in Athens. "Thank you, Schlemiel," Danny said, wishing he had stuck with Samuel. The kid appeared not to notice, tagged his bag, and wished him luck.

*

United was easy. Danny abandoned the anniversary story for one that cut to the chase.

"I'd like to see if my wife and I can change our seats for the eleven-ten flight to New York," he said as he handed his ID to the gate attendant. She smiled back at him and scanned her list.

"I'm sorry, Mr. Muldaur. I don't see you listed on this flight, only your wife, Teressa."

Bingo!

"I can't believe this!" Danny feigned outrage. "My wife has the boarding passes. I'll be right back." And then he high tailed it back to gate E4, with plenty of time to spare. *Better early than late,* his mind glibly said, to overshadow his bigger thought: *She's actually leaving me.*

*

The takeoff went without a hitch. After the day he'd had, he almost didn't care if it hadn't. That thought, like every thought, brought him to another of Teres' theories. Whenever they flew, she could only relax if she got a look at the pilot and he seemed happy. "I want a pilot with a reason to live," she'd say. *It's a good thing I'm not flying this plane.* Danny requested a nip of whiskey and a cup of coffee from the flight attendant. He would make himself an Irish coffee. Like a metaphor for his life, the two ingredients fought, each trying to cancel out the other. His mind was in overdrive anyway. There would be little sleep on this overnight flight. *Fourteen hours to dwell on the cesspool of my life.* He had better use some of that time to formulate a plan beyond *I'm flying to Greece to chase down my wife.*

*

The plane was halfway to Paris, three-and-a-half hours in. He should have been unconscious, but Danny didn't feel the least bit tired. In fact, he had hardly thought about his health for weeks. Before his ill-fated sixtieth birthday, he had felt like an exhausted old man. True, cardiac by-pass was a big surgery to get back from, but it was six months ago. No wonder Teressa had an affair. She had been married to a sick old man. *Why am I still making excuses for her?* There was nothing explainable about his inability to cast his wife as the villain.

Teres' plan to leave him hurt more than her affair had. His logical brain told him this should not be the case. If he were unable to forgive her something, that something should be her sleeping with another man, not the leaving him afterward. *Christ, I need a therapist. What's wrong with me?* Danny never had a difficult time assessing blame before now. Who is screwing you was something you learned fast in the Navy. Gregory Costa had screwed him. But try as he might, he couldn't stay mad at him. He owed Costa for saving his life. So, Danny transferred most of that anger to Philip Dixon, both a safe target and an easily hate-able guy. He was ashamed to realize he was also mad at Martha for being a friend and Seamus for handling Teressa's paperwork. He was even a little mad a Ron for his constant concern, forcing Danny to come up with one lie after another. He seemed to be mad at everyone but Teres. And now that he was finding his anger, it was about her leaving him – not the affair. *Yeah. I need a shrink.*

Danny pushed his uneaten airline dinner aside. He should try to get an hour's sleep before they landed in Paris, maybe grab some decent food in the terminal before boarding the next flight to

Athens. He shut his eyes, determined to think of something other than his wife. He decided on visualizing a parade of foods he'd eat while in Greece: lamb gyros with tzatziki, stuffed grape leaves, moussaka, vasilopita. It was going well until he recognized the gold-leaf Greek-key plates his brain had conjured up as the dinnerware set Teres inherited from her Yaya. *Every thought leads to her.* The flight attendant picked up his tray. Danny opened his eyes.

"Miss, do you have Irish Mist?"

"No," she answered, "but we do have a nice single malt scotch whiskey."

"Great. I'll take a double."

PART II

GREECE

March 30, 1992

RENTING A CAR in Athens was simpler than he thought it would be. Danny deliberately chose a small sporty car, reminiscent of his time stationed in Greece. Although he second-guessed his choice as he stuffed himself into the compact car, it didn't take long to embrace the zigzag control the little rental provided. *I'm back*, he thought to himself. It was a one-hour drive to Nea Makri. Danny was determined to enjoy every minute of it.

*

Irene Giannopoulos was excited about picking up her sister-in-law at the airport for two reasons: One was she loved and missed Teres. But the second, more compelling, reason was she wanted to tell her side of the story before her husband, Nicky, had his sister to himself. Nicky was the king of convincing. He had already convinced Irene he was a devoted husband. He had convinced his parents that his wife was a bit hysterical and making a big thing out of nothing. He had even managed to convince Irene's best friend that there was nothing to this rumor about him and Anamaria, the jewelry designer from Milan. If Irene were going to leave her husband, she would need someone from his family on her side. Giannopoulos Family Jewelry was a big enterprise to walk away from.

The moment Irene saw her sister-in-law, she knew her own plight was going to take a backseat to Teressa's news.

*

"*Είσαι έγκυος!*"

Teres, tired and mesmerized by the motion of the luggage carousel, jerked her head up at the familiar sound of her sister-in-law's voice. Irene's exclamation was quickly followed with, "You're pregnant!" apparently in case Teres had lost her ability to speak her native language. *I guess there's no hiding it anymore*, she thought to herself, looking down to confirm what now appeared obvious to everyone else.

"Irene. Yes. I'm having a baby." Teres spoke calmly, like it was no big deal. "I thought my brother was picking me up?"

"*Άγιος Θεός! Άγιος Θεός!* Holy God! This is wonderful news! Where is Danny? I can't wait to see the face of your mama and papa when they hear this good news! Where is Danny?"

Where is Danny? Teres had practiced dozens of lies to tell her family during her long, two-leg flight from Boston. Suddenly, all of them sounded stupid.

"I've left him."

*

The ride to her parents' villa was agony. Irene would not let up. "I thought you couldn't get pregnant?"

"Well, I am," Teres replied, unable to ramp up the enthusiasm her brother's wife required.

"Did you use a doctor to get pregnant?"

Oh god. How do I stick to some semblance of the truth?

"Yes, Irene. I used a doctor." Technically true.

"Was Danny okay with that?"

Stick to the truth.

"He didn't know. Please, Irene. I'm exhausted. I'll tell you everything after I've had a chance to rest.

"Just one more question. Does he know now?" Irene's persistence was legendary – and probably a necessary skill, honed in self-defense from living and working with the Giannopoulos clan. Teres suddenly had doubts about what a move back home would look like. Her imagination had led her to envision defiant independence, much like her life in the States had been.

"Irene, I'll tell you what I can." Teres conceded, hoping to put a temporary end to the inquisition. "Danny knows. It was a shock, to say the least. He feels betrayed." *To say the very least* she added silently. "We're trying to work some things out. But in the meantime, I thought it would be best if I told Mama and Papa myself – while it was still safe to travel. Danny had to stay behind to run the business," Teres said, ending her story with her first official lie. Irene's open mouth signaled another question ready to drop. Teres didn't want to start this trip with a fight. She knew if she needed an ally Irene would make a good one. But patience wasn't something anyone who knew her expected, so why change now?

"Enough, Irene! Can't you see I'm exhausted? Don't say anything to my parents – or even Nicky – until I've had the chance to tell them in my own way. And that means even if it takes me a day or two to get it out. I'm serious!"

"*Εντάξει! Σε ακούω.* I get it!"

"We have an hour's ride and I have got to shut my eyes."

*

Well this is certainly going to stall any plans I had to blow up my own marriage, Irene thought to herself, realizing she could use Teressa's misery to her own advantage. Even five thousand miles away, Teressa and Danny's life always trumped hers and Nicky's. If Danny and Teres were ready to split – especially if there was a baby on the way – Irene would have her *own* husband wrapped around her finger. There was no way he would want his parents to hear a word of scandal if he finally had a chance to be the golden Giannopoulos child. It was the thing that drove him, pleasing his father.

Irene was so lost in thought she almost missed the Leof. Marathonos turn. Teres must be tired; the quick left didn't even cause her to stir. Irene considered waking her now that they were close but decided to let this fiasco play-out whatever way it was meant to. Irene couldn't wait to see the look on her mother-in-law, Katharine's, face when she heard the news.

*

Big Nick and Katharine's villa looked exactly as it had the last time Danny saw it, five years ago. It was beautiful, ornate, antique. Sitting high atop the mountain, the view from the property was a never disappointing, but barely-visible, glimpse of the Aegean Sea lapping at the Marathon coastline below. When Danny pulled into the drive in his unrecognizable rental car, a little dog he'd never met greeted him, soon followed by his father-in-law, Big Nick – a man nearly two heads smaller than Danny but with a personality that well-carried the title "Big."

*

126

Because the sun was in his eyes, Nick didn't recognize Danny. Later he would say to Katharine it was because he'd never seen Danny without Teres, or maybe that he'd not seen Danny looking so well, or perhaps because there was something off and unfamiliar about Danny's smile.

"*Γεια σας. Μπορώ να σε βοηθήσω?*"

"Yes, you can help me. Nick! It's me. Danny."

Big Nick felt his stomach drop. *Where is Teressa?* Nicky was supposed to be picking her up from the airport. *What's going on?*

"What is going on? Why are you here alone? Is my daughter…"

*

"Teressa is fine, Nick. She's coming in on the next flight. I wanted to surprise her," Danny said quickly, scaring his in-laws was not part of his plan. He kept talking like he had something to prove. "When she planned this trip at the last minute I decided meeting her would be the perfect way to celebrate our twentieth anniversary. I know it's not till the end of the summer, but a couple weeks in Greece, maybe a trip to Italy…you know how she is. If I suggested a big trip, she would say we couldn't leave the business that long…"

Finally, his father-in-law broke out of his stupor and rushed over to grab Danny in a hug. "Danny! This is wonderful! Wait till Katharine sees you! Grab your bag and come in."

Danny popped the trunk to retrieve his luggage. The little Jack Russell yapped at his feet.

"Coco! Leave him alone! He is family! Danny, ignore that stupid dog. He is Katharine's new *μονομανία*, ah, obsession."

Danny looked at the dog with a pity born of premonition. *Wait till Katharine sees her daughter is pregnant. She won't even know you exist.* He reached down and gave the dog a friendly ear rub. *Buddy, you and me are both gonna be invisible soon.*

*

Teres awoke to the vibration of gravel. The turn into the cobblestone drive of her childhood home had a familiar crunch to it; a sound imbedded like DNA. Her eyes popped open. She felt drunk with exhaustion, then filled with dread. *I should have spent this hour figuring out what to say.* Irene slammed the car into park, a silly grin on her face. Teres had a moment of feeling betrayed, like she'd been set up. But with what? Irene had done nothing but remain silent and let her sleep. Teres realized it was her sister-in-law's grin that made her want to slap her. Irene was enjoying this, as if Teres' life was now a game. What happened to the sweet, caring girl her brother had married eighteen years ago? Teres guessed it was probably her brother that had happened. Nicky had become quite a handful over the years. Smart, cocky, a tad obnoxious. His good-natured kidding had turned the corner to know-it-all bullying. Teres wished her brother wasn't so insecure. He had everything: a beautiful wife, two healthy daughters, the ear of her father – and a future as owner of a successful jewelry business. All he had to do was hang in there and not screw it up. *Sweet mother of God. Who am I to lecture my brother on how to not screw up his life?* Teres shook herself fully awake, exited the car, and walked the path to the front door. She'd worry about her luggage, later.

*

Katharine had adored her son-in-law from the moment she met him. Yes, he was older than their daughter. Yes, he was from America. But there was a gentleness about him that impressed Katharine. She had prayed he would make a good balance for a girl everyone knew could be a handful. Danny would either compliment Teressa's fiery nature or be eaten alive by her. Happily, their love had stood the test of time. She was shocked and thrilled to see Danny at their door just hours before Teressa was due to be picked up at the airport. But Katharine wasn't stupid. Something was up. Danny was acting strange, overly jovial for the quiet man she knew him to be. It would all come out when Teressa arrived. Katharine was all about patience; she had to be with a husband like Nick and a daughter just as fiery and impulsive.

Katharine would never forget the day she met Danny, the same day they learned he had gotten their daughter pregnant. She thought her husband's head was going to blow off.

Summer 1972
Nea Makri, Greece

"It does no matter! We are in pregnant!" Teres hollered at her father.

"Δεν πάτε πουθενά!" Nick yelled back for the tenth time. *You are not going anywhere!*

Nick and his daughter had had a million fights, but never one like this – and *never* involving a boy. Teressa didn't have boyfriends. She had ambitions. For two years she'd been fighting her father about going to the University of Athens. She wanted to be a journalist, not a jeweler. Nick would have none of it. He knew a career in journalism would take his daughter far from Greece, something he could never allow. Now, he would gladly trade that argument for this one. His daughter pregnant? An American sailor, twice her age no less? *The guy looks as old as me!*

"Δεν πάτε πουθενά!"

The fight was attracting the entire household. Big Nick had already shooed away his wife, the housekeeper, the gardener, and his son, Nicky. Now his father, Papus, was banging on the door to the study.

"Πατέρας! Φύγε!" Nick commanded. *Go away!* He wasn't looking for any well-meaning advice from his father. A key turned in the lock. Papus stepped inside.

"Aς μιλήσει το αγόρι." Papus' voice was quiet, commanding. *Let the boy speak? Boy, my ass...* Nick was ready to charge at this stranger who had taken advantage of his daughter. Papus raised his hand.

"Aς μιλήσει το αγόρι," He said again. Everyone looked expectedly at Danny.

*

What seemed like a good idea in the moment suddenly looked like the biggest mistake of Danny's life. "We will only say that I am pregnant," the beautiful girl at his side had said. "My Papa have must to allow me go to America." *What was I thinking? This guy is gonna have me killed. I'll be fish bait at the bottom of the Mediterranean.* Danny wished he could understand what they were saying.

The yelling had stopped. All eyes were on him. *Oh shit. Now what?*

"It does matter," Danny began, slowly and with a voice he hoped wasn't shaking. "You are her father. It matters what you think. We," Danny motioned the space between himself and Teressa, "are in love. But, what happens here today is up to you." He waited for a positive response – any response. When nothing happened he continued.

"I promise to devote my life to taking care of Teressa. I can only do that in America, where I know I can work." Danny watched Teressa's father's face cloud over at the word 'America.' "If that is not good…" *Then what, dummy? Where you going with this?* "If that's not good, I will stay here, in Greece, until you accept me…"

"No! We are placing to America!"

Her outburst took Danny by surprise. *Jesus, Teres. You're making this worse.* He turned and put his hands on her small shoulders, letting them slide to her forearms in case she planned to back up her words with something physical. Their arguments, thus far, had given Danny a good indication of what his future wife was capable of. She was a woman his mother would have referred to as *a handful* – a woman he wouldn't have touched with a ten-foot-pole up until the moment he met her.

"No, Teressa. I will not go against your father." *Or whatever Mafia he has under his control,* Danny thought to himself. "We will stay here until he sees for himself that you will be safe and happy with me." And then Danny stared her down, as if daring her to say another word. In reality, he was silently pleading with her not to speak. Either way, she got the message and stopped herself from adding anything more – a minor miracle.

*

Papus and Nick exchanged looks. They both knew English, George Giannopoulos knowing a little less. *Maybe this is not a tragedy,* George tried to convey telepathically to his son. *Perhaps this Danny is the right man for our Teressa?* Papus hoped, for the sake of this family, that his hard-headed son had heard the same words he had.

"We will speak again, after the evening meal." Papus spoke with authority. They were dismissed. Teressa lingered behind.

"Είστε έγκυος?" Papus asked of his favorite granddaughter. *Are you pregnant?*

"Όχι. Δεν είμαι." *No. Papus. I am not.* Teressa replied, with more shame on her face from the truth than had been there telling the lie. "Αλλά σύντομα." *But I will be soon.*

*

131

Nick knew what his father would suggest: Let Teressa marry. Let them move to America. Papus had been advocating for his granddaughter's independence for months. More than once he referred to Teressa as Nick's captive. "How is your caged bird today?" Papus would ask after an evening of listening to their fights. Nick couldn't understand it. When he and Katharine married, it was assumed they would stay in Nea Makri, run the jewelry store and eventually inherit the mountainside property and the family business - which under his watch was turning into a chain of stores. Nick would need more than just his son to run the size business he had in mind. And it was clear to him Teressa had a better head on her shoulders than her brother. Granted, Nicky still had time to grow and could one day surprise him. But the boy wasn't serious about anything. He lacked the drive and determination his sister possessed, traits she would be taking to another country.

What choice do I have? My daughter is pregnant. It is either watch this drama play out under my face, and to the delight of my neighbors, or send her to America and hope for the best. Big Nick knew what he had to do. He would put himself behind this idea like it was the best thing to ever happen to his family. Have a big wedding. Invite the entire town. Boast about his daughter's life in America. *Okay, it's a plan.* Now, to tell Katharine she would soon be losing her only daughter and then go to Saint Nicholas to convince Father Mistakidis that their precious Teressa must be married to this foreigner in the Greek Orthodox tradition. After all the money the Giannopoulos family had given the church over the years, it shouldn't be hard. "Σκατά!" *Shit!*

March 30, 1992

Everyone stopped talking when they heard Irene's approaching car. Katharine tried to read the look on her son-in-law's face. Nothing, certainly not the joyful anticipation of a man waiting to surprise his wife. Instead of excitement at seeing a daughter they hadn't seen for five years, she felt dread. Katharine sensed, as her son Nicky would say, *a shit show was coming*.

*

Teresa froze in the doorway.

"What are you doing here?" It was more a statement than a question.

She felt an immediate rage at seeing Danny – rage mixed with a flutter of excitement in her belly. She had not seen him in three weeks, but had pined for him every minute. Although his absence was a punishment she deserved, Teres had hoped the distance would ease some of her pain. Apparently not. *Damn you, Danny!*

*

Danny knew he had a single chance to keep this from turning into a one-day visit to Greece. He stood, slapped a weirdly genuine smile on his face, and walked toward Teres.

"Hey," he said quietly, looking her directly in the eyes. Then, in a much louder voice, said, "How could I let you tell everyone our big news by yourself? I couldn't. So, after you left, I grabbed a direct flight that got me here before you!" Danny saw Irene's smirk, causing him to wonder what she knew. *Fuck you, Irene. I'm trying to get my wife back.* Then he waited.

The wait paid off.

"Ω Θεέ μου! Εισαι εγκυος!" *Oh my God! You are pregnant!* Danny heard Katharine scream behind him. "Αυτό είναι ένα θαύμα!" *This is a miracle!* Nick jumped up and slapped him heartily on the back.

"Daniello! How did this happen? Twenty years …"

"It happened the regular way," Danny responded without thinking, then added, "with a little help." He kept his eyes on his wife. It would seem she had no choice but to go along, but Danny knew better. Her next words would seal the lie or blow it up. A thousand silent messages translated between them. The room dissolved, replaced with telepathic communication Danny would never again take for granted. He felt her on the brink of caving into his story and wouldn't let her break away from their stare. *Please Teres, let this be our new truth, I'm begging you.* Her eyes began to water. Never a good sign. Then her face changed. It was as if she just realized what good news this was for her family.

"It is true," Teres said, her eyes still locked on his. "I am having a baby." Danny felt no relief; her words didn't include him. "I … *we* are scared - and excited."

Finally, we. Danny stepped aside to let her parents surround her, hoping no one noticed that husband and wife had yet to embrace. "Baby steps," he whispered under his breath, then tried to let himself enjoy the moment as though it were real, hoping at some point it would be.

*

Teressa's grandfather built the little cottage shortly after he married Yaya. It was constructed of stone and stucco-covered cement, just one bedroom and washroom, flanked by a tiny room Papus once used as a jewelry repair shop, and a stone kitchen with enough space for a large table and a small sitting area. Behind the house were huge flower and vegetable gardens – once a necessity, now a hobby – along with a small building housing a woodshed and the old outhouse, which Teressa's father insisted on keeping in good working order, just in case.

When Papus and Yaya built the big house, a gardener and his wife moved into their small cottage, the wife later becoming a nanny to the Giannopoulos children. And so it went. Big Nick brought Katharine to live in the cottage, later swapping residences when their children, Teressa and Nicky, were born, and Papus and Yaya were ready for a simpler life. After Papus died, sixteen years ago, Yaya wouldn't allow her son to invade her space with such nonsense as replacing a faucet or putting new stucco on the wall. By the time Yaya died, the cottage was in total disrepair. Out of respect for his mother, Big Nick left it as it was for a year of mourning. Then he pulled out all stops, turning it into the most magnificent guest house, every surface either stone, polished wood, or whitewashed, with special attention paid to the outdoor spaces. He planted dozens of fruit trees: pomegranate, fig, citrus, and pear, and created two separate sitting areas, one with a vista of the mountain range and the other looking toward the sea. During the renovations, his only thought was to create a place his precious Teressa might love to visit. *And now she is here, and with a baby on the way!* Big Nick couldn't contain his joy.

*

From her comfortable spot on the cushioned chaise, Teressa could see through the new landscaping back into an earlier time. The gardens and small vineyard, rarely producing more than a few jars of jelly and some homemade wine, used to be directly in front of her. Just past them was the winding driveway that led down the mountain to the seaside village of Nea Makri. If she closed her eyes, she could see Papus in the garden, and Yaya hanging sheets out to dry in wind-whipped sunshine. Staying in the small villa gave Teres a feeling of being wrapped in her grandparents' love. As with many Greek families, she and her brother were brought up by their grandparents. Yes, her Papa had final say. And, yes, when her parents came home from their long day at the jewelry store, Papus and Yaya stepped away from the childrearing so as not to step on toes. But it was clear to everyone who was raising the Giannopoulos children.

Teres had been in America only a couple years when her beloved Papus died. To have missed the last moments of his life filled her with regret, temporarily making her second-guess her decision to leave her homeland. She knew Danny would have stayed in Greece to be with her. It was she who had wanted out. Greek women had only a minuscule window of opportunity from which to climb out before they found themselves living their mother's lives. Teres had wanted adventure, a life of her own. She knew the lightning bolt of love she felt upon meeting Danny was her window. If she had let it slam shut, even if both of them were on the Greek side of that window, it would be years, or a lifetime, before she escaped the droning predictability she knew her life would become. So, although she missed the last years with her grandparents, she wouldn't have changed a thing. America had provided opportunity, friends, and a world on her terms. Teres loved the life she and Danny had created. It was hard won. They had been through more struggles than she could count but had always come out on top ...

Teressa's eyes sprung open. *What a hypocrite! If I loved the life we created so much, why did I singlehandedly ruin it?* Her beautiful moment of memories was gone. In its place, the self-loathing and guilt that had become her constant companion. She got up from the chair and went inside to get a glass of water. Danny was gone fishing with her father. Her mother was at the shop. Back in the day there would have been staff living on the property, a gardener, a housekeeper. But times had changed. The Giannopoulos' no longer housed workers. They now came once or twice a week; lots of workers in big trucks, who got all the landscaping tasks accomplished in one or two hours. Teressa was alone on the property with too much time to think. At least things between her and Danny had settled down. The fight they had the night she flew in made her grateful the villa was so far from the big house …

*

"How dare you go behind my back and come to Greece!" Even as she said it, Teres knew it wasn't an accusation she could defend. So, she did what she always does when she's wrong – back it up with worse behavior. She squared her shoulders, stood on her tiptoes and leaned into Danny's space as she hollered, "You had no right to come here! This is *my* home! *My* parents!"

His measured response surprised her.

"Is that really how you want to play this? I'm pretty sure your parents would take my side. In fact, I think they love me more than they love you. I'm easier to get along with."

"How dare you?" she hissed at him.

"How dare I what? Figure out that you're leaving the country? Buy a plane ticket? Make a decision on my own? How dare I what, Teressa?"

What is happening? Teres swallowed back her anger and focused on Danny. He looked positively calm. There was no resemblance to his normally flustered and tongue-tied responses to one of her offensive fireworks display. She had no idea how to fight with this new Danny. Teres went to her classic plan B strategy: walk past him and barricade herself in the bathroom. He stood in her way.

*

"No, you don't. We're gonna hash some of this out. I didn't come all this way to watch you lock yourself in another room,"

Danny said, struggling to maintain his guy-in-charge persona. "Do you need to go to the bathroom before we talk?" She shook her head no. "You sure? I know you had a long trip with that connecting flight in New York City." He watched the look of surprise cross her face. *That's right, Teres, I know what you've been up to.* Danny saw her shoulder's slump. Her head went down. *Oh, shit,* he thought, suddenly worried she was heading for another breakdown. He began to back away from the bathroom door, ready to let her have her way. Then she answered him.

"You are right. We are here, now. We should talk."

*

An hour later, the battle lines had been clearly drawn in blood. Teres agreed to keep up their pretense until a better plan emerged, or Danny gave up on them as a couple. They both agreed to be truthful *only* to each other; a silly agreement in Teressa's mind since she knew Danny wouldn't ask her anything for which he would be afraid to hear the answer, and as far as she knew, Danny was always truthful to her. They agreed sleeping in the same bed was necessary, given the size of the villa.

There was only one issue that caused their discussion to escalate back to a fight. Danny asked Teres if anyone else knew what was going on, and Teres told him Irene only knew they were having trouble and that Danny was upset about the pregnancy.

"That is just great! Make me look like some asshole who doesn't want kids! Like a selfish prick who's punishing his wife for getting pregnant with a kid she's wanted her whole life! This is fucking rich!"

She didn't defend herself. "I know. I know. I am sorry. You were not going to be here! You know Irene. She was pushing me onto the spot. I had to say something."

"Well, you said the wrong fucking thing. I *do* want this baby – sometimes more than I want you!"

The discussion was ended. Danny walked through the parlor and out to the veranda. Teres watched him stare at the mountainside, hands in his pockets, his shoulders relaxed. Other than the graying hair, he looked just as he had when they met. She thought about how much he loved Greece, at times more than she. It was the same with America: the wash-a-shore in her adored everything about her adopted country. Yes, America wasn't as beautiful as Greece, and there was a part of her that missed the old-world charm of her native land. But making her way in such a diverse country gave her a pride she could never have felt as the daughter of Nick Giannopoulos. Here, her success had been written in stone, or more's the case: gemstones. In America, it was born of her own ingenuity. Suddenly the absurdity of her plan hit her. She would leave her beloved America, banish her husband from his precious Greece, tear him away from her family – or if he was right, they'd embrace him and banish her – and bring up her child alone. *Some plan, you stupid woman.* She walked outside and stood beside Danny.

"Did you mean what you said? About wanting the baby more than you want me?"

*

A thousand responses went through Danny's head, most of them centering around his undying love for her. He took his time with the answer. He wasn't going to feed her ego or let her ride to the top of this argument. The promise not to lie to each other had just been made. Danny broke it.

"Yes," he said. "I think sometimes it's the baby that stops me from hating you." He saw his words crush her and immediately regretted them. Worse, Danny felt a sick weight as he conceded the truth of his lie. He stood there watching the sun set on their first day in Greece, too stunned by his admission to hear the bolt slide shut on the bathroom door. *Way to go, dummy.*

*

Although it wasn't true, Nick liked to think he had made a fisherman of Danny. It was the one element that induced anything resembling paternal feelings toward this son-in-law who towered over him in height and was just a few years younger. Their relationship hadn't been much the father-son type, which was fine with Nick. He didn't need to love Danny like a son – he loved him like a brother. They had bonded over a drunken fishing trip out of Provincetown, Massachusetts. The weather was bad, Nick was seasick, and the bar they hit after fishing was very gay – and Nick didn't mean lively. The way Danny had been forced to hold up his sick, drunk father-in-law made all the patrons assume they were a couple. It was a joke that lasted years. "You want to go fishing?" Nick would ask, to which Danny would bat his eyes and reply, "What kind of fishing did you have in mind?" Today, Nick knew exactly what he was fishing for: the truth about what was going on between Danny and Teressa. Something was up.

*

RIB, Rigid-hulled Inflatable Boat. Danny's least favorite.

The boat was sturdy, fast, and perfect for a two-man fishing adventure, but Danny couldn't shake the word "inflatable" from his mind. And this RIB was small, kind of shallow. For a big guy it was like walking onto a raft or an ocean kayak – both things Danny wouldn't consider with his height and lack of flexibility.

"Nick, I thought we were going deep sea fishing?"

"We are." Nick replied, with a grin stretched across his face. "This boat will take us anywhere we want to go. I got it last year and now it is the one thing I use."

Danny couldn't imagine pulling in anything over ten inches with a boat this lightweight. But he could imagine a tuna dragging their asses all the way back to the States. *Jesus, why is everything always such a pain in the neck with this family?* Like most Giannopoulos situations, he had no choice but to go along for the ride.

*

The day was perfect. A light mist covered the sea, just waiting for the midday sun to burn it off. Nick sped along, heading out of Port Nea Makri toward his best secret fishing spot. Well, he hoped it was still a secret. His wife kidded him about all his "best fishing spots." Probably because he said it about every spot where he'd ever caught a fish. It was kind of a theme for them both. Katharine had one favorite recipe for making stuffed grape leaves and they were good – but the same every time. With each batch she'd say, "This is the best grape leaves I have ever made."

Nick had packed light, two jigging rods and a small box of tackle, along with a couple sandwiches and a six pack of Heineken, Danny's favorite beer. As Nick powered out to his secluded spot he glanced over at his son-in-law. Danny looked relaxed, leaning against the bow of the boat, arms outstretched to either side, eyes shut, face tilted up to the sun. From Teressa's description of what he had been through with his heart, Nick had expected him to look like an old man. But Danny looked great. Ευχαριστώ τους Ουρανούς – *thank the heavens*. Now if he could just get to the bottom of their marriage, as if any of this were his business. But, a fool could see how uncomfortable they were together. Unlike he and Katharine, Danny and Teressa had always been openly demonstrative. In the beginning, it drove Nick to the point of wanting to scream, "Take your hands off my daughter!" Looking back, it was stupid. They were just draped over each other is all, her on his lap, or him standing behind her with his long, bulky arms crossed over the front of her. Nothing X-rated, just the normal stuff a protective father wanted to kill a man for. Nick sometimes wished he and Katharine had been more like that. He regretted how quickly in their marriage he had begun to view his wife as his work partner rather than his cherished lover. *Different time, different generation,* he thought to himself, easily forgetting he and Danny were from the same era.

Nick knew fishing makes a man open up. It was his own father's go-to method of pulling information. Nick had used it with his kids, even a business partner. Now he would use it on Danny. The technique was very much like the fishing itself. It required patience to wait for the right minute to yank the line. They had all day.

*

Danny hated Heineken beer. He and his Navy buddies used to refer to it as panther piss. He should have grabbed a couple bottles of water at the marina before they set out. It hadn't occurred to him to worry about what was in the cooler. Packing a cooler was, again, Teres' area; staying hydrated a berating theme of hers for as long as Danny could remember. The tables had turned with the pregnancy, him harping on her to drink fluids. *Well, no one is getting hydrated today, not with six bottles of Heineken, two salami sandwiches and a bag of potato chips.* His cardiologist would have died if he'd seen this meal. *He did die.* Danny's face clouded over.

"What's wrong?" Nick's voice broke through Danny's thoughts.

"Nothing," Danny lied. "I got a cramp in my leg and I can't stand up in this damn toy boat you're so fond of."

"You will love this boat by the end of the day! With it, we can go into the smallest inlets, where the largest fish hide in the rocks to get out of the sun! You will see!"

Nick's enthusiasm was contagious. Danny had missed his take-control-of-the-moment personality. Apparently, all the important people in Danny's life had big personalities: Teres, Ron, Martha, Nick – Gregory, were people who didn't mind carrying the ball with conversation, decisions, and enthusiasm. *Maybe I'm the problem with my life,* Danny thought, then quickly dismissed the notion, knowing he was the Yin to all their Yang. *Wait, is Yin feminine?* Since when did he care about this kind of philosophical shit? *Since your life became a mystery to ponder on a minute-to-minute basis*, his dual brain retorted.

"Okay, Nick. You're the boss. Show me where these fish are hiding!" Danny yelled into the wind, while unnecessarily extending his leg and pretending to knead out a Charlie horse.

*

Two hours and eight nice fish later, Nick was ready to make his move. They had pulled the boat into a rocky cavern. It was early spring so neither of them had thought about sunscreen, and Danny's hat had flown out of the boat without them noticing. Danny was burnt to a crisp. The shade of the cave was Nick's last good-cop gesture before beginning the interrogation. They had eaten their sandwiches and were on their third beer. Nick went the direct approach.

"What is going on with you and Teressa?"

Danny looked like he had been waiting for the question.

"We're having a baby." It was said in an even tone with just a bit of do-not-disturb attached.

"I know this, Daniel. I mean – you don't seem – yourselves." He didn't say happy, which was his first word choice. Nick took a short swallow of his beer. *I hate this awful beer,* he thought, waiting for Danny's reply, which didn't appear to be coming. Nick was formulating his next sentence when Danny finally spoke.

"Why do you buy Heineken? The closer it gets to the bottom of the bottle, the worse it tastes. I've had three beers, maybe enough to tell you anything you want to know, except I've poured out the last half of the first two bottles. I think the only time you and I talked about my marriage was the day I asked for your daughter's hand. That conversation didn't go well, and we're not gonna pick it back up now." Danny poured the rest of his third beer onto a rock. "I don't know how you drink this shit."

Nick was momentarily shocked into silence. Then he threw his head back and laughed with such force he fell over onto the wet sand of the cave floor. When he righted himself, he saw Danny wasn't laughing.

"Εντάξει. Ας είναι." *Okay, so be it.* "Marriage isn't easy. If you tell me not to worry, I will stop worrying." Again, the long pause from his son-in-law, followed by words he didn't want to hear.

"I'm not telling you not to worry. I'm saying stay out of it."

I was right, thought Nick. *There is a problem, and I have ruined my only chance to learn what it is.* But also in Nick's mind was a growing admiration for the strong voice his easy-going son-in-law had found. Perhaps his Teressa had finally met her match.

"Okay, Danny. Now the big question: Do we gut and clean the fishes now, before we go home? Or listen to our wives tell us what useless men we are?"

"I don't mind a little complaining if you're up to it. I hate gutting fish."

"Me too." Nick decided he was going to like this new Danny. "It is decided. Let's go, before we chicken out."

April 15, 1992

Teres was feeling great. The sun, the change of venue, the truce with Danny, were all having a calming effect on her nerves and on her body. She had read three carelessly written novels she'd taken from her mother's little shelf in the house's old library. It felt frivolous and relaxing. Each book's outcome was easily deduced before she was halfway finished. She wished the answers to her life were as easy to figure out. In the meantime, she would sit on this veranda, take walks, eat fresh fruit, and get through every day as best she could.

She thought about the last time she'd been here in the spring. April was a nice time to visit Greece, warmer than New England. Suddenly she thought about the date. *April Fifteenth! Tax Day in America!* What had they done toward filing their taxes? Was anyone on top of this? Their accountant? This was not something Ron or Martha could do for them. The Muldaurs had never been a day late paying their taxes! Teres' moment of panic was interrupted by a unique sensation. Her hand flew to her stomach.

The feeling was lower in her uterus than she would have expected, but exactly like the butterfly flutter people spoke of. At nearly five months along, her waist had thickened and pushed out higher than a pot belly would. In her imagination the baby was taking up all that room, though she knew better. There were a lot of organs being pushed up and aside to make room for her swelling uterus. Books tended to compare fetal size to fruits and vegetables. Twenty weeks gestation, as big as a sweet potato. Teres had bought a lot of sweet potatoes in her life, some were huge, and some were long and skinny. It didn't matter. Her baby had let her know he was there. Teres needed to share this miracle. *Where is Danny?* She looked toward the house, in search of his face.

*

Danny hated using the bathroom in their guest villa. It was tiny, barely any knee room. There was no exhaust fan. Discretely polluting the bathroom was not an option. He knew there were times he stunk up the entire little house. This might be one of those times. Last night he had eaten like a pig. They had gone to the village for dinner. While Teres ate a beautifully cooked piece of fish, he had eaten more than half their Mediterranean platter, two lamb souvlakis skewers with rice, pitas, and plenty of Tzatziki sauce, mastic ice cream and a piece of Baklava he was supposed to be taking home for later. He couldn't help it, he loved Greek food. But he always paid for it later, or rather whoever was near him paid.

He had forgotten to open the bathroom window. He flushed the toilet a second time, then opened the shade to unlock the window. Teres was sitting outside, not twenty feet from the house. Her hands were on her stomach, her face lost in a look of wonder. *The baby moved;* his instinct told him. He watched her, trying to imagine what was going on in her mind. He felt a brief lurch of his own stomach when he considered the possibility she might not share this news with him, then forced the thought from his mind. It was her news to hold if she wanted to. For now he would just stand there and enjoy the look of maternal amazement on his wife's face. Then Teres looked up, her eyes honed a straight line to the bathroom window. A wide smile exploded on her face, matching the one on his. Danny's heart broke into a million tiny pieces. Their baby had moved.

*

"Let me make love to you."

"I can't."

"You can. You just won't."

"How can you ask me to have sex with you while I … carry another man's baby?"

146

"You already have."

"That was different. You did not know I was pregnant, and I … I was asleep. You were a dream."

"Teressa, I knew you were pregnant." Even in the dark, he could see the disbelief on her face. "I found your pregnancy test the week before. I put two and two together and came up with conclusions, some worse than others, but all of them leading to you being pregnant."

"Why didn't you tell me? Confront me? You should have fought with me!"

Danny could sense her ramping up to a huge defensive move, as if his handling of her affair were the bigger issue.

"Stop." He put his hand near her lips, knowing she wouldn't hesitate to bite it off. "Picture who we were, who we are. I couldn't confront you about changing the brand of my shaving cream."

"That is not true!" she shot back at him.

Danny was in no mood to argue. He was in the mood for sex.

"If you say so." He rolled to the other side of the small bed, his back to her. He could feel the anger behind him. Danny knew from twenty years' experience that no didn't mean no. Teres had a quick pivot turning point, often surprising him after he'd thrown in the towel. Minutes passed. This wasn't going to be one of those times.

"Will you tell me what you thought?" her voice was a whisper.

"About what?" Danny was determined to make her work for this conversation. It wasn't payback. It was reluctance to revisit the most painful week of his life. He wasn't going to volunteer his feelings.

"About when you found out I was pregnant. What happened?"

Danny got out of bed. He walked around to her side, sliding his legs against the bed rail so he wouldn't trip over the extra quilt she had kicked to the floor. Then he sat in the reading chair facing her in the dark. After a few deep breaths, he answered.

"I was looking for the Pepto Bismol when I found the used pregnancy test," he hesitated. "I guess now would be a good time to tell you I hate peppers. You insist on putting them in everything even though they give me indigestion."

Teres started to say something, then stopped. Danny took a ten-second pause, giving her time to make the fight about the virtue of peppers. She didn't take the bait. He continued.

"I spent the rest of the night sitting in the sunroom trying to come up with a good reason for you to take a pregnancy test. There wasn't one. But, you were coming home from work later and later. And you had stopped drinking wine at dinner – made like you were doing it for me, so I wouldn't feel bad about my meds. And you were always tired. There wasn't a lot of other conclusions I could come to. I've seen pregnant women before."

She said his name and he shook his head. "Let me finish." A minute passed; he began again.

"Nothing about how you were acting made me feel like you were cheating. We went to bed every night, same routine. You hogging my side of the bed, my arm thrown over your waist. Nagging me, worrying about my health – nothing different. I made up my mind you had artificial insemination – your big secret was that you got a sperm donor. Every day that you didn't leave me gave me some hope it was the truth. I even decided you weren't telling me because you wanted to make sure the pregnancy was good – as if my heart couldn't take the disappointment. Those were the lies I was telling myself. They were good lies. I needed them."

Danny wasn't one to overanalyze or rehearse his words, so relaying a big story was always a bit of a surprise. He'd hear himself say things he didn't know he knew, like the part about how much he needed his lies to be true. When faced with a wife who cheats on you or a wife who starts a sperm-donor pregnancy without telling you, the latter was preferable by only a tiny margin. But at the time it was something he could work with.

"The night of my party, I convinced myself we could have it all: our marriage, my health - a child. I felt like I would know if there was another man involved. I decided there wasn't. Just this baby you wanted so bad you couldn't risk me talking you out of it. I was ready. I was happy."

Danny was done. That was his whole story. She was really crying, now. He wanted to save the situation, end on a high note, as if they would then fall into each other's arms and make love. *Why do I still want her?* he wondered, every thought ending with the word *dummy*. He worked to push away the guilt he felt about making her cry.

"Sorry, Teres. But you wanted to know."

He thought he heard her say, "No. This is good." *Is it?* he thought to himself. *Will it ever be good again?* Danny climbed back into bed and hugged her until she fell asleep, happy she wasn't pushing him away, but careful not to let her feel his erection. *Just go to sleep, dummy.*

April 26, 1992

"Γαμώτο αλαζονικό μαλάκα!" *You fucking arrogant asshole!*

This morning was the last straw. Just when Irene had finally decided she should drive to Easter Mass without him, her lying, cheating husband shows up wearing yesterday's clothes. Irene was done sugar-coating her disgust for Nicky. He had driven her to this moment of screaming in their front yard – their daughters, Calista and Stephanie, dressed like angels, with hands turning blue from their mother's death grip.

"Τελείωσα! *I am done*, Nicky! Look what your life is doing to ours." Irene pulled the girls toward her husband's car, whipped open the back door and practically threw the ten-year-old and her eight-year-old sister into the back seat. She grabbed the keys from Nicky's hand, spat on the ground for emphasis, and sped away toward mass to be followed by a big celebration with her in-laws. *Yippee! Let's go celebrate the miracle of Teressa's pregnancy!* What a sham, but she had to go. Spitting on her husband was one thing, spitting on the Giannopoulos family fortune was another.

*

If Nicky had to guess when his life had gone wrong, he would have said early, with the leaving of his younger sister, Teressa. He was twenty-one when she married Danny and moved to America. Everyone had expected her to shoulder some of the burden of the family business, the way their mother had. Teressa was smart, reliable – both traits no one expected of Nicky. With her gone, he was last man standing. Any expectations of carrying on the family tradition now fell on him, and he wasn't even close to being ready to settle into a life resembling his father's. At forty-one, he especially wasn't ready.

Still to this day, right now in this yard watching her speed away, Nicky knew marrying Irene was the smartest move he had ever made. When he met her, she was sweet, polished, and worshipful. That worship extended to their bedroom, where Nicky assured himself he had found the last woman he would ever need. But of course that changed. Irene's second pregnancy was difficult. It ended in a bout of post-partum depression that totally excluded Nicky. He had managed to remain faithful up until then, relying on a multitude of flirtations and masturbation fantasies to keep himself satisfied. Baby Stephanie was six months old when Nicky threw in the towel and had his first affair.

She was a summer girl from Turkey, hired to work nights in the store. Her name was Dora, so he teasingly called her Dodo. She pretended to hate it, but Nicky saw how much she loved the attention. *Women love attention.* It was less than a week's work to get her into bed. She turned eighteen on a Tuesday, they had sex on Thursday. Dora said she was on birth control pills – which he made her show him – but he always used a condom. There was no need to bring anybody's anything back to his wife, or on to the next girl. And there was always a next girl. At the end of the summer, Nicky pretended to be miserable, but he was ready to be done with Dodo. Irene had begun to perk up and she was still his first choice in the bedroom. Their sex life took a bit of work to get back to amazing. Irene told him it was her fear of getting pregnant again. They considered their options. She wasn't going through another procedure, two C-sections being enough. Vasectomies weren't performed in Greece, on top of which his parents would have had a stroke if their only son voluntarily cut off his blood line before having a son of his own. But producing an heir for a family dynasty he himself wanted no part of seemed ridiculous. After extensive research, and swearing Irene to secrecy, Nicky flew to a renowned clinic in Luxembourg where they had been performing vasectomies since 1978. *Nothing but the best for my favorite body part* Nicky told his adoring wife, who worshipped him even more for the sacrifice he was making.

After the vasectomy, it went back and forth for a bit: faithful, unfaithful – feeling committed to his wife and family, feeling like they were a noose. Irene's fear of pregnancy had helped make cheating on her easier, because, like every man practicing the fine art of infidelity, Nicky, too, had a fear of pregnancy.

Somewhere down the road, he began using Irene in whatever way suited him. His family knew she suffered depression.

Whenever Nicky didn't want to attend a family event, a conference, or any number of things required of him, he would tell his father he couldn't leave Irene. She was *in a bad state* and he was worried about the girls. Of course his father would want him to put family first. If ever Irene confronted him about his absences, accused him of having other women, Nicky would tell her she was crazy, maybe too crazy to be bringing up his daughters. That usually shut her up. Did he feel guilty? Yes, he hated being so manipulative. *But a man's got to do what a man's got to do.* Eventually, Nicky stopped working at covering his tracks. It wasn't necessary. In what was never a planned move, he seduced Irene's only ally, her best friend, Maia. Though unintentional, the silent threat of him revealing their one-week affair was enough to keep Maia a bit on Nicky's side. He didn't need some caring best friend talking his wife into a divorce.

No, this wasn't the life he had planned. Every so often, Nicky wondered if he could get his marriage back on track, make Irene love him again; be the family man he had wanted to be. This morning was one of those moments. Then he thought about his latest obsession, Anamaria, a jewelry designer from Milan. His favorite body part spasmed when he envisioned their mind-blowing sex from the night before. It was hopeless. He wasn't going to change. *Irene better have left the keys to her wagon,* Nicky thought, as he raced into the house to take a quick shower. He didn't mind being late for church. At least they would be done with the Divine Liturgy. Everyone hates that part.

*

In her head, Teressa referred to the Greek Orthodox Church of Saint Nicholas as *the first scene of the crime.* She had spent her life cataloging bad moments and then villainizing the locations in which they occurred: the church where she and Danny had stood before God with the lie of their pregnancy – also the happiest day of her life, the doctor's office where they received the original news about their chances of conceiving a child, their starter house on Wallace Road where Danny had the seizure that ended their attempt to adopt, Sea Street in Hough's Neck where a trash truck nearly killed Danny, eventually ending with the Scituate Country Club where Danny collapsed on the green, causing their lives to collide with Dr. Gregory Costa's. Over twenty years, she would view many places as scenes of the crime, not knowing there would be only one true place fitting that description: Gregory's bed.

*

Today was a joyous day. Easter Sunday, a day of celebration; *Christ is risen.* Two days ago, her mother had insisted on taking Teres to buy maternity clothes. "You do not want to pressure the baby with tight παντελόνια παντελόνι – trousers." Great Friday is a strict day of fasting for Orthodox Greeks, but clearly there were no rules prohibiting excessive shopping. Teres knew Katharine was dying to announce her pregnancy to all of Nea Makri. As if seeing their community at Easter mass wouldn't be enough to make it official, they were not going home for dinner after church, as was their tradition. Instead they had reservations at Prytaneion Taverna, the most popular eating establishment in the village; a place that might have once been on Teres' *scene of the crime* list for its part in catering her and Danny's wedding.

Teres' Easter outfit was an announcement in itself. Two pieces, consisting of a crisp white top that cascaded off her breast with the rigidity of a frozen ski slope, and a red print pencil skirt with an unnecessarily large maternity stretch panel. Teres thought she looked like a Greek Easter egg. Danny thought she looked beautiful. They had gotten dressed in the same room, unusual for their current situation. But getting ready at the same time meant using the bedroom together, neither could manage in the bathroom. Even putting on makeup was a pain with the tiny ceramic tiled wash basin and no real countertop. After cleaning out the toothpaste and shaving stubble, Teres would throw her makeup bag in the sink and work out of it, squinting into the diminutive, hand carved mirror – its antique glass causing Danny to refer to it as the *fun house mirror*. The squinting thing was becoming a nuisance as well. After having perfect eyesight her entire life, Teres was furious her eyes were failing her now. She had to rely more and more on her store-bought cheaters. Her eye doctor had announced her aging eye diagnosis in the same month her obstetrician confirmed her pregnancy. *How ironic.*

*

It was a short ride to the church, made shorter by the speed with which Nick drove his black sedan. Danny imagined the car looked like a Seventies drug dealer ride; dark tinted windows, sharply twisting down the mountainside, kicking up dust and barely breaking for the turns in the road – especially with a big guy like himself sitting in the passenger side, sporting a pair of dark Ray Ban's. *Yup. Greek Mafia.* He had his doubts whether the level of window tint was legal, even in Greece. No one would stop them, for either the windows, or the speeding. This was Big Nick's town, and by extension, his.

Danny was excited about going to church, unusual for him. His wife had long since stopped dragging him to Saint Mary's, only succeeding to guilt him into it on Christmas eve. But today was different. This was part of his new resolution not to take any portion of his former life for granted. No longer would he view family gatherings a hassle, or any request from his wife as too much work from here on out. The things he'd spent twenty years doing with reluctance, out of what he could only guess had been

154

generational cave man habit, were now the tasks he craved. Sometimes he'd wake in the middle of the night with a random memory of his failure as a husband, like the time he huffed out a deep, frustrated breath when she asked him to clean the snow off her car while she got ready for work. Before he could get out of his La-Z-Boy, she had flown from the house with a broom in her hands, dressed only in her bathrobe, and whisked the heavy snow off her car with fury. Neither of them mentioned the resulting scratches on the doors and hood. Would it have been so much to say, "Sure. No problem"? He tried to remember what he had been watching that was so important. He couldn't. Was it a re-run of *Mash*? A hockey game? The morning news? *Did it matter? No.*

The church parking lot was full. Nick parked in a spot reserved with a sign Danny couldn't decipher. He jumped out to open the back door for Teres, reaching in to take her arm in the process. She pulled away, then must have realized how odd that looked and said, "It is easier to get out of this low car if I use both of my hands." It wasn't. Danny took a step back and watched her struggle. Negotiating the white crushed-shell lot in her heels looked even harder. He stayed close but didn't touch her again. Walking beside her was awkward since holding hands was what they would have done *had she not complicated their lives by carrying another man's baby.*

*

Teres was dreading this church service. She had avoided the hours long Easter Saturday service, but now wished she had gotten it over with. It had been a while since she'd been around so many people. *Danny's birthday party.* The greeter in the church doorway was a friend of her mother's. She took one look at Teres and lunged for her in a way only a woman who already knows the news would do.

155

"Η Τερέζα, σε κοιτάζει! Η μητέρα σου μου είπε τα καλά νέα!"
Teressa! Look at you! Your mother told me the good news!

"Mrs. Lasko." Teres felt a flush of heat. She struggled to stay in Mrs. Lasko's embrace. Her head was swimmy, like she was floating through someone else's dream. She felt a hand on her shoulder. *Danny.* His voice behind her said, "I'll take one of those hugs, Mrs. Laslo." Mrs. Lasko didn't miss a beat at his botching her name. She released Teres and went straight for Danny's arms. Danny winked at Teres as he bent down low to hug the short, chubby Greek woman. Teres should have felt grateful, but all she could think was, *he's trapping me – with his husbandly rescue and charm.* It was a strangely familiar feeling. *Gregory. Danny was acting like Gregory.* The swimming feeling got worse, brown spots began to cloud her vision. She fell backwards in a dead faint, right into the arms of Christos Tsakalos: the man whose love Teres had once shunned by returning to America after a summer in Greece.

*

Christos Tsakalos had a hell of a morning. There were churches much closer than St. Nicholas he could have taken his sons to. Nea Makri was an hour away from their home in Mandra. The boys, ages twelve and fourteen, argued about getting up early to meet their grandparents for Easter Sunday mass. In fact, they had fought him on everything for the last year. He knew they were awful children. Between losing their mother and being spoiled by his parents, who had become the boys' primary caretakers, Basil and Chris were unbearable. Holidays and a couple weeks of the summer were the only time the kids saw their grandparents on their mother's side. There was no way Christos was going to let up on Easter. They hardly knew Dione's parents as it was.

It was during their worst times Christos really missed his wife. He felt selfish, missing her most when it would have been convenient to have a partner. There were days he forgot how much he had loved her. It was less painful to make it about how much he needed her; she was everything to him. Having children right away was her only condition to his marriage proposal. They said 'I do' in a small ceremony on the beach. Then what Christos referred to as *the rule of eighteens* took over: Eighteen months after the wedding they had little Christos, eighteen months later, Basil, who was just eighteen months old when Dione died in a bathtub accident. Eighteen months after her death, he fell in love with Teressa. *Or did I?* Christos hated to think how well the pieces would have fit had Teressa Giannopoulos not run back to her husband when he declared his love. *I played it wrong.* Maybe if he had given her time to realize she had feelings for him, or hadn't blurted out that they could have it all, even another baby – as if all women see having a baby as the carrot a man dangles – maybe then he wouldn't be standing in this line, waiting to be seated at a church he didn't attend, with two boys whose hateful stare he could feel at his back. Teressa was ten years and three disappointing relationships ago. She was the one who got away. *As if she had ever been mine.*

*

Christos cranked his head higher, looking inside the church to see if he could spot his in-laws. He inched forward just as a woman slumped backwards into his arms. No one seemed to notice. Christos wrapped his arms around the front of her, clasping his hands under her bosom, and above what appeared to be her pregnant stomach, and pushed his way backward into the crowd to gently lay her on the ground. She was unconscious. He scanned her face as he checked the pulse on her neck. *Teressa!*

*

When she came to, lying gracefully on her back, not a hair out of place, the voice calling her name sounded familiar.

"Teressa, ξυπνήστε, παρακαλώ πείτε μου ότι είστε εντάξει!" *Teressa! Wake up. Please tell me you are okay!*

She opened her eyes.

"Christos?" she asked. "What are we doing here?" Her disorientation was further compounded by not being able to see where she was. Christos' face blocked out everything. Teres strained to remember where she might be. *Are we at the festival in Athens?* Two breaths later, Danny had pushed Christos aside and was knelt beside her.

"Danny. You do not kneel," she said, embarrassed to be causing such a fuss.

"Only when I have to." He lifted her head and shoulders a bit, and hollered, "Somebody grab me some water! Νερό! Aqua!"

Her confusion increased, "You don't speak Greek."

"Again, babe, only when I have to."

"I only faint when I have to." *That made him smile. Everything must be fine.*

He lifted her to a seated position, gave her a sip of the water her mother had produced. "Did you drink anything this morning?" he asked her.

"We do not eat or drink before mass."

*

Danny was pretty certain there was a pregnancy dispensation when it came to Orthodox rules. He remembered having a conversation with a pregnant Catholic nurse who was eating meat on a Friday during Lent. She told Danny the church bent the rules for the sick and the pregnant – which caused him to chuckle seeing she had already bent them with an unwed pregnancy. He gave his wife more water and persuaded Nick and Katharine to go inside.

They reluctantly agreed, Nick handing him the keys just in case. Soon everyone was gone except two boys and the man – who helped Danny to his feet, then assisted him in getting Teres on her feet.

"You must be Danny," the man said.

Why do I get paranoid when someone knows me, and I don't know them? He thought of attorney Philip Dixon. "Yes," Danny said, extending his hand to shake the man's. "Thank you for helping my wife."

"Danny," Teres said, "this is Christos Tsakalos. And these are his sons, Chris and Basil."

Suddenly, the oldest of the two boys became animated, pulling his bored, pimply face into a grin.

"Σε θυμάμαι!" *I remember you!* And then to his brother, who insisted on speaking only English since he began to study it at school, "Remember Basil? We found her one morning in Papa's bed? She made us pancakes? We called her Tee Tee?"

Danny watched their father's face go crimson, then he looked at his wife's flushed face. It didn't take a math wizard to put together the timeline. It fell right into the summer his solitary bout of depression had driven her back to Greece. *Has she been cheating on me our whole marriage?* He turned away and began walking toward the parking lot. His wife obviously had plenty of people who could take care of her in a pinch. She was right on his heels, grabbing his arm. *Oh, now you want to hold my hand?* Danny jerked his arm from her and continued walking. Teres kept up with him and at the car swung herself in front of the driver's door, barring him from opening it.

"Danny, it is not what you think! Please let me explain!"

"What do you want from me, Teres? You've been trying to get me to stay away from you, and now I will. What's there to explain?"

Maybe it was her native Greek speak that made the next sentence so awful for Danny to hear. It *untruthed* everything she'd ever said to him.

"I have never cheated on you while we were away in our marriage!"

Danny looked at her pregnancy under the big, white tent of a shirt. He shook his head in disgust.

"Is Easter morning really the time to tell me this was an immaculate conception?"

She looked scared, like she'd finally succeeded in getting something she didn't want. He didn't care. He was done. She was safe here in Greece with her parents, *or whoever.* He put the keys on the hood of the car and began walking. The main road, Marathonos, was about two kilometers away. He'd thumb his way back from there. She was still on his heels. He ignored her, walking faster without looking back. Five minutes went by. As fast as he was walking, she kept up.

"Danny! Please! Why won't you let me explain? Nothing happened with Christos. I stayed at his parents because I worked the festival in Athens! Why will you never let me say my side of this mess I have made for us?" He ignored her. She kept at it. "I will tell you everything in truth. We said we will not lie to each other in Greece?"

Hearing her say that made Danny lose it. *We'll only lie in America? What a crock a shit!* Before he could stop himself, he wheeled around and yelled right in her face.

"Shows how much you know! I've been lying to you since the day I got here!"

160

He turned from her shocked expression and began walking again, but not in silence; now he couldn't shut up. The things he'd been holding in, for the hope and possibility of a reconciliation, came flying out of his mouth.

"I'm a fucking liar! Not one time when I said it would be okay did I really mean it! It does matter that you fucked around on me! I hate you more than I love you – and I hate myself because I can't hate you enough to leave! So yeah, Teressa, we're both liars!"

Somehow she was still behind him, and her reply was anything but contrite.

"I didn't fuck around on you! I had a moment of … insanity! A short lived-"

"Short-lived? Your fucking shampoo was in his shower! You were practically moved in! You were running to him when the accident happened!" Danny was regretting every word – and still he couldn't stop. "If Gregory hadn't wrapped himself around a utility box you'd already be living at his harbor view apartment – Oh wait, I mean *your* harbor view apartment!" He took a breath, tried to stem the flow, knowing he'd already gone too far. She was still behind him, close enough where she didn't have to scream. Her words were filled with pain and resignation.

"You are right about some things, but not about that night. I was not going to leave you, and Gregory knew it. I wrote him a letter – told him it was over, that I was telling you everything after the party." Her voice had become further away, still audible. He stopped walking and she finished. "He told me he would take my baby, fight me in court – that is why I went after him. That is why he raced away to his death."

She wasn't leaving me. Danny turned to look at her. She was kneeling beside the road, head down. He walked back. She looked up at him, her face streaked with dusty tears. She had taken off her shoes to chase him and her nylons were in shreds.

"I need to sit; my skirt is too narrow."

Danny was hit with the shameful reality of their situation. *She's pregnant and just fainted from dehydration.* They had no water, and there were no cars in sight. *What the hell is the matter with me?* He sat down and pulled her toward him to take the pressure off her knees. She let him wrap his arms around her, put his face in her hair. "Do you see?" she said. "It is not about my love for Gregory that I cry. It is because I caused his death." She wasn't looking for absolution and Danny didn't offer any. He just held her. *How many times had she tried to tell me about that night and I wouldn't listen, afraid to hear the truth?* He thought about their next move. They were half-way to Leof Marathonos. He'd leave her there and go back to get the car, or maybe find a shady spot and wait it out until church was over. Someone driving by – hopefully, Nick and Katharine – would pick them up. It would be awhile. Easter service was a long haul, hours of church and then endless socializing on the way out the door.

*

The shower had done Nicky good. He felt handsome in his summer suit, which Irene had laid out on their bed. Her wagon reeked of his cologne: Armani, the one Irene gave him every year for his birthday. Nicky felt slightly remorseful when he thought of how many times he'd used her present to throw her off his scent, drinks after work when he had assured her he was working late, another woman's perfume, even his occasional smoking habit. *What a mess.* Having, earlier that same morning, ruled out the possibility of changing, a depression settled over him. He had experienced the same malaise a month ago when he considered not having an affair with Anamaria. *Damned if I do and damned if I don't.*

Part of Nicky's job was writing proposals and projections. As schmoozing as he was, it surprised everyone – himself included – to find he had quite a head for business. A couple weeks ago he used that business mind to project his future, were he to stay on the same cheating trajectory. It didn't look good: divorce, watching Irene pick a jerk as the new stepfather for his girls, because women whose self-esteem has suffered as many hits as he had inflicted on hers didn't marry up; they married down. There would also be no wife at home to use as an excuse to leave a stale affair. He'd end up getting married to someone eventually. *Maybe we should try counseling?* The problem was he hadn't hit rock bottom. Nicky knew there was still some wriggle-room left in his marriage. He could turn it around without the hassle of counseling where some bitchy therapist would see right through him and take away any delusions Irene still had. It was a catch-22. Nicky was so lost in his own dilemma he almost missed seeing the couple sitting on the side of the road. *Is that Danny and Teressa? What the hell are they doing here?*

*

Teres struggled to remove her ripped pantyhose in the confines of the station wagon's back seat. She had a blister on her toe and a cut on the bottom of her foot. *I'll live.* She was surprised Nicky hadn't asked too many questions when he pulled over to pick them up. It made her wonder what Irene had told him.

"Pregnant women shouldn't wear pantyhose. It's too constricting," her brother admonished from the driver's seat. Danny looked back at Teres, a question on his face.

"It is fine. These are made for pregnancy. Or they were." She shoved the ruined hose in her purse. "Where are we going?"

"Well, I was going to drive back to church, but we have plenty of time to kill if you're ready to tell me what's going on."

Danny didn't say a word. Teres was about to spew a story about not being able to face the crowds and opting for a walk, but then she thought about how a spur-of-the moment lie would further ruin her credibility with her husband. So in true Giannopoulos fashion she countered with, "Why don't you tell us how you are driving to Easter mass late, on your own, in Irene's car? Trouble in paradise, again?" Before her brother could answer, Danny came through with a lie coming as close to the truth as possible.

"Teres felt sick and insisted a walk was what she needed. We had a fight about two minutes into it. I'm surprised it took that long. I don't know how you dealt with Irene being pregnant twice. But then again, your wife isn't a true Giannopoulos. She might be less trouble than the two of you."

An excuse *and* a well-landed punch. *Bravo, my husband.*

"No argument there. We are a tough lot," Nicky laughed, though his eyes looked serious as she caught his reflection in the rearview mirror. "Where do you want to go?" her brother asked, seemingly happy to change the subject. Again, Danny took the lead.

"Drop us off at the restaurant. Teressa needs something to eat and drink. Go finish what's left of mass – God knows you won't be lucky enough to miss all of it. Let your parents know we're fine and we'll meet them there. Maybe that'll stop your father from talking to every single person in Nea Makri on the way out of church. Oh, and I left Nick's keys on the hood of his car."

*

Those were more words than Danny normally said in a day. *Yup*, Nicky confirmed to himself, *something's changed.* His spirits lifted as he drove to Prytaneion Taverna. It was good to know he

164

wasn't the only one pretending to have a perfect marriage, or at least trying to pretend.

May 4, 1992

"No. I do not want to go to a public obstetric clinic. If you look at the research, they are more likely to do a C-section. I do not want a C-section. I want natural childbirth." Teressa's attitude said the discussion was over.

Katharine was at the end of her rope, but not finished with the fight. *What does she know about childbirth? Or medical care in Greece? Or the rate of caesarean sections?* She was done having her daughter treat her like a βλάκας, *an idiot!*

"You know nothing! I have been here! I am the one who hears the stories! You will go to the doctor I make for you! You are a … a idiot!" She meant to say stubborn, a word she knew in four languages, thanks to her husband. To her surprise, Teressa burst out laughing.

"Okay, Mama! I will go to the doctor you have set up for me."

Katharine was feeling her power. "And you will let me come with you so to be a two pairs of ears!" she added for emphasis. Teressa laughed harder.

*

Over the past weeks Teressa had seen a different side of her mother. Truthfully, she had never given her mother much thought. Kind, loving, patient were words she would have used to describe Katharine. Dominated by her husband. Perhaps Teres had gotten it all wrong. Maybe the squeakiest wheel was just louder than the rest, but no more in charge of the direction of the cart than the other three wheels. She had begun lately to think about the fluctuation of power in relationships. Gregory had dominated her, and she had been the driving force in her relationship with Danny, *although that appears to be changing*. It didn't take much to flip the dynamics. Was her mother always this forceful but Teres was too young to see it? Or had the power reversed hands over time? And what was with her mother's sudden urge to communicate in English?

"I know why you speak English to Danny, but why me?" Teressa asked.

Katharine pointed at her daughter's stomach. "That is why. My εγγόνι *grandchild* is in that κοιλιά *belly*. He will be born in America. I will not be a Yaya he does no understand!"

"Good idea," Teressa replied.

"They are all my good idea!" Katharine asserted, holding both hands on her hips. "You are not the one smart woman in this family!"

Do not work too hard to learn English, Mama, Teres thought sadly. *This baby might not be going anywhere.*

May 8, 1992

"Do we have to start over with everything?" Danny asked. "Blood work, family history, the whole nine yards?"

Teres lifted her large purse and patted its side. "No. Dr. Aarons gave me copies of my medical records." She watched his face change. She wondered if he were thinking about how nothing in those records had anything to do with him. Her spirits dropped too. It was a lot to explain to a new doctor, and none of it could be done in front of her mother, who insisted on coming despite Teres pointing out Danny was a perfectly good second set of ears. *But was he really?* Teres wasn't certain how many clinicians spoke English. She hoped there'd be a way to talk to the doctor in private, speaking in Greek meant her mother would know everything. Explaining everything in English meant Danny understood – hurtful at worst.

*

"Miss Giannopoulos?" the doctor's assistant called out. Danny stood, realizing Dr. Aarons' office hadn't updated Teressa's alleged name change to Muldaur. His mother-in-law's look was questioning.

"Long story, Katharine." *One I hope never to tell.* He and Teres exchanged looks. In an instant he knew her unvoiced concern: *Today, my mother will find out everything.*

"I got this," he whispered to his wife as the three of them followed the nurse to the examining room. Teres looked confused by his words. A young woman in a doctor's coat walked by as they neared the room. Danny touched the nurse's arm and nodded toward the woman. "Is that our doctor?"

"Yes. Doctor Helen Zygouras," she replied in perfect English.

"Great. Thanks. She looks," he stopped himself from saying young, "smart."

"Dr. Zygouras is very well respected. She could have her own private clinic, but we are fortunate she has chosen us," the nurse said, a little on the defensive side.

Why are Greeks so easily triggered? Danny wondered. He tried to choose a diffusing reply. He settled with, "Nice."

"There is a changing gown on the exam table," the nurse said to Teres. "Your family can wait in the hall if you'd like privacy."

"You go in, Katharine. I'll wait out here," Danny said, as if this were his generous offer to include his mother-in-law in the visit. He worried this new phony-baloney side of him was becoming too easy. When the door shut behind Teres and her mother, Danny strode around the corner in the direction Dr. Zygouras had walked. She was standing at the nurses' station, writing notes in a file.

"Hello. I'm Daniel Muldaur. My wife is your new patient. Do you speak English?"

The doctor looked up, aggravated at being disturbed. "Yes."

Danny catapulted to the point. "The baby my wife is carrying isn't mine. My mother-in-law is with us and she doesn't know. We don't want her to find out."

*

Thank you Jesus! Dr. Helen Zygouras almost said aloud. *Finally something interesting to deal with this morning!* She was only two hours into her shift and already wanting to blow her own head off. After being up all night with two births that were both routine, right up until they weren't, she felt like she was sleepwalking through the day. But this looked interesting, an older man whose wife is carrying someone else's baby. He seems perfectly fine with it. Clearly, he's from America. Helen wondered what made American men so open-minded when it came to their women.

"Does your wife know you're telling me this?"

"No. We didn't have a chance to talk about it before I saw you in the hall. It's what she'd say if she could. Her mother insisted on coming."

"Okay."

"It's all there in her records."

"Okay."

"So …" the man dwindled off, still standing there. Helen resumed writing her notes, her clear sign to anyone, apparently except this man, that she was finished. He didn't move. She looked up at him.

"Is there something else?" His reply was less awkward husband, more authoritative practitioner.

"I know this is just another day in the week for you, Dr. Zygouras, but my wife has waited twenty years to have a baby. It's a big thing. We're here because my mother-in-law said you're the best. Part of being the best is worrying about the patient's psychological wellbeing. Is that something you can do? Cater to my wife's emotional health?"

Helen could have reacted with indignance, or asked a dozen questions: Is your wife unstable? Is she on medication? Was it artificial insemination? Instead she asked the one question that would answer many about the woman's overall situation.

"How long have you and your wife been married?"

"It'll be twenty years in September," he answered, "September second, the same day our baby is due."

Yup. There's a lot to this story. "Mr. Muldaur, I must thank your mother-in-law for her confidence. I promise to take excellent care of your wife and child. I'll see you in the exam room in just a few minutes." His grateful stare went right to her heart.

"Thank you, doctor."

*

The weight, blood pressure and current medical history were completed. The baby's heartbeat had been heard by both *father* and grandmother. Questions were asked by all, including Mr. Muldaur's question about whether sex was still a safe idea, a topic Helen normally doesn't discuss with a patient's mother in the room. Both mother and daughter looked horrified. She gave her standard answer, "There's no reason your wife can't have sex up until the very end of her pregnancy unless she doesn't wish to. Then the answer is no." The husband's face turned bright red and he gladly left the room with his mother-in-law so Dr. Zygouras could examine his wife.

"Your husband told me everything about your baby's situation." Dr. Zygouras said, as she performed her internal exam. She kept it vague, fearing saying too much in front of the nurse might spook the woman. She needn't have worried.

169

"So, he told you that my baby's father is dead?" Mrs. Muldaur replied.

"No. I'm sorry Mrs. Muldaur," Helen attempted to mask her surprise, "he didn't tell me that." Her mind raced to a best-selling novel plot where the husband kills the lover and then kidnaps his own wife and leaves the country. *Probably not.* "Can you tell me how he died?"

"A car accident, three months ago today, in a snowstorm. We had a brief affair, resulting in this pregnancy. My husband wants the baby – he wants me and the baby."

Wow. This lady isn't holding back. "Is that what you want?" Helen asked, acting like this was the kind of conversation she had with first-visit patients all the time.

"I don't know what I want," the woman answered.

"You have plenty of time to figure things out," Helen said optimistically. "In the meantime your pregnancy looks perfect. We'll get a routine ultrasound to confirm it, but I think the baby is of good size. No blood pressure issues. Whatever you're doing, keep doing it."

"My baby must thrive on stress," Mrs. Muldaur said, with the first genuine smile of the visit. Helen smiled back.

"The hardiest babies are usually girls."

*

There was trouble brewing for Nicky and Irene Giannopoulos. Danny could feel it and was hoping to be the hell out of Dodge before an event of seismic proportion shattered the new sense of hope he was feeling.

Things had settled to a nice hum for he and Teres. Danny began to think of their episode on Easter Sunday as the *long road home.* She no longer flinched from his touch; he wanted to touch her. She looked healthy – happy when she wasn't lost in her own mind.

They walked every day, talking easily about things both inconsequential and enormously important. He still hadn't convinced her to come home but was making headway. Greece was magical. Whether their relationship could stand up to the memories and significant microscope of Scituate life was still in question. Not to mention the workload, which from this distance looked like it went just fine without them. Over the past four months Danny had watched his wife go from obsessed with Accelerated Ambulance, to not caring about its existence, to mildly curious about how things were going. As far as he knew, she had made no attempt to contact either Ron or Martha to check on things. He had promised both he would keep them up to speed from his end, and he hadn't. His father-in-law was funny about long distance calls. Out of habit he acted like they were going to financially break him. When Danny mentioned making a couple calls to the States, Nick told him he should go down to the shop to make them so he could write it off as a business expense. This trip was the most time Danny had ever spent with his in-laws. Now he could see where Teres got her irrational penny-pinching ways where she'd bargain shop for a can of beans, but then order a five-hundred-dollar stained glass window to replace a perfectly fine clear one. Making a call from the shop worked better for him anyway. He could barricade himself in Nick's office and say whatever he wanted. *But what would I say?* Maybe Teres should call them. That would handle both issues: finding out how the business is really going, and letting their friends know she was alive and doing well. *But, is she?* As easy as their conversations had become she was still fragile, a flight risk in every way, which was why he wanted to leave here before Nicky and Irene's problems blew things apart. He wasn't that lucky.

*

"Ένα διαζύγιο; για τι μιλάς;" *A divorce? What are you talking about?* Katharine shot back at Irene, then looked at her son. "Δεν έχουμε διαζύγιο σε αυτή την οικογένεια." *We don't get divorced in this family.*

"No, Mama," Nicky interjected. "Of course we are not getting divorced. It was just a little fight and Irene has not yet calmed down."

Irene exploded. "Calmed down? Are you shitting me? Why don't you tell your mother about your latest affair? Tell her about Anamaria! Maybe then I will calm down!"

Danny grabbed Teres' hand, ready to make a quick exit. What had begun as a nice Saturday lunch on the terrace was quickly going bad. Thank God Big Nick was called away at the last minute. Danny stood up, pulling Teres up with him.

"We'll just take a little walk while you sort this out," he said to no one in particular.

"Oh, don't you act so above it all, Daniel!" Irene fired at him. "I know your marriage is not perfect, either!" Then to Katharine she blurted, "Teressa was leaving Danny because he did not want a baby!"

Katharine looked like she was having a stroke. "No!" she gasped.

"You little conniving bitch," Teres leaned across the table as Danny held her back. "How dare you make your fucked-up life about us!"

Calista and Stephanie, who were playing tag in the gardens, came running toward them. Katharine regrouped enough to address her granddaughters. "There is gelato in the freezer of the big house. Eat as much as you want but eat it in the front parlor. We are having a grown-up talk."

*

172

Another grown-up talk, Calista thought to herself, as she grabbed Stephanie's hand and led her toward Yaya and Papus' house. "We are going to be fat girls from all the treats we eat while our parents fight," she said, matter-of-factly, to her sister. "Come on. I will put your ice cream in one of Yaya's good crystal bowls. It will be fun. We never get to eat in the front parlor."

*

The horse had left the gate, with Nicky attempting damage control.

"Irene, please! Let's not ruin everyone's day with our little squabble."

"Little squabble? You are something else, Nicholas Giannopoulos! I'm done!" Irene stood to leave.

Danny's voice boomed above the rest. "Everyone just sit down and shut up!" and then to Katharine he said, "Irene's right. I thought we were too old to start a family. We had a fight and Teres ran home. I panicked. I'm sorry." Then he threw a quietly said dagger at Irene. "And fuck you, Irene, for using what Teres told you in confidence as a weapon." Danny reached for Teres' hand, asked her if she'd had enough to eat, and said to the other three, "If you'll excuse us, my wife is tired. In case none of you remembered, she turned forty today."

*

Katharine needed to get control of the situation. She wasn't going to watch her son make a mess of his life. The fact that Irene was turning into a shrew was further proof of Nicky's infidelity.

"We are not going to have a screaming fight in the yard," she said to her son. "You will get your life together for the sake of those two girls. You are turning your wife into a bitch with your cheating ways."

173

Nicky's retort was unwise. "It didn't turn you into a bitch when Papa cheated with the housekeeper!"

Before she knew it, Katharine swung her arm back and with its full force smashed Nicky in the face, breaking his Greek-god of a nose in the process. Irene rushed to his side to help stem the flow of blood. Katharine felt no remorse. Her son had it coming.

"You know nothing! If you ever disrespect your father to me again in such a way I will be rid of you as my son! And you had better figure out your marriage because if you divorce, your daughters will inherit half, and Teressa, Danny and their child will get the other half of the business your father and I worked our fingers to the bone to build! Do I make myself clear?"

Her arrogant son and his foolish wife nodded their heads. "Yes, Mama."

Katharine marched back to the house while trying to decide how she would approach Nick about changing the will without going into every detail. They had agreed years ago to never bring up his infidelity again. *I need a bowl of gelato, maybe I will put it in my Sunday best crystal bowl.* She deserved a reward; a battle had been won.

*

They had gotten used to their afternoon naps. A lifetime ago, Teres would have laughed at the idea of lying down in the middle of the day. Danny was always a better napper than she, the chair and hassock in the sunroom his go-to spot. But this was nice. Every day after lunch she would change into one of the light cotton embroidered sundresses her mother had bought her and lie down on the soft woven bed cover. She always started out on her back with her hands over her stomach, hoping to feel a little flutter before she fell asleep. Most days, Danny laid down beside her. They'd fall peacefully asleep and sometimes she would awaken holding his hand or with his arm thrown over her. This afternoon would be different. From the minute Danny silenced her obnoxious family with a self-depreciating lie to protect her honor, all she could think about was how badly she wanted him. Whether her husband knew it or not, they were going to make love today.

*

Danny heard nothing but the sound of birds singing outside. Teres' family must have taken their fight indoors. The whole thing went better than he thought it would. Irene's outburst was like killing two birds with one stone, *maybe three birds* he thought to himself, mentally apologizing to the avian choir outside the window. First, it stopped his worrying about when Irene would drop the bomb about Teres' real reason for coming to Greece. Second, it gave him a chance to put a reasonable excuse to why he might not have initially wanted a baby. Third, it might put him in a gallant light with a wife he was dying to touch – and not in a saintly way. Most afternoons he wanted to rape her in her sleep. He'd lay there with his eyes shut, waiting for her to drift off, so he could put his arm around her, letting his inner arm and wrist rest up against her full breasts, breathing in the scent of her hair, marveling at the tiny strands of white mixed delicately into the black. He forced himself from rubbing his erection onto her. It was agony. Sometimes, he got up before she awoke and took care of himself in the bathroom. *What the hell?* Sex with Teres was part of the reason he never looked back longingly at single life. Marrying this crazy Greek girl had made his life better in every way. *Keep telling yourself that, dummy*. He laid down on their bed in just his boxers, his erection obvious, and waited for her to come out of the bathroom. His wife didn't know it yet, but they were about to make love.

*

175

Nicky and Irene drove home in silence. Katharine had the girls overnight, a plan already in place before the disastrous lunch. As they pulled into their driveway, Nicky tried to break the ice with humor.

"Well that went well, don't you think?"

Irene didn't smile. She waited for him to shut off the car then turned in her seat to face him.

"I still love you. What can I do to fix this? Who do you need me to be?" she asked, anxious sincerity splashed across her face.

Those were the words Nicky knew he should have said to her: *I still love you. What can I do to fix this?* Two out of three anyway. *Who do you need me to be?* wasn't in his lexicon. He was sadly, willfully unable to change who he was.

"Irene, you don't need to be anyone other than who you are. I'm the one who needs to change, not you." Nicky said, with equal sincerity.

"Nicky, we both know you're not going to change. I'm asking, who do you need me to be to keep you away from other women? What do you need me to do for you that I haven't already done? I know your cheating is about sex and not about love. Tell me what I must do, and I will do it. Nothing is off the table." There were tears streaming down her face. "I need you back."

Wow. Who gets an offer like this? he thought. It was like a reward for bad behavior. Irene hadn't been awful in bed; in fact, she was very good. She had always done whatever he'd asked, even if reluctantly. But things get in the way of a married couples' sex life, things like kids, and schedules, and boredom – and other women. Nicky shut his eyes and wondered for a moment what it would be like to go back to only Irene, except this would be a new Irene, one who lived to please him in the bedroom. He wondered if he could cross his own mental boundary and ask, no, *demand*, of her the things he easily demanded of his mistresses; the acts that made sex a beautiful game: role-playing, domination, servitude? How far would his wife be willing to go, and what did he have to lose by trying? The thought of this future made his favorite body part jump to attention, taking precedence over the throbbing pain of his broken nose. Nicky reached beside his seat and hit the recline leaver.

"Show me with your mouth," he commanded, his eyes still closed. "And it better be good."

*

Teres had forgotten how wonderful sex was. *Happy birthday to me*. Her engorged breasts and heightened sensitivity left her breathless under Danny's experienced hands. He had always been a considerate lover – a *you* before *me* kind of guy, with an exquisite amount of patience. She tried not to compare Danny and Gregory. But if she had, neither suffered from comparison to the other. They were nothing alike. With Danny, Teres could languish, completely losing herself in the moment. He knew her body better than she did. He worked his way like the methodical man he was, never moving on to another area until she thoroughly needed to be released from the last. He was silent, stealth like. Danny was the man who taught her what her body was capable of. He loved her with a firm gentleness, a knowing hand. Not so, Gregory. He commanded attention. He wouldn't let her shut her eyes and relax into what he did – *had done, never to be done again* – to her body. He wanted her to watch him while he worked his magic, answer him when he demanded to know if what he was doing pleased her. Her response was part of his sexual plan. "Oh, you don't like this? You must not, I don't hear you begging for more." And he'd stop. In the beginning she was stubborn, furious with his technique, and tried acting as though she didn't care if he stopped or not. But they both knew the truth. She needed him to keep going until he had wrung every ounce of strength, *and pride, and self-esteem,* out of her. *A pound of flesh* was the payment for her soul.

May 24, 1992

"Danny! Wake up!" Teres pounded him on the arm. Clearly, she was no longer worried about scaring him into a heart attack. She pulled his hand to her stomach. "Feel this! You can feel the baby moving from the outside now!" Danny opened his eyes as she pressed his hand down hard over the bulge.

"Teres! Don't push so hard! You're gonna hurt the baby." She ignored him, keeping the pressure steady.

"Did you feel that?" she asked excitedly. He didn't feel anything. "What about that?" she repeated. Still nothing. She pressed down harder. He felt it, like a little minnow popping through the water's surface. He grinned at her. She grinned back. It almost made him cry. Not the baby. The return of the closeness. The return of her. He was overwhelmed with emotion and couldn't stop his eyes from filling. She saw it and cried with him. *Let her think it's because of the baby.*

It had been ten days and as many afternoons of sex since the backyard fiasco. Nap time had become Danny's favorite time of the day. Sometimes they dozed afterward or talked until they were sick of being in bed. They were figuring out their new life, trying to decide if they could bring it back to America without losing it. Danny no longer cared where they lived. He had forgotten most of their previous life; this new part overshadowing everything. It reminded him of when they met. For the first six months of their marriage they were attached at the hip. He'd wake in the morning with her hair stuck in his armpit. She wore his Navy t-shirts to bed and insisted he tell her something new about himself every day.

She ran the show. He had no rules for her back then, *or now, or ever*. That wasn't true. He had insisted on only one rule, and enforcing it had been a disaster.

December 1972

"Are you sure you came?" he asked her.

"Yes, Danny. It was beautiful," she answered too quickly.

"I think you're lying. Seriously, this is my only rule: Don't ever lie to me about that. If you need more time, take it. I got all day," he said to reassure her. "I dated a woman once who always said she did when she didn't. It drove me crazy. Hey? Where are you going?"

His new wife was out of their bed before he realized his mistake. He bolted toward the bathroom as the door slammed shut. The eye-hook lock was flimsy. He could have easily broken it, but he'd already acted like a brute. "Teressa! I'm sorry!" She yelled back at him in Greek.

"Δεν θα βάλω στο κρεβάτι μου και ακούω τον σύζυγό μου να θυμίζει τους περαστικούς εραστές του!" *I will not lay in my own bed and listen to my husband reminisce about his past lovers!*

"Baby, I don't know what you're saying, but you're right. I'm an asshole. I'm sorry." She continued to rant.

"Ίσως θα πάρω έναν εραστή που θα σας συγκρίνει!" *Maybe I will get a lover to compare to you!*

The Greek went on for twenty minutes. Danny pulled a chair from the kitchen table to the bathroom door so he could sit while they both berated him. Finally Teres spoke in English.

"I am sorry I lie about my pleasure. It will no happen again." She opened the door; he scooted the chair out of her way. She walked regally past him, adding, "You will work hard for me next time. It is your choosing."

May 25, 1992

"It's Memorial Day back home." Danny said while they walked back up the hill toward the villa. They had decided to walk every day, using the altitude and incline as cardiovascular rehab. Sometimes it was a struggle. There were plenty of places to sit, or lie down if need be, along the mountainside road. Teres had spent much of her pregnancy doing nothing physical and it was beginning to show in her breathing.

"We missed the Scituate parade!" Teres replied, a little out of breath. "I love that parade, especially the part where they throw the wreath into the harbor to honor sailors lost at sea." They trudged a little farther. "We would be having a cookout today – with Martha and Bemus."

"Yup. And Seamus, Colleen and the girls. And Ron. Do you miss them? They're more your friends than mine."

"How can you say that, Danny! Ron is your best friend, and Bemus – you love Bemus."

"True," Danny said. "But they all come around because of you. You're the big draw, kiddo."

He hadn't called her kiddo in a long time. Teres thought back to what a boss she had been for most of their marriage. He was twenty years older than her; she had started out as the kiddo in the relationship. When did that change? How did she become this opinionated bossy woman who always had to be right? Not anymore. She had knocked herself off her high horse. It was a bit of a relief. Nothing left to prove to anyone. She just had to get through each day without her life unraveling again. There were still atonements to be made. Mending her relationship with Danny was healing for her. She was beginning to see the meaning behind Dr. Aarons' *teshuva*. It didn't change the amount of guilt she felt, but it made her grateful to see him so happy. She would work optimistically on their relationship and trust Danny to steer them in a good direction. As though Danny had been following the train of thought in her head, Teres continued it aloud.

"You are not the only person I must atone to for my behavior. There are others for whom I must make it right." Danny stopped walking.

"Teres you don't owe anyone anything. If you're thinking you need to say something to our friends, you don't. The truth is what we decide it is. It's nobody's business but ours."

"You are right, Danny. It is no one's business but ours. I was not meaning that. Gregory's family. It is because of me they mourn. I must make amends."

*

Danny stopped himself from saying what he wanted to say: *Costa's death was not your fault. He was a hot head, into sports cars instead of safety. Stop beating yourself up about it.* But he knew it was futile. Switching gears, he tried to think about this pain from Teres' side. What would she consider a meaningful atonement? How could he help her through her grief? *Jesus* he thought to himself, already hating the idea taking root in his mind. *Stop yourself!* cried his inner dialogue. But he didn't.

"Teres. I think we should go to Italy and see Gregory's father. Tell him about the baby. Then he'll know he hasn't lost everything; a piece of his son will live on through our child."

It wasn't a love of Gregory that made Danny suggest this – although he still couldn't bring himself to hate the man. It was his love for the life they were working to rebuild. He couldn't watch Teres fall into an abyss of misery ever again. His happiness was dependent upon hers. She was silent, her face giving no clues whether Danny should have listened to the little voice in his head.

181

"Babe. It was just a thought …" Her face shattered before he could finish. *Way to go dummy.* "Hey. Stop. Don't cry," he whispered to her while he held her. "I'm sorry. I know it's a crazy idea …" She pulled away to look up at him.

"I will never be worthy of you, Daniello. You are an amazing man. Yes. We should go to Italy. And then we should go home, where I can spend the rest of my life trying to be the wife you deserve."

*

The card from Joseph Costa to his son was still in the backpack Danny had taken from Gregory's car. Since a call to Ron was way overdue, Danny decided to ask him to check on the house, grab the letter in the backpack, and call him back with the address. Teres didn't know he had Gregory's backpack. It seemed stupid to tell her now.

"Hey, there! If it isn't my long-lost golfing buddy! Are you guys home?" Ron's voice sounded clear and close.

"I have good news and bad news, my friend," Danny slid easily into the language of their friendship. "The good news is we're fine; Teres is doing much better. The bad news is I'm calling from Greece and we're heading to Italy, so you're golfing on your own for a little longer. Although my guess is you haven't had time to play one round between the hospital and covering for us."

"Don't kid yourself, hot shot. I've been out more than a few times. I plan to kick your ass when you get home. When will that be, anyway?"

"It depends," Danny answered. "Do we still have a business to come home to?"

*

There was a split second when Ron thought Danny might already know about the lawsuit. He shook it off. *That's impossible.*

182

No one knew Accelerated Ambulance had been named in a six-million-dollar liability suit but himself, Martha, and of course their attorney, Seamus, who advised Ron not to contact Danny and Teres until they knew where this was going. He wrestled with an answer.

"Oh, you know how it is. Always something around here. Martha and I are making such a disaster of things we had to call in reinforcements." *True, but not the whole truth.* "The good news is the crap we've got going on isn't anything you can help us with from Italy, so you may as well enjoy the rest of your vacation. Seriously, when are you coming back?"

"We'll be back by the end of the month," Danny answered. "We're gonna spend a couple days in Sorrento – see Gregory's father."

"Danny. Are you sure that's a good idea? Taking Teres there might push her back to not good."

"Ron, I know. But she and I were the last two people to see Costa alive, I feel like we owe his family something. It's an hour's flight. We'll see the man, take in a couple sights, and fly home from Naples on Saturday. Plan on me being back to work on Monday."

"Hey, you don't have to rush back in – you're pretty worthless around here anyway. Now your wife, that's another story." His friend let the comment go unchallenged but hit him with a couple requests.

"I know Martha's probably set up surveillance around our house, but do you think you could go check on the place for us and do me a couple favors while you're there?"

"Absolutely. What do you need?" Ron asked.

"The code to the garage door is 0514, Teressa's birthday. In the mudroom is Gregory's backpack – I grabbed it out of the car when we were at the tow yard – I need Joseph Costa's address. It's on a Christmas card he sent to Gregory."

"What's the second thing?' Ron asked, still pondering the first.

"It's a biggie. I almost called Martha to do it. Can you empty out the refrigerator? Teres will have a stroke if she comes home to dead stuff growing mold. I should've done it before I left. You're probably gonna need a hazmat suit."

"No problem. I'm done with my shift in an hour. I'll call you with the address – and bill you for the fridge thing. What phone number?"

"Call me at my in-laws. The number's on a magnet pad on the front of the fridge. If we're not around you can leave the information with Teres' mother – I hope you've brushed up on your Greek. And thanks Ron. Thanks for everything."

"Again, no problem, buddy," Ron replied. *Hopefully, you'll still love me when you come home to the mess we got going on here.*

*

One phone call and Teres had the address and the phone number for Joseph Costa. The call was to Efterpi Lasko, the church greeter who witnessed her fainting spell on Easter morning.

"Κυρία Lasko, είναι η Teressa Giannopoulos, Teressa Muldaur." *Mrs. Lasko, it's Teressa Giannopoulos, Teressa Muldaur.*

"Ω, Teressa! Είμαι τόσο χαρούμενος που είσαι καλός! Η μητέρα σου μου είπε ότι ο γιατρός σου έδωσε μια καλή αναφορά!" *Oh Teressa! I'm so happy you are good! Your mother told me the doctor gave you a good report!*

"Yes, thank you for your worry. I need to get in touch with someone from a Catholic parish in Sorrento and I am wondering if you have any suggestions ..."

Ten minutes later, Effie Lasko called Teres with all the information, including a gossipy little tidbit about how Mr. Costa had been in prison for much of his life.

"Πώς ξέρετε αυτόν τον άνθρωπο; Είστε σίγουροι ότι θα είστε ασφαλείς;" *How do you know this man? Are you sure you will be safe?*

"We will be fine, Mrs. Lasko," Teres assured her. "His son was a friend of ours. We are just going to pay our respects." *And drop a bombshell that I hope will not blow us apart.*

*

The ride to the Muldaur's house was too short to fully unravel the turmoil in Ron's head. He was a guy who looked relaxed, like he was flying through life by the seat of his pants. Looks were deceiving. A symphony of what ifs and shoulda-couldas were his lifelong backdrop to any thought added after age thirteen – his last true authentic day. Becoming a physician had changed nothing for him, although it did give him some great psychological terms to apply to his behavior: masking, normopathy, sublimation, and then there was the transitional repressive desublimation he experienced when he began acting out his gay lifestyle from within the confines of his heterosexual life. *It's hard to be authentic when you're living a lie.* This was his everyday world, so when something additionally bad happened, Ron's brain did one of two things: gratefully push aside everything in his own head to fully attend to the problem at hand, or ravel it together, making the new bad all about himself. The latter was his neurons' route for this lawsuit. He should have been tougher with the staff. A tough gay guy – passive, yet firm, funny, but taken seriously when necessary. Ron didn't have a clue what made him straddle these two lives. He had money, enough so he could quit his job, find a tropical gay island, and drink fruity drinks all day in the sun with the cabana boy. Even that scenario wasn't truly authentic, Ron would be the cabana boy. *This train of thought is getting me nowhere.*

*

The house looked abandoned. No one had stopped the newspaper delivery, now a yellowed pile of soggy unidentifiable rolls. Maybe he could come back later and do a little weeding. *Maybe I could let them figure out their own weeds.* The garage door opened on the first try. Seeing their two perfectly parked cars made him feel better, like they were home. The backpack was on the bench in the mudroom, right where Danny said it would be. Ron walked past it, straight toward the smell in the kitchen. The trash under the cabinet was half-full. Curiosity wasn't reason enough to explore the food culprit. Ron tugged open the bin, pulled the drawstring tightly closed, and walked the bag through the garage and out to the driveway. He went back inside, grabbed a new trash bag from under the sink, and began emptying the fridge. He filled the sink with Lestoil, wiped down the refrigerator shelves and counters, then sprayed Lysol into the trash bin. The smell wasn't going away any time soon, but putting in a new scented trash bag helped.

Ron had loaded up the trash along with the old newspapers and was pulling out of the driveway when he realized he had forgotten the card from Joseph Costa. *Idiot.* He left the car running, unlocked the garage and ran back in. He sifted through the backpack and quickly found it, then jotted down the Giannopoulos' telephone number on the back of the envelope. At the last minute, Ron decided to use the bathroom before he left. It was a thirty-five-minute drive to the dumpster at the ambulance company.

Walking through someone's empty house, even when invited, was creepy for Ron – and a little tempting. It wasn't like he had a desire to go through anyone's underwear drawer, it was more of a voyeur's pause. He pictured Danny in his chair, Teres at the built-in desk in the kitchen. He would never let himself picture them in their bedroom, although man-woman sex fascinated him. Gay sex, even at its most loving, was dirty sex as far as the world was concerned. Maybe as far as he was concerned too. Where heterosexual sex had a Hallmark quality, nothing nasty about it. Of course Ron knew better. And his feelings toward Danny weren't sexual, they were brotherly, worshipful. Danny took things at face value. He was emotionally neutral, bordering on oblivious, when it came to social interactions. It allowed Ron the freedom to be as close to his real self as possible. Giving each other shit was just bro-flirting, a teasing one-upmanship, perfectly acceptable when it came to playing golf or shooting pool, even cooking over the grill. Danny never misunderstood Ron. Their relationship had balance. Ron, as a doctor, had larger title credential than Danny did as a respiratory therapist. But Danny, twenty years his senior, a veteran, and a man who had logged more hospital time than Ron, was way ahead of him in real-life experience. It made them equals. And they shared a loyal love for Teres, who was more Ron's partner in crime than Danny's.

Ron tiptoed through their bedroom and into the bathroom. He sat on the toilet, wishing he'd done this before he drove over there. Danny's bloody bandage from three-and-a-half months ago was sitting in the plastic-lined wicker basket at his feet. He would take the bathroom trash away too. Finished, he stood to wash his hands and saw a letter on the windowsill, with one word written in Teres' handwriting: *Gregorio.*

Holy shit! The letter was sealed. He held it against the light of the bathroom window. It was a good envelope, the kind Teres used for payroll, nothing to be seen. Was it a letter to her lover? A letter to a guy who was *trying* to be her lover? Saying yes? Saying no way? For a second he considered using steam to open it. Why would she have left it here? There were too many possibilities that didn't matter anymore. Gregory was dead.

Danny said they were doing good. Seeing this letter might ruin everything. Ron decided to destroy it, throw it in the dumpster with the trash. If he were going to do that, it wouldn't hurt to read it first. Right before he tore into it, he came to his senses. It wasn't his to read – or throw away. He settled on burying it in Teressa's top bureau drawer. *So now I really am a perp, rummaging in my best friend's underwear drawer.* He couldn't wait to get out of their house, but took one last look over his shoulder as he exited, imagining the ghost of Gregory Costa right on his heels.

PART III
ITALY

AN HOUR'S DRIVE to the Airport in Athens, the flight to Naples, and a shuttle to catch the ferry for what should have been a very relaxing forty-five minute coastal boat ride to Sorrento, was all more than his wife could take. With each leg of the journey her anxiety became more apparent. She had stopped talking halfway to Sorrento. Her eyes were closed and facing the sky. The weather was perfect, sunny, a breeze but not too much. Danny hoped she might be enjoying the warmth on her face, but then heard the telltale sounds of her measured breathing. *My girl's in trouble* he thought to himself.

"Teres, we don't have to do this," Danny said, trying to gage her level of distress. "We could just enjoy a few days on the Amalfi coast before heading back to the States."

"No. I will be fine. But if I cannot do this, promise me you will do it for me."

"Babe, I plan on doing most of the talking. Let's check into our hotel, have a bite to eat, maybe a nap, and then I'll call him and we'll decide what to do next." Danny had pulled Teres tight to his side. "That sound good?"

"Yes," she answered. He felt her shoulders relax. "It is a plan."

"And we both know how much you love a plan," Danny kidded, internally acknowledging this plan to let another man into their newly acquired peace was his. *What the hell was I thinking?*

*

Joseph Costa had made one tiny mistake in life: trusting his good friend, Ugo Fallaci. Other than that indiscretion, he had been a good son, a hard-working student, an honorable businessman, a doting husband and father. His Sundays were spent thanking the Holy Father for his many blessings. Joseph had lived his entire life in Sorrento, Italy, *minus the twenty-four years spent in prison.*

The courts don't give points for a life well lived when it comes to the embezzlement of government funds. The contract he signed with his friend, Ugo, was a fortuitous sign of God's good favor – right up until it wasn't. By the time Joseph figured out it was a scheme, it was too late. He was in it. It took the Italian Finance Ministry a dozen years to catch onto the plot – a dozen years of waiting for the other shoe to drop. When it did, Joseph lost everything, including contact with his only son, Gregory, who he had managed to relocate to America before the shit hit the fan.

Joseph was an old man when he left prison. Sixty-four. His wife was long dead, his daughters under the thumb of his sister, Elena, a hateful bitch whose social standing had plummeted with the disgrace of their family name. By some miracle he reconnected with Gregory just before his release from prison. His son was now Dr. Gregory Aldo Costa, a famous cardiothoracic surgeon in Boston, Massachusetts. They exchanged letters for a year before Gregory used his financial influence to get Joseph released six years early. Picking him up from prison was Gregory's first visit to Italy since he had left as a boy of fourteen. Joseph would have recognized him anywhere. Gregory was the spitting image of the man he himself had been the last time they had seen each other.

For the next two years, Joseph and his son exchanged letters and monthly phone calls. Gregory came to visit twice, once to help Joseph set up his little apartment in Sorrento, and the second time to talk about a statue he was commissioning in memory of his mother, Louise, for the garden at St. Leonard of Port Maurice Parrish, a church built by Italian immigrants in the North End of Boston. Gregory had remembered his father pointing out the stonework to him as a child. Joseph was moved to tears by the blessing of knowing this son who had built himself a wonderful life despite the misery his father's mistakes had inflicted upon him. *My cup is full.* Then everything changed.

Joseph's phone call to Gregory on the night after his death was three weeks into the month. He couldn't make himself wait another week to congratulate his son on the news he had received in Gregory's latest note:

Pa – I met a woman. She's important to me, but it's so complicated. I finally know what you meant when you said not all of life's decisions are black and white. We're going to have a baby. I'll let you know more later. Happy New Year! Love, Gregory

And now my son is dead. It was difficult to find a reason to dress in the morning. When he was a prisoner he vowed never to let himself succumb to depression. Yes, he had bouts of darkness, but he held on to the idea he would someday be free and able to make amends to his children. Reading, daily workouts, writing letters to his parents, which he found out later Elena didn't give them, kept him moving forward. There was also the knowledge that he was guilty. He had committed the crime for which he was charged. Living a lie had been his only choice when the alternative was being separated from his family. Being free of it was a kind of freedom in itself. The first thing he did when he was extradited from America back to Italy was confess to a priest. For all these reasons Joseph was able to keep a sense of optimism while in prison. Even though he couldn't see his future, he knew he had one. Not anymore.

*

Getting a call from Gregory's friend, Daniel Muldaur, was a surprise. He was relieved when the man suggested they meet at the café around the corner. Joseph hadn't swabbed out the toilet or done a dish in three months. His daughter, Maura, had offered to clean his apartment, but he wouldn't let her. Somehow, he deserved to live in squalor. They were meeting at five o'clock. Maybe he could buy Gregory's friend a nice meal with the money that was piling up in his bank account. Joseph had no need or desire for money. Receiving the news from Gregory's lawyer, Philip Dixon, that he had become a rich man upon the event of his son's death had made Joseph unable to leave his bed for a week. Thinking about it now made him want to crawl right back into that bed. Thinking about how dirty his sheets were made him crawl into the shower instead. *I hope I have what it takes to keep it together for this friend of Gregory's.*

*

The man was right on time. Joseph was surprised to see Daniel Muldaur was closer to his age than his son's. *Probably more like a father figure* he surmised. Joseph wanted to give the man a hug, but the handshake didn't turn into one.

"Hello, Mr. Costa. I'm Danny Muldaur."

"Please. Call me Joseph. Any friend of my son's is a friend of mine." Joseph's smile wasn't answered in kind. They sat down at an outside table. The man got right to the point.

192

"Mr. Costa, please let me first tell you how sorry I am about your son's death, He was a great surgeon and an amazing man. He saved my life and we became good friends – and my wife ... loved him as well."

Joseph was already tearing up. He reached out to grip Danny's hand and it was pulled back. Their eyes met and something flickered across Mr. Muldaur's expression. *Humanity? Sympathy?* Joseph suddenly felt like he was at a business meeting, not a friendship call. He straightened his back, unsure if he could handle more bad news. *What news could be worse than losing my son?*

"My wife, Teressa, is pregnant with your son's child." Daniel said to him without wavering his stare. Joseph was flooded with relief. Part of the anguish of losing his son was knowing he might never know his grandchild. He had toyed with the idea of hiring a private investigator to uncover details of this pregnant woman. And now, here sat her husband, sharing the news. *Not all of life's decisions are black and white.*

"I … I am speechless. I do not know what to say." Joseph's decision to pretend this was his first knowledge of the pregnancy was instinctual. If he had to pull out Gregory's letter at some point in order to lay claim to this child, he would do so. But for now he was keeping his cards close to the vest. "Is she … the mother … is she well?"

"It's been a rough time … and we're … committed to each other and this baby," Daniel answered haltingly, but not in a way that sounded rehearsed. Joseph got the sense he was feeling his way through the conversation. *So am I.*

"Can I meet her? Your wife, Teressa?" he asked.

"She planned to meet you. She wasn't sure she could tell you on her own. Maybe now that she knows we've talked it will be easier."

Mr. Muldaur stood as the waiter arrived, reminding Joseph how lousy the service was at this café. Joseph stood.

"I'll call you tonight and let you know what my wife decides. But you need to know, Mr. Costa, Teres has been through a lot. If you say anything to upset her, our meeting is over."

"Thank you, Daniel." Joseph replied, again shaking his hand. "I'll wait for your call."

*

Teres heard the hotel room door open from her corner of the bathroom, where she was soaking away her anxiety attack in the clawfoot bathtub. *It can't be Danny. He left less than a half-hour ago.* She jumped from the tub, then slowed her movements, remembering the untimely death of Christo's wife from slipping in the shower. She wrapped a large towel around herself and hesitantly opened the bathroom door, sure she would see an intruder. It was Danny. He was already lying on the bed with his arms crossed over his face.

"That was fast. How did it go?" She asked.

"He was nice, respectful, sad. When I told him about the baby he looked shocked. But you know what, Teres? He didn't look too shocked. Do you think Gregory already told him?"

"I don't know," she answered. "Gregory told me they spoke at least once a month since his father got out of prison a couple of years ago."

Danny popped up to a seated position. "Got out of prison? How long was he in for?"

"I think it was twenty-four, twenty-five years or so."

Danny was clearly agitated. "Jesus Teres, you could have told me I was meeting with a convict. I mean what if I told him you were pregnant, and he pulled a gun or something?"

"Danny, Joseph Costa isn't a gangster. He got involved with a crooked deal with government money. By the time he figured out it was shady he was stuck in it. Gregory said he was a good man and prison had not changed him."

"You could've told me."

"No." She answered, turning her back to leave the room.

"No what?" Danny asked.

Teres stopped where she was. She could feel anger washing over her. She was ready to defend her choice not to tell him about Joseph by resorting to the same poison dart tactics she had always used in an argument. *What am I doing?* She took a deep breath, turned around and sat on the bed beside him.

"No, I could not tell you because I know it hurts you to hear about things between me and Gregory. But since we are having his baby, we should decide what is comfortable to talk about."

*

Danny lowered himself to a lying position again, feet on the floor, arms back to being crossed over his face. He felt Teres lay back as well, also positioning her arms over her face. *Since we are having his baby ...* He couldn't have said it better. *We are having Gregory's baby. I'll be the only person Teres can talk to about this. She'll be my only person if I choose to talk.* He tried to imagine what a casual conversation about Gregory might look like. He couldn't. But letting Costa be the elephant in the room wasn't going to work if he wanted to stay married to this woman. Maybe *he* could keep his darkest fears to himself, but not her. For a woman to whom lies and secrets were like acid corroding her soul, his wife had picked a couple of whoppers to tell during their marriage. It occurred to Danny maybe he should be saying all this out loud. Maybe sharing his thoughts, being bold and honest in their relationship, could work. Changing his modus operandi had gotten him to this point: brainstorming together on a hotel bed in Italy. *Here goes.*

"A big part of me wants to never hear Gregory Costa's name again. I want to get both of us a lobotomy so we can pretend the guy never existed. I've spun this situation any way I needed to, to make it okay. But Teres, I'm excited about the baby. I know it's not mine. But it *is* yours, and that's good enough for me. The next spin we put on this pregnancy, it's gotta be our spin – one we're both good with, and if that means me knowing more about how things were with you and Gregory then I guess that's how it's gotta be." He stopped talking, waited for Teres' reaction. There was nothing predictable about either of them anymore.

"I can't hate him," she finally said.

"I know. Me neither, and I want to. But I don't want you to be in love with him either."

"I'm not. I was drawn to him, in a way I could not stop."

This was what Danny feared most, Teres saying things that put a permanent image in his mind – a silent moving picture of his wife being drawn to Gregory like a moth to a flame, *the way she had been drawn to me.* It was already too much. *Okay, stop! I was kidding. You don't have permission to tell me how things were with you and your lover!*

"Danny?"

"Yup."

"Can we talk about this later? I think we should get dinner and talk about what we want to say to Joseph Costa tomorrow."

"Sounds like a plan." Danny wished he had a dollar for every time he'd uttered those words.

They had a plan, but neither moved, and both were sound asleep within minutes.

*

Il Ristorante 'o Parrucchiano La Favorita was magnificent. They ate outside, under a canopy of lemon trees, grapevines and ferns, bordered by stonework fountains and beautiful flowers. The dress Teres wore was meant to be loungewear, black, silky, deeply cut V-neck, skimming just above her knee. Her shawl was a tapestry of Yaya's her mother had just given her. It still smelled of Yaya's perfume, Chanel No. 5. "Never wear a little black dress without a little black dress perfume," her Yaya had told her. Words to live by. Because Teres had fallen asleep with her hair twisted in a towel, it was dry and untamable by the time she woke up, and had to be pulled into a messy bun at the nape of her neck. Curls and wisps incorrigibly escaped, framing her face like a halo. It couldn't be helped. When she and Danny had awoken and realized the time, they rushed to get ready, fearing there would be nothing open at that late hour. Between the nightgown dress, the hair, and no makeup, Teres was sure she looked a mess.

*

Danny couldn't take his eyes off his wife. It wasn't the dim lighting of the stone patio, or his not wearing the glasses he'd tucked into his shirt pocket to read a menu whose language he didn't understand. It was her. She looked exactly the same as when they'd met. Her skin was flawless, her eyes clear and radiant. Without makeup, Teres had an innocent quality, less sophisticated than the look she normally donned when in public. It had been a long time since he thought about the girl she used to be. The responsibilities of running a business, traveling in circles which included insurance executives and hospital presidents, had quickly taken his wife to another level. The command in her voice, the sureness of her decisions masked the person she still showed to him, just much less often. This was pure Teressa Giannopoulos

Muldaur, and he couldn't get enough of it. Eventually his lustful stare made her uncomfortable.

"Danny, please. You must decide what you are eating. Look at the menu like you understand and then ask for whatever you want."

"I know what I want," he replied not taking his eyes off her. Her blush was more than reward for his use of a cliché. He couldn't help himself. Their relationship seemed brand new, a do-over. He swore this time he'd pay more attention to her needs, stop taking the easy way out. If Gregory Costa had taught him anything, it was that his wife could be won over, and that's what Danny planned to do, win her over every day of his life. He'd do it by being more involved, letting her know she could count on him – standing up to her fierceness.

The waiter came by to take their order. Teres ordered the salmon.

"I'd like a dish with chicken… pollo… and any kind of pasta. Insalata, a bottle of Valpolicella, two glasses – and a bottle of San Pellegrino," Danny said, with a little more stumbling than he'd hoped. Valpolicella was a wine he and Teres drank at home. He saw a bottle of sparkling San Pellegrino on someone else's table as they were being seated, and he didn't care what kind of chicken and pasta dish they served him, but sort of hoped it was Parmesan. The salad he ordered to prove he was planning to take care of his health. His wife was duly impressed.

*

Teres couldn't remember ever having a nicer time with Danny. He was funny, sweet, and they talked about everything except the reason they were there. Dinner was exquisite on all counts. Her salmon had been prepared with an encrusted pistachio topping and served over broccoli rabe with a side of parmesan risotto. The sparkling water, topped with just enough wine, was crisp and satisfying. She said no to dessert, but yes to cappuccino, while Danny looked over the dessert cart. Involuntarily, Teres' thoughts turned to the night she and Ron dined with Gregory at Legal Seafood while Danny was in the hospital. She had asked him what his favorite dessert was.

"Biscotti and a good espresso," Gregory had answered. "But since they don't serve that here, I normally get the Boston cream pie." Teres was lost in thought when Danny answered the waiter.

"Since you don't have my favorite dessert, Boston cream pie, I'll take a couple of biscotti to go."

The déjà vu was too much. Teres' head began to swim, much like it had on Easter morning. She took a sip of her coffee. The waiter returned with the bill and dessert bag. The swimming feeling wasn't going away.

"Danny, this has been perfect, but someone pulled the plug on my energy. I am done with this day."

"Okay kiddo. Let's get you outta here," he responded, quickly standing to help her up from the chair. Teres gratefully leaned on her husband, knowing he wouldn't let her fall.

*

Joseph woke with a sense of dread and depression. Daniel Muldaur had not called back last night to arrange a meeting with his wife. He also hadn't left an address or phone number, giving Joseph no indication that contact from him would be welcome. The feeling was a second death. He wished he could think of his daughter, Maura, as a reason to live. She was sweet, married to a nice man, two daughters of her own. But it was Joseph's son who had been his greatest source of pride, and the largest casualty of his mistakes. The only reason he was out of bed at all was his need to urinate. His bodily functions overrode his lack of will to live. As he stood in his filthy bathroom, unconcerned about his aim, the telephone rang. It was three rings before he could end the stream and race to the phone in the kitchen.

"Ciao."

"Mr. Costa, it's Daniel Muldaur. I'm sorry I didn't get back to you last night. Would noon be a good time to meet? My wife is anxious to see you?"

"Yes," Joseph answered.

"Same place?" asked Mr. Muldaur.

"Perfetto." Joseph said. "The service is so bad they'll probably never know we are there."

*

"You are beautiful," were Joseph's first words upon meeting Teressa. "You look like my daughters." The woman had no reply to that. Joseph got straight to the point. "Your husband tells me you are carrying my son's child. I have to admit; I am both overjoyed and confused by this news." The woman was still silent. "He also assures me you are not here to seek money …"

"I do not want money from you. If anything, I owe you a debt. My husband and I could not have children. Your son, Gregory ..."

The pain on her face at the mention of his son's name was pure and obvious; a pain he had felt for over two decades at the sound of Gregory's name. She either loved him, or … no, she didn't hate him, that much Joseph could see. And maybe the guilt he saw was a reflection of his own guilty pain.

"Your son and I lived a lie for a short time, a lie that gave me the gift of this pregnancy. I, we, couldn't let you live out your life not knowing a baby had been conceived." Teressa Muldaur began to cry, which caused Joseph to do the same. Her husband took over the conversation.

"We've chosen not to tell our child about Gregory. The baby will be brought up as mine in every way, including my heart. If that's something you can live with, we'll send you pictures and letters, keep you informed about his life."

Our child, the man had said without malice or shame. Perhaps a good man. Joseph made the only decision he could.

"I am grateful for whatever you will share with me of this child's life," Joseph said. "It is more than I deserve."

PART IV
HOME

May 30, 1992

THE RED-EYE FLIGHT landed uneventfully in Boston. Typically, Danny would've slept through most of the flight, while Teres, always unable to get comfortable, would remain awake. But she had slept from the moment the flight attendant removed her dinner tray until the pilot made the announcement to land. He, on the other hand, couldn't shut off his mind. He had called Ron to relay the details of the flight, hoping he'd pick them up or send someone from the ambulance company. The news Ron told him threw a torch at their happy homecoming. Accelerated Ambulance was being sued. Danny spent the nine-hour flight wrestling with whether or not to tell Teres about the lawsuit. Her peaceful, flight-long slumber made the decision easier; the bad news could wait.

The Miller Family Lawsuit
Wolfsberg, Austria

The biking trip through Austria was supposed to unite them as a family. After her husband's five-month deployment to the Persian Gulf, Joan Miller wasn't certain she could stay in this quasi-military life. Dana Miller had a great job with John Hancock; staying in the reserves was by choice, not necessity. He came back a different person after each absence. His rocky re-entry into their domestic life eventually ended as they all did, in counseling and apologies to his wife and their sons, Robert and Francis, for the hell he had put everyone through. One more time, their marriage-war was over and, once again, they were celebrating with a fresh-start family trip.

At ten and eleven years old, the boys were the perfect ages for a bike trip, not so little they had to be micromanaged, and not yet in the antisocial, can't-stand-my-parents years. The tour company Joan had chosen held fabulous reviews on all counts, including safety. Safety was very important to Joan, whereas adventure took top billing for Dana. This trip fit the bill for both. Most of the day trips were moderate rides through little towns, lake regions, and backroads, with the poop-out van close by, ready to pick them up if the outing became too taxing. But it wasn't. On day four of their tour of the Austrian countryside, the Millers were riding in unison, chatting comfortably, looking like the perfect family.

Tonight we'll be taking the bus to Vienna, thought Joan, as she daydreamed about someday returning to Austria for Christmas. She let her mind wander toward visions of Christmas trees and baked goods, wrapped packages, and Catholic boy's choirs. She let her bike wander, as well. Her front tire hit the back wheel of her son Robert's touring bike, ramming him down the mountainside.

After eleven days in intensive care, doctors determined Robert's broken neck was stable enough for him to be med-flighted home to Boston. As stressful situations go, Dana and Joan were killing it in the unified team category. No blame games, no decision-making fights, they were sailing into the homestretch of this major event in their family's life. With care and rehab, Robert looked to make a full recovery.

Their flight landed in Boston. The family had been cleared by customs while still onboard the plane. They breezed through the terminal, and were whisked away to the private ambulance, which was waiting along with Dana's company car, complete with driver. They would drive straight to Massachusetts General Hospital on Fruit Street. Dana could have hired a med chopper for the jaunt from Logan to Mass General, but it seemed like more work for the same outcome. Robert was in no imminent danger. Joan would ride in the ambulance, Dana and Francis would follow directly behind for a trip that should take under fifteen minutes. Besides, Joan hated helicopters, having experienced a terrifying open-door helicopter tour in Oahu on their honeymoon.

*

Doug hated working the nightshift. His circadian clock wasn't set up to sleep during the day. As Accelerated Ambulance's longest and most reliable employee, Doug had earned the right to skip night duty. He was doing the shift as a favor to Ron. The schedule was a mess this month, between another new guy leaving and Teres still out of town. Now he was stuck with the newest recruit. At least this guy had experience. If Doug had to train one more guy just to see him leave for the next available fire department or hospital job, he was going to shoot himself. The night had been quiet, a couple impromptu nursing home runs, and later a planned trip from Logan to Mass General. And, thankfully, the FNG (*fucking new guy*),

Travis Paddock, was pretty easygoing and kind of a cut-up. His one liners were doing more than keep Doug awake, they were giving him material for tomorrow's bowling night. He was currently onto blonde jokes.

"Why can't a blonde dial nine-one-one? She can't find eleven on the phone! Why were there bullet holes in the mirror? A blonde was trying to commit suicide!" Travis was cracking himself up.

"Okay, Rodney Dangerfield," Doug said, shutting down the act. "It's almost twelve-thirty. That flight from Germany comes in at one-forty-five. Let's get over there a little early and I'll buy you a cup of Dunkin's. Everything all set in one-oh-nine?"

"Yup."

"Checklist by the book?"

"Yup."

"Okay, let's get outta here." Doug said, grabbing his bag and heading for the driver's seat of ambulance 109.

*

The roads were empty for a Friday night. Bar closings at 2:00 a.m. would fill them up a little, but Patriot's Day wasn't for another week so Doug had no real concern about traffic. Callahan Tunnel was without a slowdown. Rare, even at night. Doug followed the route to international arrivals, terminal E. He backed into the special zone parking area between two cement walls and told Travis to stay with the ambulance while he checked on the flight and grabbed coffee.

"If you're a very good boy, I'll get you a donut."

"Make it a jelly stick if they got one," Travis responded. Doug went inside. A John Hancock Insurance Company car pulled up behind the ambulance, wedging them in.

"Sir, you can't park here," said Travis to the driver.

"You here for the Miller boy?" the driver asked.

"Yup," Travis answered.

"Me, too," said the man. "Let's not make the family have to go to the remote lot or meet me at the pickup curb. And there's nowhere else to park."

"Sounds good," Travis said.

"Great. I'm gonna go take a leak. I'll be right back." The driver pocketed his keys, leaving the sedan unlocked and sauntered off to the bathroom.

*

Matty LeVeque had been transporting somebody or something for most of his life, beginning as courier for a local pharmacy. His driving gigs had gone from boring to exciting and back to boring. In his glory days he worked for a talent company picking up celebrities at Logan and driving them to their hotels and concert venues like Great Woods, Cape Cod Melody Tent or the Boston Garden. That was back in the seventies and early eighties. At sixty, he shouldn't have been a has-been, but he was. His life had been up and down like a yo-yo since he and his wife got divorced over him giving their home number to Laura Branigan. It wasn't like they were sleeping together; it was in case she needed to be picked up in the middle of the night. But having Ms. Branigan call at three in the morning and ask for him resurfaced a lot of *feelings* from the times he did cheat on her. At least that's what the marriage counselor said. Being innocent at that point didn't matter.

Matty felt sick. He was overtired and had a whopper of a headache which sometimes happened when he had to take a dump. He found the first available bathroom, the private family handicapped access room. It was empty, he hurried inside and locked the door. As he sat down he wished he had brought something to read. He reached into the back pocket of his pants, lying in a wrinkled pool around his feet, and grabbed the Suffolk

Downs racetrack betting program from earlier that day. Maybe he could learn something from his mistakes. Matty blinked a couple times. His vision was off. *I need new glasses.* He felt constipated, not like him. Knowing his time was limited, Matty bared down with all his strength. He felt something pop in his head, accompanied by the worst pain imaginable. The aneurysm killed him before his head had a chance to hit the floor.

*

The patient transfer hadn't gone well. The boy, who by all accounts had an uneventful flight, woke up in an acute sense of discomfort. If Doug had known the flight came in early, he might have come into the terminal with his own stretcher. Once it became apparent Robert wasn't going to transition well, he was grateful to have the team from Germany accompany him to the ambulance, where there'd be four sets of hands and a full ambulance of supplies. The kid's mother wasn't making things any easier. She couldn't keep up, but wasn't letting go of the stretcher.

"I don't think he can breathe," she kept repeating, while running alongside her son.

"I think it's a little anxiety, Ma'am. We'll give him something the minute we get outside." *And you should shut up. You're adding to his anxiety* Doug wanted to say but didn't. The younger brother was crying and the father looked pissed. The patient's breathing was getting worse. Doug stopped to grab an accurate blood pressure. It was falling.

"Did your son have a chest injury with this accident?" Doug asked.

"Oh my god! You think he has a chest injury?" the woman replied, going quickly to level ten.

"No Ma'am, just trying to get a history on the fly." Doug answered calmly. The father spoke.

"He had a broken ankle, and fractured C5, but not misaligned, no spinal cord damage."

"Did he have surgery?" Doug asked.

"Yes," the man answered. "On his foot."

Blood clot, deep vein thrombosis, long flight. No activity for eleven days. Pulmonary embolism. Doug and one of the med flight nurses exchanged looks. He wished they could exchange places. He would have loved to be the person handing this one off.

Travis must have seen them coming. He had pulled the stretcher and was ready and waiting as they came busting through the door. They quickly transferred the patient to their gurney, with Doug barking orders. "Get on the horn and tell them we're coming it with a med flight transfer – possible post-surgical PE of an eleven-year-old." He calmly put an oxygen mask on Robert, who was pushing him away, struggling to breathe. "Hey, big guy. This will help. Why don't you close your eyes, hold your mom's hand." Doug grabbed an 18 gauge needle, large enough for the contrast CT the kid would be headed to the minute they got to Mass General. In the meantime, he'd use this second IV to push as much fluid as possible to get the boy's blood pressure closer to normal. He turned around to say something to Travis, and that's when he saw the big black car blocking their only exit.

"What's that car doing there? Tell him to move it. Now!"

"It's the driver for the kid's family. He went to use the bathroom. We thought he had time." Travis looked apologetic. "Want me to go find him?"

"No. Find out from Mass General what's the most norepinephrine I can give this kid." The boy's heart rate and chest pain were rising. The med flight nurse had climbed into the ambulance beside him, forcing the boy's mother toward the back. The nurse was securing the line while Doug pulled out the norepinephrine vial. He asked Joan Miller how much her son weighed. No answer. She had mentally checked out. Doug looked out the ambulance door. Dana Miller was trying to calm his other son. "Mr. Miller, run inside and find your driver. He went to the men's room. We need to leave, now." The man and his son took off at a run.

"Travis, call in another ambulance in case we can't get this thing moved in time."

"I think he'll be out any second." That's when Doug lost the show.

"You think? You think any minute a guy might come busting through those doors, a guy you shouldn't have let park behind us?"

*

That was the quote Mrs. Miller gave to the attorney when they added Accelerated Ambulance to their wrongful death suit, *you shouldn't have let him park behind us*. It went deeper than that, though. When eleven-year-old Robert went into cardiac arrest, just after Doug injected medication designed to constrict the vessels and force up the blood pressure, performing CPR caused further damage to his cervical fracture – not enough to sever his spinal cord, but enough to make the case for a lawsuit a bit more substantial.

Airport Security had to bust down the bathroom door when they couldn't find a key. When the second ambulance arrived, Doug was manually ventilating the patient with an Ambu bag, no heartbeat on the monitor. Joan Miller was screaming for her husband and fell from the back of the ambulance, breaking a wrist and lacerating her cheek. Travis called for a third ambulance for Mrs. Miller, and eventually a fourth for the driver, Matty LeVeque. Doug and Travis had done everything by the book, resulting in two dead bodies, an injured woman, a traumatized child, and a father with herniated discs from trying to single-handedly move a car in parked gear.

May 30, 1992
Boston, Massachusetts

After a surprisingly nice breakfast at an airport café, Danny called a cab for their ride home. Ron had offered to pick them up but since Danny hadn't filled Teres in on the lawsuit, the drive to Scituate would have been anxiety provoking. He was already beginning to regret their return home. Yes, Greeks could be abrupt, easily offended, and snappy. But there was no comparison to Bostonian rudeness. They had been hollered at three times since they landed. Once, when Danny leaned on someone's sky-cart at the baggage carousel. "That's not for you, buddy. You have to rent these, ya know!" A second time when they went in search of Teres' other bag. "I have no idea," the woman said without looking up. "Fill out the claim check form in front of you." Danny reached over to point at Teres' bag in the pile behind her counter.

"Ma'am, I think ..."

"Did you not hear me? Fill out the form and we'll get back to you."

The third rude moment was from a cab driver in the smallest cab Danny had ever seen, who angrily informed them when they became next in the taxi line, that they needed a cab big enough for luggage. After the long, sleepless flight, Danny wasn't at his best. "We're at an airport, for Chrissake! Why would our luggage be a surprise to you?" *Welcome to Massachusetts.*

*

They were almost to the house when Danny remembered the letter he had left on the windowsill of their bathroom. *Gregorio.* He wasn't going to let that be Teres' welcome home moment. It was over three months since she'd stepped foot in their house. This was going to be hard enough for her as it was. He set the stage for a mad dash to the bathroom. "I know you're the pregnant one, but my bladder isn't going to make it another minute. Have the cab driver leave the luggage in the driveway. I'll grab it when I'm done – and don't even think of lugging it in yourself." Danny handed her his wallet to pay the driver and raced out of the cab the second it pulled to a stop. He really did have to go to the bathroom.

Forget the letter thought Danny as he hit the light switch in the mudroom. *How about I worry about the stolen backpack of Gregory's I left on the bench!* He grabbed it on the run, deciding he'd stuff it under the couch for the moment. The house smelled good as he rushed through. Ron must have lit a candle. Everything looked just as he had left it, better actually, more like how Teres would have left it. *Thank you, Ron.* Then he turned on the bathroom light and the windowsill was empty! *Thank you, Ron?* Had he removed the letter? He must have. No one else had been in the house. Did he read it? Does he know everything? *Oh Jesus. Do I have two secrets from my wife, now? A company lawsuit and Ron knows about the baby?* The promise they'd made to share everything, good or bad, was already gone straight to hell. He heard Teres come in the house.

"Oh, Danny! It is so wonderful to be home!" she hollered as she came down the hall. *I hope you still think that tomorrow* was Danny's desperate thought.

"Yeah. I tried to keep things on the neat end." *Why are you talking, dummy? She doesn't need a reminder that you lived here without her for a month.*

It didn't seem to bother her. "Well, you did a very good job of it," was her happy reply. He took the credit. There was no sense telling her now that Ron had tidied up for her arrival.

Danny flushed the toilet, washed his hands, and came out into their bedroom. Teres was sitting on the bed with a look on her face that said, "You should join me on this bed." He almost begged off, told her he was too tired, then came to his senses before saying something stupid.

"How about if I drag our suitcases in, and then we take our afternoon nap? I know how much you liked our Greek nap routine." He tried to give her a sexy look that ended up more of a leer. She nodded her head yes. *Maybe this is gonna be okay* he said to himself as he went out the front door to get their bags.

*

Sex at home was as good as sex in Greece. Within minutes of his impressive performance, Danny was snoring. She felt bad about coming on to him the second they got home. She could see he was exhausted. But making love here, in this bed, in this home, was a christening of sorts - holy water on a sinner's forehead. She needed to keep the hard won intimacy they had reclaimed in Europe. There was no going back now. She and Danny had laid out the roadmap of their relationship: trust, love, openness. Teres promised herself she wouldn't revert to task mode, taking over everything and leaving Danny behind. To that end, she forced herself not to begin organizing by getting up and dragging their bags to the laundry room. She decided, instead, to take the long nap her husband was surely headed to. They would order delivery pizza and a salad when they got up, and tomorrow go grocery shopping together and get the laundry done.

*

212

May 31, 1992

Teres couldn't leave the house. She told herself it was just temporary, a result of jet lag. She didn't tell Danny about the anxiety, instead sending him with a list for the grocery store. She would get the laundry done, take a shower and relax until he came home. Then she'd make them a big Sunday dinner. *It's no big deal* she told herself, eating a can of pineapple chunks and wishing wine were the preferred breakfast drink for pregnant women.

*

Danny was grateful Teres opted to stay home. It would give him a chance to find Ron, tell him they were having a baby and feel him out about the lawsuit and the missing letter. Then he'd whip through the grocery store, proud of the shopping skillset he acquired over these last months.

*

Ron wasn't an alarmist. Being an emergency room doctor cured you of that pretty quickly. But things were looking bleak with this suit. Of course, Accelerated Ambulance had ample insurance. He wasn't worried about a judgement taking them down financially. He was worried about their credibility taking a hit. They were a private ambulance company – a choice. Nothing was public yet, but it would be. That was the reason so many suits settled out of court: you could attach a gag order to the situation. There wasn't any version of the Miller boy story that made AA truly appear at fault, but every account of the event sounded cartoon-like, horrendous – a circus act. It had appeared in the newspaper as a small story, *Man Found Dead in Logan Airport Restroom.* The three-line article went on to say the man was a driver for John Hancock Insurance and had died of natural causes. It was treated as a separate incident from the med flight patient death. Ron knew, from hospital reporting procedures, that the police daily gave a list of every type of crime and accident to the newspaper, and each paper determined what might be of interest to its readers. Some of the biggest news never made the papers, some of the smallest stories were given a platform to grow. There was no doubt in Ron's mind the media drove the story, the story didn't drive the media. Either way, he didn't want the Miller suit to be driven anywhere.

When Danny had called about meeting him this morning, Ron jokingly tried to convince him they should discuss this over nine holes of golf. Danny didn't bite. He sounded intense, serious, not like himself at all. This was normally a situation Teres would have taken the lead on, made a decision, and then force them all to see it her way. Why didn't *she* call him this morning? Was she still that fragile? He hadn't seen or spoken to her since February eighth. It was almost June. *What the hell is going on with them?* It couldn't all be about Gregory's death, or could it? *Gregorio.*

*

"We're having a baby," Danny said to Ron as the waitress poured their coffee. He had decided it would be weird to hold back something this big until after they talked about the lawsuit. Ron's expression looked genuinely shocked.

"Wow! That's amazing news! We are happy about this little miracle?" Ron asked, with what sounded like equal doses of enthusiasm and caution.

"Yes." Danny smiled back at him, letting the genuine sincerity of his excitement about the baby show through.

"You old dog! Congratulations! How is Teres feeling? When is the baby due? Will she be back in the lineup at work, or is she sitting out the season until after the birth?"

"I'm trying to talk her out of going back to work. She's…" He didn't know where to end the sentence. Everything was riding on what Ron already knew. *Okay, my friend. I've told you about the baby. Now is the time for you to tell me you've read Teres' letter to Gregory and you know about everything.* Ron didn't bite.

"Well, there's plenty of time to decide about that. I'm glad you're home and I'm thrilled about your news. Give Teres a big, fat kiss for me. Tell her if she needs anything – and I mean anything – I'm just a phone call away. And that goes for you, too, Danny."

*

Holy shit! Holy shit! Holy shit! Only one time did Ron hear Danny allude to he and Teres' lack of children. He had dangled the sentence, "If things had been different..." in reference to Seamus and Colleen's growing brood. Martha once confided to Ron that the topic was off limits for her and Teres, as well. Everyone just assumed they couldn't have kids. Why else would such a great couple be childless?

Danny hadn't responded about the baby's due date, but Ron's gut told him the conception took place before Gregory's death. He wondered what Danny knew. The guy sure looked happy. Ron wasn't going to stick a knife in his best friend's stomach with conjecture or mentioning a personal letter to a dead guy. For all he knew it was an arrangement between the three of them, with Gregory donating sperm to the project. It was none of his business. The Muldaurs were headed for enough hassle with this lawsuit. *Here goes nothing,* Ron began to relay the gory details of their company's disastrous night.

*

Teres was pleased by how much she had accomplished. The suitcases were empty, the laundry almost finished, a fresh scrub to the bathrooms, and their bed sheets had been changed. It felt great to fuss around her house again. The outside was another story. This was the week they would have opened the pool. She needed to

215

make a list of yardwork to be done and hire someone to do all the work. She and Danny needed a break. Just this bit of housework had worn her out. She was craving red meat and glad she told Danny to pick up a steak. It must be the baby. Despite the supplements, her iron was still low when they checked it in Greece. Dr. Aarons would do another hematocrit when she saw him next week. *Wouldn't Danny just love it if I became a meat eater like him?* The thought of pleasing Danny pleased her. *This is going to be okay*, she reassured herself.

Her bed was laid out with clothes to be put away, including Yaya's beautiful silk shawl. Teres gently folded it, placing tissue paper between the layers like her mother had taught her. Because the shawl was old and the dyes had been hand-created naturally, the colors had a tendency to bleed into each other if the fabric got too humid. Teres would put it in the top drawer of her bureau, where she kept her evening purses, gloves, and scarfs. Teres loved her special accessories drawer. The items were mostly family hand-me-downs, mixed with a few well-chosen pieces she had purchased over the years. She opened the drawer, ready for the heady whiff of nostalgia that accompanied each item. As she lifted some things out of the way to place the folded shawl where it was less likely to get wrinkled, she saw the envelope. *Gregorio.* She lifted the letter and turned it over. It was still sealed. Teres backed away; her knees buckled as they hit the edge of the bed causing her to plop awkwardly into a seated position. She thought about that night, the last time she had seen the letter …

February 8, 1992

Teres had just finished Danny's birthday speech and was relieved when she looked around and didn't see Gregory. She hoped he had left before her tribute. Soon he would read the letter she had given him and they would figure out the details of what she had planned. Teres headed to the coat closet to retrieve the checkbook in her coat pocket. She would settle the bill and try to enjoy the rest of the party. *One last perfect night.* She stepped into the back hall and jumped when she heard Gregory's voice behind her.

"Jesus Christ, Teressa! Did you ask me here tonight so you could torture me? I get it! He's amazing! You love him!"

Teres reached for his arm. "Gregory, I do not want you to be in pain, and I do have feelings…"

He angrily ripped his arm away. "Just stop talking! I don't want to hear about your feelings!" Gregory pulled her letter out of his pocket and threw it onto the floor at her feet. "You think you can wrap this up in a letter? It's my baby, too! I will fight you in court for this child! Fathers get custody all the time these days!" Gregory grabbed his coat from the rack and stormed out the back door of the restaurant, leaving Teres standing there in shock. *Oh my God! He wouldn't dare!* Teres reached down and picked up the letter. He hadn't even opened it. If he had, he would have seen that Teres planned to tell Danny everything, beg his forgiveness and offer joint custody to Gregory. She was tired of the lies and wanted it all out in the open. And now Gregory had run off, with a threat to take her baby! She needed to get to him and make him open the letter for himself so he would know she wasn't trying to take anything away from him. If this escalated into a custody fight, Gregory was not a man she wanted to battle in court. He didn't know how to lose.

The next thing she remembered was a crumpled red sports car and Gregory's bloody face.

May 31, 1992

Why didn't Danny tell her he found the letter? Or just read it then destroy it? Teres tried to recall their fight on the road in Nea Makri. He called her a liar. What were the words she said that made him come back to her? *"I wrote Gregory a letter telling him it was over."* Danny turned around because he knew it was true. He had seen the letter with his own eyes. *He found it and was too afraid of what it might say to open it.* Teres felt the familiar wave of gut-wrenching guilt she would carry forever. She wondered if they should talk about the letter, open it together so he could read it. She couldn't remember the words she had written. Was there a phrase, a declaration, that could cause more harm than the good it would do? She decided not to say anything. She would lock the letter in her mother-of-pearl jewelry box, never to be mentioned again. She had caused her husband enough pain.

*

Martha was done being a patient friend. When she heard the news about the pregnancy, she was too mad to be happy for them.

"What do you mean six months pregnant? That's impossible!" she sputtered out at Ron. "They can't have children."

"I didn't see it with my own eyes, but Danny wouldn't make something like that up. He said it's been a tough pregnancy. Martha, it explains a lot. She was newly pregnant, hormonal, and traumatized by witnessing Gregory's death, and had kind of a breakdown. It happens. Danny said she's doing good, but not coming back to work. He still hasn't told her about the lawsuit."

Martha whirled through the list of questions storming across her mind and settled on one.

"When will we be able to see her? I mean, should I call her?"

"I don't know. When I finished telling Danny about the Miller case, he asked if I could come to the house and give them both the

218

news together, make it like he was hearing it for the first time, too. Before I could decide on a good response to a weird request like that, he said to forget it – telling her that way might upset her even more. I felt like he wasn't looking for my advice, just brainstorming out loud."

"Well this is crazy. What kind of friend would I be if I didn't call to congratulate her as soon as I heard the news?" Martha said, building a case for the call she planned to make the minute Ron left the office. "You should call her, too, Ron. She probably needs us more than she'll admit. You know how pig-headed that girl is."

*

"I do," Ron replied. He thought about how pig-headed they all were – all except Danny. There were many times Danny had been the voice of reason amidst a threesome of pig-headed opinions. Maybe Martha was right. They should be their supportive selves, act the way they normally would. Danny hadn't told him to keep the pregnancy a secret. Telling Martha was expected behavior; and of course Martha would call when she heard the news. Normalizing this whole announcement was exactly what they should do.

"Martha, you're right. Call Teres and congratulate her – see if she wants to do lunch or something. I miss our monthly bitch and fix work lunches. It's high time this place returned to normal. And call Seamus and Colleen and make them invite us all to a cookout. Does Teres even know you became a grandmother? Let's get this summer rolling, for God's sake! Before you know it, it'll be Labor Day. Life's too short for this bullshit."

He could see he was hitting it just right for Martha: enthusiasm, mixed with a plan, and none of it anything he had to generate. Hopefully, Martha's bossiness could knock their lives back into normal. Ron was counting on it.

*

The night was clear and warmer than usual for the last day of May. Teres had suggested they eat outside, Danny vetoed the idea with his newfound honesty.

"Let's eat in the sunroom instead. We can open the windows, put on the Red Sox game, and when we're done, I'll do the dishes."

"Why would you do the dishes?" His wife seemed seriously baffled.

Why would I do the dishes? he asked himself. An answer came from his mouth before he had a chance to edit. "You're having a baby. You're gonna need to start asking for help, and I'm gonna need to start doing more. We're a team." She was happy with this answer so he stupidly continued. "Plus I have something to tell you after dinner, and it might be safer if you're not holding a steak knife." He meant it as a joke, an opener to a difficult conversation. But Teres looked shaken, unable to handle any bomb he might drop. *Dummy, now you've ruined dinner.*

"Danny, what is this news? Tell me now." She was holding their dinner plates – steak, roasted potatoes, and sautéed green beans. Danny took the plates from her and brought them over to the little table in the sunroom.

"Babe, let's just enjoy dinner. We can talk about it later." He gave her his award-winning smile.

"Okay," she replied, bringing over their drinks. "I have something to tell you, too."

Danny's head shot up. He tried to judge her look. Maybe their conversation couldn't wait. "You wanna go first?" he asked.

"You go first. I am starving. I will eat while you talk."

"Okay," Danny wasn't going to prolong the agony. "I talked to Ron and he told me our ambulance company is being sued." He waited for the barrage of questions he knew was coming. They didn't come. Teres continued to carefully chew her steak. It looked like she was lost in thought, not a hint of panic on her face. "Teres? Did you hear me? I said we're getting sued."

"I heard you, Danny. But it will not help the situation if I choke on my steak."

*

A suit meant attorneys. Somehow Teres had forgotten about Seamus. He was the one friend who knew everything. As their attorney, he would never reveal the identity of their baby's real father. But it would be forever awkward knowing he knew the truth about the lie she and Danny were planning to live. Certainly, Seamus won't be handling this lawsuit, it wasn't his forte. But they would be conferring with him, maybe daily. *Does Danny know I told Seamus everything?* Teres was tired again. There were mental obstacles to thinking about the lawsuit, the first one wrapped around another betrayal of Danny.

"Have you talked to Seamus?" she asked, followed by, "Danny, I need to tell you that before I left for Greece, I went to Seamus and asked him to handle the apartment transfer and go over Gregory's will. And I tried to get him to transfer the house and business into just your name. He knows about the baby. I am so sorry." She teared up, thinking how this would make him feel, but he was completely fine.

"Teres, I saw Seamus before I came chasing after you. He didn't tell me everything, but he had read the brief from that jerk, Philip Dixon. I knew what was in it." Smiling, he added, "I was like a man on a mission when I thought you might leave for Greece. I chased everyone down to see what I could find out. It was Martha that spilled the beans – she thought I was going with you."

Teres didn't know what to say. She was done underestimating him. Clearly he could handle whatever came his way. She had to stop managing bits and pieces of information and just throw it all out there when there was something to tell. *A full partner in this life* was what they had promised each other in Europe.

"Before I ask about the lawsuit, let me tell you my thing. I cannot go outside. I tried a few times and I get as far as the doorway before I start shaking and sweating."

"I wondered why you gave in so easy about eating in front of the TV," Danny said. "I was getting worried you were losing your edge."

"No," she joked back. "I am still neurotic. Now tell me about the lawsuit while I eat this steak for the baby."

June 5, 1992

"Sometimes my mind plays tricks on me. Danny and Gregory are very different – opposites – but they get blended together and it makes my head swim. I feel nauseous and weak, like I can't walk."

Dr. Marion Lamoreaux-Aarons didn't respond right away. She sipped the tea Teressa had made for her and looked around the sunroom. Her gaze rested on the scene outdoors. The yard was filled with activity. There was a man cleaning the pool. Two gardeners pruning and weeding the flower beds, a riding lawn mower skimming back and forth at breakneck speed.

"Your yard is beautiful. How long have you lived here?"

"We bought the land in nineteen-eighty-five, so seven years," Teres answered.

"Well, it's lovely. Your house has the perfect mix of formal style and inviting sanctuary. It's a big house. Did you know when you built it you wouldn't have children?"

"Yes. Danny didn't want to go this big. He said we didn't need it, but I was looking to the future. Someday we would downsize, a family would own this house. The area has big homes, I wanted it to fit in even though you can't see it from the road. And I needed room for my family in Greece to visit."

"Have they?" Marion asked, hoping this information gathering still sounded like polite conversation.

"My parents, only one time," Teres answered. "My mother does not like to travel. She gets anxious."

Family history of anxiety. "And your brothers and sisters?" Marion asked.

"I have one brother. He came for the first time last summer, with his wife and two daughters. He runs the family business; they are not able to get away."

"Well, it's a great house and now it will be getting the joy and laughter of a child. Maybe you could see the future," Marion said, risking Teres might think she viewed the pregnancy as premeditated.

"No. That door was closed." Showing no sign of offense, Teres added, "I worry it might still be closed."

"Teres, your pregnancy is going well. You're healthy." Marion smiled. "In spite of my reservations about you running to Greece, it turned out to be what you needed to put your marriage on track. Are you afraid something's wrong with the baby?"

"Nighttime is the worst. I wake up frozen with fear something bad will happen. How could I end up with what I always wanted after what I have done?" Anxiety flooded Teres' face.

"That's not how this works," Marion replied, as though everyone knew this to be true. "If healthy babies were only rewarded to perfect people, all babies would be sick. Your guilt is something you have to find a way to live with. Everyone knows the sorrows they keep. They just don't know the damage it's doing. Do you think Danny deserves a terrible outcome for this pregnancy?"

"You sound like your husband," Teres said, chidingly.

What an unexpected response, Marion thought, considering how different she and Abel were. "How so?" she asked.

"Teshuva. Repairing what I have broken. My penance is Danny's happiness, which is then my happiness."

Well I'll be damned, thought Marion, keeping her face neutral to hide the delight she felt. Her husband never ceased to amaze her. It's true that when a Goy marries a Jew there's going to be a word or two that drops into the marriage at unexpected times. It's also true that those words will be followed by a lengthy lesson, most handed down for generations. *Teshuva.* Marion wracked her brain to think of what the word meant and the story that accompanied it. She knew it was forgiveness but not the unique slant the parable took. "My husband is a smart man. Tell me about *teshuva.*"

Half-way through the telling, Marion remembered all of it. *The broken vase story.* It was a good one. She'd likely pirate it for future use. Their hour together was flying by. Teres had begun today's session with a fear of intertwining Gregory and Danny. Marion dove right in.

"Is it important for you to keep Danny and Gregory compartmentalized? It would be normal for some of their personality traits to overlap. Usually, people are attracted to similar personality types over and over again."

*

This is different, Teres' thoughts shot back. She often felt crazy. As impossible as it seemed, Danny and Gregory were becoming the same person in her mind. Logically, she easily recognized their differences; they were nothing alike. But whenever Danny was decisive, even forceful, it reeked of Gregory. When he took over doing the hard thing, or pushed for her to let him handle it, she felt both relieved and panicked. *Gregory pushed, not Danny. Danny was sweet, easy-going.* Over the last few days, Teres had spent hours pulling apart her short life with Gregory. Had there been anything about his behavior that reminded her of her husband?

"I don't know how to explain it," Teres said, honestly. "There are times Danny does things that are totally out of character. We've been married a long time. I know how he acts."

Marion began a parable of her own.

"Marriage is an ever-changing scale. It's all about compensating strengths and weaknesses. If one partner is strong in an area – let's say decision making – and the other partner is less adept, the stronger person will not only win out in that category, they will become more and more powerful, causing the weaker spouse to become less powerful. The scales will tip." Marion paused. "I can see from your expression you hate this concept. Most women do. But look at it from Danny's perspective. You're good at steering the marriage. Your choices lead to success. Danny may have balked a bit in the beginning, but time proved you extremely capable of making the big decisions in your life as a couple. So Danny steered less and less until you were doing all the driving and he was going along for the ride. It happened gradually."

"Yes, but how could this make Danny and Gregory seem the same?" Teres asked.

"Teres, even bosses get sick of their jobs. You gravitated toward Gregory because of his ability to take over as the boss. His insistence on being with you relieved you of some of the guilt and responsibility. It wasn't your idea to have an affair. Of course there were more factors that went into creating the right dynamics for your relationship. From what you've told me, it was like the perfect storm – all forces coming together at once." Marion pushed on.

"So, picture you became passive, indecisive. Gregory becomes the driving force. Then he dies and you have what could only be considered a breakdown – decision-making, gut instinct, caring for yourself, all compromised. In walks passive Danny. He quickly rises to the occasion and takes command, for your safety and with the hope of getting some semblance of his life back. The less capable you are, the more capable he becomes. He now makes choices for the two of you that turn out to be good. He is forceful with his opinion – taking charge and getting things done. His confidence is boosted, and this more confident person reminds you of Gregory. Add to that Danny's true desire to bring up this child with you – the same desire Gregory had. Neither would take no for an answer. I can see where the lines are blurred. Is this making sense to you?"

"Yes," Teres nodded. "Like a pendulum, power swings back and forth."

"It does if you let it," Marion answered. "Now let's talk about goals. Fear will keep you in this house if you let it. It's an unconscious desire to control what you can, in an out-of-control world. It's not unusual to become agoraphobic during pregnancy. Your body is in a natural protection mode. But the longer you stay inside, the harder it is to get out. If you weren't pregnant I'd put you on meds to help break the cycle. But we can't. So, let's choose small goals. This week I want you to go outside in your fenced back yard and enjoy some sun. Think of it as vitamin D for your baby. Thursday is your appointment with Abel. I think you should try coming to the office with Danny – even if you have to lie down in the backseat to do it."

"Yes. But, I do not want to make him my security blanket."

"Let him worry about that," was Marion's quick response. "Call me if you need to set up something between now and next Tuesday, but I think you'll do fine."

"I hope you are right," Teres eyed the comfortable chaise by the pool. If Danny wasn't home by nap time, she would make herself test it out – just ten steps and less than five minutes before she would be asleep. *I can do that.*

June 10,1992
51 Federal Street
Boston, Massachusetts

Doug was sweating through his shirt and tie. An insurance deposition wasn't a court trial, but he knew it was all being recorded. Whatever he said today could come back to haunt him. He was told by Jim Daigle, the insurance attorney for Accelerated Ambulance, the session would likely take a couple hours, *enough time for me to slip up and say something stupid.* Seamus and Ron had prepped him, and assured him he hadn't done anything liable. "It was a bad night," Ron had said. "Nobody's fault." Travis Paddock was scheduled to be interviewed right after Doug. Who knew what he was capable of saying? The kid was smart, but always with a quick comeback. The one thing Daigle had stressed was to take their time with their answers. "You'll get one chance to make the perfect response. It's the first answer that counts in a case like this. No matter how many times or different ways something is asked, stick with the same answer."

The room was filling up with people. Doug hadn't expected that. In his mind it would be him, Ron, Jim Daigle, and the Miller's lawyer, plus a court stenographer. It wasn't obvious who the extras were. They weren't the Miller family, maybe just more people to be disposed. He wished it were cooler in the room. Normally, he wasn't the kind of guy to sweat. In fact, they called him "Cool Doug" at work. Little did they know how uncool Doug was. He was like a Clint Eastwood character: strong and silent exterior to hide how fucked up he felt. *Here goes nothing.*

"Do you swear to tell the truth, the whole truth and nothing but the truth?"

"I do."

*

Three hours later, Doug felt better. The questions had been clear and expectable:

Attorney: Was there a designated sign in the space where you parked the ambulance that night?

Doug: It's the normal parking for transport ambulance pickup. I believe the sign says, "Emergency Vehicles Only."

Attorney: Were you the senior paramedic for the ambulance that night?

Doug: Yes.

Attorney: As senior paramedic, what are your duties?

Doug: To oversee the entire call, from cradle to grave – *why did I say that?* – from start to finish, including shift inspection of the ambulance and follow-up paperwork.

Attorney: Did you have every supply you needed?

Doug: Yes.

Attorney: What was Travis Paddock's position with the company?

Doug: He was a new hire, but not a new paramedic.

Attorney: Were you his boss?

Doug: No.

Attorney: So you weren't in charge of him?

Doug: As senior officer, I was in charge of the entire event. *If he makes me say it's my fault one more time...*

Attorney: So, technically, you were in charge of Mr. Paddock that night.

Doug: Yes.

That was the worst it got, with the attorney replanting over and over again he was the paramedic in charge. Doug tried to hang on to what Ron had told him, "Just because you're the guy in charge, it doesn't make you the guy at fault. Stop reverting to your military training. Being in charge doesn't make you responsible when things go sideways." *Yes it does.*

*

Doug made a hasty exit from the conference room. He could smell himself and was glad he'd packed an extra shirt to change into; it was out in his truck. He looked at his watch, three o'clock. He had been too wound up to eat before the meeting and was starving. There was a sports pub right down the street where he could grab a couple beers and a burger, try to wipe this day from his mind. As he headed for the parking garage to grab his shirt, he felt a hand on his shoulder. It was Ron.

"You did great," Ron said.

"You think?" Doug asked. "I don't even know what I said."

"You told the truth," Ron smiled and began intoning in a preacher-like fashion, "The truth will set you free."

Doug wanted to make a joke about Ron quoting scripture, but couldn't. He was too drained to see the humor. He opted for a thank you instead.

"This has been horrible. A dozen years on an ambulance, and nothing like this has ever happened to me before. I guess I've been lucky. I know you're supporting me because it's your company, but this would have been so much worse without your help. Thanks." Doug put his hand out to shake Ron's. Their eyes met.

"Doug, I'd have done this for you anyway. It's been good getting to know you better," Ron replied, his stare direct and… something else.

229

Holy shit! thought Doug, as a current of electricity shot through him with the touch of Ron's hand. *What the hell is happening?*

*

Did I just feel what I think I felt? Ron forced his hand to stay in the handshake a few seconds longer, to better gage the moment. *Yup. He might not know it yet, but this guy is into me.*

The thing Ron hated about being gay was that it was never clear cut. There were two things to worry about, instead of one. With heterosexual relationships, most people had only to figure out if the object of their affection returned their feelings. Once you know you're gay, half the battle becomes figuring out if the guy you like is gay, let alone if he likes you back. Ron was finished having crushes on straight guys. It was an avenue to heartbreak. He had even had crushes on straight married men, ramping up the number of obstacles to three. But Doug? Ron had known him for years as the quiet, reliable staple of the AA crew. Now that he thought about it, Doug never brought anyone to the cookouts and parties Teres organized *for bonding and work-place happiness*, as she put it. The guy had a great sense of humor, was handsome as hell – if you liked somewhat short, slightly balding, middle-aged men with piercing blue eyes. Yes, this was worth a second look, Ron decided. *Nothing ventured, nothing gained.*

"You up for lunch and a beer? I just called the ER and got another doc to cover my shift. I'm done with this day. I'll bet you are, too."

"There's a sports pub down the street, toward Congress," Doug replied without hesitation. "Let me grab a fresh shirt out of my truck and I'll meet you there."

"Sound's good." Ron was a big fan of anyone who carried a fresh shirt in his truck.

June 11, 1992

When the packet came in the mail, Danny was tempted to tear it open. He knew what Teres had asked of Seamus, which Seamus had promised to stall. With so much to catch up on, Danny had put Gregory's apartment out of his mind. He'd seen Seamus only once since coming home, a lawsuit conference that included Ron and Martha, giving them no chance to speak privately. Just walking into that meeting had been tough. He wasn't concerned about an indiscretion on Seamus' part; he was concerned about looking him in the eye. He needn't have worried.

*

"Daniel! Ron tells me congratulations are in order!" Seamus jumped from his seat and strode to Danny in two steps, handshake at the ready.

Danny hesitated, wondering if any answer would be construed collusion. He slapped a smile on and enthusiastically took the handshake. "Thank you. Seamus. Yes! We are having a baby."

"Ye have no idea how happy this makes me," Seamus said, a double meaning they both understood. "Fatherhood is going to suit ye well."

"I'm not sure how good I'll be at it. We'll be looking to you for advice," Danny said, with a weird bit of Irish accent that always came upon him in Seamus' presence.

"Ah, go way outta that – of course, ye'll both be fabulous! Colleen can't wait to get her eyes on Teressa, she has a medal of Saint Briget of Kildare for her to pin – protect the leanbh."

It was a genuine congratulations. Danny couldn't wait to relay every detail of it to Teres. Maybe it would calm her fear of social interaction with the Flannigans, who were such a great couple. Now their three closest friends knew the news – of course, Seamus already knew – and they reacted with support. He began to feel that things would be fine.

*

And then, with just one trip to the post office, the whole apartment thing was shoved in his face again. In ten minutes they were leaving for Teres' doctor appointment. It was gonna be tough enough to get her out of the house without dealing with this apartment shit. Danny walked through the garage. He opened the door of Teres' car and threw the thick envelope onto the floor of the back seat. He'd deal with it later. He almost laughed when he considered the concept of dealing with something now or later. Just a few short months ago, his dilemma-dealing strategy would have been later or never. Right now he was dealing with his anxious, pregnant wife, who looked perfectly calm and able to get in the car this morning, but could flip the situation into something that resembled getting a cat into a bathtub. *Let the show begin*, Danny thought, walking into the house.

"Teres! I'm home."

*

Although Marion had already told him how the Muldaurs were doing, Abel was thrilled to see it with his own eyes. "Teressa, you look wonderful. Weight is right on track, good to see you're finally gaining. Blood pressure, normal. Urinalysis, good. Just this low hematocrit."

"Is it better than it was in Greece?" Teres asked.

"No. It's actually a little lower," Dr. Aarons answered. Her look of panic made him quickly add, "Not by much, but we still have to get it up. Your blood is carrying all the oxygen to your son's blood."

"Our son?" Teres and Danny replied, voices overlapping.

Abel knew the minute he said it, he shouldn't have. He had not made a mistake like that in ages. But to be fair, most times he was the one who ordered the ultrasound and orchestrated the follow-up appointment.

"Oh guys. I'm sorry. I thought Dr. Zygouras told you. It was clearly noted in the paperwork she faxed to our office. Did you decide you didn't want to know the sex?"

"Nobody told us finding out was an option," Teres answered.

*

Our son. Gregory's son. Danny's elation fought with his despair. A baby was a theory. A son was a reality. He tried to keep his face excitedly neutral, whatever that looked like. *Shape up, buddy. You knew this baby had to be one or the other.* Until this moment he hadn't realized he had conjured up a baby girl who looked just like Teres: curly dark hair, huge eyes. Wrapping his head around a son was going to take a minute. Teres turned to him, a teary look of wonder in her eyes.

"Danny, a boy! This is the best news!" *Okay, your minute's up,* he thought to himself, realizing this was the look he had battled so hard to see on his wife's face. He pulled her into his arms to avoid eye contact, lest she see his fear.

"Baby, this is the best news, ever. I can't believe it; we're having a boy."

*

After a visit to the lab for more blood work, they were on their way home. Danny couldn't stop thinking; his wife couldn't stop talking.

"A boy was something I never expected. It is so crazy!" *You can say that again.* As hard as Danny had worked to pull Teres into raising this baby together, he would have thought any trepidations of his own would have already surfaced. He spent the car ride trying to pin down just what was bugging him. With a jolt, more like the whack of a baseball bat than a lightning bolt of thought, Danny realized his fear wasn't about having *Gregory's* son, it was about having *any son*. He had not one clue how to parent a boy.

*

There had been many things David Muldaur had taught his son, none of them had anything to do with being a father. Danny spent his childhood staying out of the way, and playing at other kid's houses – mostly Teddy Wilkinson's. His father had two rules: Stay out of trouble and listen to your mother. Of course, stay out of trouble was really a hundred rules, the kind of rules Danny couldn't possibly guess until he broke one. Not taking off your shoes at the doorway was an offense. But taking your shoes off too soon while your father was bagging trash for you to bring down to the street was also an offense, even if you had no way of knowing this was his plan. Somehow, in second grade you were supposed to come home from school on a Tuesday knowing trash pickup day was Wednesday. Figuring out what his father wanted was a full time job. When David Muldaur wasn't busy working or being disappointed by his son, he was hanging out with his friends or watching TV. Throwing a ball or having a chat with a kid was of no interest to him. Danny quickly felt like the burden he was. The first time he experienced true camaraderie was in the Navy. Occasional parental feelings came much later, when he'd mentor a young recruit or co-worker. But for the most part, Danny liked to keep his life simple, mind his own business, don't make waves.

A daughter would have fallen primarily into Teressa's hands. Not a son. The duty of role model was going to be his, and it terrified him more than it would have had he become a father earlier in life. But who knew if that were true? Maybe he would have already been a failure at parenting if he had done it years ago.

This was like a do-over, without the first do. Would it be easier to raise another man's child with your own ego completely out of the picture? Kind of like being a good uncle? Danny was obsessing and unable to hear words by the time they entered Scituate.

*

"Danny! Are you listening to me?" his wife had raised her voice.

"Sorry, babe. What'd you say?"

"I said we need to stop at the post office. Deidre called Tuesday to tell me Seamus was sending paperwork for me to sign about the apartment. It should be here by now." *It is. I hid it in your car.*

"You had a long day. How 'bout I drop you at home, then go get the mail? Do we need anything at the store?" he asked in his best amazing-husband voice, inwardly chastising himself for the phony he had become.

June 22, 1992

Danny's favorite bakery was in the harbor area of Scituate, where summertime parking was a pain. But Finn's was worth the hassle. For a guy who loved pastries as much as Danny, picking them out should have been easier. He could never keep the names straight: scones, croissants, turnovers. He knew he should make it quick and just grab a dozen of the same thing, so he could get home in time to help Teres before Ron and Martha came over. He had talked her into having this lunch. Her isolation needed to end. She was going to want friends more than ever once the baby came, and Danny wasn't in the mood to get to know a whole bunch of new parents from some birthing class. Their current friends were just fine with him. There was no need to break in anyone new. Danny pointed his way through the pastry order and hurried home.

*

"Teres! I'm home," he hollered, making his way to the kitchen where maybe she had pulled out a platter for the desserts. Martha insisted on bringing everything else. Ron said he'd grab a six-pack. Then Danny saw it: Gregory's backpack laying open on the kitchen table. *Oh Shit!* After stuffing it under the couch when they got home from Italy, the backpack never entered his mind again. Clearly it should have. Danny dropped the pastry box on the counter and went for the bedroom at a run. Teres was sitting on the side of the bed, holding the bottle of aftershave, and choking back her tears. *Oh shit!*

"Have you had this the whole time?" she asked, the pain in her eyes reminiscent of those first days in the apartment.

"They gave it to me," he lied, "at the impound lot."

"You saw everything in it, the ultrasound picture – that's how you knew I was pregnant." Her statement was an accusation.

"No. I told you how I found out. The pregnancy test and Gregory's last words…" Danny worked at keeping his voice even, at the same time wondering how she makes him feel like he's the liar in the room. She stood and walked past him. He could feel the wall she had already raised between them. She was getting ready to either shut him out or shut down entirely. *Here we fucking go again.*

"This is not going to work," she said dismissively, as though she were talking about rearranging the bedroom furniture. "Every time I am ready to forget for a minute what I have done, it slaps me back in the face. I cannot do this." Teres put the aftershave lotion down on her bureau. "I need to be somewhere where remembering doesn't hurt so much." Suddenly staying calm seemed stupid. Danny lost it.

"And where is that, Teressa?" he bellowed. "Where is it you can go that the smell of Gregory's cologne won't make you fall apart? You're having his baby, for chrissake! Are you gonna have a nervous breakdown if the kid looks like his father – or will it only be if I'm standing beside you while you're looking at him?" Danny knew he'd gone way too far. He was mentally packing his bags, deciding if he could survive living alone again, when she touched his hand.

"I am sorry, Danny. I am an idiot – a woman who acts like she will run away and cannot even leave the house. I do not know why you want to be with me. Can you forgive me for this one more thing?"

"Yes." He folded her into his arms, breathed in her hair. "What can I do to help you?"

*

What can he do to help me? It was the one million dollar question. What could anyone do to help? Every time Teres thought she had it under control – not anything as complete as making peace with herself but was keeping it together – something happened to derail her. Finding the letter in her drawer, opening an old purse and pulling out a napkin from their first dinner together at Legal Seafood, vacuuming under the furniture and hitting an unfamiliar object. She thought she was going to faint when she pulled the backpack from under the couch. It was like a horror movie, where the parts and pieces of her dead lover kept coming back to haunt her. It made her suspicious of everything. What does Danny know? Does Ron know anything? Had they all been talking behind her back? She knew she seemed paranoid, but there were just enough loose ends to have her constantly waiting for the other shoe to drop.

"I have an idea," she said to Danny, pulling away so she could look at him. "There are too many things about my time with Gregory that you don't know. Some I wonder if, yes, you do know.

237

Some are things I can only say one time, but I have to say them."
She hoped she was making sense. "Have you ever heard of a
couple's retreat?"

"No."

"It's where-"

"No. I'm not going to a couple's retreat. Jesus, Teres. I'm not
gonna let a bunch of strangers judge us, or our lives, with the lame
hope of making it better. We're doing fine!"

"No we are not. I am not. Every time something happens I get
confused about things. For a minute I thought *I* put Gregory's
backpack under the couch. Can you see how trying to figure out
what you know, or what I am hiding, is going to hurt us?"

"Couples meditation yoga hocus pocus is not going to help. We
could just talk about things, right here in this house. What about if
I join your sessions with Marion?"

"No." Teres was surprised by her own quick response. "Marion
already thinks you are amazing. "She will hate me if she spends
more time hearing your side of how this has been. I need her for
me."

*

Maybe I will hate you if I hear your side of things, Danny
thought to himself.

"Well, I'm not gonna go to a couple's retreat." He looked at his
watch. "Martha and Ron are gonna be here in fifteen minutes.
Anything you need me to do?" As was usual with his wife, the
change of subject didn't work.

"Just hear me for one more thing. I did not mean a place where
other couples go for therapy. I meant a place where we go for the
weekend with the sole purpose of saying whatever we need to say,
or ask what is on our minds, and to never bring it up again."

Danny could tell she was in railroad mode, her accent had slid backward by a full decade. He needed to end this conversation, get his wife to regroup before their friends came.

"Teres, I feel like we did all that while we were in Greece and Italy. But if you need one more weekend for us to just say more stuff, okay, let's plan it." *That should do it*, Danny foolishly thought, happy again with his newfound husband skills. But then she knocked him for a loop.

"I want to do it at Gregory's apartment."

Danny was shocked into silence and thinking she had finally lost her mind when he heard the doorbell ring. "I'll get it," Teres said, completely composed, as though she hadn't just asked the impossible of him. Figuring out his wife's latest plan would have to wait. One hurdle at a time.

*

Martha was finally going to visit her best friend. Luckily for Teres, she had already seen Danny, to whom she had planned to give the brunt of her displeasure over being the last to hear about the pregnancy. One look at him, and Martha forgot how mad she was. You'd have thought by his happy glow he was the one carrying the baby. He bounded toward her, arms outstretched.

"Martha!" He exclaimed. "I know you want to kill us. I almost told you about the baby before we left for Greece, but Teres was such a mess I was afraid to." Just like that, all was forgiven. But it was still two weeks of illusive behavior before Martha managed to nail Teres down for a visit. Her phone calls had been short, always a phony excuse at the end. "I've got to go, someone is at the door," or "This baby – sorry, Martha, I have to run to the bathroom. You know how it is…" Teres seemed reluctant, almost disinterested, when Martha suggested they catch up over lunch, and invited them only after Martha had told her Ron was off on Monday and planning to surprise Teres with a visit.

So much for girl talk, Martha thought, armed with sandwiches and a dozen pictures of her new grandson, Estefan. She deliberately arrived ten minutes early, hoping to get a little one-on-one time before Ron got there, but was disappointed to see his car, and further disappointed to see Danny home. Hopefully, the guys would wander off to another room at some point, and leave Martha to uncover every detail about this out-of-nowhere pregnancy.

*

Ron felt like he was in the Twilight Zone. Teres, who he had expected to be a mess, was calm, laughing, and looked completely at ease. Danny was darting back and forth like a chicken with his head cut off. He had retrieved luncheon plates and set them out, put the sandwiches and desserts on a platter, gotten frosted mugs out of the freezer for their beers, and made Martha a cup of tea – *with honey!* He was the perfect host. Ron had never seen him go to the kitchen for anything other than a second beer. And he was talking, telling him and Martha about everything from getting in shape with their mountain walks, to the differences in European prenatal care. It was crazy. In social settings Danny was a listener, not a talker. Ron sat back, kept his mouth shut, and observed this new, weird couple. After hearing Teres tell Danny he forgot the napkins and Danny's response of, "Oh babe, yeah that's right," then scurrying back to the kitchen, Ron stopped observing and started giving him shit.

"What the hell did you do to this boy, Teressa?"

"What are you from the South? Calling me *boy*?" Danny shot back at Ron.

"Be grateful," Ron replied. "My first choice was *old man*, a little harder to throw out there with your staggering virility so

240

obvious." He regretted his words immediately and waited for a hint of an arrow hitting its mark. Nothing. Danny shot right back at him.

"*Son*, you wouldn't get away with calling me *old man* even if my wife wasn't pregnant. I don't know if you've noticed, but I'm in pretty good shape these days. And you're looking a little soft. I think I could whip your butt!"

Ron smiled warmly. "You probably could, my friend. It's like you drank from the fountain of youth while you were away. I don't think I've ever seen you look this healthy – or happy for that matter." Just to twist the knife a bit, he added, "Or helpful."

He watched Teres look up at her husband, pure adoration in her eyes. Maybe he was way off base with this whole thing. Maybe they'd hired Gregory as a sperm donor. *Shit, maybe it's not Costa's baby and I'm a suspicious asshole.* Ron had resisted the unscrupulous urge to access both Danny and Teressa's medical records, knowing there'd be an answer in there somewhere. It was hard being a nosy doctor and having legitimate access to everyone's health information. *Repeat after me*, his brain admonished: *This is none of your business.*

Martha chimed in, "Teres, I gotta say, I've never seen a more beautiful pregnant woman in my life. Danny told me you were as sick as a dog in the beginning. It's no wonder, pregnancy's hard enough at your age, let alone with what you've been through. It's amazing how healthy you look. When did you start to feel better?"

*

And why did you not call me the minute you did? was what Martha was obviously asking her. Teres had known the conversation would include questions she didn't want to answer. How could it not? Her friends deserved some kind of explanation after four months of radio silence. This morning, with the backpack discovery, she didn't have time to think about what she might say.

What if she blurted out the truth? *Gregory was my lover and I'm pregnant with his baby. Danny and I spent the last four months trying to decide if we could put my affair behind us and raise Gregory's son together. Yes, it was a tough start and I still don't feel better.*

"It was a tough start. I was scared and nauseous." she answered, looking for her next sentence. She was relieved when Danny jumped in.

"Yeah. It was like day and night. One minute I was trying to figure out how to get her to drink a few sips of water, and the next minute she's saying she feels good enough to take a flight to Italy."

Martha persisted. "Oh I get that, how you can go from feeling horrible to normal in a day. I just don't see why you went to Greece in the first place if you were feeling that bad."

That was a good question. Teres wished she'd thought of the answer *before* she invited her friends over to interrogate her. But, clearly, Danny had.

*

"She wanted her mother. Crazy, right? I guess most pregnant women do. Katharine's fear of flying's getting worse. We probably could have talked her into coming if we told her Teres was having a baby, but it seemed too early to get everyone's hopes up. Then the doctor said it was okay to fly – that getting outta town might do her good." Danny grinned and looked down at Teres from where he was standing guard-dog at her side. "And it did, right babe? Just what we needed."

"It was exactly what the doctor ordered," his wife answered, looking up at him with such a grateful look of love that Danny thought his heart would burst. He wasn't sure how much longer he could continue saying all the right things. It was time to change the subject.

"Hey, let's get this lawsuit conversation out of the way so it doesn't wreck our dessert. I got us a bunch of different stuff from Lucky Finn's. Elephant flaps? Lobster tails? I don't know what they're called, but they look good."

*

An hour later, they were walking their friends to the door. The groundwork had been laid. He and Teressa were a happy, lucky couple who, by some miracle, were finally having a baby nearly twenty years into their marriage. There was no reason for anyone to think otherwise. The Muldaurs were cashing in on a reputation of integrity, build by a lifetime of telling the truth. And Danny didn't feel one bit guilty. In fact, this might be the happiest he'd ever been.

July 4, 1992

For the past five years, Seamus Flannigan had hosted a bash of an annual fourth of July cookout – yard games, Irish football – the only kind as far as he was concerned – a clam boil, and an impressive neighborhood fireworks display. It was the perfect excuse to mix business with pleasure, thereby making good on Seamus' favorite saying: *"A business that makes money is a good thing, indeed. A business that makes friends is worth its weight in gold."* Nearly every one of the Flannigans' friends had begun as legal clients. His wife, Colleen, often worried it might be a bit uncomfortable to be friends with a man who knew all your secrets. Seamus assured her none of their secrets were too harsh; it wasn't as though his clients were hiding bodies in their basements. But he had to wonder if the Muldaurs would finally prove Colleen's fears as truth. He and Danny were fine. Seamus had enthusiastically wished him well and assured him he'd be a fabulous father. The problem was Teressa. Without a true conversation to clear the air,

243

Seamus wasn't certain what part she would want him to play. Would he become confidante, as well as counsel? Or would they both pretend Seamus didn't know about the baby's father? There were still legal issues to finalize. Seamus had already dropped the ball there. Normally, he would call Teres himself when paperwork required a signature. They'd catch up on the Flannigan girls, Danny's health, and the ambulance business. When it had come time to finalize the apartment transfer, Seamus had chickened out, asking his secretary to make the call instead. Teres had signed the deed at home, with Martha as Notary Public, and sent it back to him in the mail. Now he wished he'd broken the ice before this cookout. The Muldaurs were friends, the loss of which he'd feel.

Fate goes as she must Seamus thought to himself, as he dragged the last of the porch furniture onto the lawn. He couldn't remember which famous person said that before him – an Irishman, no doubt. Seamus tried to surround himself and his daughters in homeland culture, hence his reason for living in the heavily Irish-populated town of Marshfield. Yes, it was a hike to his office in Boston, but well worth the effort. He and Colleen had a modest 1950's built home in a family neighborhood in Ocean Bluff. It was not as pricey or desirable as the homes directly on the water in the Bluff or Brant Rock, but it suited them. Three bedrooms, wide porches, large green lawn. They were simple people, no need for swimming pools and fancy dinner parties. Although they hadn't known each other then, both Colleen and Seamus grew up in little villages off the Wild Atlantic near Galway. Seamus' family ran a bed and breakfast, more of a boarding house for fisherman, in Roundstone. Not far away in Tully Cross, Colleen's family, the Bragans, had owned a sheep and goat farm for four generations. Neither grew up thinking the world would be their oyster. So when fate brought them together, under the awning of a Boston hotel in the middle of a summer downpour, Seamus, in only a moment's time, grabbed hold of her flying umbrella, her Irish lilt, her pale upturned face, and her sweet *cailín* heart. After that, the world was their oyster.

Three daughters, many friends and good fortune later, he and Colleen were still in love. Their family was everything to them, which was, regrettably, the reason they had to return to Ireland. Today was the day they'd be telling their friends. Tomorrow they'd be telling their daughters. Seamus wasn't looking forward to the telling of any of it. His wife, on the other half of the coin, though sad about his family's misery, was giddy about the consequence it provided. She had quickly whipped everything into place. Their house was rented for the winter, the business set up to run from a distance, confirming Seamus' biggest fear: he would never get Colleen to leave Ireland again. *Cac!* Maybe it was for the best. The economy in Ireland was finally making a comeback. Why fight it? Their hearts were in The Emerald Isle. But he would keep this house, a place to visit, a legacy for their girls. *This will be a tough Independence Day, indeed*, he acknowledged, as he saw the first of their guest arriving. It was Ron and Doug, not quite arm and arm, but clearly together. Seamus had seen it coming. As he ran toward the driveway to greet them, he congratulated himself on his keen powers of observation, ignoring the fact that Colleen had put the bug in his ear in the first place. No matter. Seamus, contrary to most attorneys, was a man in love with love. He near broke his face with the stretch of his grin as he bound toward them. *This is fettling to be the best party ever!*

*

Teres never said she was coming to the party. Danny had tiptoed around the conversation, asking things like, "What do you think we should bring on the Fourth?" and "Was it last year

Colleen's sister came for the summer?" He was back to being careful with his words and he hated it. It had been over a dozen days since Teres floated the idea of a retreat. Danny was fine with getting away, but he wasn't spending one more night in Gregory's apartment, *Teressa's apartment.* It was a stupid idea. He couldn't imagine what she was thinking. But, once again, a wall had been erected. It was more like a fence where a little air and light came through but you still couldn't see to the other side – definitely not a white picket fence. Eight weeks until the baby was due. Could he do this for eight more weeks? Danny decided he would give it a couple more days and if nothing improved he'd make reservations for a weekend on Cape Cod. Maybe they'd stay at The Seacrest, where no one would care if they never came out of their rooms, unlike those bed and breakfasts he hated, where the inn keeper asked polite questions that required polite answers and then wanted to know your breakfast choices in advance.

The moment of truth had arrived. Seamus' party was starting any minute.

"Babe, do we have sunscreen to bring to the cookout? Colleen probably has buckets of it. Those girls have skin you could see through." Then he waited. She was sitting at the kitchen counter, dressed like it could go either way. Everything she owned was new so it was hard to tell. Today she was wearing a sundress, blue and white, sleeveless, and tied in the back. *It looks like a cookout kind of outfit* Danny thought to himself, knowing how deceiving looks could be. She didn't answer, but got up, opened the refrigerator, and pulled out a glass pan with her famous strawberry, blueberry American flag cheesecake.

"Tell Colleen to keep this in the refrigerator until just before she serves it. I made it this morning and it is supposed to chill for four hours." His heart sank.

"Teres, come on," Danny pleaded. "How could you miss this? It's your favorite party of the year." She didn't dissolve into tears. In fact, Danny realized her tears had pretty much dried up over the last couple weeks. He didn't know whether to take this as a good thing or a sign of the apocalypse. He tried again.

"Babe, really. Everyone's dying to see you. Colleen will have a stroke if you don't come. Seamus says-"

"Please, stop. Who knows what Seamus says? I cannot go there and pretend everything is normal. Ron and Martha, yes. But not everyone." Her words were a simple statement, not the prelude to a meltdown. Danny tried a different tact.

"You can't stay here forever. If you can get to the doctor's and to the lab, you can make it to the Flannigan's. It's twenty minutes away."

"It is not about distance, Danny, and you know it. There will be a crowd of people. I will stick out, an older woman having a baby. Everyone will ask the same questions. Do you have other children? Do you think the baby will look like your husband? Are you going to breast feed?"

"Hey. Forty isn't old. Try being sixty. *Are* you gonna breast feed?" Danny asked, having never given the question one bit of thought.

"Probably – or maybe not. See? I do not know the answers. I am just trying to get through this." Her voice was still surprisingly calm. Danny knew she was right about the attention pregnant women get and was beginning to see this party through her eyes. Maybe it wasn't all about Seamus.

"Okay, babe," he said. "But, one of us still has to show up. I won't stay long and you have their number if you need me. In fact, call me an hour after I get there so I'll have an excuse to leave." Danny kissed her on the forehead, grabbed the cheesecake –

accidently sticking his thumb into the stars – and headed out the door. Although Teres' love of friends and family had rubbed off on him enough to attend a party without her, he didn't like the idea one bit.

*

Overnight everything had changed for Lori. After not hearing from the Muldaurs for almost three months, she got a call from Mr. Muldaur asking her to come to Scituate and help his wife with some things around the house. Lori was happy to help Danny, but reluctant to go back to being a regular in his crazy wife's depressive world. She was feeling normal these days, having survived the birth of her best friend's daughter, celebrating the baby's entry into the world by trying to re-enter it a little herself. She had bought some clothes, treated herself to a perm, and had dinner out with the baby's mother. Hopefully, her new attitude wouldn't take a hit at the Muldaurs'.

Being greeted with an enthusiastic smile and hug from Mrs. Muldaur was a surprise. "Call me Teres," she'd said, and told Lori she needed help emptying "junk" from their spare bedroom. This Mrs. Muldaur was nothing like the melancholy woman Lori had met four months ago. She was talkative, funny, laughing at all the crap she and her husband had accumulated through the years. For hours they sorted through bureaus and closets, putting aside donations for Goodwill and items to store elsewhere, along with a couple bags of practically new clothes Teres insisted Lori take home. They ended up having a great afternoon, with Lori promising to be back in a couple days to finish up. It would be tough setting up a nursery for someone else's baby, but she was glad she didn't say no. She would have missed out on two important opportunities: a part-time job-offer as dispatcher at Accelerated Ambulance, and meeting Travis Paddock.

*

Lori was a wreck on her first night of work at AA. It wasn't that the job was hard, she had a medical background and was a quick learner. The training had been accomplished during the day. But her shift was the middle of the night, in an office tucked in the back of a big warehouse-like building, and she was alone with men she didn't know. Tuesday night was quiet, just as they assured her it would be. One call so far, a nursing home run to Quincy City Hospital. Realistically, Lori knew she was safe. Emotionally, she felt completely vulnerable. Like driving without brakes. Like standing by yourself on a city corner after the bars let out. *Like waiting for your husband to come home in a foul mood and beat the shit out of you for making rice instead of potatoes.* She was practicing four square breathing when Travis Paddock walked into the office.

"New girl. Hello. We haven't met. I'm Travis Paddock. I'm sure you've heard my name. I'm the guy who holds the record for the biggest mistake ever made at this ambulance company."

Lori looked up from her desk and saw the most beautiful man she had ever seen. His eyes were caramel-chocolate brown. His hair was short, with a hint of stubble heading toward his face. But it was his smile that stopped Lori in mid breath; it was the most genuine smile she had ever seen. Travis Paddock's smile was an experience. She couldn't speak. She just looked up at him, dumbstruck by the impact he created. Without missing a beat, this adorable man went right into a comedy act.

"Oh, wait? You aren't the girl from the office of equal opportunities? I thought they were sending us a blind dispatcher. I've been working so hard on my Braille. Now I have to figure out sign language, too? Okay. Give me a minute." And he started to sign the alphabet. "A, b, c, d …"

"I'm Lori," she sputtered. "What did you do that was so awful?"

His face dropped; his voice lost the joke. "I let a guy park behind our ambulance and he died in the bathroom with his keys in his pocket, so we couldn't move his car to get our patient to the hospital. Our patient died."

"Could you have saved him?" Lori asked.

"The guy in the bathroom?"

"No. Your patient."

"He was probably gonna die anyway," Travis responded. "That's not the point."

"I think it is the point," she said, not certain if it were.

"Let's hope the judge feels the way you do. It's going to trial."

They spent the rest of their shift talking. Before she knew it, Lori had told Travis about her husband and the baby, a girl she had named Cheryl after her mother's sister who died in a car accident as a teenager. Two dead Cheryls, one paying tribute to the other. He was easy to talk to, like a big brother, but not. She didn't fool herself into denying the effect he had on her. It was a surge of terrifying, unwelcome attraction. Everyone had told her time would heal the part of her she was certain was dead. But until she saw Travis, she didn't believe them. In the morning, they went out for breakfast. At breakfast he asked her for a date.

"There's a cookout in Marshfield on the fourth. Everyone from AA goes to it. They're friends of the Muldaurs. I won't be able to drink because I'm working that night, but they have lobster. You wanna go with me?"

Lori didn't overthink it. She said yes. Feeling good felt good, like a reward for getting through the worst thing a woman could go through. Later that day she realized how much fun it would be to decorate a nursery. She hadn't had the opportunity to buy one thing for her own baby. She couldn't wait to go back to the Muldaurs' and help Teres set up the room. She knew now wasn't the time to tell a fragile pregnant woman about her own sorrow, but saying it once had opened a floodgate. Maybe one day she would tell Teres about baby Cheryl. In the meantime she would do everything possible to help the Muldaurs welcome their own little miracle into the world.

*

The cookout was fun, but would have been more fun with Teres. She could talk to anyone. Even when they first married and her English wasn't fluid, she never let it stop her from being a social butterfly. His wife wanted to know everything about everyone. It wasn't gossip. It was true interest. She was especially interested in how people got to where they were now. *When did you know you wanted to be a doctor? What was it that made you come to Boston? Did you come from a big family?* All Danny had to do was sit back and listen, occasionally adding a word or two to the conversation. If Teres were at this party right now, she'd have all these new relationships figured out in a heartbeat. Danny almost fell over when he saw Lori and Travis together. That was fast. *He better be a decent guy,* Danny thought, protectively. And when did Doug and Ron get so cozy? He couldn't wait to go home and tell Teres. Whenever they speculated about Ron's love life, Teres would territorially state, "It better be somebody we like!" She'd love this news about Doug, if it actually was news. Danny sometimes had trouble reading relationship situations correctly.

Thinking about her response made him realize he'd been there almost two hours and she hadn't called. Then he saw Colleen heading his way.

"Daniel! I've barely time to chat with ye. Tell Teressa she's in a heap 'o trouble fer not coming today! But, truly, I do understand."

"Well, I'm glad somebody does, Colleen. She looked dressed and ready to go when she handed me the cheesecake and pushed me out the door," Danny kept it light.

"When I was pregnant with Maeve I wouldn't go anywhere there be a gathering of people," Colleen replied. "It was as though my responsibility to protect the *leanbh* was too great to put me in a crowd."

Maybe this is more normal than it looks, Danny thought hopefully.

"Daniel, Seamus wants a private word. He's in the kitchen. He'd have come to grab ye himself, but could not abide the twenty conversations it would take to get to this part of the yard." She touched his arm and smiled like she was skirting bad news. *Does she know about the baby?* Danny could feel his face redden as Colleen moved on to another guest. He marched up to the house like a man on a mission. *Seamus better damn well not be telling anyone about our private business!*

*

Danny was further alarmed to see Seamus had the same weird look on his face as his wife. Before he could confront him about the suspected treachery, Seamus grabbed Danny into a bear hug.

"Daniel. We thought to make a public announcement of our news, but Colleen got a call from Teressa an hour ago ordering her to make you stay at the party a wee bit longer. So I'll be telling you first, so you hear it from me before ye have to be going." Now Danny was really confused. He let Seamus continue without responding.

"We're packing it in, Daniel. Me da is doing poorly. I canna leave me mother to deal with the lot of it. We'll be moving back to Ireland by one, September. Colleen, you know, has always felt the pull of home. I, myself, am a man in two camps. I'm sad to leave me business and friends behind, but I know where the need be."

Danny took a shameful minute to process the news. Apparently, everything didn't revolve around him and Teres. Apparently, other people had things going on as well. He couldn't deny the quick thought that the only man who knew the truth about their baby was leaving the country. Danny felt guilty for his flash of relief.

"I'm sad to hear this, Seamus!" Danny rose to the importance of his friend's news. "Teres will be crushed. She was counting on Colleen to walk her through this whole parenting thing. Me too. Of course, you're leaving Teresa Rose behind, right? I don't think you can legally take our goddaughter out of the country."

"More's the reason to visit us, Daniel. I canna believe an Irishman such as yourself has never set foot on the Land of Saints and Scholars!" Seamus replied, pouring each a dram of Irish Whiskey. "Let us toast to the day the Muldaurs bring their leanbh to visit the Flannigans! Sláinte!" In the clink of a glass, Danny was reminded how valuable this friendship was, and that he could trust Seamus Flannigan with his life.

*

The minute Danny left, Teres wished she had gone with him, even more so after her phone call with Colleen. Facing their friends was something she would have to do eventually. It wasn't like they were moving out of Scituate any time soon. *Maybe we should move?* Even as she thought it, she knew it would never happen. Getting Danny to move once was nearly impossible, he loved living here. So did she. Their house was an oasis – *or it used to be.* Teres made herself a glass of iced tea and went to sit outside. The day was perfect. They didn't make Fourth of Julys any better. She tried to relax, enjoy the day for what it was – *another day of solitude.* She looked around the pool and yard. Her plan when they put in the pool last spring was to christen it with a huge summer party. She had envisioned having the party at night, all lit up and catered by Barker Tavern, a place she loved for its old-world history and great spanakopita. It was a party that was supposed to happen last July, but then Danny had a heart attack, and quadruple by-pass surgery - *and I had an affair.*

Suddenly Teres couldn't stand the beauty of the day. She didn't deserve it. In one motion she stood and attempted to grab her iced tea glass from the side table. It slipped from her hand and shattered on the concrete apron of the pool, some of its pieces scattering into the water. As she went to retrieve the dustpan and broom she stepped on a shard of glass, lacerating the bottom of her bare foot. Teres sat back onto the chaise, examined the cut, and determined that even though it seemed a lot of blood, it was not deep and wouldn't need stitches. She carefully stood and made her way to the slider off her bedroom to grab a band-aid from the master bath, then hobbled to the mudroom for the broom. As she swept, she wondered how you get glass out of a pool. "I guess you call the pool man," she muttered to herself. Cleaning up the messes she made had become her new life. She dumped the dustpan of glass into the trash under the sink and went to put away the broom. It didn't use to be like this. She wasn't the one to wreak havoc. She was a fixer. *Not anymore.* The tears she thought were long gone exploded from her eyes. Within minutes she was kneeling on the mudroom floor, sobbing. When she heard Danny's car pull into the drive, she felt a sense of panic. She couldn't let him see her like this again. She got up, opened the back door and ran into the woods behind her house.

*

"Teres, I'm home!" Danny optimistically sang out. He had decided on his way home to convince Teres to come back for the lobster feast. Once he told her Seamus and Colleen were moving back to Ireland and this would be the last Flannagan cookout, she couldn't refuse. He'd save the Ron-Doug thing as his trump card. There was no way she could resist that! He trotted to the bathroom, figuring he'd run into her on the way. He didn't. What he saw instead were bloody footprints leading from the pool to the bathroom, then nowhere. Bloody footprints meant one thing: something bad had happened to the baby!

"Teres! Where are you?" Danny called out in a panic, running from room to room. He hollered her name again as he ran toward the telephone to call the hospital, sure she'd been taken in by ambulance. He picked up the telephone receiver, ready to dial South Shore Hospital when he saw the bright red 9-1-1 sticker Teres had just placed on the phone that week. He dialed it.

"You've reached nine-one-one emergency," The dispatcher intoned. "Please give me your location and nature of your emergency."

"I'm at thirteen Kent Street, Scituate. My wife is missing. I think she may have been-"

"Danny? Is everything okay?" Danny jumped at the sound of Teres' voice.

"Teres! I thought something happened to you and the baby! The blood!" He was beginning to shake, adrenalin sending mixed signals through his body. Teres took the phone from his hand.

"Hello, this is Teressa Muldaur. I am sorry. It was a false alarm. My husband could not find me and got worried."

"Please put your husband back on the phone, Mrs. Muldaur," the dispatcher responded. Teres handed the phone back to him.

"Mr. Muldaur, do you require any assistance at this time?" the despatcher asked.

"No, sir," Danny answered. "It was a false alarm. I'm terribly sorry."

*

Even after she explained everything, he still wanted to know why she was in the woods. Teres didn't have an answer. How was she going to tell Danny that her ever-shrinking world was closing in on her more each day. Going out to the rock wall at the back of their property made her feel like she wasn't trapped. "It is cooler in the woods," she decided to say. She wanted to tell him how scared and miserable she felt, but couldn't bear to upset him further. She changed the subject.

"Tell me about the party. I should have come with you."

"You think?" he responded sarcastically. Then he launched into telling her everything she had missed. It was a lot. She was pushing him for more details about Lori and Travis when the doorbell rang. It was the state police.

"The emergency dispatcher heard you use the word blood and we needed to be certain you weren't speaking under duress," the officer explained, after going through the home and hearing the Muldaur's story.

"Only if you consider pregnancy duress." Danny responded.

"Oh, I get it. My wife put me through hell with our pregnancies," the officer replied.

"How'd everything turn out?" Danny asked.

"She's pregnant with the fourth – so, not good." He joked.

Listening to these two men talk about pregnancy like she wasn't there was disturbing. *Lighten up*, she chided herself. Aloud she said, "I can assure you I will only put you through this once." The joke dropped like a stone when Danny seriously replied:

"I sure hope so, babe."

Teres didn't know whether to laugh or cry.

August 3, 1992

Danny pretended not to be worried, but he was. Other than OB appointments and counseling with Marion, Teres hadn't left the house in four weeks. Martha had come by a couple times, bringing gifts of food and conversation. Ron was a regular, keeping them up to date on the lawsuit and the business. And Lori filled in all the gaps in the day-to-day household, including asking Travis to come by and drag boxes to Goodwill, then lug the excess furniture out of the baby's room and down to the basement. He seemed glad to do it. Nobody said no to Lori.

*

"Well. I'm finally meeting the amazing Mrs. Muldaur!" Travis said good naturedly, when Danny introduced Teres.

"And I am finally meeting the man responsible for putting a smile on Lori's face," Teres answered.

"I wasn't sure where you were going with that, Mrs. Muldaur. I thought you were gonna say 'the man responsible for putting my ambulance company out of business.'" Teres' laugh was loud and genuine. Danny had to hand it to the kid, he spent every minute keeping it real. It was good he had come by, Danny planned to work his ass off as payback for the lawsuit hell.

"Travis. You are exactly as Lori said you would be," Teres said.

"She did a good job describing you, too. She said you were beautiful and you had a sense of humor that sneaks up on a person." Danny loved the smile Travis' reply put on his wife's face. Sometimes he wondered if he were overreacting about her depression. But then their visitor would leave and she would go back to barely keeping it together.

*

The woods had become a thing. Whenever Danny turned his back, Teres would go missing. She'd leave a note on the sliding glass door: *Out back*. Sometimes she'd be gone for thirty minutes, sometimes hours. On those longer absences Danny would wrestle with whether to go check on her. Just as he'd be getting up to go out there, she'd return. Her mood was always the same, upbeat like she had just returned from a shopping trip. It was a coverup. He could feel her receding. He went to Barnes and Noble to find a book on fatherhood, hoping to get an idea if Teres' behavior was normal or because of their situation. He ended up buying *What to Expect When You're Expecting*. After leafing through it a bit in the car, he decided everything was normal and nothing was normal. He walked back into the store and returned it. His answers weren't in somebody else's book. When he got home, his wife was still in the woods. It was almost dusk and getting buggy out. With that as his excuse, Danny grabbed the bug spray from the cabinet and went out to find her.

*

She was beautiful, like a movie star. Half on her knees, arms thrown over the smoothest boulder in the rock wall; her eyes were closed with her hair cascading over her shoulders and trailing down the side of the wall. It had been hot that day and she was wearing one of the billowy dresses she'd brought back from Greece, her pregnancy hidden in the folds. Her feet were bare, sandals kicked to the side. Danny stood there, unable to speak. He was touched by such beauty and sadness that he felt like he had stepped into another world. Teressa had done this to him before, transported him somewhere unexpected. She needed a blanket, or a yoga mat, or a fairy-tale like bed with a crystal dome cover. *Sleeping Beauty*. His wife was the Greek version of Sleeping Beauty. He took one step toward her and she startled awake.

"Danny."

"It's getting buggy. Are you being eaten alive?" He awkwardly held out the can of spray.

"They do not like me. I am not sweet." He didn't argue with her. He watched her try to push herself to a standing position. She couldn't. He rushed to help her.

"My foot is asleep and my stomach grew again," she smiled. As he came closer he saw her face was streaked with tears, like she had tried to wipe them with a dirty hand. Maybe she looked like this after every trip to the woods. He always assumed her rush to the bathroom was for her bladder, not to wash her face. He helped put on her sandals.

"What can I do for you?" Danny asked her, knowing her answer might be dismissive.

"You're doing it Daniello. Just keep things normal when I cannot."

It was a heartbreaking answer that acknowledged the essence of his question. Danny knew keeping things normal wasn't proving to be enough. He knew what more he could do.

"Teres, let's go to the apartment on Friday. We can stay till Sunday or Monday – get everything figured out. How does that sound?"

"It sounds like a plan," she answered, filling up with more tears. "Thank you, my sweet man." Danny helped her walk back to their house. He couldn't imagine what a weekend at Gregory's apartment would change, but he had to do something. He couldn't witness his wife's internal struggle for another minute.

*

Dick was a renaissance man. Having retired early from a rather mundane job in the production end of journalism, he now had plenty of time to feed his interests. For the moment, it was landscaping. Being outside after a career in a windowless printshop was a gift; physical labor, the perfect companion to a mind that never slept. This was Dick's second year working the Muldaur property. The job had changed considerably. "Yard Boss" was the title given to the homeowner in charge of landscape decisions. Last year's yard boss was Mrs. Muldaur. This year the word Mrs. was crossed out and Mr. written in its place. It was like night and day. Mrs. Muldaur had a plan and a preference for everything. Mr. Muldaur led with, "That sounds good," or, "Is this how we did it last year?" By the look of the property, the regime change hadn't made much difference; it was an established yard and just needed to be kept up.

Dick wasn't attached to the drama of things. He liked learning about plants and the chemistry that goes with growing things. He also liked getting to know the customers. Mrs. Muldaur had been one of his favorites for a couple reasons: she was direct, asked questions without assuming she knew the answer, and she was married to a man Dick's age to whom she was clearly devoted. Week to week, Dick had watched the events of last summer unfold: The Muldaurs being excited about their new pool and landscaping. Mr. Muldaur having a heart attack at the beginning of July. Mrs. Muldaur taking residence at the hospital, only coming home for a night's sleep and change of clothes. Finally in August, Mr. Muldaur returning home. Dick wasn't a voyeur. He was an observer. Maybe someone else would have let the job slack off, taken advantage of the lack of oversight. Not Dick. He made certain the crew did everything by the book. His diligence didn't go unnoticed. After the fall cleanup, Mrs. Muldaur sent a generous tip, along with a gift certificate to Mill Wharf Tavern, large enough to buy the crew a nice dinner. That was last year. Other than a head nod and half-smile, he and Mrs. Muldaur hadn't spoken one word this entire season. It didn't take a genius to see Mrs. Muldaur was in trouble.

When Dick first saw her pregnancy he had a reaction that included pride, as though he'd had something to do with it. Instead of chastising himself for his foolish thought, he spent the afternoon analyzing his emotions and came to the only conclusion that made any sense, *Way to go, team!* Danny Muldaur, by getting his wife pregnant despite his age and health, was a hero in their shared age category. There was nothing more to it. After that realization Dick continued to work hard on the property, now with Mr. Muldaur as his favorite homeowner. He was thrilled when Danny approached him with a special project.

"Hey, Dick. How's it going?"

"Good, Mr. Muldaur. How are you?" he replied.

"Call me Danny. It's good. I need a little help with something for my wife. I don't know if you've noticed that she's pregnant."

"Congratulations," Dick said, since they hadn't mutually acknowledged the fact before then.

"Thanks. It's been hard on her … she seems to be most happy in the woods by that rock wall that runs along our property line. She needs a comfortable bench – I could pick it out, but I trust your judgement. And can you make sure there's no poison ivy growing in that clearing? It's the last thing she needs, a raging case of poison ivy."

"I'll get right on it. I can check out benches today. You want wood? Metal? Stone?"

"I think wood. It's probably the most comfortable," Mr. Muldaur concluded after a minute.

Dick was happy to be part of this. He could help Mrs. Muldaur get through her pregnancy. He understood the dark cloud of depression.

"Have you ever heard of a labyrinth?" Dick asked, not realizing he was going to.

"I think so," Mr. Muldaur replied. "It's a circle puzzle, like a maze."

"They're also used for meditation, as a walking path to contemplate life. We built one out of cobblestone for a woman in Cohasset last month. They're supposed to be very calming." *I felt calmer just laying out the stones.* Dick let himself feel the solitude the project had invoked in him.

*

A walking labyrinth. An image came up in Danny's mind. What he saw wasn't his pregnant wife, but a woman holding a baby close to her heart, her face pressed into the bundled infant, walking the path and soothing the baby to sleep. *A labyrinth.*

"How long do they take to make?" Danny asked.

"I can get it done in a weekend if you want the same size and design I did for that woman," the landscaper replied. Danny thought about it. He would be making a 'Teres' decision – clearly out of his wheelhouse.

"Is there any chance you can do it this weekend? I'm taking Teres away for a couple days. It would be a great surprise. And could you pick up a comfortable cushion for the bench? One of those outdoor ones that dries really fast."

"Absolutely!" Dick's face exploded in a grin. Danny patted him on the back, almost gave him a hug. *What a great guy!* he thought to himself, mentally adding one of his wife's favorite lines: *Decisions are easy if you surround yourself with smart people.* Now to call Lori and see if she can get the apartment ready for their weekend, maybe grab groceries, too. Hopefully, her answer is yes; Danny had no desire to step foot in that apartment without his wife – or *with her* for that matter.

*

It had taken the whole day, but Lori was satisfied. Everything was freshly washed, dusted, and inviting. Along with the list Danny had given her, she purchased a bouquet of flowers which she put in an empty Maxwell House can on the table, pulling a few buds out for a bedside glass. In the outside storage, Lori found two spider-ridden deck chairs and a small table. They looked brand new once she cleaned and positioned them on the little balcony facing the harbor. She had never opened the bedroom closet before now, but did so in search of something to throw over the chairs for comfort. Lori was surprised by its contents. It was meticulously filled with men's clothing – not cheap stuff, either. White shirts and suits lined one side and shelves of casual pants and sweaters lined the other side. The bottom had three rows of shoes: dress, casual, and athletic. She could tell at a glance they weren't Danny's. On the top shelf, along with some boxes, she found two old crocheted afghans – the kind your grandmother makes. She tossed a throw over each chair back, adding some pillows taken from the couch in the living room. After putting away the food, she prepared a tray of cheese and crackers, leaving an apple and paring knife on the tray. Red wine and sparkling water were chilling in an ice bucket she'd found under the sink. She wasn't sure if red wine needed to be chilled, but it was hot August and she was pretty certain it shouldn't be served warm. At the last minute she remembered the candles she brought from home and she placed them beside the wine, leaving a book of matches close by.

With one last look and a cheesy grin on her face, Lori left the apartment, locking the door and slipping the key under the mat like Danny had said to. *Maybe someday I'll have a husband who cares enough to surprise me with something this nice.*

August 7, 1992

Gregory's Apartment

Figuring out what to pack for a weekend at her ex-lover's apartment was more difficult than Teres thought. She put her flowy silk nightgown back in the drawer. She wanted this to be her and Danny's weekend, not a reminder of the sex she had there with Gregory. Suddenly she was having second thoughts. Why had she pushed this plan? It was too late to change it now. How many things fell under that heading? Too late to take back her affair. Too late to go back in time and work harder at adoption. Too late to have the most glorious pregnancy a mother ever envisioned. Or was it? She had less than four weeks left of her pregnancy. Could she become a mother filled with joyful anticipation, sharing every movement and mystery with the man she loves? Could she put the ghost of this baby's father behind her? She would know after this weekend.

*

Danny didn't have a clue how the next few days were supposed to play out. Should he treat it as a vacation, a normal weekend away with his wife? Or was there going to be an official agenda with uncomfortable questions written on lined paper, hoping to get to the bottom of things. He didn't want to get to the bottom of anything. There was sludge and muck and crap you could cut your foot on at the bottom of most things. As far as he was concerned they had already been to the bottom. Yet here they were, willfully driving back to the lowest point in their marriage.

"Let's stop at the store and pick up some food," Teres said when they were almost to Gregory's. Danny could feel her stalling. He was also perplexed by her sudden ability to leave the house without a full blown anxiety attack, and now wanting to stop at the store – although she didn't say she would go in.

"Teres, we're almost there. Let's get settled in and make a list of what we need." She nodded. They drove the rest of the way immersed in independent thoughts. *So much for sharing our feelings.*

The silence continued into the elevator and up to the sixth floor. Teres had used her own key to open the main entrance. But when they got close, Danny dashed ahead to snag the key Lori had left under the mat so he could open the door with a flourish, hoping his ta-dah moment lived up to the gesture. It did.

*

Teres took in the flowers and the bright light streaming in from the open blinds, which she had shuttered to cave-like darkness before she left for Greece. The air conditioning was set to a refreshing chill; a cheese tray, plates, napkins, and wine glasses sat invitingly on the counter. Everything smelled freshly cleaned. She smiled to cover the nauseating déjà vu of seeing this apartment intentionally designed to charm a woman. *The wine bucket.* Teres knew she would not be able to stay conscious if she looked inside to find Gregory's favorite wine. "Did you do all this?" She tried to keep her voice pleasantly surprised instead of accusatory.

"I wish I could take the credit," Danny said, happily. "It was Lori. She did a great job, huh?"

"She did," Teres answered, irrationally feeling like the left out partner of a threesome. She worked to reroute her attitude. This had been her idea. And while Danny was busy making the best of it, she was acting like a zombie, keeping her emotions bland and guarded. *This has nothing to do with him!* she chastised herself, pushing Gregory and his smooth, calculated behavior from her mind. *My husband wanted to make this nice. It is nice. I am not nice.*

"Everything looks wonderful! I thought we would have our work cut out for us making things clean for our stay." She said, as she walked into the kitchen and opened the refrigerator. There was ready-made salad and a piece of salmon from the fish market. Eggs for breakfast, and odds and ends like mustard left from when they lived - *survived* - here.

"Teres, we can order out for dinner – we don't have to cook. I just wanted you to have what you like to eat. There's bread and coffee in the cabinet. Lori-"

"Danny, it is perfect. You know me. It just takes a minute when something good happens that is not my idea. I am a crazy woman."

"Yes, you are," her adorable husband confirmed.

*

Yes you are, Danny repeated in his mind. His thoughts shifted to the surprise he had planned for her space in the woods. If she was this freaked out about him cleaning the apartment and buying food without her input, what the hell was she going to be like when she saw the construction project he had arranged. *Well, it's done.* Danny didn't have Dick's telephone number or last name to call and back out now. Thinking about a call made him wonder about phone service. He walked to the living room and picked up the receiver of the aqua princess phone. Dead, of course. Clearly he hadn't thought of everything. Danny grabbed his duffel bag and followed Teres as she rolled her small suitcase to the bedroom, *Gregory's bedroom.* He suddenly wished he hadn't insisted Lori buy a new set of sheets for the bed. He and Teres both knew the linen closet had stacks of fresh white sheets, along with white towels, white wash cloths, and a shelf devoted to toilet paper and bars of Irish Spring deodorant soap. What else would a confident bachelor want – *aside from my wife and the baby she's carrying?* It was difficult to remember Gregory was dead and no longer a threat. Or was it his death that made him a bigger threat to their happiness? *Take the lead, dummy, before it's too late.*

"Babe, do you want to take a walk by the harbor or just sit on the deck and have a snack?"

*

The sun was beginning to set. They had been on the balcony for two hours discussing nothing important, but with simple ease. Danny felt relaxed. It was probably the wine. There were a couple times their conversation could have gone south, but didn't. Teres mentioned she had never been on the balcony before. He knew her reference was more about seasonal opportunity, but his mind quickly shot back, *because you couldn't bring yourself to leave his bedroom.* His mouth replied, "It's beautiful out here. Remember that client we had, Mrs. Pierce? The one we had to drive to dialysis once a week? She lived on this side of the building. I'd hate to own an apartment on the other side – a great location, but you can't see the water." *You are so lucky to have inherited an apartment from your lover that's on the good side of the building.* He wondered when they were going to get to the awful part of the weekend. If he were a different guy, they would be in the awful part already. If he were a different guy…

*

Teres couldn't decide why Danny was so okay. She had expected this weekend to cause him the kind of stomach acid that accompanies a case of Pepto Bismal. He was smiling, conversational, like he didn't care. *Jesus, Teressa Muldaur! Of course your husband cares! Why else would he go through all this bullshit? Why would anyone go through this bullshit?* The guilt began to weigh her down. She couldn't concentrate on what he was saying.

"Okay. I think that answers my question," Danny said.

What was his question?

"We definitely need to take a nap before we figure out dinner." Danny stood, grabbing the cheese tray, but leaving the wine and seltzer water behind. He held his other hand out to help her from the low chair. Then he opened the slider, the coolness an immediate contrast to the August heat.

"Maybe we need to get air conditioning," her husband said to her, placing the tray on the counter. "Or we could just come here when it gets too hot in the summer…"

Come here? He hates this place. Teres could feel the dizziness overtake her. Was she mixed up? Getting it all wrong? She couldn't clear her head. She felt her body go sideways. She caught herself before her distress became obvious, or so she thought. The next thing she knew, she was laying on the couch with a cold compress on her forehead.

"I think we need to call the doctor," Danny had his hand on the pulse at her wrist.

"I'm fine," Teres replied. "I think it was the heat."

"Teres, you nearly passed out," he persisted. "This has happened before. Stop saying you're fine." He looked mad at her. She'd forgotten how mad he got when he was worried. In the past, it would have made her smile, his angry face imploring her to stop worrying him. Not today. There was nothing funny about having your head swim without notice.

"Danny," she said, "let me tell you what I think is going on. If you think I am wrong we can go to the hospital, or call the doctor, or whatever you say." She sat up. He waited for her explanation.

"It is anxiety. I become emotionally overwhelmed and my pulse begins to race too fast, then suddenly slows. Being pregnant takes more toll on my blood flow. It does not get to my head so quickly and makes me feel light-headed. The minute I put my head down, it passes. It is a classic vasovagal response – nothing to worry about."

*

Danny had no argument with the mechanics of why she passed out. But what had triggered it? He was being so careful not to upset her. If only there were a way to find out what was going on in his wife's head. *Just ask her, dummy.*

"What made you overwhelmed?"

"It was nothing. Sometimes I get confused." Her answer didn't make sense. Teres was the queen of clarity – or so she always said.

"Listen," he persisted, not as sweetly as he hoped. "We came here to be honest. Tell me what was going through your head that caused this." He waited for her to answer. She didn't. "This is stupid. What are we doing here? What is it you think can be solved by me pretending I'm okay and you falling apart?" It was a bit more of a tirade than he intended. Her sarcastic response surprised him.

"Thank you, heavenly father! I feel better. My husband is just pretending he is okay!" Danny looked at her like she'd lost her mind.

"Of course I'm not okay! What did you think? That I suddenly forgot whose apartment we were in and why we're here?" Danny fought to keep his anger in check. "Jesus, Teres. What do you want from me?"

"I want you to be honest with me."

"No."

"No what?" she asked him.

Danny thought about how to make his answer simple.

"If you ask me a question, I'll give you an honest answer. But if you expect honesty in the way I behave, I can't. Think of it as faking it until you make it, or putting up a good front, like walking around with a bad headache and telling everyone you're fine.

269

That's what this is like. I'm gonna make the best of it. There are days I'm gonna slap a smile on my face and pretend I'm okay even if I'm not. And I'm gonna do it with the hope that someday it will be real. But the part of it that's already true is I love you, and I want this baby. That's the truth."

He watched her face, trying to gage her reaction. He wanted her to understand. She didn't.

"So now I will never know if you are happy? I will look at you, see you smile and maybe inside you are a man filled with misery? And that is okay?" Her expression was still unreadable.

Danny was sure with a few well-chosen words he could turn this conversation around. But then he didn't choose his words well.

"Teres, this isn't too different from what I normally do. Do you think I'm wild about every decision you've ever made? I'm not. But I keep my mouth shut, put up a good front and eventually when I get used to things – or they work out for the best – I can genuinely say I'm happy about it. That's what this is like."

"So, you have been faking your happiness for our entire marriage? You hated the choices I have made – for our success and our happy future – you put up with it instead of telling me what you really feel? Our whole marriage is a lie!"

"That's not what I'm saying …"

"I do not know you at all, Daniel Muldaur." Teres got off the couch, steady as a rock, and marched self-righteously into her lover's bedroom, slamming the door behind her.

Danny chuckled to himself. *There's my girl*, he thought, as he went into the kitchen to put away the rest of the cheese plate and see what else Lori had bought. He hoped she remembered the eclairs. He also hoped Gregory's Pepto Bismal was still in the medicine cabinet. He was going to need it.

*

Slamming the door had knocked Teres out of her self-centered fit. She sat tearless on the bed, running through the list of her emotions. It was a long list. If she were having a session with Marion right now, her list would have warranted a pen and paper. Organizing her emotions was one of the weekly tasks Marion required of her. Almost always, guilt was at the top. Marion explained that guilt wasn't truly an emotion. It was a thing that brought about emotions like shame and feelings of responsibility. Eventually Marion threw in the towel and let Teres refer to the entire sum of those attached emotions as guilt. *Today I slammed my husband for making the best of a situation that I put him in, over which he has no control.* That would be today's heading.

Teres laid down on the bed, putting aside the comforter as she did. The sheets were an unfamiliar paisley blue. *Danny.* Of course he wouldn't want to sleep on Gregory's sheets, or be in his apartment, *or be reminded the baby wasn't his.* She almost called out his name, told him to come nap with her – that she was sorry. She decided maybe she should spend a couple minutes organizing her feelings, and figure out what she really wanted out of this weekend. That was when it hit her like a boulder from an avalanche: *I'm trying to get Danny to leave me before it's too late!* Why else would she have insisted their soul-searching weekend take place in this apartment? Teres pushed everything else from her mind and concentrated on the main question. Was this what she really wanted? Danny to be gone from her life? She thought she had already committed to stay with him, but clearly she hadn't.

Whenever Teres made decisions in the past, she used pros and cons to judge the merits of her choice. If she applied that strategy to Danny it was grossly lopsided.

The pros of staying with Danny:

He is going to be a great father.

271

He knows everything about me and loves me anyway.

I love him.

He wants the baby.

Our business, friends, home, and family can remain intact.

The cons of staying with Danny:

I am reminded of my betrayal every time I look at him.

Push away the love of my life so I can feel less guilty? It didn't make sense, even to a hormonal, desperately confused woman such as herself. Leaving Danny would be the true definition of cutting off your nose to spite your face. Maybe that's what she was trying to do, punish herself completely. Why did everything keep coming back to this? Was it easier to give up and go forward as a single mother than to live with constant guilt? If she were truly punishing herself, she would choose to live with Danny, in a state of guilt and contrition – and *teshuva*.

Teres was exhausted. She could feel a tight knot in the small of her back, crampy pain running down her buttocks. She practiced her meditation breathing, trying to release the knot. A light tapping on the bedroom door interrupted her meditation.

Danny's head poked in.

"Hey. You okay?" he asked in a low voice. She patted the bed beside her.

"I like the sheets," she said, by way of a truce. Her husband grinned. "Come lie down with your stupid, pregnant wife." His grin widened. *How could I think of leaving him?* She rolled to her side so he could squeeze up against her back. She gratefully felt his erection. "Up for a nap?" she kidded, an old joke they had shared many times.

"I think my wife needs a real nap," he answered. Within minutes they were both asleep.

*

She knew it was a dream. Her contractions were coming closer together. She wasn't in the hospital. She was on the road beside the wrecked sports car. Lying in the snow felt good on her back. Danny was yelling at her, "Go get help!" *Who does he want me to get?* She concentrated on timing her contractions, like she had done once with a pregnant woman on an ambulance run. Without a watch, she counted the numbers in her head while looking up at the snowflakes falling from an imaginary point in the dark sky. She was hot. The snow melted the second it hit her face, making her skin glossy. *One, two, three, four, five* ... She felt like she had to push. Someone was walking toward her, kneeling down beside her. *Oh, good. I need help with this baby.* The hand on her stomach felt reassuring. She looked at the hand and saw Danny's wedding ring. Drops of blood were falling onto it and splattering across her rounded abdomen. She raised her gaze to the source of the blood and saw the detached scalp flapping above intense, familiar eyes. His lips wore the smile of an expectant father. She felt another contraction start and she began to scream.

*

"That's it. We're going to the hospital." Danny tied his shoes and reached for his wallet on the nightstand.

"We should wait a little longer and see if this feeling goes away?"

Teres was pale and shaking, the kind of shaking women in transition get. She could be eight centimeters dilated for all Danny knew. He would be calling an ambulance if the phone worked. He calmed his voice.

"Babe, that feeling is a baby. At this point it doesn't go away. What's the worst that happens? We go to the hospital, they check you out and say, 'Go home, it's not gonna happen today.' A month early isn't something you fool around with. And if that contraction was strong enough to make you scream …"

"I told you, it wasn't the contraction. I had a nightmare," she reiterated, but at least she was getting her things together while she argued. She headed into the bathroom.

Danny stood by the door and listened. Everything sounded normal. He heard her brushing her teeth. *Maybe I should brush mine*, he thought, wondering if Gregory's toothbrush were still here. He spent a few moments of thought on the toothbrush dilemma. That was when he realized how nervous he was. "Babe, we should get a move on."

*

Teres had been so busy worrying about her pregnancy she had neglected to think about the birth. The idea of it happening now, a month early, produced the kind of fear that made speaking almost impossible, as though her lower jaw were held together by a rusty hinge. Their ride to the hospital was quiet, Danny's support displayed by how tightly he gripped her knee. *Don't let go of me!* Teres silently begged of him. *I can't do this alone.*

The emergency room at Quincy City was jam-packed, typical for a Friday night in August. Being a woman in labor propelled her to the front of the line. While Teres ineptly answered questions, Danny dug through her purse for the insurance card. Two minutes later she was in a wheelchair headed for maternity on the third floor. The elevator door was closing when Ron Watters' arm popped in.

"Hey! Is this it? Are you in labor?" he asked excitedly, shoving his way through the closing doors.

"We don't know," Danny replied. He started giving Ron the story. It was too much for Teres to hear. Her anxiety level upped with every word.

"Danny. Tell him later." They both stopped talking. The elevator opened, revealing the OB-GYN nurses' station, behind which sat a pretty, blond nurse. She glanced up from her work.

"Give me one second to finish this note and I'll be right with you." She went back to scribbling.

"Karen. Thank god you're on today," Ron said. "These are my best friends, the Muldaurs. I know you'll take good care of them."

Karen grinned without looking up. "That's what you always say, Dr. Watters. You have a lot of best friends."

"Yeah, I know it's my standard line when I send patients up from the ER, but this time it's true. Danny used to be a respiratory therapist here, and Teres and I own an ambulance company together."

If Teres could have moved her jaw, she would have laughed at Danny's injured expression over being omitted from ownership of the company.

"That's why you look so familiar!" Karen exclaimed, cranking her neck to look up at Danny. "I think we've worked on a couple sick babies together."

"We did," Danny said. "Hopefully, *this* delivery will be smooth sailing."

Teres cleared her throat. It wasn't to get attention, her throat was closing up from anxiety. Danny made introductions.

"Karen, this is my wife, Teressa. We – might be having a baby today."

When the nurse came around the counter to the front, Teres was surprised to see how little she was. Apparently she had been standing, not sitting, behind the desk. Her diminutive size didn't stop her from taking charge of the situation. "We've got it from here, Dr. Watters." the nurse said cheerfully and dismissively, ushering Ron back into the elevator. She scooted in front of Danny, taking control of the wheelchair, and spoke over her shoulder to him as she pushed Teres down the hall. "We're headed to room three-oh-eight. Grab yourself some scrubs and change while I get your wife settled in – don't forget booties for your shoes!"

Teres felt herself relax. *Clearly this petite powerhouse of a woman knows how this is supposed to go – even if I don't.* She looked at the name tag. *Thank you, Karen Olsen.* Then she gratefully surrendered the burden of her worry to the competency of the nurse, putting out of her thoughts the men in her life and the chaos her duplicity had caused. Her only concern was the health and safety of the baby she carried. *I'm going to be a mother!* The thought filled her with joy and wonder.

*

"It's called prodromal labor," Dave Almer, the obstetrician on call, said. "It's from a Greek word meaning precursor."

"Of course it is," Danny interjected.

"It's stronger and more consistent than Braxton Hicks contractions. For some women it comes on hours before real labor, for others weeks before. We see it happen early with first time mothers, especially if they're under stress – or older. It's nothing to worry about, just your body getting ready for the big day."

Relief and dismay fought for space in Teres' emotions. "Will it stop?" she asked.

"We never know. What we do know is you're not in actual labor right now. Your cervix is closed and uneffaced. We did a PH test for premature rupture of the membranes – negative. And that monitor we put you on was to make certain your baby isn't under any stress; it looks like he's doing great, a nice steady heart rate through the prodromal episodes."

"So, what do we do now? Go home and wait?" Danny asked.

"Nope. Go back to your normal lives." the doctor replied. "Babies come when they come. I see situations like this where the baby ends up being late – or it could happen tomorrow. Though, I'd like to see him hang in there another week or two. But if he comes early he'll do just fine. My guess is he's about five-and-a-half pounds."

*

I could handle a five-and-a-half pounder Danny thought to himself, acknowledging how excited he had become. Dr. Almer left and Ron strolled into the room.

"So? What's the verdict?"

"Looks like we're headed home," Danny replied with a more somber expression than he felt. "Turns out she's in Greek labor. It could take another two months." Danny's joke landed right where he wanted: his wife smiled. Danny's face lit with an idea.

"Ron, do you have your bag phone?" he asked.

"Yes." Ron replied.

"Is it charged and can we take it? We were trying to have a weekend away when this happened."

"Danny! We need to go home. This could-"

"Take forever, the doctor said. Besides, where we're staying is closer to the hospital than Scituate." Danny wasn't taking no for an answer. Ron interjected.

"How about you two fight it out and I'll be downstairs. Whether you go home or not, I'm giving you my phone. It'll make you look cool, and you can answer calls from people I regret giving the number to."

*

Teres was exhausted. The adrenal rush had come and gone. Now that she knew she wasn't in actual labor her contractions seemed less painful, something she could sleep through. She wanted her own bed.

"Danny, why do you want to go back there? We should go home." She said, confused by him not running back to Scituate at a gallop while he had the chance. His answer surprised her.

"I was excited today. I want this baby – our baby. I say we go back to that apartment and get anything standing between us out of the way. When we come here again, I want it to be like everyone else gets it to be – just two parents who can't wait to meet their kid. You owe me that, Teres."

You owe me that, Teres. If he had thrown a sentence like that at her a year ago, she would have gone ballistic with 'how dare yous!' But that was a year ago, when she owed nothing to anyone.

"Okay. Go get your cool bag phone from Ron and I will meet you when I am discharged." Danny leaned over to kiss her. Teres knew he was aiming for her forehead, but she pulled him into a kiss fueled with passion, apologies, and promise. It was the type of kiss her husband deserved, but seldom got; another thing she vowed to change.

*

Teres was settled comfortably on the couch. She had suggested they stop and get dinner to go, but Danny said he had it covered. By the sound of things, Teres wasn't sure that was true. Pans rattling, the occasional curse word – the kitchen wasn't far away.

"Danny, I would be happy with more crackers and another piece of cheese," she hollered over the backdrop of the evening news. Miraculously the cable was still on, as was the electricity. Gregory's attorney must have paid the bills. It had been six months since his death; an eternity or just a day, depending upon how she looked at it. Certainly not a lifetime. *Maybe when this new life comes into the world I will think of it as a lifetime ago.*

"You need something healthy," her husband yelled back.

The kitchen sounds had turned into the tambourine-like shuffling of the utensil drawer. Teres went back to watching the news. Shaquille O'Neal was signed by The Orlando Magic. This was more Danny's kind of news. Of all the sports, basketball was her lease favorite. "If it always comes down to the last five minutes, why do they not play for just five minutes?" she had complained, irritated that the end of any basketball game seemed to take an hour. Teres would give her right arm to be fighting about silly things with her husband again,

*

"Dinner is served," Danny said theatrically, setting a glass of water next to Teres' plate. "You okay with these bar stools, or do you wanna eat on the couch?"

"It smells good," Teres replied, cautiously getting up. He helped her onto the stool. The meal consisted of poached salmon with honey mustard sauce, broccoli, and Far East Rice Pilaf. It came out better than Danny had dared hope. He watched her take a bite.

"When did you learn to cook like this?"

"You kidding? I got to drink wine and watch the best cooking show in town – this crazy Greek woman. She ends every show with, 'This is the best blah, blah, blah I ever made.' I figured poached was the safest way to cook it and the honey mustard is my own concoction, just French's and a squirt of that bear honey." He tried to make the cooking sound like an everyday occurrence instead of the feat it really was.

"It is really good." Teres said between bites.

"How are you feeling?" he asked her.

"Better. The contractions are still going, but not painful. I am tired, though – ready for bed."

She didn't look tired. She looked beautiful. Her hair was pulled into a simple band and looked like a horse's tail, flowing nearly to her waist. Twenty-five weeks had gone by since the accident, roughly five missed haircuts. He wondered about Norma, her hairdresser for years. Did she just think Teres had moved on to another stylist, or had their life become the topic of salon gossip?

"Your hair is so long and pretty," he said, thinking there was a better way to say it.

"It is the wiry, dry hair of an old woman," his beautiful wife answered.

Why does she do that? he wondered. She was hard to figure out. If he didn't comment on her looks or clothing, she'd chastise him for not noticing. But when he did, she dismissed it as a lie. *Women.* Or maybe *woman* was a better exasperated word choice. He had spent twenty years trying to figure out this one woman. Every time he thought he might be close, the game changed. With empty satisfaction, Danny realized he, too, had become a puzzle.

"This apartment is amazing," Danny said, adding, "I wish I could love it. Can you imagine how easy it would be to live in a place like this? No maintenance? Water view? Close to everything?" He waited for her response, not knowing what he was going after. She finally spoke.

"I could never live here. No yard, or privacy. Truthfully, Danny, I never gave it a thought."

"Are you saying you never considered moving in here with Gregory?" Then he couldn't stop himself. "Or that you and him wouldn't have gotten yourselves another place? Maybe kick me out and keep the Scituate house?" *Stop, you complete asshole, before it's too late!* "You must have thought about living with him – for the sake of the child."

*

280

Teres tried to remember that saying about fighting dirty. *The gloves are off.* Finally Danny was being mean, even sarcastic – a tone he didn't often use. It was in his last words, *for the sake of the child*, as though her pregnancy hid the real reason she might consider leaving him – being in love with Gregory. She wrestled with whether she had the strength to begin this conversation tonight, while it was here at the surface. Tomorrow would look optimistic, as mornings do. Could they work their way back to this moment? Teres doubted it.

"I considered leaving you because of the pregnancy. The pressure from Gregory was overwhelming. He gave me a deadline to decide." Teres made it sound like a business transaction, not the emotional rollercoaster it had been. She pushed her plate aside. "Let me help you with these dishes. Trying to look at you while I sit beside you is hurting my back." It was true, but not the reason she stood.

"I'm sorry, babe," her husband said, clearly walking back his anger. "It's stupid to get into this now – it's practically midnight. Eat the rest of your dinner."

Misplaced or not, Teres felt her anger rise.

"Danny, this is what we are here for, yes? To get things off our chest, right? You want to know, did I love Gregory? Was I going to leave you? Do not ask me a question and then stop the answer! Maybe this is stupid and we should go home!" She was flinging the dishes into the sink as she spoke, running hot water for nothing but the comfort of it. Maybe this argue and run tactic was inherent with the apartment. She and Danny didn't fight like this at home. It suddenly occurred to her that the only place they *didn't* fight was at home. In their beautiful Scituate house they were civilized with their anger and their sorrow – no banging plates and slamming doors. She tried to think of one knock-down, drag-out fight within the walls of their house and couldn't. Maybe that was another reason she wanted to come here, so she wouldn't sully their home with Gregory revelations.

"Teres, I'm just saying you had a long day. Maybe this should wait till tomorrow."

She whirled around to face him. "I had plenty of sleep in my nap! It was not pain that woke me! It was a vision of Gregory, with your hands, and blood covering his face! He was going to deliver my baby on the side of the road! We need to get this done! You both are mixing into one person, and I am losing my mind!" She knew she sounded crazy. She could see the reflection of her insanity in Danny's expression. There was a moment of stillness, then Danny threw a plate into the sink, the sound of breaking china like the starting bell of a heavyweight fight.

"Fine! You wanna do this now? Is that what you want, Teres? Everything out on the table?" He slammed the refrigerator door, causing them both to shutter. "Okay, here's the real thing I wanna know – what the hell made you fuck Gregory Costa in the first place? Were you that hard up for sex while I was laying in the hospital practically dead?"

*

It was the question she asked herself a thousand times a day. *Why did I have an affair?* Unwanted memories invaded her mind, beginning with the day she met Gregory …

Danny was unconscious and in critical condition as they waited for the heart surgeon Ron had recommended. Teres, asleep at his bedside and dreaming about Greece. In her dream, she was adrift in a small wooden boat that looked to be homemade. The sail was a triangle of material sewn from her wedding dress. It was too small and too sheer to stand the winds. She was alone and couldn't remember how to sail. Just when the boat was ready to capsize,

Teres heard the sound of breaking glass from the heavens above the storm clouds. She awoke with a start, unsure of where she was. Standing in front of her was a beautiful man. He merged with her consciousness as though he were part of the dream. His name was Gregory Costa – and he had come to save her husband's life.

And then another memory floated before her eyes …

She was frozen in the doorway of a hospital room while Gregory worked frantically to resuscitate Danny. He was in cardiac arrest, just days after the open heart surgery. It was so much pain Teres couldn't bear to stay and watch him die, so she fled.

Gregory found her in the Chapel an hour later. Her head was hanging down between her arms, both hands gripping the pew in front of her. She looked up from her distress, knowing it would be him standing there.

"I cannot do this. It is killing me. I would rather not love him. It would be easier." Gregory pulled her up from the chapel bench, and held her tightly while she cried. And then he said the strangest thing. He whispered it into her hair.

"He's alive, Teressa. Your husband is alive. I'll help you get through this, Il mio piccolo gattino." *My little kitten.*

And finally, the scene that sealed her fate …

Teres was exhausted from weeks of going back and forth to the hospital. Gregory offered to drive her home. She gave him directions to her house, then reclined the passenger seat of his red Ferrari and shut her eyes, unexpectedly unnerved by his closeness. It was dark in the car, intimate. Gregory's hand was partly on her seat, planned, but casual. She could feel him, even though he wasn't touching any part of her. And then, for reasons she will never understand, he said, "I think I love you, Teressa." She took a deep breath. It was the kind of inhale that normally precipitated a tirade. She let the air flow slowly out of her body, and then she took his hand in hers.

"I know," she said, her acknowledgement of his feelings becoming the first step toward betraying the only man she had ever loved.

*

It was three months before they slept together; three months of Gregory doing everything he could to right Danny's heart, while doing anything he could to wrong hers. In fairness, Teres would not make this his fault. She had known what she was doing. Hers were the vows that were broken. While Gregory was obsessively pulling her into the deep end, she was hesitantly feeling her way through every emotion. She hated herself. But to feel butterflies unattached to the dread of her husband's health was intoxicating. It made her find ways to run into Gregory, be alone with him. When he began taking Tuesdays off, her day on the road, the die was cast.

Teres had promised herself the first time they made love would be their last. She even swore to God she would stop in exchange for Danny's health. But then the next time happened. Each Tuesday she vowed to end it. Whether it was hormones or the return of sanity, this involuntary pull toward Gregory changed after she got pregnant. The comfort and safety of her husband's arms was suddenly the only thing she craved.

How would she find the words to explain her treachery to Danny? She had to try. She owed him that much.

"Danny, this is only worth the pain if I tell you the truth, which I cannot do here in this kitchen. I am too ashamed to say these things in the light, and you deserve to know everything."

*

Danny looked at the clock on the nightstand. They had been talking for over three hours. There were moments during his wife's tale he thought he should have been hooked to a heart monitor. But he laid there beside her in the dark, in Gregory's bed, forcing himself to listen to the story of how his heart surgeon came to have an affair with his wife. In the beginning it was painful, but soon it became a story that had almost nothing to do with him. Eventually, he began asking questions.

"So it happened every Tuesday? No other times?" he asked her.

"Mostly," she answered. "Once Gregory had a long surgery that was cancelled. It was a Friday afternoon, and I got home very late because of the traffic."

Danny remembered that night, worrying about her stuck in the weekend traffic to the Cape.

"And we were together for that emergency medical conference I went to in Connecticut in January," she continued.

Okay. That one hurts. The thought of them together day and night for three days was a lot. His visions went to romantic dinners and laughing over private jokes. Taking their time in the bedroom. Lingerie. As if she could read his thoughts, she added:

"If it is any consolation, we fought the entire weekend. Actually, Danny, if it helps at all to know, we fought every time we were together."

It didn't help. Danny thought about all the fighting he and Teres did at the beginning of their marriage, each fight ending in a session of earth-shattering makeup sex.

"When did you find out you were pregnant?" he asked, painfully recollecting the day he found out.

"It was Christmas eve. I was shocked – and elated. I could not wait to tell you. That is how delusional I was. I was living two separate lives. Gregory got me pregnant, but I wanted to rush to tell you the happy news. Knowing I could not made me feel suicidal. Marion would say it was a symptom of a psychotic break."

"What did Costa say?" Danny knew calling him by his last name hurt them both, since he had always been 'Gregory' or 'Doc' and was now 'Costa' or 'the father.'

"He was very happy. He immediately began his campaign to get me to leave you," her words sounded teary in the dark.

"Did he love you?"

"Yes."

"Did you love him?"

"No," she answered without hesitation.

"Did you tell him you loved him?" Danny pushed.

"I never said 'I love you' to him. In fact I told him I was not in love with him."

Jesus Teressa! No wonder the guy had to have you! She couldn't have planned a better strategy for getting his attention. Gregory Costa loved a challenge. Even Danny's heart problems seemed to make him more excited than frustrated. Danny was done asking questions. The baby moved, an enormous roll from one side of Teres' stomach to the other, pushing out at Danny's ribs.

"This baby is always moving, like his father," Teres said. Danny sat up, surprised after all she had told him it was her comparison of the baby to Gregory that hurt so much.

"I don't want to think about this baby being his, but we can't pretend he isn't," Danny said. "We need some rules."

"Like what?" she asked.

What do I want? He needed to make a permanent statement, something that put him in a better position than 'acting father.'

"From now on when we say 'father' we mean me. If you want to refer to the baby's genetic father we say 'Gregory.'" He put his hand on her large stomach. The baby was still rolling. "Teres, I'm going to be this baby's father, not just because he doesn't have one, but because he is yours, and you are mine."

*

Of all the words and weeping that had happened that day, this simple declaration drove straight to her heart. *He is yours, and you are mine.* Her husband was a beautiful man, an unintentional poet, an angel she didn't deserve. This child had done nothing wrong, and would be blessed to have a wonderful father like Danny. She was sobbing as he continued to talk.

"Me and the baby need you to be okay. We need you to forgive yourself and give us a good life. You and I both know you're the kingpin in this relationship. If you're happy, I'm happy. And Teres, I wanna be happy. It doesn't have to be like before, but we can do all the talking in the world and you're still the only one who can make yourself okay with what happened."

Teres pulled him back down to the bed. "I love you," she said.

"I know," Danny replied, then he shifted onto his side and draped his arm over her. She felt his hand reach for hers. They knit their fingers together. "Let's get some sleep," he said. Teres rolled over, forming her back to fit into the curve of her husband's body, and drifted into a peaceful, dreamless sleep.

*

At nine the next morning, Danny awoke to a weird ringing sound coming from the kitchen. He reached for Teres and she was gone. The ringing stopped. "Teres!" he hollered, as he scrambled from bed, grabbed his pants, and headed toward the kitchen.

She was leaning on the counter, talking into Ron's bag phone. The kitchen mess from last night was gone. Danny could smell breakfast cooking.

"This is wonderful news!" she was saying. "So that is all we have to do? There is nothing else for us to worry about?" Danny assumed it was Ron, and tried to figure out what they were talking about. "We are at Gregory's apartment," she continued. "He left it to us in his will." Danny gave her a look. She smiled back at him. "Ron, we did not tell you because it was such a big thing to inherit, and we did not know if he left you anything." There was a long pause. "Oh, I am sorry we were not there. I would like that. You should meet us here for breakfast." Again Danny gave her an exasperated look. "Thanks. I will tell him. Bye." Teres hung up the phone.

"They dropped the lawsuit," she announced triumphantly, "in exchange for Travis' testimony that the chauffeur knowingly parked in a restricted area."

"That's great," Danny said, feeling another burden lift from his shoulders. "I think your omelets might be burning." Teres rushed to the stove, declared them perfect, and began setting out breakfast. Danny grabbed his morning pills and a cup of coffee, and sat down to eat. "Why'd you tell Ron about the apartment?"

"I have an idea." She wore a look that usually meant trouble. He waited for her plan, temporarily happy to see her excited about something again.

"Ron should live here," she said. "It is close to the hospital and the ambulance company. His place is small. If he and Doug become a real couple, it would be perfect for them."

"I think Ron knows the truth about the baby." Danny blurted. "From your letter to Gregory – I found it." He expected her to look shocked. She didn't.

"Yes. And you put it in the top drawer of my bureau," she responded.

"No, I didn't. I left it on the windowsill in the bathroom." Danny countered, his mind beginning to put two and two together. "Before we came home from Europe, I asked Ron to come by and empty the trash – freshen up the place," he admitted, wishing he hadn't been so quick to take credit for how nice the house looked.

"He must have found the letter and put it in your drawer. When it wasn't in the bathroom, I figured he read it and threw it away. Was it open?"

"No," she said. "Why are men so stupid? Why did you not read the letter when you found it?"

Danny could feel her turning this on him. *Sorry I didn't handle your affair exactly the way you wanted!* was his knee-jerk response. But he wasn't up for a blowout first thing in the morning.

"Do you think telling him about the apartment added to his suspicions?" he calmly asked, watching her think everything through to its most likely conclusion – a trait he loved and hated.

"Yes. Probably," she answered. "Nothing to be done about it now."

"Should we bring it up? See what he knows?" Danny suggested.

"No," she said, firmly. "Ron had plenty of time to say something if he were going to. We let it go and offer him the apartment. Have you ever been to Doug's place?"

His wife was back to boss mode. It made him unexpectedly happy. He couldn't wipe the smile off his face. "So, that's it? We're done working on our love life, and on to someone else's?"

"We are not done," she replied. "We still have things to figure out, but maybe the apartment thing is solved."

Danny had to admit it was a good idea. "What did Ron say when you flaunted your inheritance in his face?"

"He said Gregory's last request was better than our stupid apartment – Ron did the eulogy." Her face went pale. "He has a copy of his speech for us."

Danny tried to decide how to feel. Did he want to read the eulogy of a dead man he was working so hard to bury? "You know what, Teres? I feel bad about not going to the funeral. The man saved my life. And yeah. I think it would be great to have Ron live here." His words were sincere and rewarded by his wife's smile.

*

Teres watched Danny butter another piece of toast. In her self-absorbed haze, she hadn't nagged or overly worried about her husband's health in months, and he never looked better. He was trim and strong, his graying hair just a bit longer than usual – the picture of health. She had Gregory to thank for it. She protectively put her hands on her stomach. *And for this.* Teres decided she would say a special prayer for Gregory each morning. When Danny went to take a shower, she bowed her head and began with today:

> *Dear God, I will get better at this prayer. But for now I thank you for bringing Gregory into my life. He has left me with more blessings than I deserve, my husband's health and the baby I carry. I will try to be worthy of these gifts.*
> *Amen*

Then, instead of cleaning the kitchen, Teres decided to join her husband in the shower. She had no idea what would come of it, but smiled just thinking about the possibilities.

*

Dick couldn't wait for the Muldaurs to return home. The project had exceeded his expectations. The labyrinth was the same basic design as the one he had already created, except instead of laying the cobblestones the long way to form the path, he had placed them horizontally, side-by-side, creating a more impressive walkway. The wood bench he selected was long with curved arms. Mrs. Muldaur would be able to sleep on it if she wanted. Since it didn't come with a cushion, he asked a friend who worked for a marine supply store to make one from foam rubber and blue vinyl. It was meant to be used on a boat so it was totally waterproof. When Dick saw the two perfectly spaced pine trees shading the rock wall, he grabbed a double-sized hammock made of rope and varnished wood, and chained it between them. He also bought an outdoor storage table they could use to put things like warm throws, pillows, and bug spray. Then Dick added a little lighting for safety: two of his own battery operated lanterns, which he hung from tree limbs.

There was one more item he had found at the little store beside the garden shop – a beautiful statue. He wrestled with whether or not to place it. If he knew for sure Mrs. Muldaur was religious it would have been a no-brainer. His gut told him it was perfect for the center of the labyrinth – perfect for her. *But you never know when you're going to offend someone.* He rolled it to the center using his small hand cart, deciding the worst that could happen was they take it down. When everything was done he took pictures, good advertisement in case he ever built another one. Then he totaled the receipts, making the statue his gift, and wedged the envelope into the sliding glass door near the pool. By then it was dark. The project had taken every minute of two twelve-hour days. Dick looked at his watch and decided he had time for one more walk around the labyrinth before he went home to his empty house.

August 12, 1992

They had been home for two days and despite still having contractions, Teres had become a ball of energy – Danny her unwilling side kick. With each task he kidded, "Shouldn't you be in the woods? I haven't had to drag you out of there once this week?" It was true. She felt calm and healthy now that she and Danny were on the same page. There was no reason to run to the woods – until a delivery man came to the door with a package requiring her signature. Teres was sitting in the kitchen staring at the envelope when Danny came home from errands.

She held the packet in the air. "It's from Philip Dixon."

"Throw it away," Danny said.

"We cannot just throw it away. We have to see what it is."

"I'm serious, Teres. Whatever it is, we don't need it. And Seamus probably got a copy anyway."

Teres tore it open and quickly scanned the cover letter. She felt nauseous, like she might throw up. She handed the letter to Danny. He pulled the reading glasses from his pocket and reluctantly began to read. Halfway down the page he went wild.

"That son-of-a-bitch! He told us he would stay out of this kid's life! He said he'd be happy with pictures and letters. What a fucking crock of shit!" Danny swiped the countertop clear of the groceries he had just brought in. "We shoulda never gone there! Fucking jail bird!"

Teres grabbed hold of him. "Danny stop! You will give yourself a heart attack! We will call Seamus and figure this out!" His face was beet red and filled with rage. In all of it, she hadn't seen him look like this – as though he could commit murder. She pulled him into a chair and grabbed the phone on the wall. With shaking hands, she dialed Seamus' office.

"Deidre, hello. It's Teressa Muldaur. Yes, thank you I am fine. We are excited too. Can I speak to Seamus? It is a bit of an emergency." She held on.

*

Danny had stopped hearing words. *Will this fucking nightmare ever end?* His mind exploded. Every time he had a foothold in this situation, somebody kicked the ladder out from under him. *Fucking Joseph Costa! Legally asserting his grandparent rights?* The shit thing was that meeting Costa had been his idea. *Now what? A fucking paternity test?* He looked at the kitchen floor and saw splattered pasta sauce and wondered how it happened. Danny took a couple deep breaths. His sanity was returning. His wife was getting her purse.

"Come on. He can see us now," she said.

"What about the mess?" he answered.

She took his keys. "I will drive." He got up and followed her out of the house, wondering when she started driving again.

*

"It's called paternity fraud," Seamus said, getting right to the point. "When a man knowingly signs a birth certificate without being the father they're breaking the law. Now, if I tell you true, it happens all the time. Sometimes the mother has convinced the bloke he's the Da, and sometimes both signing parents know the truth. It's only an issue if the biological father chooses to make it one."

"And if the father is dead?" asked Danny.

"Mostly it's not a thing ye need worry about. Surely, Joseph Costa could make a bit of trouble, forcing his way into ye lives. But can he take your *leanbh?* No he can't. That is not to say the court cannot order a paternity test if pushed, proving you're a liar if you've put your signature to the birth certificate."

"What would you do?" Teres asked.

"I'd call him and ask him what he wants" Seamus said.

"You do not think we should call Philip Dixon?" asked Teres.

"No. He's a bit of a wanker. Let's go right to the horse's mouth on this one. It's a half past two – seven-thirty in Sorrento. Do ye have his number and I'll ring him up right now?"

Teres rummaged through her purse while Danny shifted in his seat. "I don't know, Seamus," he said. "This could go bad. The guy's a career criminal."

"All the more reason. No court in the world would give custody to a dodgy chancer like that. Let's call his bluff." Seamus dialed the number and put the call on speakerphone. Joseph Costa picked up on the eighth ring.

"*Pronto.*"

"*Buona sera, è questo* Joseph Costa?" Seamus asked.

"*Sì,*" Costa answered.

"Mr. Costa, my name is Seamus Flannigan. I am an attorney representing Teressa Muldaur."

"Is Teressa okay?" His voice showed immediate distressed. "*Per favore* tell me you are not calling with terrible news. Is the *bambino* okay?"

"Mrs. Muldaur is fine." Seamus assured. "She's sitting right here in my office. Today she received some disturbing paperwork from your attorney, here in the States."

"I do not understand. I have no attorney in America."

"Mr. Philip Dixon,' Seamus prompted.

"Ah. Gregory's lawyer. Yes? What did he want?" Costa asked.

"He wanted to secure grandparent rights for you," Seamus replied, leaving out the part where Dixon wanted Danny excluded from parental rights.

"But I have already done that – with Teressa and Daniel. I got a card just the other day saying the baby was growing, and it is a boy."

Danny looked at Teres. She shrugged her shoulders.

"We just want to make certain there is nothing else you'll be needing in the way of information." Seamus said, giving them a thumbs up, and a smile. "You have the Muldaur's address. Can I give ye mine as well?"

"Per favore. Hello Teressa – Daniel, if you are there."

"We are," Danny said. "Joseph, we'll let you know the minute he arrives."

"*Dio vi benedica entrambi,*" he said.

"God bless you, too, Joseph," Teres said. Seamus relayed his address and phone number, and then all said their goodbyes.

"Fucking Philip Dixon," Danny blurted, the minute the call ended. "What do we do now?"

"You let me handle it," said Seamus. "More's than not, he wants control of your son's inheritance. We won't give an inch, and he has no claim to make on behalf of a deceased client."

"Do I sign my name to the birth certificate?" Danny asked.

"Are ye the father?" His attorney volleyed.

"Yes I am," replied Danny.

"Then you should do as you must," Seamus replied with a smile. "Never cross an angry Irish father, I always say."

*

Teres was drained. They both were, with barely enough energy to clean the mess Danny had made in the kitchen.

"I don't think I can handle another shock like that," Danny said, sweeping up the last of the broken spaghetti jar.

"Me too," Teres agreed. "No more surprises, or letters, or revelations. Let's be the most boring couple we know for the next three weeks."

Danny pushed the mess into the dustpan and left it on the floor, an odd look on his face.

"Babe, I got something to show you. I thought you'd see it by now." His expression was anxious, like a confession was coming. He took her hand and guided her through the slider and into the back yard. They were headed to the woods. Teres' mind was blank with possibilities as they walked the narrow path to the clearing.

*

Danny was never good at spin. A savvier guy might have presented an enthusiastic buildup to his surprise. He wasn't that guy. He was a guy who had done something without his wife's okay, to a territory belonging strictly to her. He was a little scared, especially since he hadn't even seen it yet. At the last minute, in an attempt to control his own dread, Danny said, "Close your eyes. We're almost there." He was shocked when she did as he asked without a fight. He half-backed toward the clearing, leading her with both hands. "Okay, you can open your eyes," he said, moving aside so they both saw it at the same time. "I thought you needed to be more comfortable ..." his words drifted off as he took in the full scope of the changes.

*

Her eyes went right to the statue. It was a small replica of the one in front of Saint Mary's of the Nativity, the church beside their house – the reason she had been drawn to this property in the first place. The sculpture wasn't a typical rendition of the Madonna and child. Its gloriousness was in its simplicity. Mary stood tall and solemn on a cube of granite, an unadorned robe covering her head and shoulders. Her eyes were downcast, focused on the baby in her arms. An expression of pure maternal rapture was frozen upon her perfectly chiseled face. But the Infant Jesus was another story. He was lifelike, balanced precariously in his mother's arms, suggesting he might at any moment struggle from them to get down and play. His fat little hand was reaching toward Mary's hair as though he wanted to yank on it. Surrounding the statue was a labyrinth that had somehow landed in the clearing without disturbing a thing. The soft ground covering from years of fallen leaves and pine needles looked untouched, as did the surrounding bushes and rhododendrons. The transformation wasn't something new to get used to. It was magic to be absorbed. Teres walked to the bench and sat down, her hand running along the smooth curve of its arm. The lowering sun created sparkling shafts of golden light through the trees. She studied the cobblestone pattern.

"You know the labyrinth is an ancient Greek structure. It was designed by Daedalus to hold Minotaur, the half-man, half-bull monster. Whenever I was obstinate, my father called me 'Little Minotaur.' He said my May birthday and my stubbornness made me the sign of the bull in every way." Danny sat beside her. "How did this happen?" she asked him, holding back the full surge of emotion she felt.

"I wish I could take the credit. Dick did all of it, from building the maze to picking out the bench. I also had him check to make sure there wasn't any poison ivy around. Someday you'll be out here with the baby ..." his voice trailed off, clearly he was waiting for her approval.

"Danny, this is the most beautiful thing I have ever seen." Her words didn't do justice to what she was feeling. "You have taken a place I filled with sorrow and turned it into one of tranquility and peace."

"So, you like it?" His face lit up.

"I love it. And I love you." She punctuated her words with a passionate kiss.

*

When it got dark, Danny switched on the lanterns which shed just enough light for them to safely walk the labyrinth one more time. Then, after Teres assured him their combined weight was well under the four-hundred pound limit, they laid crosswise on the hammock with their feet touching the ground, gently propelling themselves back and forth. Neither wanted to get up. It was a beautiful night, just breezy enough to keep the bugs away.

"I don't know why I was never a hammock guy," Danny said. "This is great."

"Did you have a hammock as a child?" Teres asked.

"We didn't even have a yard. My uncle was so possessive about the bottom floor of our multi-family that we thought the yard was his. The basement too, for that matter. We had a back porch, and come to think of it, my father was the only one who ever used it. He sat out there and smoked every night after dinner." Danny let his thoughts drift to his younger years. It was an effort.

"Our childhoods were so different," Teres said. "I had such space, so much area to roam." Danny could hear the sympathy in her voice.

"Don't feel bad for me," he said. "I had a great childhood. It just wasn't with my own family. And you got me a hammock when we lived in Quincy."

"You never used it."

He chuckled. "I was busy resisting the good life you kept trying to shove down my throat. Maybe I thought I didn't deserve it."

"You deserve a wonderful life," Teres said, quietly.

"Yeah, I know. So do you," Danny responded. "So let's have one." He rolled over to kiss her. The curve of the hammock and the size of her stomach made it impossible, causing them to laugh rather than kiss.

*

"I love this," Teres said. "You might never get me back into the house," She positioned her head onto Danny's shoulder, the rope beginning to feel uncomfortable. Normally this was when her husband would have called it quits, the minute his physical comfort began to suffer. She heard him begin to speak, then stop himself. "What, Danny? Just say it."

"There's something else. I wasn't supposed to tell you, but Martha's having a baby shower for you on the twenty-second. She tried to move it up after she heard about your Greek labor and I wouldn't let her."

Teres' first instinct was no. She fought it.

"Where is it?" she asked.

"The plan was to have it at Accelerated. I wasn't sure if I could get you there, so I told her we should have it here. I can call her back and change it if you want."

"Don't. That sounds nice. Is there anything I have to do?" Teres asked.

"Nope. They're bringing everything, and if this nesting thing continues we won't have to worry about getting the house cleaned. They'll be able to eat off the floor by then." Danny laughed at his own joke, a thing that always caused her to laugh harder.

"Speaking of floors," Teres said, "maybe we should go back and clean up the kitchen." Danny agreed.

After a less-than-graceful exit from the hammock, they each held a lantern and made their way back to the house. Teres was happier than she had ever been.

August 22, 1998

Bemus Bertakis didn't get it. Why was his wife making him lug all this stuff over to the Muldaurs' for a baby shower that was no longer a surprise? He had loaded Martha's car to the gills with platters, coffee urns, paper goods, and a giant cutout stork that she saved from their grandson's baby shower. Now he was putting extra folding chairs and coolers into his SUV. He was pretty sure Danny had plenty of coolers and folding chairs. Actually, now that he thought about it, these might be theirs. He had lugged them back and forth so many times he couldn't remember who bought them. *Jesus fucking Martha*. His wife would kill him if she heard an ugly reference to her, such as that. *Good thing she can't read my mind* he thought, taking a deep breath and reorganizing everything to get the liftgate to latch.

Bemus was a man who loved his wife. They had been married for more than forty years and he had given up trying to change her fairly soon into their marriage. She was a good woman, the pillar of her church, smart, efficient and occasionally a lot of fun. Like most Greek women, she was bossy. Like most Greek men, he had learned to function around it. And he knew how to put his foot down when totally necessary.

"Bemus! You forgot the stuff for the punch! It's in the refrigerator!" His wife's voice cut through the pat on the back he was giving himself for being so long-suffering. He put the SUV in park and got out to retrieve the Fresca, White Zinfandel and rainbow sherbet, Martha's go-to, secret-recipe punch. "Danny's gonna owe me big-time for this!" muttered Bemus, juggling the bags back to his car. Then he smiled, thinking how good it would be to see his friend. It had been way too long.

*

Having a Jack and Jill shower sounded like a great idea until Danny found out what it was. His wife couldn't stop laughing at his reaction to the news he was required to be there the whole time, his plan to hit the links with Ron foiled.

"I thought Martha was doing a nursery rhyme theme, you know, like Jack and Jill," he said to Teres, still explaining his confusion an hour before the guests were to arrive. "Seriously, Teres. How the heck would I know what a Jack and Jill shower was? I never went to a baby shower."

"Did Ron say he would golf with you today?" her mocking grin stating the obvious.

"He said 'see ya tomorrow.' I figured ..."

"He said see you tomorrow because he is coming to our baby shower," she said, still smiling.

"Okay. Okay. I get it. What's the father supposed to do at one of these, anyway?" Danny asked her.

"What we are all going to do: whatever Martha tells us to." Teres answered.

Jesus Fucking Martha thought Danny, as the back door opened and Bemus spilled in with armloads of stuff. *Let the games begin,* he decided, watching Bemus drag in a couple coolers.

The coolers weren't heavy, filled with just ice. And yet, when Danny went to help, Bemus protested.

"I got this, buddy," his friend insisted. "Today's your day, no sense hurting yourself. Just grab the food from Martha when she comes in the door."

Danny had been lugging stuff for Teres all month. He was done being treated like an invalid. Apparently his wife thought so too.

"Bemus! Danny is fine. Give him those coolers and go help your wife!" She snapped at their friend like it wasn't the first time they'd seen each other in months. Danny appreciated the normalness of the moment.

"Where do you think she wants these?" he asked Teres, feeling the comfort of being a soldier under her command again.

"Put them on the back deck. Martha will tell you if she wants them somewhere else." She got up and opened the slider for him, kissing him on his way out. The dread of the baby shower fell from him. He lined the coolers beside the sliding door and went back in to help. *Normal, normal, normal*, his brain repeated, and then a random phrase popped up from his Navy days: *All is well in the land of hell.*

*

The Jack and Jill shower turned out to be more fun than Danny expected. Teres was seated in the place of honor on the patio beside the pool. The women, consisting of Colleen, Lori, Martha, her daughter-in-law, Angie, and Marion – who was added at Teres' insistence once the event was no longer a secret – surrounded her in rapt attention. Every gift elicited an appropriate ooh or ahh. Danny and the men stood on the outskirts, ignoring the gifts and talking amongst themselves. They had already survived a baby-food-flavor-guessing contest and a game where you had to determine the number of toilet paper sheets it would take to go around Teres' waist. The number was fourteen, not forty-four which was Travis' guess. Ron had won the timed word scramble, solving fifteen baby-related words in just three minutes, ten seconds. Over delicious food and drink, the men had covered a number of topics: fatherhood, the weather, and their shared relief at having the lawsuit dropped. Doug took a moment to reiterate to Travis he had better not blow his end of the testimony.

"Jeeze, Doug! Seriously. All I have to do is tell the truth. How hard can that be?" Travis said, no real ire to his voice.

"Sometimes the simplest truths are the hardest to tell," Seamus said. "Especially the kind told in so few words."

The remark hit Danny like a baseball bat. *Was that meant for me?* He knew of course it wasn't. Seamus wasn't one to insinuate. But how simple would it be to blurt, "Gregory Costa is the father of our baby." *So simple.* Especially now that they had reduced some of the pain attached to it.

"Daniel!" Colleen's voice shot through his thoughts. "Come here for the opening of the present we've made for your *leanbh.*" Danny went over to his wife. Piled around her were more gifts than people in attendance. Bemus scooted a chair under him and he sat. Teres handed Danny the gift bag. He pulled out a box.

"Not that one," Colleen said. "Go for the wee one."

302

Danny retrieved the small box from the bag. It was wrapped in rustic oatmeal-colored paper with a blue bow. He began to unwrap it.

"All the *leanbh* in the Bragan family have one of these," Colleen began.

It was a tiny silver baby spoon with an embossed black sheep on the end, a shamrock and the word 'Ireland' in raised letters along its handle. Seamus came closer to explain the spoon's meaning.

"Colleen's people came from Tully Cross, where they raised sheep and goats. Along with the wool, milk, and meat they put forth, was the occasional black sheep." Seamus smiled and winked at his wife. "Quite a few generations ago, there was a *gurrier* – a hooligan you might say – among them. He spent more than a bit o' time in the clinker, and his people, knowing he was a chancer, referred to him as the black sheep of the family. It seemed every Bragan generation had one. Colleen's grand da was wide to the problem, and determined to change their fate. He decided every *leanbh* be given a black sheep at birth – putting the pressure off to be pegged as one later in life. At first they were real sheep. Now, each babe has a spoon like this – reminding them to get their black sheep behavior outta them early on. Your son is now part of our Bragan Black Sheep clan."

Danny couldn't speak. He handed the spoon to Teres, wiped the water from his eyes and stood to hug Seamus. "I'm going to miss you," he managed to choke out.

"And I you, Daniel." Seamus said, tearing up as well.

From the background, Bemus' voice boomed strong, "Well that's just great! Now our present's gonna look like nothing. What did we get them anyway, Martha?" Everyone laughed.

*

Teres was grateful to have Danny at her side while she finished opening the presents. The day's emotions surpassed her expectations, Marion's gift adding to the tears. It was a simple brushed nickel picture frame, engraved with the words: *this is what LOVE looks like*... "For your first family photo," Marion's card had read. And the big package from Greece was truly a surprise. Her mother must have been knitting day and night since they left. It was filled with baby sweaters, hats and booties, along with a delicate white christening shawl. There were two baptismal boxes. Teres didn't have to open them to know what they contained: olive oil, soap, white candles, Martirika witness pins for everyone in attendance, and a tiny cross pin for the baby. The other box would be the white satin baptismal outfit, complete with socks and tiny shoes. Nicky and Irene's gift was a beautifully carved Greek crucifix for above the crib. But their real gift was a card saying their life was back on track and focused around their family, signed *Theo Nicky and Thea Irene*.

Once all the presents were opened, Martha ordered everyone to grab what they had brought and march it to the baby's room so Danny and Teres wouldn't have to lug it later. Then they feasted again. Bemus Jr. arrived with baby Estefan fresh from his nap. Colleen and Seamus left to get home to their girls, promising one more visit before their return to Ireland. The Red Sox game blared on the television in the sunroom, their team finally not losing. Danny and Bemus were engaged in a heated argument about whether or not they'd keep Butch Hobson as manager for another year. In the corner of the room, Ron and Doug were busy putting together a changing table. Martha and Marion, unknown to each other before that day, happily chatted while cleaning the kitchen. Travis and Lori had walked to the labyrinth under the pretense of being excited to see it, as if everyone wouldn't know better.

This was what her world looked like just over a year ago, before Danny's heart attack. *Before she met Gregory.* A wave of protectiveness overtook her. *This is my real life. I will do everything to keep it.*

But for now, there was nothing to do except wait for their son, and pray for his safe arrival.

September 1, 1992

After countless opportunities to happen at home, Teres' water broke in the office of Danny's new cardiologist, while listening to him chastise her husband for missing his follow-up appointments.

"I think staying away from doctors has done my husband wonders," Teres said, only half joking. The cardiologist didn't crack a smile.

"If you mean living with your head in the sand and hoping nothing serious happens is doing wonders, then I'll agree," the doctor said tersely.

"We've been a little busy," her husband defended, referencing her pregnancy. Teres smiled like a conspirator. Their eyes met; her water broke. It wasn't subtle. It was a gush that ruined the chair and spread to the floor. The cardiologist wanted to call 911. They ignored him. Teres began to laugh with fear and excitement. Danny hopped off the exam table and put his shirt back on. "Let's go, babe. It looks like Greek labor is officially over."

They headed out the door with barely a goodbye to the doctor.

*

Abel Aarons hung up the call from Teressa Muldaur's nurse at the Brigham. Apparently his lecture about the potential complications of age-related, high-risk pregnancies worked. He had been more than a little miffed when Teressa went into pre labor a month ago and didn't go straight to Brigham and Women's

Hospital, but instead went to Quincy City. He took off his lab coat and donned the gray sportscoat he had worn into work that morning, then buzzed his receptionist to let her know he was leaving. Mrs. Muldaur's labor wasn't going smoothly. Rather than up-to-the-minute reports, normal for an obstetrician located just five-minutes from the hospital, Abel opted to see what was going on for himself. He had been through a lot with this couple, and any outcome other than perfect would devastate his wife, Marion.

*

Danny could easily see the decelerations on the fetal monitor. With every contraction the baby's heart rate went down and didn't rebound as quickly as it should. He wasn't certain if Teres was aware of it. She didn't appear to be.

"How you doing, Babe?" he asked for the millionth time.

"Stop asking me that," his wife replied between pants and groans. "This is going to be harder if I keep having to say I am fine. I am not fine!" *Yes you are*, Danny thought to himself. *You're a trooper. Let's hope this little guy is too.*

*

Teres was on her hands and knees, the nurse having repositioned her for what seemed like the tenth time: right side, left side, sitting up, and now onto her hands and knees. She was dilated to six centimeters when they checked her a half-hour ago. *Or six hours ago,* she thought dramatically. Teres had decided the only way to handle this pain was to clam up entirely. She was determined not to take pain meds, but afraid of what might happen if she gave in to the urge to let go and scream. The mantra in her head seemed reasonable: *How hard can this be? Every person is born.* Which eventually dwindled down to *How hard can this be?* and later *How can this be so hard?* She was trying not to panic. She knew the baby was in a bit of distress, she could tell by all the repositioning and the swishing beat of the fetal monitor, which increased then decreased noticeably. "Turn the sound back on!" she demanded when the nurse had tried to lower the volume on the monitor. She saw Danny nod his head at the nurse who then raised the volume back to normal. That was when she realized Danny, too, thought something was wrong.

"I'd like to talk to Dr. Aarons," Teres said calmly to the nurse, not interested in the on-call doctor's latest opinion.

"We've already called him. He's on his way right now," the nurse replied.

Teres looked up at Danny. His face had lost its bravado. In a flash of insight, Teres knew if something bad happened to this baby, she and Danny wouldn't survive as a couple. She would lose everything in her grief. She began to pray:

Please God, which was subconsciously mirrored by the words *Please Gregory. I beg of you to watch over this baby. I have done nothing to deserve this miracle, but please let our child be born healthy.* Teres thought about how stubborn Gregory was, how he would never let anything bad happen to his child. They were, all three, on the same side in this. She felt reassured, thinking of Gregory taking control of the situation like he had taken control of her husband's health -*like he had taken control of me.* Another hard contraction washed over her. Danny rubbed her lower back.

*

He thought it would be difficult to watch his wife in pain. It wasn't. Her distress was so overshadowed by the baby's distress that his "Hang in there. You're doing fine," was said in complete sincerity. She *was* doing fine, but the baby wasn't.

Danny had seen a lot of deliveries go bad. Respiratory was always on hand when things were going down the tubes. Danny didn't want to see a respiratory therapist today. After all their work

307

to get to this place, he didn't want to see his life go down the tubes either. He began to silently pray. The crazy thing was when he thought about the most powerful being to whom he could direct his prayer, god was number two; Gregory was number one.

Costa, I know you're listening. As much as I've blamed you for screwing up my life - you didn't. You gave us a gift. I want you to know I'm planning on being an amazing father to your son. I won't ever forget he's your child, and that you left him in my care. I swear to god I'll take good care of them both. I'm asking you to watch over this delivery and make sure our son gets here safely.

Doctor Aarons came through the door just as both his prayer and Teressa's contraction ended. He seemed cheerful, calm. Danny wasn't buying it, and didn't wait for the doctor's friendly hello to finish.

"The d-cells are too low. She's been repositioned and nothing's changed." Danny intentionally made the comment sound clinical rather than hysterical. As he spoke he walked around to the top of the bed and turned on the oxygen, placed the cannular into his wife's nose, and wrapped the tubing over her ears, pulling some of her hair out in the process. Her lack of protest was proof to him of how scared she was.

"You can take the man out of the job, but you can't take the job out of the man," the doctor joked, looking over the accordion-folded sheets of contraction and cardiac history. He addressed his comments to Teres. "Your husband's right. The baby's heart rate is taking more than a little dip with every contraction. There can be a number of reasons for that. Let's see if we can figure it out. I'm going to have you roll over onto your back so I can examine you."

The exam was painful, causing Teres to cry out with a yelp that cut Danny like a knife. "How am I doing," she asked when it was over.

"I'd say a generous seven centimeters – getting ready for transition. I'd love to see this end in a quick vaginal delivery. I'm sure you would too," Dr. Aarons said. Teres nodded yes as Danny broke in.

"No. We'd like to see this end in a healthy baby, so we'll do whatever it takes."

"Danny. I do not want a C-section," she said to him, panic rising in her voice. He leaned over and put his face down to hers.

"Babe, you want the same thing I do – a healthy baby. I think a C-section is where this is going." Danny looked up at Aarons. "Am I right, doc?"

"Maybe, but I want to try one more thing before we jump to surgery. Based on your last exam and your account of how much water was lost when your membranes ruptured, my guess is the baby's head wasn't fully engaged in the pelvis, allowing a substantial amniotic fluid loss. That factor alone can be pretty stressful on the baby. I think we should do an intrauterine transfusion to replenish his fluid, and push more IV fluids for you, Teressa. It might take the pressure off the baby." The doctor helped Teres back onto her hands and knees while he spoke. "What do you think, team?"

Danny thought about it for a minute. His first choice was to get the baby out fast. Seven centimeters sounded like a lot, but he knew better. It could take hours to get to the pushing end of things. *An oxygen deprived baby. A brain injured child. A life of hell.* His mind screamed, *Do the C-section! It's not worth the risk!*

"You're the expert," his mouth said. "Is that what you want, Teres?"

"Yes. We should try it. I really do not want a surgery."

Stubborn, stubborn, stubborn. "Sounds like a plan, babe."

*

Six hours later, the plan looked like it was working and Danny decided his bad feeling was paranoia. Six hours and five minutes later, he wasn't so sure.

Teres was proving herself the warrior he knew her to be. Other than barking out the occasional demand, "Don't touch me! Rub my back! Don't touch my back!" she had remained on her hands and knees, stoically focused on her goal. Danny tried to keep his attention on her, but spent most of his time obsessed with the monitor. Other than a few decelerations, the baby's heart rate had remained stable. All that changed when they flipped Teres onto her back to begin pushing.

"Doctor, I can't get a heartbeat."

"Recheck the monitor," Dr. Aarons said, calmly. "It must have come lose when we moved her."

"I'll check again," the nurse replied, reaching between Teres' legs to feel for the internal monitor. "It's in place."

The heartrate resumed its steady beat. Another contraction began.

"Teressa, do you feel ready to push? Let's see if we can get this done," Dr. Aarons said.

"Yes," his wife grunted. Clearly, the pushing had already begun.

"Take a deep breath and hold it," Aarons said. "I want you to put everything you can into it and we'll see what we got."

Teres started pushing in earnest, with Danny and the nurse holding her legs lifted and flexed. "Push! Push! Push!" the nurse commanded like a coxswain in an eight-man rowing sweep. Danny remained silent, straining to hear the fetal heart monitor over the yelling and grunting. He couldn't hear well enough to time the heartbeat in his head. The contraction peaked and subsided. The baby's rate didn't perk up fast enough for Danny. He was done being a bystander.

"The baby's in distress. We should do a C-section," Danny's voice was firm. He lowered himself to Teres' face and spoke quietly. "You have to trust me. I know in my gut it's what we need to do."

*

Teres had forgotten what her objective was. Through the pain of the last ten hours, she had stopped thinking about this ordeal as a baby and had begun to consider it a torture, her sole goal getting to the other side of it. Danny's words shook her out of the gladiator ring. She opened her squeezed-shut eyes and concentrated on his face. Everything fell away except the two of them and her sudden knowledge that Danny would get them through this, like he had gotten them through the past year. "My husband is right. Do the surgery."

The activity in the room changed. "Okay, let's prep for a cesarean," the doctor commanded. Nurses filed in, unhooking and re-hooking tubes and equipment. Teres couldn't hear anything but Danny's soothing voice. Within minutes she was being wheeled to the operating room. She felt strangely calm, her thoughts centered on the man running by her side – Daniel Muldaur, the love of her life.

*

The baby was born at 12:02 a.m., weighing six pounds, twelve ounces. His umbilical cord was abnormally short – barely enough length to lift him out of Teres' womb, let alone provide a vaginal birth. It took everything in Danny not to grab the blue-hued infant out of the nurse's hands. He watched her pivot the baby into the incubator and expertly suction his mouth and nasal passages to clear his tiny airway of the prematurely released meconium bowel movement. He was limp. She held him by his purple feet, aggressively rubbing and thumping his torso to get him going.

"Come on, baby. Just take a breath – you can do it," Danny's whispered prayer were the only words in the room. "I swear to you, little man, it's gonna get better. You're gonna have a great life. Please, just take a breath …"

Time was running out. Danny didn't dare look at Teres.

Finally they heard a cry. It was faint, but got progressively louder until the infant was an appropriate angry red. It was then that Danny turned his attention to his wife. He wanted to hold and reassure her, but his legs had become quivering pillars of stone. He backed away from the baby and fell into a chair he hadn't seen was there, then covered his face and started to cry. *Thank you, God. Thank you, Gregory.*

September 2, 1992

They had been to hell and back. Danny remembered a saying about a battle only being worth the win if you couldn't bear the loss. He stood in the doorway and gazed upon the win.

Teressa Giannopoulos Muldaur. She looked like a sunny day. Her hair was piled in a nest on top of her head, the strain of the previous day's trauma replaced by serene maternal beauty. There was a baby in her arms, sharing the same dark curls, full lips, and defiant profile as his mother. Danny could have stood in that doorway for the rest of his life and not gotten enough of the scene before him. He walked inside, interrupting his wife's reverie.

"Unless you have something picked out, I know what we should name him," he said, leaning down to kiss them both. She shook her head "no."

"Costas," Danny said. "It's a name for the three of us. Costa is Italian, it means the edge, or the coastline – like Sorrento, Nea

Makri, and Scituate. But Costas is Greek. And it means steady and consistent. That part's for me." Danny waited for her response, not sure how she would view his choice. Her answer overwhelmed him with emotion.

*

"I prayed to Gregory while I was in labor, thinking he would keep us safe. But when it got bad – when maybe we would lose everything – my heart told me to put our lives in your hands, knowing you would not let us down." Teres looked at their son. "Baby Costas," she whispered into his hair. "It's perfect, Daniello."

The nurse walked in, speaking cheerfully as she checked the baby. "What a cutie!" she pronounced. "He looks like his gorgeous mother."

"That is surely the truth," replied Danny, nothing but love in his voice.

Teres trembled to think she had nearly succeeded in pushing this beautiful man from her life. Only in this moment could she have known what the cost of that loss would have been.

"Yes, this baby has my dark looks," she replied to the nurse, though her eyes were fixed on Danny. "But make no mistake. He is an Irishman's son."

Teres watched her husband's smile light up the room. Her heart filled with unprecedented joy. A full repentance of *teshuva* had occurred, and the broken vase of their love was mended.

THE END

Teressa's letter to Gregory,
opened and read by their son, Costas Daniel Muldaur,
twenty-three years later.

February 7, 1992

My Dearest Gregorio,

This is the hardest letter I have ever had to write. You have been so much to me these last few months, a savior in so many ways. Whatever the reasons for what we have done, it has appeared to be out of our control. I'm not making an excuse for my part in this. I wanted to be with you. The pull toward one another was more like a remembering than a meeting. It could not be stopped.

As if the debt I already owed you for saving my husband's life was not enough, I now owe you my soul for the creation of this little being growing in my womb, whom I already love and cherish more than my own life. I know, Gregorio, that you feel the same way as I do about this baby. You would give your life to make certain that your child is well.

But Danny doesn't deserve any of this. He is a good man. He is the only man I have ever loved. I know it's difficult for you to hear this. It was difficult for me to admit. What I feel for you is a connection and a love, but I am not in love with you. I know the difference.

Tonight, after Danny's party, I am going to tell him everything, and beg for his forgiveness. Whether or not he forgives me will not change my reasons for ending our relationship. We are over as a couple, but just beginning as parents.

I don't want this to be done in secrecy. If you are willing, we will tell the world this baby is yours and let them think what they want. It won't matter to me. We have created a life. I am willing to suffer whatever arrows are slung my way in return for this baby's health and happiness.

Please believe that I never meant to hurt you and I am forever grateful to you for the life I am carrying. I plan to contact a lawyer to make a legal agreement of joint custody between us. I have every confidence that you are going to make a wonderful father.

With love and shared devotion for our child,

Teressa

ABOUT THE AUTHOR

Kathy Aspden is a lifelong resident of Cape Cod, Massachusetts. Along with her writing, she enjoys painting – both artistically and the occasional wall, and construction projects of any kind. With a background in the study of psychology, Aspden loves writing character-driven tales that explore the frailty and resilience of being human, finding meaning in life's most difficult moments.

Her first novel, BAKLAVA, BISCOTTI, AND AN IRISHMAN, was a finalist for the Multicultural Fiction Category of International Book Awards, May 2017. Aspden lives with her husband in Marstons Mills, where she is a contributing writer for LitLovers.com and Her Circle News. She is currently at work on her third novel and fourth feature screenplay.

For speaking and book club engagements, please contact the author through her website: www.kathyaspden.com

PRAISE FOR THE AUTHOR

"In her book, AN IRISHMAN'S SON, author Kathy Aspden shows us the ripple effects of one decision and its lasting impact on many lives. Her prose is crisp, her characters speak to you, and the journey she takes you on will stay with you long after you've finished reading.

AN IRISHMAN'S SON is a penetrating and well-crafted tale."

~ Casey Sherman, New York Times Best-selling author of "The Finest Hours"

"Can even the most devoted love withstand the trauma of a devastating betrayal? This question is at the heart of AN IRISHMAN'S SON. In Kathy Aspden's moving novel of a marriage under siege, Daniel and Teressa Muldaur must not only confront the truth about the child Teressa is carrying, but also the truths about themselves, and the many contradictions and complications of the human heart."

~ Anne D. LeClaire, Best-selling author of "The Halo Effect" and "The Orchid Sister"

"An exceptionally insightful story of a husband trying to save his marriage after his wife's infidelity. Set in a multicultural community and spanning events in Greece and Italy, Teressa and Danny hope to survive while they wait for the birth of their son. A good read, and a model for the power of love."

~ Madeline Miele Holt, Producer, *Books and the World* – A Cape Cod Writers Center Television Broadcast, enjoying more than 40 years of literary programming.

BOOKS BY THIS AUTHOR

BAKLAVA, BISCOTTI, AND AN IRISHMAN

"Kathy Aspden's debut novel, *Baklava, Biscotti, and an Irishman*, is written with quick wit and a sincere heart, weaving a twisting tale of passion, deceit, and redemption. It made me feel the weight of life (or as Milan Kundera put it, the unbearable lightness of being), with all its trade-offs, and conflicting desires/emotions/ideals."

~Tim Miller, Cape Cod Times Film Critic

A novel that reads like a movie. A love story that leaves you wanting more.

Artfully blending three lives, three coasts, and three generations, *Baklava, Biscotti, and an Irishman* is a dazzling pastiche of love, deception, acceptance, and forgiveness – proving there are no accidents in life, only fate and its consequences.

When the choices that Teressa Giannopoulos and Daniel Muldaur make intersect with circumstances out of their control, each must straddle the fine line between what is right and what is unimaginable to live without.

Baklava, Biscotti, and an Irishman was a finalist for the Multicultural Fiction Category of International Book Awards, May 2017

319